anyway and Don and her powerful friend, the multimillionaire Vance must figure out how to free her. Since security is in the hands of Diana's enemies, Wildwood and Vance cannot inform the police. They must free her by themselves.

Books by H. R. Coursen

CRITICISM
Hamlet's Mousetrap
Christian Ritual and Shakespearean Tragedy
The Leasing Out of England
Why Poetry?
A Jungian Approach to Shakespeare
Shakespeare on Television (with James Bulman)
Shakespearean Production as Interpretation
Watching Shakespeare on Television
Reading Shakespeare on Stage
Shakespeare: The Two Traditions
A Guide to 'Macbeth'
Teaching Shakespeare with Film and Television
A Guide to 'The Tempest'
Recent Shakespeare on Screen
Shakespeare Translated
Contemporary Shakespeare: Essays in Production

DRAMA
Richard II (New Kittredge)
The Second Part of Henry IV (Blackfriars)
Compton Hall
Ben and Julie
After the Play is Over
Euripides: 14 Plays
The Aeneid: A Dramatization
Iphigenia at Aulis and Four More by Euripides
Euripides: Five Lost Plays
The Iliad: A Dramatization

FICTION
After the War
The Outfielder

H R Coursen has written thirty novels. Howard Nemerov called Coursen's *After the War* a "great story."Of his *The Lake*, Nancy Grape says "A polished and urbane novel. Coursen is masterly at keeping the reader focused on the brightest balls he has tossed in the air." Robert Taylor calls Coursen's *Moment of Truth* "a stunning achievement." John Cole says of Coursen's *Return to Archerland* "Harry Potter and more!" His adaptation, *Five Plays of Euripides*, has just appeared from JustWrite.

His *Contemporary Shakespeare* was published recently by Peter Lang. His thirty fourth book of poetry, *Blues in the Night*, has just appeared from Moonpie. His latest novel, *The Werewolves*, about a para-military group attempting to destroy the U.S. government appeared in the spring of 2010 from JustWrite. He is a graduate of Amherst, Wesleyan, and the University of Connecticut. He teaches Aviation History at Embry Riddle Aeronautical University and Shakespeare at Southern New Hampshire University, and lectures on Shakespeare at Bowdoin College. He lives in Brunswick, Maine.

And She a Shade

Death in Sevilla: Agent Scott Winthrop is called out of retirement to help Spanish authorities thwart an attempt on King Juan Carlos during the April festival in Seville. Posing as a journalist and accompanied by a beautiful young photographer, Winthrop soon finds himself the target of the would-be assassins. He makes an escape from their headquarters and a hair raising crash landing in Sevilla's cemetery, but finds he has only increased his own problems and those of the authorities he is trying to help.

Full Circle: Bill Chambers receives a call from the wife of his best friend in the Air Force, a man to whom Chambers owes his life. His friend has been killed – in an "accident" – and his friend's wife, Karla, is in trouble. She and her late husband have run afoul of the powerful Sheriff of their California country. Chambers finds that he, Karla, and her young daughter are trapped within Sheriff Duclos' jurisdiction. Any escape will be a close call at best.

One More Chance: Harry Marston receives a call from a former lover, Alexandra Chamberlain, who has been incarcerated by the Homeland Security Police and is being held in a prison camp near the Canadian border. He visits her but is himself arrested because she has slipped him the names of other prisoners trying to contact friends on the outside. With the help of a guard, Ken, Marston, Alex, and her friend, Marianne plan an escape during a storm that has battened-down the rest of the camp. But even if they get across the border to Canada, they will still be fugitives.

Ready on the Right: Harry Chambers receives a call from a woman he has never met – Mim, the wife of his friend from the Air Force. Charley has been killed in a car crash near Valley Junction, SC, where he was teaching history. Harry decides to attend Charley's funeral, but quickly realizes that Charley's 'accident' had been staged by a right-wing group that perceived Charley as a threat. Now Harry becomes that threat. He is captured by the local fascists and must now not only escape from immediate captivity but figure out how to get Mim and himself out of isolated Valley Junction.

Contrary Winds: Don Wildwood gets a surprise visit from long-ago lover, Diana Gregory, who is being pursued by the para-military action wing of a powerful corporation. Don decides that they will go south rather than try to cross the border into Canada. They stay for a while on Cape Cod, then flee to Florida, and from there to an island in the Gulf of Mexico and from there to an even more remote island. Diana is captured

When Life Is Young (editor)
Growing Up in Maine II (editor)

WHAT CRITICS HAVE SAID ABOUT COURSEN'S FICTION.

"Coursen is one of our best writers line by line. When he gets a structure, he's a killer."

Barry Malzberg

"We're in the hands of a person who loves words. More than that, he loves the power of words to communicate, especially through stories. The main characters, Benjamin and Rose set out on a trip that sheds light on all aspects of the hero's life, from the nightmares he brought home from Vietnam to his relationship with his father and a secret his father has guarded since World War II. It is a warm and inviting love story, a trip worth taking."

Nancy Grape on *And Less than Kind*

"The scene between Hoeft and the Countess is a comic masterpiece."

Eugene Walter on *Moment of Truth*

"This is the kind of book – intelligent, beautifully constructed and fascinating from beginning to end – that discerning readers are always hoping to discover but seldom do. This extraordinary book is not like any other I have ever read."

Robert Taylor on *Moment of Truth*.

"An extraordinary job of catching what it was like during World War Two for the ballplayer."

Robert Creamer on *The Outfielder*.

"*The Outfielder* is warm and moving, but it doesn't slip into sentimentality. The characters are wonderfully drawn and George Roger's inner struggle is quite convincing."

Stephen Topping on *The Outfielder*.

"Everyone in *The Outfielder* comes achingly alive. Millicent is heartbreaking and for that reason the ending is so powerful."

Barry Malzberg on *The Outfielder*.

"This book has beautifully evocative language. A larger consciousness works here, and it delights in an illumination of the world beyond the pages."

Jim Glenn Thatcher on *Ask for Me Tomorrow*.

"A polished and urbane novel. Coursen is masterly at keeping the reader focused on the brightest balls he has tossed in the air."

Nancy Grape on *The Lake*.

"A great story!"

Howard Nemerov on *After the War*.

"Such good writing!

Gordon Clark on *After the War*.

"Armed with only the cryptic runes of Killbeard, the former king, and a magic amulet, a young man sets out to free his land from its cruel overlords. Coursen's lead character journeys through magical forests and icy wastes in a rite of passage not only for himself but for the people he is destined to rule. Libraries seeking to add to their holdings of Christian fantasy should consider this gracefully told allegory, which is suitable for both young adult and adult readers."

Library Journal on *The Search for Archerland.*

"Coursen's book is Potter and more! A free-flowing tale of good and evil, heroes, heroines, villains, monsters and magic, this book has all the magic, all of the sinister devices of darkness and the bright lights of virtue that give such fables their profound capacity to carry us off to another world. And Coursen's book has a language you won't hear in Harry Potter's company. It pulses with poetry. You make an agreement with these kinds of books. You give yourself to the writer and let him take you where he will. Coursen is a splendid guide."

John N. Cole on *Return to Archerland.*

"*Storm Warnings* is a page-turner from start to finish. It reads like an updating of George Orwell's unsettling novel, *1984*. Coursen does a superb job presenting unsavory characters, such as Cyrod the prison camp interrogator. *Storm Warnings* is a well-written and fascinating book."

Lloyd Ferriss on *Storm Warnings.*

"You'll need no compass, no notches on trees to guide you to the theme of this novel. Coursen has created a bare-knuckled assault on the policies and practices of George W. Bush. And that theme whirls through *The Wilderness* in furious prose. And while the dominant notes sounded throughout this novel are political, there are lyrical passages that make points worth savoring."

Nancy Grape on *The Wilderness.*

AND SHE A SHADE

Stand close around, ye Stygian set,
With Dirce in one boat conveyed.
Or Charon, seeing, may forget,
That he is old, and she a shade.
                    Walter Savage Landor

H R COURSEN

IUNIVERSE, INC.
BLOOMINGTON

And She a Shade

Cover: Vincent Van Gogh, "The Asylum Garden."

For Moose

iUniverse books may be ordered through booksellers or by contacting:

iUniverse
1663 Liberty Drive
Bloomington, IN 47403
www.iuniverse.com
1-800-Authors (1-800-288-4677)

ISBN: 978-1-4502-7772-3 (sc)
ISBN: 978-1-4502-7773-0 (ebk)

Printed in the United States of America

iUniverse rev. date: 12/6/2010

DEATH IN SEVILLA

The chill rides down from the mountainride,
just ahead of a white ghost of snow.
It crawls into my backbone, deep inside.
Once there, it stays, and won't let me go.

Rolf Manheim, *Matterhorn*

"Home."

It was a concept, a word without meaning, like "Spring" in New England on January 15th.

That is where home was, of course, but I did not say, when I get home, or if I get home.

It was enough to reach the end of each day and drag my sorry ass over to the "Lower Four" club for a beer.

The club was in a musty tent with a couple of light bulbs strung across. When you entered, it looked like some worm-eaten scene from the Limehouse district in a 30s film. Shadow-stained faces stared up without interest and wavered as the bulbs rocked back and forth as the wind from the north reminded the canvas of its presence.

But the beer was good. Kirin, product of a previous enemy.

At least I, Scott Stanley Winthrop III, knew where home was. Some of these guys were lifers and thus had no home except where the USAF sent them. Others had probably moved so many times that even a war zone was a stable world for them. Home – it was an oak tree in a friend's backyard. It was a word you shouted when you touched the rough and welcoming vein of that oak tree. Funny, though, the pleasure faded quickly. It was more fun to hide.

I could not hide during the day. I sat in the back seat of a T-6 Texan. The waggish Brits called it The Harvard, because it was a trainer. But it had been reconstituted for the Police Action as a spotter for artillery. The enemy held the higher ground, of course, so we sputtered along at traffic pattern altitude, racing on downwind, scarcely moving when we came into the wind, or wingdown against whatever breeze was blowing from north or south. I called in coordinates for our artillery: anything that moved below in the hard ridges that reminded me of the closed faces of the North Koreans. We were an easy target. Even their small arms could reach us. Captain Cochran, my pilot, and I each put a flat piece of iron under our chutes before we ascended from the muddy field just south of Seoul. That was strictly against regs, but I had discovered that regulations were to be circumvented where possible. No one was playing by the rules. And this wasn't even a war.

So home was another murky tent that smelled like a moldy wash not hung up to spank itself dry but just dumped in a wet pile on the floor. You got used to it and really only noticed it when you stepped outside into the wind. That brought a different kind of stink, depending on which way the blow was winding – the garbage of the city or the stench of rotting mud. Can mud rot? Here it could.

The other smell was Gunk, the stuff they used to liquefy the frozen grease of the big radial that blatted in front of the T-6. It smelled like the tar they used between the cracks on the macadam roads of summer. I did not have time to be reminded of home then, except way, way back of my mind. And that is where I was living.

"So, Scott, what are you going to do when you get back?"

That was Dave Remington, a big, dark-haired airman from upper New York state, one of the few northeasteners I had found in the Force. Most of them were Christers from Alabama, finding God in making war, or hillbillies escaping from the starving hollows and desperate eyes, and the long, thin mannerist faces of West Virginia. Dave refueled our planes. Like me, he'd been pulled into the sudden vortex created by a need for young bodies.

"Back to school, I guess."

That was a standard answer. The specific was erased by the vagueness that usually deflected further questions and perhaps elicited a "good for you."

"Where?"

"When I get back..." I paused. I hadn't really thought about it. Life was in compartments. Even when its stately progress got interrupted, it was segmented. I had to get this part out of the way before I even thought of anything beyond it. It wasn't that I thought I wouldn't get back, just that any life beyond this chilly, scent-heavy, and ear-splitting existence didn't seem possible. I did not realize then, of course, that life was mostly interruptions, mostly visits from the unexpected.

"I may reapply to Hadley."

"Think they'll take you?"

"Our parting was not acrimonious. It was just official. Technical."

"You flunked out."

I clicked the beer that remained in the bottom of the bottle and poured it into my glass. A momentary golden light suffused a tiny area in front of me.

"I had a sophomore slump."

"Must have been a bad one."

"It was. I just didn't see the point anymore. I broke up with Anne. And I figured I had some growing up to do."

"The Air Force is great for that."

"Not bad. I think time is what does it. I was a kid. That seems a long time ago. Last year. And, hell, the other guys still have their military obligation ahead of them."

"Yeah. That is an advantage. These couple of years won't count in the long run."

"Right, Dave. But it's not a race."

Home then was a comfortable house on the hill in Lexington toward which the statue of the Minute Man pointed. It was a place I associated with the sudden fume of lilac in the darkness near the kitchen door and the explosion of forsythia at both sides of the front door. I did associate home with spring. Home was also the third floor of the fraternity house at Hadley, way down Route Two in Western Mass. The aroma of stale beer managed to waft up from the basement at unnumbered hours of the early morning. Home was the enjoyment of coming over the top of a hill and seeing the new, lighter green pushing up from the dark stoicism of the pine trees. Home was also winter, the twist and turn as crystal congregations settled down to stay. Outside the window was a world where only the wind could move. Home was a place that often lost power when the storm's voice became too strong. The power company apparently expected that its customers would evolve into creatures who could use echolocation. We were suddenly in a cave and even the distortions that we might have made out in Plato's allegory, were dark. It is often thus in New England.

But the place I remember from those days is New York City.

Anne lived on Sutton Place. Since her parents were often away and since the servants had a separate entrance, we had the apartment to ourselves most of the time. I could get down there on most weekends. We'd go to Jimmy Ryan's on 52nd, between Fifth and Sixth and listen to jazz – Muggsy Spanier and his group -- down to the Village, to Nick's, where Phil Napoleon held forth, or Condon's, which often featured Wild Bill Davidson, puffing on a cigarette between trumpet solos, and for a change of pace to cooler jazz of Oscar Pettiford at Birdland, at Broadway and 52nd, or to the Blue Angel on East 55th, right around the corner from where she lived. The entertainment there was varied – Dinah Washington occasionally, and, one night, a very funny magician who kept fouling up what he called his "illusions." Those were all expensive places, but Anne paid the checks. And I didn't mind. I think I was supposed to mind and I guess it was some defect of character that I did not give a damn. I was having so damn much fun. Of course, my studies at Hadley suffered. Sunday was when you got most of your reading done, but on Sundays, after brunch and Bloody Marys at P. J. Clarke's, I was driving numbly back up the Hutchinson River and the Merritt, then across Massachusetts to the Deke house at Hadley. Massachusetts was supposedly building a new east-west highway at the time, but what one saw along detours and muddy patches of non-road were ubiquitous signs that said "Pardon the Inconvenience, while Massachusetts Builds Another Link in its Great Highway System." It turned out that the guy who owned the sign company was the Governor's brother.

On some Sundays, of course, we'd take the long subway ride and both laugh at the train broke out of its starless dark and burst into a windy October noon with the iron facade of the Stadium coming into view on our left. And there, in the slanting columns of light sliding down the Watergap, Connerly, Rote, Gifford, Schnelker, Clatterbuck (only rarely), Herb Rich, Cliff Livingston. Eddie Price, Emlen Tunnell, Tom Landry, Toeless Ben Agajanian, Ken MacAfee, Dick Nolan, and the rest of the Giants would cavort in their dark blue jerseys. The Patriots could come to New England whenever they wanted to, but I would always be a Giants fan. But going to the game with her father's tickets meant that I did not get much sleep at Hadley before the Monday morning grind of classes began.

And I remembered moments vividly. One time we were in a mixed doubles tournament at her little club – two outdoor courts on a rooftop above a garage on Sutton Place. Anne had a good forehand return of service and a deft lob when the other team came crowding up to the net. But we were in the third set of a long match and I was beat. I was serving for match from the north side of the courts, and the sun had just drifted into a spot in the sky that sent a blinding zone between my hand and the ball as I tossed it for the serve. I could see the ball at its apogee and could hit it, but as I moved forward, I had to blink away the brightness. I was going to lose serve. And if that happened... Sometimes you know when the only point of the match is being played. And this was it. Anne had hit a great lob that caught the other team flatfooted and had given me the add point. But the damned westering sun! I sliced in a tepid second serve, came forward, and saw the man on the other side lash a forehand down the middle of the court. I saw him that is through the mishmash of colors that you see when you are getting knocked out. But some other sense must have kicked in. I flipped a forehand half-volley that I could not have made in practice down the middle of the other court for a point. We had won. But what I remember is Anne's fierce, sweaty hug, accompanied by a rough lurch of her body against mine. The exercise and the win and my wonderful shot had turned her on. We did not linger there on that rooftop for a celebratory cooling down, as the towels around our necks savored the sweet sweat of victory. We went to her place and made love like slippery seals.

I could reproduce that elegant little corner of the world step by step, from the art deco foyer onto which the elevator opened, to the sky blue slip covers on the couch in the living room on which we cavorted from time to time, to Anne's bedroom, with the chaste, raised polkadots of the white bedspread that often crumbled like a discarded confection to the wine-colored wall-to-wall carpet at some irrelevant hour of day or night. The place was a personal archetype that would erase itself as my consciousness and memory dropped instantly into the darkness and silence that was nothingness. Were I to go back and look at how it had all changed in those years, it would be the changes that were the unreality, the things that were not.

"All you want to do is fuck me," she said.

That was true, certainly first priority, after beer, squash, and tennis.

But it came out so bluntly and with a word that ladies of Anne's background did not use. Or, at least, my perception of them did not include that word.

But I didn't reply in time. A simple yes or no might have sufficed. Silence signaled agreement – and guilt, since her tone had been accusatory.

We were at Nick's, having finished our sizzling steaks –and they really did come sizzling to the table – just after Phil had finished his set with a souped-up version of "Who's Sorry Now?"

What I did do was to look around to see whether anyone else had heard her. Nick's packed people in.

"There's nothing more than that to our relationship," she continued.

The dark hair and the dark eyes gleamed in Nick's permanent twilight. But the mischievous hint of laughter was not there.

I finally mustered a reply.

"That's not true."

But it was. We played tennis at her club on top of that garage – listened to Dixieland, went dancing now and then at the Starlight Roof, the Roosevelt Grille, or the Rainbow Room, but all of that was foreplay. I couldn't say, What's wrong with that? She, clearly, wanted more. And I, then, had nothing more to give. That is, assuming I ever would.

And even that night – it was a Saturday – she did not say no as the quiet flowed with the shadows into that sheltered nook of a noisy city. But our final love-making, though intense, focused, with plenty of eye-contact that said very positive things about the moment that the eyes were considering, had a valedictory quality. You seldom know when last times come around. But this time, I did.

We made love one last time as dawn hardened on the buildings in back of her place. We skipped the bloody marys and brunch.

And, as I drove north that day, I began to go through a zone of desperation, grief, disbelief, and all of that. No denial, though. Up to then I'd only lost the occasional squash or tennis match. But this was Anne. Had been Anne. And the thought of her in the world without me – I was too young for jealousy and could not conceive of her with anyone else – was overwhelming.

Memory is strange. For some reason the bad things jut out like rocks from a snowscape. They wake me at night. My mind can't get away from them and sometimes I get up and wander around. It is post-traumatic stress from life itself. Only rarely, when I was tired and when my senses somehow grabbed the wrong signals, did I go back to the combat stuff. The joy, the infatuation, the youthful narcissism fades away. It was an illusion. It is only embarrassing to recall the words you spoke then, believing them, but learning that they had tumbled forth because their object was, for a brief moment, reflecting your own intoxicating self-image and because you wanted to get laid and felt that a few words were a token entrance fee. So that stuff drops away. It is replaced by pain, often the self-hatred that rises from your recognition of how stupid you had been back then. Who the hell was that? But Anne. No. It all took on the luminous glow of a time before responsibility began, an ontogenetic Eden. Why had I loved her? Who knows? But one reason was that she never said no. Even after she had told me that our love affair was over, she had not said no.

That all came flowing back – those two absolute years with her and within her – when I learned that she had died. Breast cancer. I could recall those breasts. We called them boobs back then.

"Yes, I had heard," I said, when a college classmate had told me during a phone call about something else. I hadn't heard.

"We did have fun," he said.

"We did."

I stared at the walls of my apartment for the rest of the day, not really seeing anything. I knew that I would die. I did not expect my response to word that she had died.

II.

The ageing process involves the hardening of memories. This development can only be partially attributed to changes in the brain. It also has to do with personal preference. The mind – as opposed to the biological brain – prioritizes an individual's distant past, privileging certain moments and particularly certain people from a specific and unique set of experiences so that they become larger with time, more insistent, both in conscious perception and in an individual's dream life.

Nadine von Lodz,
A Jungian Approach to Memory,
trans. Fritz Popple.

Ben Maclin paused, waiting for a reply.

"No, Ben. I am through. I can't even drag a bat up there to pinch hit anymore."

That was probably not true. I would bet that I could still drive a softball up the middle and into center field. I might even get to first base before the center fielder threw me out.

He looked at me with the crinkly, I'm doing my best to understand you expression of the man who commissions other men to kill for whatever the latest policy may be. Policies change, but their lethal consequences do not.

"Scott, we'd be paying you damned well."

"So you said."

And that – though I hated to admit it – was tempting. I had eaten into my principal for years, figuring it would outlast me. Suddenly, moth and rust had corrupted it to levels so low that things had become a kind of race to the finish line. It looked like I would win. That meant that I would die broke.

"And you are the perfect person for this assignment. Believe me, I searched."

"I believe you."

I spoke Spanish and actually knew enough about the bulls to throw the bull about them with experts.

"And you'd have help."

"So you said."

"You'd have a photographer, as I mentioned. And you'd be briefed by our man in Spain."

I was weakening.

"And who is that?"

"A guy who says he knows you."

"I assume as much."

"Not someone you've worked with, Scott. This is a guy named David Remington."

"No shit! Haven't heard of him in years. We shared a tent in Korea."

"So he said. He's been in export/import. Semi-retired now, but he really knows what's going down. We have used him in the past, most recently on the Madrid bombings, and, of course, on the Basque separatist issue."

"Station chief?"

"He'll be in Madrid."

Whether he knew I'd be in Sevilla or not was something I did not need to know.

"I'll expect you to report to me when you get back."

That meant that he would receive reports from someone else, probably someone in Spanish intelligence. I would be freelancing – and that is an excellent mode for someone who

11

hates bureaucracy. I would not even be a field agent. I would not exist and therefore had some scope in defining my existence.

"Look, Ben, I'll think about it."

"Scott, this cannot wait. I either put the thing in motion this week or go back to square one. You need this as much as we need you."

He knew that, of course. You work on weaknesses. Fear of rats. Fear of insects. Fear of poverty. Damn him!

"Say again what you suspect."

"We have promised to help Spain. They have been a target for terrorists for much longer than we've been. They liked what we did in Germany."

We had identified an al-Queda cell that was planning attacks on locations near U.S. military installations, places outside the fence where our troops tended to congregate. That had been good old-fashioned intelligence work. The information was not obtained through torture.

"The latest threat looks real enough, but we can't find out who is behind it. As you know, Spain is undergoing a bad deflationary spiral. Manufacturers have cut production. They've also cut jobs. So consumption of everything is down. That feeds the cycle. Unemployment of those under twenty five – they are always the first to get laid off – is over thirty per cent. Unrest is relatively mild, because healthcare and other social services exist in Spain, but the Nuevofalange has picked up recruits like crazy, just as the Brownshirts did in Germany in the early thirties. They are, as best we can tell, planning a series of assassinations, perhaps even including the King."

"But aren't they monarchists?"

"The right-wing in Spain has always been fascistic."

"Franco."

"He was good to his supporters. If they kill the King and a few key government people... But, to answer your question, their hero is Primo de Rivera."

"Yes. Founder of the Falange. And he was anti-monarchy as I recall."

"That's right."

"Do they consider themselves anarchists?"

"It would seem that anarchy is a means to an end."

"Do they have a potential national leader?"

"Maybe. Frederico Breva. Wealthy real estate tycoon. Ranch owner. Family long supportive of Franco, came to him when he landed in Andalusia in 1936 from Morocco, headed his fifth column in Madrid. Supplied his troops from their lands in Andalusia. Vastly wealthy. Don Frederico keeps out of the spotlight, but they think his money is behind the current right-wing conspiracy."

"And mostly young recruits, of course."

"Yes. Get them before the cortex grows a space for peace. We do the same thing."

And I thought of a time before plastic toys, when all we had were wooden replicas and voices. "Bang! Bang!" we'd say to invisible Japs in our woods. And then, after a few years they gave us real toys – tanks to drive, aircraft to fly, carbines to shoot with. When I'd been overseas I had not thought of peace as an alternative. Mine was a Hobbesian point of view. I might make it home, but the world would never make it to peace. Convince enough young people of that impossibility and you do achieve the permanent state of war that Dick Cheney and his oligarchy want. And the Democrats, of course, go along with it. They have a vested interest in a wartime economy. Their districts have within them palpable manifestations of the military-industrial complex. Smokestacks are votes, even empty smokestacks.

"Again -- why do they want us on this one?"

"Not just our expertise, of course. Our willingness to do some... unusual things."

"That's what I thought. But they may indict the Bushies who wrote the torture memos."

"Maybe. Doubtful. It's one reason we want to help them, though."

And, of course, your guys are off the hook."

"Right. But it will not help us if John Yoo and Jay Bybee and the other guys who created the rationale for the invasion of Iraq get indicted. The whole structure is fragile right now. We will do what we can to shore it up."

That was not a good argument as far as I was concerned. What the lads had done by way of interrogation had weakened our ability to gather useful intelligence -- regardless of the yelpings to the contrary of Cheney and Michael Hayden. We panicked after 9/11 and abandoned the usual means of gaining information. We forgot that torture produces confessions, as it did for the NKVD and the Chinese, but it seldom delivers useful information. Nothing I have seen argues otherwise. Bob Mueller of the FBI agrees with me.

"I remind you," Ben said, as if I had already accepted this assignment, "that you would do nothing operational. You don't disturb a speck of dust. As far as the rest of the world is concerned, we are not there. No running with the bulls."

I appreciated the warning. It was flattering to think that he might believe that I was capable of anything other than sorting out what bits and piece came my way.

"They don't run with the bulls in Sevilla. That's Pamplona."

"I speak metaphorically."

"You think my cover would be good enough?"

"You have never operated on the Iberian Peninsula. You have been behind a desk for most of the past twenty years. You've written enough on a variety of subjects to pass as someone covering the Feria – the annual festival that most Spanish towns and cities celebrate -- for *East Coast*. They are known for bringing in celebrity writers."

"Ha, ha."

"You'll take it?"

"I'm not sure."

"It will not involve anything physical, Scottie."

I do not like 'Scottie.' I think of two little dogs cuddled near a bottle of Scotch. I do like Scotch.

"You will be the one who figures out where the pieces of the puzzle fit. You'll have several contacts, most of them unconnected to each other."

Actually, I would have preferred something slightly physical. I'd been walking, playing tennis a couple of times a week, and I considered myself fitter than most old men.

"I'm in pretty good shape," I said.

I had not exactly said yes, was merely acceding to the format, not the agenda. But Ben was a skilled negotiator. He heard 'yes' and so it became.

He handed me a folder.

"Needless to say..."

"Yeah," I said. "I'll guard it with my life, what's left of it."

And why, I wondered should it still be precious to me? Perhaps because there was so little left of it.

"Credentials. All official and capable of verification. Tickets – you'll meet Marie Vasquez, your photographer, at the Virgin lounge at Logan. You'll be met at Heathrow. Private jet from Heathrow to Seville. Priority clearance at customs. You'll be met by a car at Sevilla. Hotel reservations. Alfonso Trece. They'll have all the other tickets and passes you need at the desk."

"Por que Sevilla?"

"Everyone will be there in April. Including Juan Carlos. And the authorities will have their hands full. The feria attracts pickpockets from all over the Latin-speaking world."

"And you want me to do what?"

"Find out what you can. Use your own judgment."

"Meaning that I turn everything over to someone in Spain who wants it."

"Probably."

"Assuming I have anything to turn over."

"You will."

"I want to keep this low-tech."

Mumbai had told us that much. How easy it is to launch an attack when all eyes, mostly electronic, are focused elsewhere – looking at the sky, for example. Just put a few well-armed men willing to die in a couple of boats and look what you accomplish. We should have learned the lesson earlier – it's known as "under the radar" -- but some of the lads had been seduced by Robert Ludlum's fantasies. It could all be done from some magic room that connected to the rest of the wide world and spaces beyond. Life is not a video game, but many professionals have opted for that vicarious substitute for human intelligence. Ex-VP Dan Quayle championed a particular weapons system because "it worked in that Tom Clancy novel."

"We will."

"Anyone inside?"

"Apparently not."

Much – perhaps most – of what we learn comes from informers. That is why al Queda is so difficult. It is almost impossible to infiltrate – "Any one here speak Arabic?" as Donald Rumsfeld had asked a group of reporters plaintively after 9/11. And the Spanish are a fiercely loyal people. It is hard to find traitors among them.

"NCS?"

"No."

"Good."

I had asked because I could believe that I was on my own and still have that branch of the CIA known as the National Clandestine Service hovering – or hoovering – over my back. No "operational traffic" – super secret messages – would be zapping off to Langley. I would not cast a shadow.

And, of course, I dreamed of Anne. They were dreams in which senses got merged like colors running together. Synesthesia. I could hear her laughter, a throaty chuckle. We all smoked back then. But the chuckle was part of some untold joke. The punchline was our own wordless merging, not quite without syllables – an "um" an "uh" maybe the hissing part of a "yes" with the exclamation point washed out by the extended sibilance, but implied and inferred. But in the dream the sound was something said by the eyes that became their own source of shadows or the frisk of hair, luminous as it moved through whatever was allowing me to see within that dreamworld.

The imagery for one dream came from the horrible portrait at the end of the old flicker, *The Picture of Dorian Gray*. But it was Anne, and her breasts were ravaged, torn and full of holes. And on her face was a savage grin. This is what it all comes to, it said.

If you know someone is still alive in the world, some sense of possibility still lurks at the edges of consciousness, even if you know that she is old and gray and nodding by the Newshour. Her voice on the phone might sound as it did all those years ago. Her eyes might still be young within their network of wrinkles. And you, after all, did not stand as straight as you did once. But death. It is a cancellation of the past because that past can lead to no present now. It is the falling of voices behind a boat that sails on. Or, the dropping of power back down the lines when the lights go out and your surroundings become strange oblongs of shadow. It may be just yourself that you mourn for, as the poet says, an ultimate version of narcissism, but the pain is real and the reality is constellated around someone you once knew who is no more. I realized that I had always expected to see her again.

And now Spain. I had not expected to be there again.

17

III.

The soul of Southern Spain has been formed by many elements. It has picked up the sound of water moving in conduits and rising in fountains with an insistence that catches light at its height. That light is part of the sound. The soul of Southern Spain hears the rattle of palm leaves in the hot wind coursing from the sands of Africa. But -- above all – is a sun that touches the brow by day with a demand for recognition and a moon at light, red with the reflection of deserts, blue as it rises over the sea, and making no claim for recognition. It is greeted ungrudgingly as it turns the huddled buildings and the stones of the narrow streets to silver. It is the ultimate artificer in an already crafted work of art.

Pedro de Granada,
Planetas Sobre Andalusia,
trans. Rosa Calderon.

And so I trundled down the dreary highway toward Logan, leaving jocundities of daffodils behind me

Airport lounges are some of my favorite places. They persuade by contrast. The outside is loud, plastic, bright, metallic with announcements – "please meet your party in the third circle of the Inferno" – and trembles with an uneasiness bordering on panic. The first class lounge is hushed, carpeted, discretely lighted, offering groupings of comfortable chairs, computer linkups, newspapers and magazines, and a bar. In the bar's fridge is a dewy supply of imported beer.

I was pulling a Heineken from the Virgin Upper Class lounge when I looked across at the woman sitting by herself at a table, her carry-on at her feet. It was Anne!

Dark hair and that pale skin that I had never seen on another woman, with a luminosity that argued the rare energy of the inner creature.

I walked across, holding the green bottle as if it were incense meant as an offering at the altar of a goddess.

"Scott?'

"Hi. Maria?"

"Si. You look as if you've seen a ghost."

"I hate airports."

I set my bottle on the table and slung my carry-on to the carpet.

"May I?" I asked, pointing at the chair opposite her.

"Of course."

I had experienced that welling up within that squeezed my lungs and tightened my throat. I felt my forehead go numb. I forgot that I was an old man.

I worked the cap loose from the bottle and took a swig. I noticed that she had a glass in front of her. Ice and, I assumed, Scotch.

"Just that you look like someone I once knew."

She didn't really, of course. But the eyes. The skin. I could not get over that first impression. I realized that I had been searching for Anne for almost fifty years. And I remembered for the first time in almost all those years the moment I had first seen Anne. She was sitting on a couch on the second floor of the Deke house at Hadley. And she had looked up as I came in the door. I had not looked away. Neither had she. I could still see the light that touched her through the shadows of the room. That pale translucence – and the eyes, seemingly aware of the long lashes above them and inviting –

19

something – a word? a smile? Inviting something beyond just a first impression. Why had that glance been directed at me? I did not ask. I had been determined to find out.

"How much do you know?" I asked.

"Enough, I think. I take the pictures. And in that capacity, I give you a second set of eyes with a zoom lens."

"Right. Of course, if I knew what I was looking for..."

"If you did know, we wouldn't be going to Spain."

"True."

And I was looking forward to the trip. She probably had no concept of the scope of the conspiracy. Nor would I tell her. This was strictly a "need to know" operation. And, fortunately or unfortunately, she probably knew as much as I did.

"Your Spanish, of course ..."

She knew that I was not asking her whether she were Spanish.

"Fluent. My father worked at the UN."

"So you're from New York?"

"Ya lo creo!"

And she had that confident New York posture, with a white sweater slung over her upright back here in the chilly stillness of the Upper Class Lounge.

"Have you been to Sevilla before?"

"No. You'll have to show me."

"I love certain cities. Paris, of course. Prague. London. I used to spend a lot of time in New York, back when the Dodgers were still in Brooklyn. But there's no city like Sevilla."

She was older than Anne had been when we parted. Small wrinkles had etched themselves almost invisibly into the zone beside Maria's eyes. Late 20s. Wait a minute, old man, what are you thinking? Just that she reminds you of Anne?

The hotel was ready for us. One mark of a good hotel is that the people at the front desk affect delight at seeing someone who has been there before.

"They remember you," Maria said, as we followed the bellboys to our rooms, one across the hall from the other on the third floor overlooking the pool and the park to the south of the vast palace known as the Alfonso Trece.

"They enjoy my Spanish," I said.

Each of us had crossed the polar ice caps cocooned in the cubicles that Virgin Atlantic provides. We had showered in the Virgin Arrival Lounge and had breakfast and bloody marys served to us on the tight little Beach that had wafted us from Heathrow to Sevilla. I was ready for a nap. I would not be contacted by anyone until early afternoon at the earliest.

"Glass of wine?" I asked.

"Be right over," she said, following the mozo into her room.

I slung my bag on top of the big bed in the bedroom and opened the mini-bar in the living room.

Maria came in.

"How's your room?"

"Luxurious, of course. As is yours I see."

It was a vast space. I indicated a table with delicate curved legs that overlooked the palm trees below. We sat on either side of it.

I poured half of a small bottle of Torres Sangre de Toro into a glass for her.

"You look tired," she said.

"I don't travel as well as I used to do. Even with a good nap on the plane."

"I had one too. I feel like exploring."

"We will. Right now I am going to take a nap. We can go out after lunch if you like."

And then, something unexpected happened. It has happened to me perhaps five times in a lifetime. Suddenly, as if a rheostat has been twisted up, a globe of energy vibrates and two people find themselves within it. I have never heard an explanation of this resonance. It can happen between people who are in love, of course, but also between people who scarcely know each other. It is somewhat like being "in the zone" during a tennis or squash match. Everything you hit is a good shot from the center of the strings. That is a very good feeling. You actually chuckle between points, enjoying it while it lasts. Or, it is like the coming of that second wind when the good shape you are in asserts itself against the exhausted tension of competition. But neither analogy is right. What had been created in this opulent room in Sevilla was a zone of energy that had nothing to do with hitting a full boast or a backhand volley just inside the baseline. And, it was occurring between two people. Just the pleasant release that arrives when you've gotten to where you wanted to go? Who knows? The question is – what do you do about it?

Just enjoy it, old man, I said to myself.

But she said something else.

"Long trip. For both of us. Lie down. I'll give you a soothing massage."

That felt good in advance. It sounded like pleasure.

"Take your clothes off! I won't look until you are face down on the bed."

At some point her fingers, discovering all kinds of places that hurt and didn't know they hurt and soothing them, lulled me into pleasant daydreams and then into sleep. When I woke up, the sun had moved directly into the room. Maria was in bed beside me. She, too, had taken her clothes off when I wasn't looking.

I had not anticipated the sudden resurgence of long dormant libido. But libido, I guess by definition, is irresistible, no matter how unexpected. We were no longer within that electro-chemical globe of shared whatever, but that did not matter. Was I pretending that it was many years ago and that Maria was someone else long gone? Hell yes.

Lunch was that celebratory meal that two people share who have become lovers since the last time they ate together.

Nothing has changed. Everything has changed. It is relaxed, full of unmotivated laughter, a sacramental moment.

Nor did I think that it had been too easy. Things had always come easily to me. Most things had been just handed to me. The only challenges to my assumption of entitlement had been in the military. I would guess that a lot of men would say that. Nothing really gets you ready for basic training. You can be in great shape, accustomed to the breath-challenging and sweaty two-a-day drills of football practice before Labor Day, but you are preparing to be Saturday's hero, running with lampblack from the locker room in spanking-clean game uniforms into the cheers that make the grass tremble. Basic wipes out your assumptions. And if you become a hero it is only because you kept the fear at bay for a few moments as you responded from the hard-wires of your training. I could remember a few glints of resentment from other men – mostly from men fairly close to my status. That is, white and well put together, but from less affluent situations. They could sense the nonchalance about money that I displayed, and they could resent it for a moment with their eyes and the compression of their lips. But, then, I was always good for the next round.

So, I was pleased, but primarily surprised at my own performance. It was, I recognized, the response of the narcissist enjoying his reflection in the mirror of youthful memory. The narcissist enjoys that replication, perhaps particularly when it is unexpected. Narcissists would like to believe that only other people grow old.

Neither of us had any messages, so we swung out of the front door and walked down to the Tower of Gold. The wind was coming down the river from the north, but it was gentle and scented – orange blossoms, jasmine, with a mild subtext of river murk. It was the perfume of springtime, but tropical with no salty reminder of snow attached.

"We can walk up the embankment along the Paseo de Colon, look in at the Cortes Ingles – it is an elegant department store – cross to the Plaza Neuva and then swing back past the Cathedral and the Giralda."

"In this and in all things, you are my guide."

When we got back I had a message from Dave Remington. I would meet him here for lunch tomorrow. They were in no rush – the feria did not really begin until mid-week – and I was in no rush either. I was enjoying the return of a desire I had long since consigned to the realm of pleasant memory of past tumescence unexpectedly present again.

We would go to the corrida later. Maria had a pass to the callejon – the fenced-in corridor between the ring and the stands. She would take pictures that we would study later just to see whether we noticed anything untoward. I assumed that Spanish security – probably an agency of the Policia National – would contact me to tell me what they were doing. And I would have something to tell Dave tomorrow, even if it was only to report that I hadn't found a thing.

That evening, I was in my room, working on my laptop, assembling my notes on yesterday's corrida. Nothing spectacular – just sound and interesting work from competent matadors who had been applauded by the knowing Sevillanos. Maria was shopping for "regalos" – gifts – among the small shops that stayed open to capture the drift of people away the historic Plaza de Toros and past the Cathedral nearby. We'd wend across to Triana to the Rio Grande later on for dinner – through the unfortunate clump of smell that gathered around Sevilla's McDonald's..

I had not turned on the lights, so the night drifted in past the open windows with the scent of southern blossoms riding the atoms of shadow. I watched the darkness play with the effect of moonlight across the chair where Maria had tossed her pajamas – cream colored with thin maroon stripes – a candy cane effect, like ones I could remember that had a sweet interior.

Anne had worn pajamas, one of the few other women I had known who did. Most of them wore filmy nightgowns, easily invaded by hands, readily tossed away like a frail summer's cloud. One time, Anne had visited me at Hadley. I had put her up in cabins in West Auburn. They were wonderful old units, creaky but clean, with crisp starched sheets on the bed. I showed up on Saturday morning to pick her up. Actually, I woke her up after a late Friday at the Deke House.

She came out of the john after having brushed her teeth and paused by her open calfskin suitcase that lay on a stand across the room. I sat on the bed.

She took off her pajama top and folded it into the suitcase. Now, I thought, she'll put on a bra and a slip and doff her bottoms. No. The bottoms slithered down. She held the top of the pjs with her right hand, leaned down to create an elegant droop of boobs, stepped deftly from them, and folded them into her suitcase. Morning flooded into the room with the minty-green flavors of springtime in the Connecticut Valley. But she needed no exterior lighting.

She paused and smiled.

"I got enough last night to last me for awhile," I said.

She nodded, selected a variety of garments from her suitcase, and walked across to sit beside me. She began to dress. After a few moments, I pulled her left shoulder close to me and kissed her.

"Sorry to make you do all that work," I said, as I took off my tie and slid my jacket off. I scrunched out of my loafers and tossed my pants onto a chair with a ching of change.

"Oh, that's okay," she said, crossing her arms and tipping her slip over her shoulders.

Just a kiss was all it took. Nothing else.

Sitting there in the room in Sevilla, I thought of the cartoon that the great cartoonist for the *Syracusian*, Don Peterson, had drawn. A minister with a prayer book in his hand was looking down and saying "No, no, my children – just a simple kiss!"

Maria arrived.

"Ready?" she asked.

"Oh yes!" I said. "Estoy listo!"

I had not expected to be this ready ever again.

IV.

The genius of any tyranny is fear. The government makes its citizens very afraid. The technique works best if the fear is vague. Invisible jihadists are preparing in some remote cave for a suicide attack against our way of life. Or, as in Orwell, everyone hears the constant background chatter of a war being fought somewhere. The government, of course, is protecting its people and solemn leaders appear occasionally with that cliche on their lips. But the technique takes on a will of its own when a substantial portion of a country's citizens can be encouraged to repeat the lies of their masters. Hitler's Goebbels encouraged that repetition. And nowadays, people on the right parrot what they have heard from the ranting of talk radio. They utter easy cliches whose power lies in the fact that their promulgators believe that they understand what they are saying. Thus do vague fears take on a tangible reality. The monster rises as the electrodes flash and sputter.

William F. Spear,
When Beggars Die.

A Purple Heart will carry you a long way. You can put it on your license plate. It does not confer impunity or immunity, but it can help. The purple lapel pin with the white borders is distinctive, more so than a couple of decorations I got that are higher on the honors list than is the Purple Heart.

And it permits me to say, honestly, "Some Unguintine and a couple of aspirin."

I tell the truth and am credited with modesty.

While no one questions my patriotism, I question the value of patriotism. Cheney has proved Dr. Johnson right. He avoids military service – and, hell, Vietnam was to be avoided, I think – but like so many who have not worn any uniform since Cub Scouts, then poses as patriot. If *he* is a patriot... I probably would have avoided the military had I had the chance. For a kid of 17, whose cortex has yet to catch up with the pleasure center located behind his zipper, the military is a grim prospect. But because I had some education, the brand new Air Force pulled me away from the Infantry. And that was good. So I have ridden the patriot wagon for years without really believing in what the country is doing, internationally at least. And I have, too often, served dubious goals, most of them involving enemies that exist only in the conditioned minds of a Foster Dulles, a Dean Rusk, or a Don Rumsfeld. Why, for example, could we not have befriended Ho Chi Minh? He ruled a country just below a huge Communist power and could have been enlisted to countervail that power as our ally. Impossible to Dean Rush who saw red. But Tito was the precedent we might have applied at the time. Or, so I argued. Instead, we did not permit the elections that would have made Ho president of all of Vietnam. We took over the colonial responsibilities of the French. We then assassinated our own puppet. Mistake after mistake, even including Kissinger's sabotaging of the peace talks in 1968, an act that trembled on the edge of giving our enemies "Aid and Comfort" in 3.3 of the Constitution – the section on "Treason."

And I am trying to work from within the system to prevent such catastrophes? No. The system is rigged. Powerful interests – politicians, contractors, military manufacturers – want war. You get a company like Halliburton that is favored by the Pentagon to the point where allegations of corruption are met by the assigning of bonuses. And you get the former head of Halliburton – who almost bankrupted the outfit by taking on the asbestos liability of Dresser Industries and surely knew of his company's complicity in bribing the Nigerian government – suddenly in charge of things. You have a seeing-eye trust that burgeons as you make policy designed to make it grow. Outrage should ensue. But the result is silence. People who believe they are not threatened by war are indifferent to it. Poor kids are doing the dying on both sides, after all. And agencies like the CIA ultimately cooperate with the warmakers. Tenet is merely a recent and egregious example with his trendy basketball metaphor. The world is shocked and awed by a hubris that, like most tragedies, is not a single doom.

Patriotism may be the last refuge of scoundrels. It is also the first casualty of thoughtful people. But thought is another enemy. It leads to helplessness.

I almost got fired when I leaked to Senator Mansfield how many North Vietnamese troops were in the south when Johnson escalated – "in the face of mounting pressure from the North." We invited the pressure, of course, by our escalation.

"Where did Senator Mansfield get this figure. 400?"

"I have no idea, sir."

"It could only have come from your desk."

I listed the number of desks from which it could have come.

Did he want to run them all down? Did he want to launch similar accusations against a vast swath of the agency? I thought not.

"The figure is wrong."

"It is now, sir. Mansfield is not claiming that it is current."

We had, indeed, forced the North to respond by sending more of their troops across the line. What had we expected?

"We have got to button things up."

"I completely agree, sir."

Fortunately, I had not been asked to take a polygraph. Ways exist to defeat the procedure, and I had been trained in them. But I did not want to put that training to the test. I am pretty sure that I would have been one of the eighty per cent that the test catches. I had trouble controlling my pores.

I did forget for a moment – the current mission, the past, love won, love lost. It is dangerous, of course, because it is just as you forget for a moment that something strikes. You forget you are driving at forty miles a hour, about to turn into your driveway, about to open the fridge and pull out that first Heineken of the afternoon, green and icy and about to be consumed in a few grateful swallows. A car comes around the corner on the wrong side of the road. Your situation comes back to you in an instant and you calculate sudden equations in speed, distance, space, and options. You consider death.

I walked along the river, among centurions guarding this southernmost port of the Roman Empire, Moors in flowing garments, darting eyes, and right hands near scimitars, Conquistadors in blooming pantaloons, rakish hats, and cynical smiles touching the edges of their moustaches, wagons laboring with casques of wine through the Jerez gate, gold being lugged by gleaming, barechested laborers from the gaudy galleons, and women in mantillas, averting the eyes above their fans just as those eyes have said what they meant to say, the rattle of palm leaves, the sudden excitement of a fountain, reaching down from an alleyway with the sound of light, the shaggy smell of horses riding under the scent of bougainvillea, the gray shrug of the river as thunder trembles above Extremadora, the minaret calling people to prayer with a cry like that of an exotic bird, the belltower echoing the oval of the bullring with outgoing vibrations, like a stone dropped into a silent pool, the sudden flare of musica as a subtext for the matador working the bull out there in the afternoon sun, an obbligato behind the slow flow of the cape, the almost endless nave of the cathedral pulling people toward that dying man, scalded on Spanish oak, and, for me, above all, the gate opening across the ring and the coming forth of the death that will die only minutes from his ramping entrance, and the sweep of the Veronica across the lowered horns. I had not expected to experience again the shoots of joy that I could remember from a long, long time ago.

The crowd takes in its breath and several thousand excited voices emerge. It is not a cheer, rather a calling of others to attention. The matadors have assembled at the far side of the arena – the side called Sol. The band rides slowly on a glissando into *Cielo Andaluz* then breaks into its 4/4 tempo, the cheer accompanies the transition, and the three men stride through the shadows, their left arms wrapped in ceremonial capes, their right arms swinging, their eyes distant above their smiles. They are ready to do those equations of time and distance and confidence – or fear. They come from the sunlight into the shade, their suits suddenly alive with a thousand, golden fires, their black monteras – the hats that they keep on their heads, since each has fought here before, -- aligned with one of the arches across the crushed rock and rising from the ancient plaza, below the bells of the Giralda that will keep the afternoon aligned with its destiny. Blood, death, disaster are on the way, but for the moment the moment redeems all time that was or is to come. The three men doff their monteras and bow to the judge. It is going to be a great afternoon.

And when some idiot gringo at a cocktail party says "I root for the bull," I say, "So do I." If the bull is not good, if the bull does not have the stamina and will to charge and charge again, the fight itself will fail. It will lose its rhythm. It will be denied its ability to rise to that sequence of passes where the matador pulls the bull around his still body the horns down, the matador's head observing them. When that happens the crowd becomes a single, focused set of eyes, and no other event comes close to the emotion shared within the circle radiating outward from the series of passes. None. Let the gringos sneer.

It was wonderful to be here again. I had to admit that. It had been one of those long New England winters – relentless snow accompanied by the usual inability of our power company to keep the juices flowing. One became a stranger in his own surroundings, like a ghost revisiting shadows. I had not expected to be here again, ever. I smiled at my response. The palms crackled, the purple flowers clambered down the riverbank, the barrio of Triana glowered across at resplendent Sevilla with envy. How do the two horses who pull the carriages keep such perfect rhythm? If you watch, they merge into one horse for a moment as they go by. Careful, I kept saying to myself. You canot be a tourist! And tourists had better beware. Men ripped handbags from the shoulders of ladies and three-man groups patrolled and lurked in the scrum waiting for traffic lights to change. One to divert attention by brushing a cigarette against your trousers and then apologizing profusely. A second to pick the pocket from the preselected spot that has opened up with your turn. A third to keep a lookout. But I was on heightened alert, waiting for contacts, aware that someone might have "made" me as I bumbled along the elegant park that ran along the Paseo Colon from the Tower of Gold up to La Maestranza. I had to discipline my sensory delight, though it was there as my eyes flicked across faces and my ears sent their radar sweep outward for some returning blip – my name spoken by a voice other than my own. I had to keep telling myself not to enjoy this. It was the New England attitude – the world is to be endured. If it isn't cold it is hot. Spring is something that often happens somewhere else. And, no, it is not hot long enough to call for air-conditioning. Push on. Don't smile.

But I had to smile. I was sharing all of this with this beautiful young woman. I was re-experiencing Sevilla through the prism of her delight.

Her backrubs did feel good. She gave me another one after our return from our walk around the old city. She had confident fingers, finger tips that knew that they were getting to where I wanted them to be, in and around that old disc that I'd torn when hitting a tackling-dummy too low and whip-lashing back onto the grass rather than tipping it over, rolling into the sweet scent of cleat-pocked turf, and getting to my feet again for the next attack. She reached down to places I didn't know were hurting until she touched them, like a chance and unintended remark then made up for.

"Walker Evans," she said. "I didn't know what I meant or was trying to mean until I saw of photo of his taken in Sprout, Alabama in 1936. The U.S. Post Office in small letters above a giant Coca Cola sign. The corporate giant has donated the sign, no doubt, and it tells everyone who is in charge. A Negro stands to the left of the soft drink dispenser, no doubt icy cold to the hand that reaches in and pulls a bottle out to be beheaded in the slot on the side of the dispenser. Would the Negro dare put his hand inside, or would he give someone a nickel and wait to be handed the dripping bottle? A white man in a boater and white shirt stands to the right. He might be waiting for a letter. A gasoline pump anticipates an automobile arriving in that cloud of dust that would have followed Achilles at Troy. The building is of ramshackle wood that seems ready to be consumed by flame. But the porch teeters on pillars of brick, so that the structure seems more likely to collapse into shingles than to burn. And I, looking at the photo, wonder whether a lynching is hovering in the invisible stars that wait for night. The photograph says nothing, but implies a way of life and a way of death. I knew when I looked at it who I would try to be."

The restaurant in the Alfonso Trece is located discretely to the left of an enclosed courtyard up the steps from the magnificent blue and gold tiles of the lobby. It is a place for rendezvous and other secret meetings. The tall white haired man sitting with his back to me at a table along the wall must be David Remington.

"Dave!"

He stood, turned, and held out his hand.

He was tall, but the gravity of years had pulled his shoulders down.

"Long time," he said.

"Cruz Campo, por favor," I said to the waiter.

"Clara, por favor," Dave said. A clara is half beer and half a tonic water that holds a trace of lemon within its fizz.

Inevitably, we spoke about where we'd been and what we'd done in the years since we'd said goodbye at Travis, after the long, lumbering ride back from Japan in a C-54. But, also inevitably, that small talk was precise and covered by "not much." Certainly, I felt that way. When I woke on most mornings my first thought was usually – what a waste it has all been. Not that you didn't try, a voice would say as consciousness crept in with a seep of morning light. But so what? I would reply.

Dave took a careful look around. It was early. No one was at any of the nearby tables. And lunch in Spain is hardly what it is in Manhattan, where people seem to converge on the city primarily for lunch.

"We don't know very much," he said.

"Any intercepts?"

"A lot of movement of people."

"To Sevilla?"

"To places close enough to Sevilla. Carmona. Cordoba."

"A tightening circle."

"Yes. They close in. It's all in the timing. They close in, then disappear."

"Who are they?"

"That's the problem. Not Basques. Not Muslims. Apparently a carefully recruited cadre of Spaniards who blend in, and with the Feria de Abril..."

"Right. The population will double. Any one inside?"

"Wouldn't that be nice. Someone may give a warning, though."

Sometimes, the Spanish with a strange sense of fair play that can mingle with a remarkable savagery, will warn the police to vacate an area about to be attacked. The point, sometimes, is to show that the terrorists can do it. That is what induces terror. Mere carnage can be counterproductive. People can be more angry than terrified.

"An assassination? What do they hope to accomplish?"

"They cause chaos. They already have a well-trained security force."

"They do?"

"Breva does. He is president of a security service – Securidad Iberia. It's a legitimate company with all sorts of contracts. It is also a perfect cover for a paramilitary organization. And they can move in just like the FBI did in Memphis after King was assassinated. Arrange everything according to their already written narrative."

"With AK-47s."

"And plenty of other weaponry. Their forces are trained with the XMT Lightweight Parasniper and the XMT Compact."

"How'd they get them?"

They were recent additions to the U.S. Army arsenal.

"Probably from Iraq. But most of their weapons have been acquired legally. They have the Steyr AugA1 Carbine and the Steyr AugA3 with flashlight and telescopic sight. What the group does is cause a huge disruption. They take over train stations, air ports – in the name of security – and television stations. They create roadblocks in response to orders from some central command. They'd outgun the police, if it came to a confrontation, just as they do in the U.S. They'd be in a very powerful position and able to dictate terms. Breva would be the man."

"So we go after the money."

"I think so," Dave said. "But we have to be certain."

"And how do we find out?"

"I have some contacts, Scott. I may be able to track some expenditures. And if I can, we will know more."

"In other words, unusual expenses paid to suspect agencies."

"Precisely. This sort of thing does not take much money. 9/11 was low tech until they commandeered the aircraft. Mumbai."

"Thanks. I kept telling them that they couldn't use all their gadgets on jihadists who have been functioning in the third world for most of their lives. When will you know?"

"Soon."

Our sandwiches arrived. They make a good turkey club at the Alfonso, moist and with only a trace of rich, Andalusian mayonnaise.

Dave's cell phone rang.

"Good. Good. Yes, send it to the office."

"Economy of energy," he said, clicking his phone off. "I think we've found what we are looking for."

Again, he looked around.

A couple had settled in at a nearby table.

He leaned forward.

"It looks as if Breva is our boy. Money going to accounts in Morocco."

"So?"

"And back to a bank in Granada."

"From which withdrawals have been made recently."

"Exactly."

"So what does that mean as far as action is concerned?"

"I am going up there."

"Where?"

"Breva has a ranch outside Carmona. I can invent a legitimate reason for being there. I know his estate agent. I have just found a rug he's been looking for – a rare Turkish that has just become available from Heidelberg. Never underestimate the hunger of the Spanish upper class for the best that the planet's cornucopia has to offer."

"You work at the high-end of the cornucopia?"

"Let's say that my clientele permit me to be very selective when I examine the flow. And, these days, I work only now and then. For some reason, that makes my services more valuable than ever."

"What will you look for?"

"Up there? It's a beautiful spread. High above the river valley. Eloy Martinez will give me the tour, as usual. We will look at the bulls of Rancho Montanoso. Their famous stamina derives, they say, from their having grown up in the mountains."

"Yes, we'll see them on Thursday. First really big corrida of the Feria."

"I'll be back before then."

"Do you think you'll see anything?"

"Who knows? Suppose I see rifle ranges, obstacle courses, buildings in which to practice house to house fighting. That is just his training facility. That's one of the devilish things about this. The war on terror has made all of that legitimate. And in the case of a significant assassination..."

"Yeah. Everyone would panic, as they did on 9/11."

"Not you. Not me."

"What a lot of difference we made!"

"Tell me about Obama's 'global justice' initiative," he said.

"It's overdue in my opinion. It gives the FBI power to interrogate. That means that potential criminals can be tried."

"Since anything gained by torture can't be used."

"Right. Whatever the FBI gets will be clean. And it translates terrorism into a law enforcement mode as opposed to a military approach. Cheney said recently, and I quote, 'With many thousands of lives potentially in the balance, we did not think it made good sense to let terrorists answer questions in their own good time.'"

"As if a bomb were ticking."

"Yes, as if the attacks were spur of the moment events. As if sleep deprivation would produce instant results. Besides, the FBI often had the background needed for effective questioning. The damned contractors were told to get results."

"They did."

"Right. As Ali Soufan testified recently, we got bad information and had to track it down. A waste of time and resources and a potential cover for real terrorist activity."

"Yes," he said, "intelligence gathering and the legal process are not mutually exclusive. People who know nothing about either – like Cheney – notwithstanding."

"I will see you Thursday."

"I'll call you when I get back. I may have something."

And he might have nothing. But it was a start. Things were falling into place. The thing to do in a situation like this was to go after the money. It you stopped the flow from the top, trickle down did not work. It was a technique already perfected by successive American governments. But seldom, in intelligence work, was it as easy to find out where the money was as it seemed to be this time. Yes, it had been too easy, I thought as I headed upstairs for a siesta. I had expected more of a challenge.

V.

The worst thing was the utter isolation. I mean not merely the blank walls and the windowless corridor outside. Not merely no book, no paper, no pen. I mean not merely the absence of another voice, another face. And not merely your fears for those you love. They know, after all, where your family lives. And you have no chance to warn them. But what could they do if you did? No place to run. But it was the closing in on a self that had no world to which to respond and no world to from which any response could be expected. No sunlight from which to turn. No wind into which to bend. The idea, of course, was to welcome interrogation. You were anxious to talk. To anybody! That did not mean that you were eager to betray any one. But it made the odds greater that you would.

Roger Moray,
No Escape

When I was a little boy, I had sets of soldiers and a Tootsie Toy fleet. Some of the soldiers were the lead combat types who would kill Nazis and Japs during WWII – olive drab and in various postures, exhorting their comrades forward with an inferred sweep of a rifle – a holdover from the "over-the-top" mentality of 1917 -- or lurking behind a machine gun, or marching and implying a thousand others, all in step, marching off to death. I had two stretcher bearers with loops for arms and a photographer with a big Speed-Graphic in his belly. Some of my soldiers lived in the elegant boxed sets of British troopers, eight identical and colorful warriors of various periods that cost a dollar a box in 1940. The ships had little wheels on the bottoms – battleships, carriers with tiny blue aircraft on their decks, cruisers, armed merchantmen, destroyers, submarines. With them I would design vast battles on the green rug of my bedroom. The enemy fleet did not exist, of course. All Japanese toys had disappeared from Woolworth by 0900 on Monday, 8 December, 1941. That was okay with me since the Japanese naval fleets were made of wood, with vast flags depicting the rising sun flying above. And – they were out of proportion to the smaller Tootsie toy armada. I did not mix proportions even as an eight year old. Or styles. My heavy, leaden soldiers fought their own battles. My fleets fought only in oceans of my choosing. They did not do anything as mundane as support amphibious landings with shells. They exchanged broadsides and executed turn-abouts a la Jutland, and churned away from enemy divebombers turning the ocean into a white serpent behind them. My British soldiers marched on ceremonial occasions, as Christopher Robin and Alice observed from the iron fence around Buckingham Palace.

The distinctions I was drawing then were a matter of taste. I did not get a lima bean on a fork with any mashed potato upon it. I recognized much later that that habit of mind help me in my role of analyst. I was a competent interrogator, though I admired the skill of others, like Maclin, who could close deals with a brilliant, rapid-fire zeroing in on the right answer. I was okay in the field. A lot of playing sports had sharpened my situational awareness and helped prepare me for the inevitable bad bounce or underthrown pass. It was the subtlety of the integration or differentiation, though, that had made me a valuable member of a team playing, at best, a dubious game. I could sense the basic equation within the process. That could save a step or two.

We missed the collapse of the Soviet Union, though, in retrospect, we should have sensed Gorbachev's desperation. You have to read pores. We did not miss on Bin Laden's determination to strike inside the U.S. or on his determination to use our own airliners to launch his attack. I say that to anyone foolish enough to say of Bush "he kept us safe." Not on 9/11 he didn't. Who would have imagined that they'd use planes? little Condi Rice asked in wide-eyed innocence, her buck teeth gleaming with wonder. The CIA did.

The problem with the Spanish assignment was that is was cut and dried. Whether anyone could get Breva or not was another question. But that would not be my concern. If I could connect the dots convincingly, I would leave it to another jurisdiction – the Spanish National Police – to complete the process.

The danger of my childhood games, of course, was that I still treated war as a metaphor. Metaphors are real – they are one way to understand how our minds work – but bullets represent a more concrete reality. And they are not "apparently unlike" anything. They are. Or, if metaphor, they link those unlike things life and death. I was still, then, as an old man likely to miss the hard side of the metaphoric equation. I was not manipulating toy soldiers. I was living in my imagination, though. Maria was responsible for that.

Diego Contreras, Colonel in the Policia National, did not wear a uniform exactly. He wore the light brown sweater of the Grupo Expecial de Operaciones with their emblem on the left shoulder. It depicted an eagle grappling with a serpent. Agular con serpiente. One assumed that the eagle was winning. Contreras was a subinspector within an elite unit that could do everything from dangerous deepsea diving to precision parachute jumping, to helicopter driving. They were in charge of counter-terrorism and had foiled the ETA effort to sabotage the 1992 summer Olympics in Barcelona. They were good – a domestic para-military unit that was much more professional than the standard Swat team in the U.S.

But what was tricky here were the politics. Various Spanish law enforcement agencies like each other about as much as the FBI likes the CIA. And they do not cooperate any more effectively either. After the Madrid bombings of 2004, PM Anzar attempted to blame the ETA – the Basque separatists – even though the evidence did not point that way. The ETA denied responsibility and suggested that they usually issued warnings before their attacks – though not always. They had blown up Franco's successor, Admiral Carrero Blanco in 1973, an action meant to produce chaos but that actually encouraged the simultaneous return of democracy and the monarchy. We – the CIA – had assisted in the counter-assassination of Argala in 1978, by providing explosives from the Navy base at Rota. Argala was the only person who could inform on the person who had given Carrero Blanco's schedule and route to ETA, so we erased any connection that might have existed between the CIA and the earlier assassination. Was there such a connection? If so, it is buried somewhere back in the cobwebbed corridors of the myriad abandoned tunnels that the CIA constructed under the earth's surface. Even I don't know. If my conjecture is correct, though, the assassination of Carrero Blanco marks one of the few times in Spanish terrorist activity where the culprits had someone inside the target's organization.

What happened to Anzar, though, was our fault – the US of A's. He had supported the invasion of Iraq, a stance wildly unpopular in Spain. He could not blame the Madrid bombings on Muslims since it would be said that he had invited such an attack. This was, after all, a week before the elections. But the attack actually came from one of the shadowy groups that falls under the al-Queda label. This fact became known almost immediately and Anzar was defeated at the polls. For me, the issue was very much alive, since the U.S. had refused to let the Spanish interrogate Mustafa Nasar, a.k.a al-Suri, whom we had

had in custody at Diego Garcia and then Guantanamo since late 2005. That, apparently, had been Condi Rice's decision and, needless to say, it infuriated the Spanish. But they had just pulled out of Iraq after Zapatero's election. We were not about to reward them, were we?

Suffice it that our own ineptitude – and I chose a kinder word than I should – at the top in foreign affairs complicates the efforts of those of us who labor in the vineyards.

And I was balancing all this conflict as I eased my fanny into that chair at Contreras' headquarters.

"We appreciate your cooperating with us," Contreras said. "We need an objective and experienced eye to look at what we have. As you probably know, our own jurisdictions sometimes collide in the instance of domestic terrorism. In this case, the Commissariat of Intelligence, which is also an agency of the Policia National, wanted to handle this problem."

"But your training is far superior," I said. "And certainly more suited to response to whatever threat emerges."

He smiled and held out his hands, palms outward.

"You understand!"

He had the tough, olive-colored face of a combat veteran – a few white nicks in that skin that suggested healed wounds – and the stocky body and shoulders of a man who enjoys pulling his weight up and down a hundred times in rapid succession. I wanted him on my side.

"They have given us what they know," he said. "And left it at that. Actually, that's preferable. We do not want to collide with them in the traffic pattern."

I appreciated his use of an aviation metaphor. Yes, he had studied my own background.

"And what is known to us at this point?'

I used the word "nosotros," meaning "us."

We were in a basement office deep below the concourse of the airport northeast of the city on the A-4, the road to Cordoba and to Madrid beyond.

It was a spartan room with charts and details of weapons on the walls – organizational hierarchies that seemed intentionally indecipherable, and detailed pictures of the Mauser SP 66 and the Glock 9mm automatic pistol that were much clearer.

"It is not ETA."

They no doubt did have informants among the Basques.

"And not monarchists," I said.

"No. Not when the King himself is apparently a target."

"Why would he be a target?"

"For several reasons. First, he is a democrat."

It is difficult for Americans to understand that a king in a constitutional system supports the constitution and the parliament that a) grant him his position and b) give him the money to maintain it.

"And therefore anti-fascist," I said.

"Yes. Franco was the only one of the old fascists to die in office and name his successor."

True. It was hard to believe that he had been a contemporary of Hitler and Mussolini.

"And, second," Contreras continued, "the assassination would cause chaos."

"And call for a strong man to take over."

"Exactly."

We had maneuvered ourselves into that position in Iraq. We knocked off the man who held power and created a vacuum. The bastards had forgotten the *Julius Caesar* they had read in tenth grade.

"So it is the Nuevofalangists," I said.

"Yes. And we know who some of them are."

"But at the operational level..."

"Exactly. They can send out men we don't know. And they can select their targets at the last minute. And, as you know, he already has a perfectly legal organization in place."

"That achieves considerable economy of scale."

Most individual terrorists require a considerable support system. Here it was built-in via Breva's security service, though he seemed to be pulling assets in from other places. His own people had not necessarily signed up as terrorists, but as mercenaries. They were young men, probably well-educated, possibly well-connected, and definitely unemployed. They had not been recruited from the barrios. The poor are usually conservative. They hold right-wing values because the list is short and simple, and they often believe they have failed the system. They don't share the fanaticism or the sense of victimization of jihadists. The poor mirror the well-off who defend the system that got them where they are. Free societies don't spawn terrorists – but grievances do, as in the case of McVey, Nichols, and Oswald.

"Must the King come to Sevilla?"

"He is a man of the people. He wants to be here."

"He usually sits in the first row of the barrera."

Contreras' brown eyes stared at me.

"Often, yes. You have been there?"

"Tourista. Aficionado de los toros."

I got another stare. His background check had been incomplete. But then, my aficion was not something I publicized. It was an aberration within the waspish persona.

"But he will occupy the royal box this time," he said.

It was high on the Sombra – or shady – side of the Plaza.

"Yes, where the late Duchess of Barcelona could usually be found."

"Yes, she loved the bulls."

"A framed target."

"Unfortunately."

"Does the King have a double?" I asked.

He laughed.

"Like Churchill?"

"And Hitler."

"No. It has been suggested. But he is a Spaniard."

45

"Duende."

I used the Spanish word that cannot be translated – guts and self-worth and personhood, an inner pride that did not strut. They hated Bush. The matador strutted in his golden suit, of course, but if he stood still as the horns sliced by, and if the blood of the bull stained his belly, he earned the privilege to manifest duende for the rest of us.

"You understand."

I hated to admit it and it was self-serving as hell, but I understood why Ben Maclin had chosen me. You did have to be simpatico, that is, to glimpse the Spanish soul even if you could share it only vicariously.

"I called you here, though, to go over our security arrangements. And to get any suggestions you might have. I've asked two of my subordinates to participate in the briefing."

He flicked a switch below his telephone.

"Send in Ramirez and Diaz, please."

They joined us immediately, two men in their mid-thirties, both majors, each olive-skinned, dark-eyed, and fit. I stood and shook hands with them. Yes, I would want them on my side. I would not want to be a member of the Nuevofalange if either one were looking at me.

The security arrangements were impeccable.

"The focal point is the Plaza," I said, "because the Corrida makes the King an available target. Any body armor that he might wear..."

"He won't," Contreras said.

"And it would be irrelevant. They'd go for a headshot, as Oswald did, and at that range..."

"A scope won't be necessary," Diaz said.

"Would they try to attack him on the way to the Corrida?"

Carrero Blanco had been killed when the ETA had loaded a tunnel with explosives. His car had been blown over a building.

46

"I'm thinking of an IED."

"And so have we. The streets from the Alfonso, where he and Queen Sofia will be staying, to the Maestranza will be swept and monitored. We'll have snipers on the rooftops of the buildings facing the River. His limo, of course, is armored."

"He gets out with the Queen..."

"And is escorted through a cordon established through the crowd in the plaza in front of the arena to the elevator to the royal box. He will appear and acknowledge those inside the arena."

"A moment of vulnerability."

"La hora de verdad," Contreras said, using the phrase for the matador's going over the right horn of the bull to kill.

"But," I said, "while they may not attack the motorcade, they might borrow a technique the Basques often used."

"Which one?" Ramirez asked.

"What they call 'kale barroka' – starting a disturbance in the street to pull security away from the point of attack."

Contreras smiled.

"Yes. We have a cadre of local police – and they are very professional here in Sevilla – ready to respond to such an incident. Our own deployments will not be disturbed."

He went over the location of his people in the Plaza de Toros, men and a few women with binoculars who were assigned specific segments of the arena and who would scan the crowd while simulating attention to the bull and his antagonists.

"Logistically, it is a superb plan," I said. "Congratulations. I enjoy working with professionals."

"But," Contreras said, "you said, 'logistically.'"

"Yes. If we can crush the head of the serpent, rather than wrestle with it...."

"Precisely. The heavy boot. At this point, however, we are in the position of foiling their plot."

"And we must do that."

"We must," he said. "The country is still jittery after the Madrid bombings and the discrediting of the government's response."

Yes, the climate for a para-military takeover – "for your safety and that of our beloved Espana!" – was favorable. This was particularly true since the new and avowedly temporary government would be composed of Spaniards. No one could point a finger at any foreign power or group.

"Do you have a sense of timing?"

"Only a guess. The King will attend the middle three corridas."

Yes, when the greatest of the Spanish matadors would perform – Juli, Ponce, Fandi, El Califa, Amador, et al.

"The third day, then," I said.

"Probably," Contreras said. "It will give them the chance to check out our security."

"And it will give us more time. Any chance the King can be persuaded not to attend on the third day?'

"No," Diaz said. "We have asked."

"I did not think so," I said to indicate that I understood and – emotionally, at least – approved.

It was wonderful to be working in this environment. I was merely confirming the plans that had already been made. But the appreciation of that confirmation was palpable in this subterranean chamber. I had not expected to be a professional again working with other professionals. It was typical of me, I thought. I had resisted doing something that I really wanted to do, and that I was good at doing. Thank you, Ben Maclin! !

VI.

For all of his wealth. Belmonte never learned the ways of the aristocracy. True, he enjoyed riding a beautiful horse around his vast ranch along the river north of Sevilla. But he did not enjoy his money. The poverty of the Triana barrio had imprinted its lesson indelibly. He was always afraid of losing the fortune that he had gained through so many dusty and sometimes nearly fatal afternoons in the bullrings. He had not been called "The matador of four oles and one shriek of terror" for nothing. And he treated his servants with the contempt that he could recall from his days of raggedy youth. They hated him. So, when he put a bullet through his head, it was no surprise. They said, of course, that he killed himself because he could no longer fight the bulls. No. He had only leaned to live in hunger and poverty. Other lessons beyond placing the sword deep down into the bull's aorta were beyond him. It should have been Belmonte and not Joselito who was killed that afternoon in Talavera. Joselito would never have killed himself.

Augustino Flores,
Juan Belmonte, Killer of Bulls,
trans. Hector Valdez

Sometimes things happen to children that should never happen. I think of a photo of a little girl crying. Little girls cry. So do little boys. But this little girl is part of a family being brutally taken by the Nazis. Why? No answer exists. None did when I saw the photo in 1943. *Life* had a section at the end of each week's magazine called "Speaking of Pictures." And they were often pictures that should not be seen by a kid like me. The world was good. We had food – roast beef on Sunday, with Yorkshire. Summers in Maine. Maids and Buicks. But they could not keep at bay the raids on consciousness by the photographs in *Life*. Not just that they kept sleep away, but the image that they kept roping in, when something else was going on, inside the pause of a waltz, a fragment of silence along the line of scrimmage – the body crumpled after its fall from the ledge. "Deleted" said the caption. At night, the threat of hanging, the man crawling the hempen edge of noose, his companion laughing, the last heartbeat of the girl looking, knotted by fascist rage, like a sophomore at the highschool down the street. *Life* was full of people out of breath. Why, in those days, was it not called *Death*?

Dave and I were in the Irish Bar at the Inglaterra, on the Plaza Nueva, where he had a suite.

"No," I said. "Pelosi did not ask a single question."

"How do you know?"

I looked at him.

"Oh. Was she lied to?"

"Just not told the whole truth. Misled, yes, but as much from her own lack of curiosity as anything else. I don't think specifics were mentioned. Just 'enhanced techniques.'"

"But she could have asked."

"Right. Whether she would have been told anything more specific, I don't know. It was not my call. I had been asked to observe," I said.

"She says that if she had objected, it would have done no good."

"That may be true. But you heard her. She said she was intent on getting a majority for her party. Translate that as – 'I wasn't about to make a peep.' You remember how everyone was in panic mode. Can you imagine how popular she would have been if the headline were 'Senior Minority House Intelligence Committee Member Objects to CIA Interrogation Methods'? And Goss, who was Chairman of the Committee, would have gone through hoops to try to block her or to refute her charges."

"Goss hasn't backed the CIA on this one," he said.

"No. And he was there. Needless to say, he raised no objections. Of course, you can't object to an Orwellian obfuscation. You'd have to ask for more details."

"Yeah, and at the same time Tenet was lying to Bush. Are you sure the orders came down from Cheney?"

"His office. Memos were initialed D.A."

"Addington," he said.

"One must assume as much. We were doing well with the few we could identify as terrorists. What could we get out of the great majority of detainees? Not a damned thing. They'd just been vacuumed up or turned in for a bounty that was a lifetime's earnings for the informants. But Cheney wanted results. The actual wording was that we were being 'too gentle.'"

"Yeah. Rumsfeld stands all day. But that's why they went to contractors?"

"Right. People with no experience. Privatizing the gathering of intelligence! The incompetence of that administration will never be fully comprehended. The FBI had scruples. Scruples, for Christ's sake! And even the CIA was too fucking slow! And, of course, they were trying to get something that couldn't be gotten," I said.

"A rationale for the war they'd already started."

"Yes – that elusive Saddam-al Queda link."

"They couldn't even get those guys to confess to it after being water-boarded?"

"If the detainees had known what answer they wanted, they might have. But no one – least of all us – believed that the Saddam regime and a fanatical religious group like al Queda could possibly be in cahoots. Fucking ideologues in the White House said that it had to be so," I said.

"Cheney said..."

"I know – 'it's been pretty well confirmed' that Iraq and al Queda met in Prague. He said that on 'Meet the Press' in December '01. We knew it wasn't true, but what good did that do?"

"The guy is walking around free."

"I'm sure he owned at least one congressman and probably several judges."

"But they did get a confession from Al-Libi, didn't they?"

"Yeah. Sent to Egypt. You know what he said?"

Dave shook his head.

"'I had to tell them something, they were killing me.'"

"How'd they get the right answer from him?"

"Something like, 'So you continue to deny that Saddam was providing training to Al Queda?'"

"And he gets the point, " Dave said.

"'Oh yes. Saddam is providing that training you mention.'"

"In poison gas, as I recall."

"Yeah. That's what the lovely cupcake, Condi Rice, told Jim Lehrer in September '02."

"Bush had already exempted al Queda and Taliban from the Geneva rules."

"True. It didn't matter whether we gave them to a foreign country to torture or not. And that exemption widened to include all of our prisoners. Even the innocent unfortunates that we swept up were likely to become our enemies once they were set free. They experienced who we were. Didn't Bush wonder why the insurgency in Iraq kept growing? It wasn't just angry Baathists," I said.

"The SEER people told the government not to use their techniques."

"I know. Those techniques were designed to get confessions. Those confessions made subsequent legal activity – executions – perfectly, ah, legal. The stuff the Nazis and the NKVD and the Red Chinese did were not designed to elicit useful intelligence."

"Or to prevent a ticking bomb from going off."

"Right. By the time you've deprived a person of sleep for 3 days, even assuming he's capable of anything more than gibberish, the bomb has long since gone off. Besides, if a terrorist has a timeline in mind, he will hold out for as long as he can. Those bastards – Cheney, Yoo, Bybee – had absolutely no experience with or knowledge of intelligence gathering."

"They had a hypothesis," he said.

"Yes. One. Actually, a conclusion. All activity had to serve that predetermination.

"Cheney okayed torture a year before the invasion. Al-Libi was cooperating with the FBI, but he was given to the CIA and sent to Egypt. Powell used the Iraq-al Queda link in that damned UN speech. And al Libi committed 'suicide,' they say, in Libya. It would not have been good to have anyone hear him deny the narrative for which they said he was responsible."

"The foregone conclusion is dangerous," he said.

"That's right. The CIA thought it could force Kennedy to use the Air Force in support of the Bay of Pigs operation. He wasn't about to do that."

"And the poor bastards were cut to ribbons."

We lay on my bed. She had nothing on at all and her rear end rose enticingly, twin curves capturing the last vestiges of sunset deserting the room.

"Here," she said, pointing.

"Yes. The binos. He must be security of some sort."

"And here."

She pointed at a man high along the sunny side of the Plaza.

"Good eye."

"I had him in mind when I took this one. Here."

She slid another photo from the stack.

"Zoomed in."

Yes, he too had the binos. And the neutral look of a guard or a cop, reserved, watchful, uninvolved with the temporary images – the flow of a Rebolera past lowered horns -- that caught everyone else's attention.

"I was told that the Spanish would contact me. I think I can tell them where most of their people are."

"Most," she said.

"Exactly. If it is this easy for us it will be just as easy for the bad guys. And the Policia will know that."

"Food?"

I got up and pulled the room service menu from shelf on the telephone stand.

"I can recommend the club sandwich with a bottle of vina sol. That's white wine. Or smoked salmon and Iranian caviar, excellent anchovies, Jamon, of course, from Iberia, and cheesecake with strawberries."

"All?"

"Be selective."

"The salmon and caviar. But can we have red?"

"Marques de Caceres?"

"In that and in all things..."

"And truffles, too. Or, as I call them, trufas heladas."

"We'd better..."

I could still sense the earth wobbling on the gravitational pull of sun and moon.

We each pulled on one of the terry cloth robes provided by the hotel. She had worn hers across the hall from her room.

We ate with the abandon of sybarites, which we were being, polished off the bottle as if by rapid evaporation and looked at more photos.

I had been in that Plaza many times but had never studied it from a security standpoint. It did have slender columns that arched upward toward the inner facade but it was open, accessible, a place where an assassin could conceal himself easily. A suicide bomber, of course, would be a different story. They'd nab him before he got inside.

And, suddenly, for all my napping, I was exhausted. I woke at some unconcerned hour of the dark to pad to the john. Maria had, I assumed, gone across to her room.

It was the third day of the Feria. The King would be coming in tomorrow. Maria was off shopping in the Fiat she had rented. "Just to keep us both a little independent," she said.

I was strolling along the irresistible walkway that borders the Guadalquivir between the Torre del Oro and the Maestranza. I was watching passengers board the tour boat, La Luna, that cruised partway down the River and then up to the beautiful Triana Bridge, constructed of ever smaller circles within arches that supported the span, when someone nudged me.

It was not a pickpocket. I turned and saw a man walk toward one of the many benches on the Paseo Colon side of the park. Good. I had been making myself available for any possible contacts.

I got a flyer from the ticket booth for La Luna and wandered over to the bench. I sat on the far side and pretended to study the flyer.

"Senor, cuidado," said the man from the side of his mouth.

I was being careful. But what specifically was he warning me about?

"Things are not as they seem to be."

Before I could question him, he got up and scuttled away, as if on urgent business.

Okay, I thought, things are never as they seem to be. I wondered what more he had to tell me before something – a face in the crowd? -- spooked him and he fled. I expected to find out the hard way.

VII.

The guiding principle of American politics has been its election of persons dedicated to maintaining and extending the power and wealth of the oligarchy. It becomes a self-perpetuating system. Money flows to the politicians. They pass legislation favorable to business. The rationalization, of course, is that big business provides jobs for the people. That thesis has been undercut by globalization. Unions, once the countervailing force against unregulated capitalism have lost their leverage. The agents of the status quo no longer rationalize their agendas with rhetoric about the good they intend or are accomplishing. Since the election of 2000, American politics has not claimed to be wearing any clothes at all. And it does not seem to matter than most citizens can see that the emperor is striding along in his birthday suit.

Samuel Whither,
The Defense of the Status Quo

I handed my heavy brass key to Pepe.

As he took it, he looked over my shoulder.

"Cuidado," he murmured.

As I turned to go out the front entrance, I saw a man leaning against the window of the men's shop in the lobby as if waiting for someone. Me.

I thought of contacting Diego immediately. No. I might find something out this way. We were still groping in the dark on this one.

I turned left at the bottom of the steps outside the hotel and began to walk down the semi-circular driveway. A car had just pulled up in front and the staff was busy opening doors and lugging bags. Halfway down the driveway, I saw a car door open. A voice behind me said, "Senor, please get into the car."

I was in the back seat of a Mercedes, with tinted windows. We drove past the entrance of the Alfonso and on to San Fernando, past the statue of Carmen and past the cigarette factory where she had worked and sung songs written for the mezzo soprano that she had been. I was seeing it all in a strange yellow light, as if it were an ancient photograph.

"Senor, we regret the necessity of interrupting your visit, but it is important that you leave Sevilla for the time being."

"Porque?"

"Let us just say that we want you to spend a pleasant few days elsewhere."

Not only were they bringing their people toward Sevilla – I could sense the various experts, mostly lookouts and communications people and a sharpshooter or two, closing in on the city – but they were exporting those who might try to stop whatever it was that they had in mind. But they were not about to bring the U.S. into things. They would prefer to hate us from a distance.

The car turned down Avenida Kansas City toward the Estacion de San Justa. Yes, they'd put me on a train, probably under guard. I was relatively helpless since my passport was in the safe back in my room. I also felt helpless. What would I be able to do anyway? I might as well lean back and enjoy the inevitability.

They'd leave Maria alone. She knew nothing. And it would do no good for her to raise an alarm.

The man beside me took my cellphone, extracted the battery, and handed it back to me.

"No harm will come to you, Senor, as long as you cooperate with us."

The vast new station offered me one opportunity. I said that I wanted to go to the men's room. The man who was escorting me looked at his watch and nodded.

"I will wait right outside the door," he said.

What had I accomplished? I had gained control of the timing. I waited right inside the door and watched as it swung open and shut with entrances and exits. Two police men were moving across the center of the concourse. I rushed out past my guard and gesticulated to the two cops.

"Policia! Policia!"

They turned. I pointed back in the direction of the Caballeros. But my escort was no where in sight.

"I wish to see Colonel Breva, Policia National. Airport. Can you give me escort?"

I flipped open my wallet and showed a very official looking U.S. Government identification card. Did that carry any weight here?

"Venga conmigo, Senor Winthrop," one of the men – a lieutenant – said to me.

We went to an unmarked office along the west side of the station.

He made a call.

It was very brief.

"Senor Winthrop esta aqui. Quieres hablar con usted." "Si." "Si." "Si, senor!"

"Venga conmigo, Senor."

And, very quickly, I was on the road to the airport.

The day was clouding over. As I settled the tension out of my system, I recalled my dream of the very early morning. I was in a house watching the Red Sox, who were ahead. Maria came in with a friend, changed her clothes and left. Out the window, to my right I saw a cloud, creamy and thick, covering a hillside. I called out. The two women exclaimed about it. I woke up, thinking of Maria. My feelings for her – yes, they were there -- had been recharged by the dream. But what was the cloud? She had not conjured it. I had. It was the unknown.

I gave Contreras a brief description of my abduction.

"And I think they've got Remington."

"What makes you think so?"

"We were supposed to meet tonight. He was going to call yesterday. He did not."

He nodded.

"They have identified you, obviously," Contreras said.

They had identified both of us, Dave and me.

"So I am of no further use to you."

I would have been happy had he agreed. The tourist in me was tugging at the creaky intelligence officer.

"I wouldn't say that. Go back to your hotel. They won't try that one again. They were probably going to take you to Madrid or Barcelona and keep you there for the next few days. But you are not on top of their list and they go into another phase of their operation when the King arrives tomorrow. They would have had you shot if they felt you were that much of a threat to them. You are an annoyance to them, but they don't want the Americans involved. That is, even if you were here, and you are not. We will relocate you as soon as possible. When did you say you were to meet Remington?"

"He was going to call me yesterday."

"And, as you say, he did not. That is troublesome."

"You think they've captured him?"

"Yes, it is possible."

"They'd be holding him at the ranch?"

"That, too, is possible. I would still like you to look at everything we've gathered. See whether we've missed anything. I'll contact you tomorrow morning."

"My photographer?"

"You can continue your observation at the Plaza de Toros. We will have increased security, of course, starting tomorrow. They won't be after you, but we'll move you just in case."

"And?"

"Yes, your photographer, too."

I know how people sneer about the relationships that develop in the military. But they can be close, emerging from shared privation, shared danger, shared ennui. People who have not graduated from basic training – boot camp – have not gone through a primary rite of passage. All of us who wore the uniform did that – with the exception of Ronald Reagan, of course – even my fraternity brother, Dan Quayle.

Dave Remington had been a friend when I was a homesick kid in a godforsaken mudhole. I could remember the hollowness opening up in me and threatening somehow to swallow me – a physical impossibility, of course, but the mind has mountains, as the poet says, and abysses that fall infinitely away from those cliffs. Daily routines took care of much of the threatened paralysis – procedures and checklists were attention getting devices – and Dave helped me over those several nighttime Kirins. Would he have helped me were I a prisoner? Yes. I would try to help him.

I could not tell Diego Contreras. He would forbid it on any number of grounds, primarily, I would guess, that I had absolutely no authority to take any action whatsoever. I was supposed to sit around as information came to me and interpret it. Sometimes, though, the information called for action.

I told Maria that I'd see her tomorrow at noon in my room.

She asked no questions. This was, after all, more than a pleasure trip.

61

Two things permit men to endure military service. First, you are young and do not believe that this is all there is. Despair when you are young is momentary. It is not like starving to death or being young and Jewish in Poland in 1940. Second, you are sharing it with other young men with the same belief – this is not all there is. And you can grouse with them and joke about officers and laugh about women. That is the only thing I did not do back then. The memory of Anne was still pervasive and it was no laughing matter. And any bragging would have diminished what we had been. And, of course, the shared hardship of the military does build fierce loyalties.

I did laugh at myself now, though. I was preparing to go on a single-handed mission to find Dave. I did not dare tell anyone. I was defying the orders I had been given by Ben Maclin, of course, but I snuggled into the notion that the agent in the field has to make decisions. Ha! – this one was supremely counterindicated, as we used to say. My GPS would track me, but it would not contradict me. Should I do this? Absolutely not. Could I do this? Once upon a long time ago I would not have asked the question. I had been less cautious, of course, but had never doubted my physical ability to do about anything short of leaping tall buildings like a speeding bullet. I do not like heights. I could remember getting agoraphobia when Captain Cochran banked to final approach and I looked down the wing to the mud below. But now, it was fear of my own physical condition – annihilaphobia – that lurked behind my actions. I tucked my Glock into my belt behind my back with a brief prayer that it need never be deployed. And, in a rental car that the hotel made available, I began driving up-river and up-hill toward Carmona. The ranch lay northeast of the town. I'd have to find a place to leave the car and wend my way to whatever I would find. Night surveillance. Dark pants and a navy blue LaCoste sweater. I was also afraid of dogs, so I had bought a bag of dog biscuits and tucked some into my right pocket. Nice doggie! Did Weimereiners in Spain saben ingles? Bueno perro! Cuidado con sus dentes!

A long dirt road led up to the gate of the Rancho Montanoso -- the roads near and within ranches are always dirt, of course, because of the horses – and I hoped that I was not generating a plume of dust against the moon. As I had seen on the map, another road ran to the left for several miles along the wall of the ranch. I left my car at the end of that road and proceeded on foot along the path that bordered the wall. And then, the wall gave way to an old metal fence. It was designed to keep the cattle inside. Cattle, for whatever reasons, seldom challenge metal fences. Bulls will rip the wood of the bullring with their horns but that is usually because they want something for their horns to dig into after the tantalizing sweep of that cape that keeps collapsing as they charge it. But metal fences are not designed to keep people out. I wondered whether, years ago, kids from the barrio of Triana had made their way up here to cape the bulls by moonlight. Perhaps I was treading where the great Belmonte and Gitanillo had trod. I did not, though, wish to whisper "heh – toro!" tonight as I swung a tattered jacket in front of its snout. Back then, mounted guards rode those moonlit nights the bambinos would choose – with shotguns. A couple of barrels into the air would send the boys scrambling. Tonight, under this half-moon, if they rode, they would shoot to kill.

The ranch complex was to my right. I found another dirt road about two hundred yards inside the fence and began padding in that direction. If they were holding Dave prisoner – and that was my assumption – it would be in one of the smaller buildings of the several that surrounded the hacienda. I had studied the layout, of course, and had chosen the buildings I would check in order of priority. I had no idea, of course, whether my priorities were accurate. But I had to have a plan simply to keep me motivated. A voice somewhere deep inside was saying, this is stupid, Scottie.

I did see a couple of bulls, horns absorbing moonlight. They are herd animals and seldom charge if in a group. These just looked at me with sullen curiosity. Don't you guys ever sleep?

I changed my plan almost immediately. In the pond that I approached, the hacienda lights were bright. I looked up. The windows on the side facing me – long, large windows set in arches of plaster – were open to the mild winds that coursed across these upland meadows. I tried to ignore the shadow I was casting as I crept closer and looked into the window. Dave! He was talking to a large man with a sun-creased face and black hair. Breva? Each held a glass of wine and a bottle stood on a small table between them.

I crouched below one of the windows.

The Spanish was rapid, but I could pick most of it out.

"No, don Frederico. They will be led to believe that the money went to Morocco. The transfer to Granada will not be recorded until two or three days from now. When they look…"

"Yes. That's good. We only need a false scent for a little while."

I had set out to save my old pal from USAF days?

"That's right. Have you picked a target yet?"

"Why do you want to know?"

"Please ignore the question."

"I will. I can tell you that we do not select a target, or targets, until the last minute."

Damn! I could have learned something useful! And, of course, he was right. Unless you are Oswald and have been given a clean shot at your target due to a last-minute change of route that he had to know about in advance, you don't fix a plan ahead of time. And even when you have someone on the inside feeding you information, many factors can shift. You balance several possibilities and issue a "go" only at the last minute and only when your target is as open as

Kennedy's head was that day in Dallas. You may even want the would-be assailants caught. Archduke Ferdinand survived the first assassination attempt that day in Sarajevo. But not the second. While everyone is has gathered to a point around a first attempt, target acquisition becomes muy facil, as they say. Very easy.

But – damn! – all I had learned was that Dave had betrayed me. Us. And I had to get that information to Diego. After than, I would recuse myself. I had proved to be just another silly, old man. Hadn't I tried to tell that to Ben Maclin only a fortnight ago?

Going back the other way always looks different. And it takes longer. I heard the dog as a kind of whisking sound, followed by a growl. This one was not sending an alarm. This one was out for my throat. I got over the wall, but not without scraping my hands and punching a hole in my pants. The hole was wet with blood from a mild contusion on my right knee. But dog was on the other side, waking the starlit countryside, and only an open field lay beyond the wall, a field adrift in moonlight. I'd be an easy target and my shoulders did not savor a shot between them.

Most people who haven't done something for a while recognize that what they recall as easy can be difficult. If it's a physical activity – wow! I'm not as fast as I thought I was. Or – I didn't warm up enough – there goes that hamstring! Of course, a righthanded hitter has to be careful. He swings. He makes contact. He follows through. Then his entire muscular structure insists on going the other way toward first base. And the right hamstring bears the strain of that decision. Or – does not. What had happened to me was mental. I had forgotten to read the signs. And now I was paying for it.

What sign should I have missed? That damned phone call while Dave and I were having lunch at the Alfonso Trece. He'd set me up perfectly. "Soon," he had said. And soon evolved into now.

And now, I was crouched behind a wall, while, on the other side, a large dog was announcing my presence to the moon and other lookers on. I could tell he was large. He was not yapping, but snapping between full-throated growls. And I had almost made it!

If I just stayed here...

I could expect to be captured.

VIII.

A tunnel with light at the end? And ones you loved
waiting with smiles and open arms? Oh no!
Even darkness is gray, and closed eyes slide
in after-images of day. And in the ears
the hum of consciousness persists, before
the swim of dreams. But this? It was complete.
It was blackness. Total. Silence absolute.

Reginald St. Clair,
Closer Than Near

"Ah – the other American!"

So said don Frederico Breva as I was escorted into the room I had observed through its window.

"Wine?"

"Cerveza, si lo tienes, por favor."

"Por supuesto."

He indicated a chair. I sat down.

"How is your knee, Senor Winthrop?"

A dutiful medic had swabbed my contusion with alcohol – I swallowed my "ow!" – put some salve on it and taped a piece of gauze across. They'd given me a pair of green pants. In Spain it is gardeners not golfers who wear green pants.

"I think they saved it," I said.

He looked at me without smiling, his leathery face creasing into a question.

"May I ask you what you were doing here?"

He used the past tense. Whatever I had been doing, I was no longer doing it.

"I was looking for my friend."

"Senor Remington."

"Yes."

My cerveza arrived. A bottle of Damm, which the white coated servant poured into a pilsner glass.

The other American? Good, that meant Dave and me, but not Maria. I did not want her pulled into this. I deserved to suffer from my own stupidity, but I hoped to do so alone.

"What made you think he was here?"

The best answer was the truth.

"He told me he was coming here."

"Why?"

"Something about a rug he wanted to sell you."

Don Frederico laughed.

"Oh yes, a rug. But why would you come looking for him?"

"He had not returned."

"And you were worried about him."

"Yes."

It all seemed so innocent.

"Senor, it will be necessary for me to detain you for a few days."

Time is defined by what occurs within its reach. Or --what does not. I was not a ticking bomb. But the ticking was loud down the hillside in Sevilla.

We could have been at a gentleman's club, sheltered from the hubbub on the streets outside, carpeted, hushed, brushed by the scents of good cigars and of the sole and ribroast that trickled from the dining room down the hall.

"You see, Senor Winthrop, the world is controlled by a very few. It has always been thus, and at times the site of the control has been obvious. It was obvious just before World War One, and the Anarchists responded. But anarchy is only a means to an end. Those of us who propose to rule the world today will do so in an enlightened way. That I can promise. Mussolini started out well, for example. It was not just a matter of getting train schedules under control or removing beggars from the area around the Coliseum, but a question of social justice. Mussolini still might have stayed on as leader had he not become anxious to cash in on Hitler's conquests. Fool! Franco would have done much better had he not carried out a series of reprisals against his enemies. Absolute rulers do have to guard against absolute paranoia. Believe me, the hatred of Franco exists to this day. But Franco was smart enough not to ally himself with that madman in Berlin. And I tell you this. If we build schools, parents will be happy. Most of the middle class consists of parents. If we support the industry we have and expand it, people will have good jobs. And people with good jobs are happy. Or, at least, hopeful. Power need not be tyranny."

No. But absolute power inevitably became tyranny. Lord Acton's thesis could not be refuted or repealed.

"We will keep each other in check," he said.

I think he believed that. Oligarchs often seduce themselves with mythologies of their own benevolence. Breva was basking in his good intentions. I recalled an ad of some years back, where an executive jet had been made available to a young cancer victim. The gray-haired, gray-suited executive smiled at the lad. See what a good man I am!

Like so many who would gain power, though, Breva's indictment of the system he would replace was accurate. But, as we discovered when we toppled Saddam, you'd better have a replacement ready. I fear a worse may come in his place. The boys had forgotten their Tito. And they had forgotten how easy it would have been to let Uncle Ho win his election in 1956. We would have had to coexist with a communist regime and that was anathema to Dulles and Rusk. But now

Vietnam is our trading partner. Could not that result have been achieved less expensively?

Someone – Dave perhaps – had told Breva that I was an aficionado. So, the next morning, I was invited to the inner courtyard of the hacienda, an enclosed walkway of slate and plaster surrounding an ancient fountain that may have dated back to Moorish times. It still produced a whispering mist. On the wall, above the tiles of blue and gold, were wooden plaques with the heads of bulls staring out. When I saw such trophies as a kid, I always thought the body of the rest of the animal was somewhere behind the wall. The bulls' heads had no ears. They were the great bulls of the Rancho Montonoso – Recuerdo, con Manolete, Valencia, 1944, Coterrear, con Arruza, Cadiz, 1946, Helado, con Belmonte, San Sebastian, 1934, Duradero, con Ordonez, Ronda, 1949, Terclopelo, con Dominguin, Madrid, 1951, Contraparte con Julio Aparicio, Pamplona, 1963. If there were bodies behind the wall, they had no tails either. These bulls represented "dos orejas y rabo" – two ears and a tail that had been awarded the matadors, as don Frederico informed me.

I stared at the glass eyes, murmured appreciatively, and joined don Frederico for wine in the dark paneled bar room adjoining the courtyard.

He poured purple wine into two glasses from a carafe and pushed one of the glasses toward me. I found it strange that he was spending so much time with me. I had very little to tell him that he did not already know. I felt as if I were being sized-up, as if I were being rushed for a fraternity. Surely he did not believe that he would persuade me to his point-of-view.

"You see, Senor Winthrop, the old systems are collapsing – liberal democracy, self-regulating capitalism. They were myths. They stayed alive for a while, just as long as people believed in the mythologies and as long as money existed to support them. But democracy became a rule by a few, an oligarchy, and markets were always manipulated by a very few who made the money. They went too far, true, not so much out of greed, but because with their shareholders and boards demanding performance they could not sit back. They had to perform. They inevitably over-leveraged themselves in their competitive frenzy. And with the old order washing away like a child's castle in the waves, someone has to take over. It will be an age of strong men, not unlike Germany after the destruction of the 1920s. The Jews may not have been responsible, but some people were, and some of them were Jews. But, as my grandfather used to say, 'Hitler gave anti-Semitism a bad name.'

"And it is easy to find scapegoats, easy to claim that we are under attack. One simply includes the victims in the definition of who 'we' may be."

Of course he was right about the collapse of the revered institutions of the western world. The idea of an attack was easy. A new Pearl Harbor, a new 9/11 was easily posited since those attacks had been real. As Goring said at Nuremberg in 1945, "The people can always be brought to the bidding of the leaders. That is easy. All you have to do is to tell them that they are being attacked and denounce the pacifists for lack of patriotism and exposing the country to danger. It works the same way in any country." Cheney proved that and keeps trying to prove it. Whether a new dark-age of fascism is about to descend upon us is another matter. I, at least, would do my best to defeat that prospect. But I was a prisoner, however pampered, of the powers that I would resist. Yes, I had considered escaping, but it had only been a thought. The place was guarded and I could no longer feel the recklessness of even yesterday coursing though my hardening arteries.

"We won't blame the Jews this time, of course. We have many more tangible enemies."

It was not as bad as I thought it would be.

71

In fact, it was quite comfortable. I could do no more. Let Contreras and his professionals handle the rest. I could just relax and watch what happened. The wine was good and it made me sleepy.

The guard in front of my room was the same man who had warned me a couple of days ago along the Paseo Colon. But he glanced at me neutrally as I came back, with escort, from an interview with don Frederico Breva. Perhaps a flicker of contempt. I tried to warn you!

I was ensconced in a room that overlooked the vast, upland meadow where bulls blended with the shadows of the oak trees that grew randomly amid the lush grasses and frequent ponds. But the window was barred. A guard sat on a chair outside the room with a shotgun between his knees. My food arrived punctually via a man with a tray accompanied by another guard. I received clean undershorts, sox, and polo shirt on my first full day there.

I heard voices in the hallway.

"I have been sent by Senor Breva."

"He said nothing to me."

"You want to ask him? He'll be very happy with you."

"All right."

The door was unlocked.

It was Dave.

He made that characteristic look around tour with quick side to side darts of his eyes. He put a finger to his lips and pointed again at the light fixture in the center of the room.

"I have been sent to ask you why you are here," he said loudly.

He reached into a pocket and handed me a folded piece of paper from a legal pad.

"Please consider your answer. I will give you time to think."

He pointed at the cream-colored light fixture in the ceiling.

"No cameras," I whispered, unfolding the paper. But I had missed the microphone in the light fixture.

"I came to look for you," I said.

"You hold to that story?"

"It's the only story I have to tell."

"I have infiltrated this group," the note said. "But they don't trust me. I can move around the complex, but they won't let me leave until they have accomplished whatever their goal is. Tell me that you suspect Breva and came here to investigate. Tonight, I will come for you. Can you fly a 180?"

I nodded.

"Keys?" I whispered.

He wrote. "I will have them."

"Well," I said, feigning reluctance after a long pause, "As I said, I came here to look for you. I also suspect that Breva is behind the right-wing group known as the Nuevofalange. And I now know that you have gone over to them. Please get out of here. I am ashamed to be in the same room with you."

He smiled.

"All right. I shall report back to Senor Breva that you have been cooperative."

"I want to be released immediately."

"That is not for me to decide."

"You are a traitor."

"To whom?"

Good question.

"I will ask about your release and let you know."

He rapped on the door. The lock clicked, the door opened, and he was gone.

Good. We had someone on the inside. If we got out of here, we might be able to stop them. This time. But that's what it amounted to – momentary stays against chaos.

As we left the room, I noticed that the chair where the guard had been was empty. Perhaps Dave knew the guard. Perhaps the man who had tried to warn me had been persuaded to abandon his post for the moment. I'd ask Dave. That is, I'd ask him once we got out of here.

That Cessena 180 had to be an ancient craft. I don't think they'd built any since the 1980s. But they were rugged, suited to short, unimproved runways, and had enough range to get Breva to Madrid when he wanted to go. They were also hard to insure, since their tail wheel make them tricky to land and take off, but I assumed that insurance was no problem for Breva.

I was running through the procedures as I followed Dave down a long hallway toward an "Exito" sign. For some reason, during our lunch at the Alfonso, I had told him that I had been flying for years. Now I knew the reason that I had mentioned that. And I learned right then the reason why I'd learned to fly after getting back from Korea.

The hillside was drifting with mist. That was a good thing in one way. No one would think we'd try to steal an airplane, particularly on a gray and misty night, but it meant that I'd be on instruments and that would make navigation tricky. Our goal was a tiny field a few miles south of the main airport. It would be hard to find if visibility were limited. I would be able to turn on the runway lights from the cockpit, but I had to find the damn runway first.

We detached the guywires.

I could hear the whisp, whisp of a dog running toward us.

"Get in!" I shouted, as I climbed in the left side of the aircraft.

The dog leaped against the thin door of the old aircraft, his paws scratching, his breath steaming the window. If a watchdog comes, can a guard be far behind?

I mumbled about fuel switches, mixture, carb heat, and throttle.

I got the engine started with a great snort of exhaust, checked to make sure that all the external surfaces were free, spun the nose toward the thin dirt strip and taxied to the end of the runway. The dog was making repeated leaps against the frail door on my side of the aircraft. As I throttled up, I noticed the instrument panel. Damn! Like any oldtimer, I was accustomed to air speed, altimeter, vertical speed, and artificial horizon. They had upgraded this ancient crate. I was in a TAA – a Technically Advanced Aircraft – with a glass cockpit. That meant on-the-job training. But the pitch information was represented by a vertical line. And that is basically all I would need to take off. I lifted the nose and let the plane slip the surly bonds of tamped-down dirt.

And the fact that I did not know exactly what I was looking at became irrelevant. I could hear air being disturbed below me as I lifted off. The warping of sound was followed by the slash of shells through the aircraft's fragile framework.

"Hang on!" I shouted calmly.

Dave said nothing. But suddenly he slumped against the yoke in front of him, pitching the nose down sharply and filling the windscreen with a mist-threaded valley. I pushed him back with a straining right arm and pulled the nose up with my left hand, but my right hand came away thick with blood.

"Dave?"

Nothing. He fell off toward the door at his right shoulder.

Carmona is on a ridge overlooking the Guadalquivir River valley, along which Sevilla stretches. It was going to be a basic glide – but to where? They'd have someone at SVQ – the airport – before I got there. And I doubted that I'd get beyond it, to look for the small strip below. The river? No. I had to get help for Dave.

The aircraft was struggling. I could smell fuel, meaning that one of the rounds must have hit the petrol tank. How fast was it leaking? I did not know. The weather was closing in. The sweep, sweep of the beacon at the airport was wasting itself among the lowering clouds. I could barely make out the A4 highway that ran beside SVQ. And the engine was sputtering in front of me. If I turned toward the airport, I'd never make it to runway niner – even if no one else was contesting me in the traffic pattern. I'd stall out and crash into the city. If I continued straight ahead, I'd fly into the old city, probably near the Iglesia de Macarena. I didn't have enough altitude to make it to the train tracks that had begun to sink into the horizon to the left of me. I was out of options. And I was pretty sure that Dave was dead in the seat beside me. That had nothing to do with whatever decision I might make. It just made it less important.

The old part of the city, the section that runs along the river, winked at me. I was at a thousand feet and descending to hold airspeed at about 110, according to my Primary Flight Display. Could I make it to the river and set down without contacting one of the many bridges? I glanced to my right. I could not see the river. It nestled somewhere beneath a cottony quilt. And then I saw a great blank area in front of me. A lake? No. It was the old cemetery, a vast city of moss-invaded marble, crosses luminous under the mist, and angels stained with time. No place for a forced landing. Except... I strained my eyes through the prowl of murk. Yes. I could see the gate at the far end of the cemetery, its bars outlined in the light from the circular street outside. The gate led back along one long avenue, from the most recent monuments to the ones surrounded by trees and overreaching bushes that went back to forgotten years. I lined up, nose toward the distant gate, and trimmed the aircraft against 15 degrees of flaps. A flick of landing lights showed me that I was over the avenue. I held it off, then touched down. Too hot, but better than stalling out at fifty feet. Dave slumped forward again against the straps. Metal screamed and bolts snapped off like rounds from a Winchester. My right wing collapsed against a pillared sarcophagus, swinging the aircraft to the right with a violence that twisted my face to the left and threw poor Dave against me. The nose broke itself against an angel of death, its folded wings mocking my crushed boxkite.

I unstrapped and opened the door. The heavy air of an unused space flowed into the cockpit from the rows of cypress trees on either side of this section of road. But I smelled no fuel. I did not sense the burning-water scent of an electrical fire. I reached across and put a forefinger on Dave's left wrist. Nothing. But my finger stuck there for a moment in blood as I pulled my hand away. I pushed him back into his seat with both hands and climbed out.

"Sorry, Dave. Damn!"

The gate would be locked. I doubted that anyone had reported the sound of an aircraft in trouble and descending. Those who might have said something were quiet. And those quiet people around me had never seen an airplane. I was deep in the 18th century.

I pulled out the flashlight next to the seat and snapped it on and off. It worked. The air was damp with rot, and rain began to pock down on hollow tombs as I wandered through the scratch of cypress, toward the fence. I don't think they built it to keep people from sneaking out.

I got out easily enough, squeezing between an old service gate that had brought bodies to this necropolis two hundred years ago and the iron fence. I went in and out of several cul de sacs, and finally found myself on an avenue that said Ronda. Good. It led to Recaredo, which would get me back to the Alfonso. My cell phone had been confiscated, of course.

Otherwise, I did not exist, as the Colonel had said. And, of course, that is how an agent often feels. He is incognito, or posing as a cultural attache, or undercover. Who is he? If he is any good, he had better be his identity. We assume so many personae that our existential being is some stranger we would not recognize. He introduces himself in dreams and at moments when one is told – you do not exist. And, if my GPS was still working, I was still up at El Rancho Montonoso. Too many of my colleagues in the Company believed in that artificial world and would still have me up in the Carmona hills even if I walked into the room and proclaimed my presence.

My expression as I asked for my key -- "llave, tres, uno, tres, por favor" – said to Pepe, don't ask. I was wet with rain, but still sweaty. My shirt was black with blood where I'd rubbed my right hand against it. My eyes were probably still wide with the stare I'd used to bring in enough light to land the damned aircraft. I was glad they knew me at this hotel!

I poured the two tiny bottles of Chevas in the mini-bar into a glass, took a huge swallow, and called Diego.

"Stay there. I am on my way," he told me. That was good. I did not want to go anywhere. I did take a shower before he arrived and consumed a can of Cruz Campo from the mini-bar, having unexpectedly run out of Scotch.

IX.

The secret of my success is clean living and a fast outfield.

Vernon "Lefty" Gomez

I wonder how many investment bankers and ad men still believe that being from the right side of the tracks is an advantage. Most do, I suppose, assuming they realize anything. You get a 90 yard head start in a 100 yard dash. But – you only cover that ten yards. Much of my growing up, such as it has been, involved unlearning what I took for granted, going back to examine that 90 yards I had been ceded. My superiority. My splendid education at Hadley College, pride of the Connecticut Valley. What I learned, of course, was how to justify the system that got me where I am. It was not education. It was indoctrination. But at some point I did ask, just exactly where am I?

It may have started when I was playing hardball in a park on the other side of 128. I was twelve. A big Italian kid, Tony Musso, threw me a curve. I lunged back as it twisted across the plate for a strike.

"What'sa matter, kid," said the ump, a janitor from one of the Lowell junior high schools, "Ain't you never seen a curve before?"

No, Mr. Ump, I haven't.

I stood in for the next pitch.

It was a fast ball that hit me below my left knee.

The ump could have said that I had made no effort to evade the pitch. That was known as "taking one for the team." But I think he understood.

"Okay, kid. Take first."

I limped down the line. Tony Musso jutted his jaw at me.

I think I realized then that people existed who wished me harm, who would enjoy hurting me. Not all – I don't think the umpire took any pleasure in what he had to know would be a welt, with stitches in it, and perhaps the signature of "William Harridge, President, American League" in black and blue on the pale side of my calf. But the big kid who lived in one of the small, frame houses on the wrong side of 128 or in one of those three story fire traps close to the mills? Yes. He held a weapon in his hand, and he did not mind firing it at God's little gift to the world. We do have enemies. I have never been convinced that one treats most of the rest of the world as enemies – the Bush-Cheney Doctrine – but it is salutary to know that there's a lot of rage out there. And it may help to know that there's some rage inside you as well. Inside me, at least. Part of it came from believing that I was privileged. Part of it comes from knowing that others never question their privilege. And a lot comes from knowing that they are the guys in charge. But let a black man be the guy in charge and watch the rage crash in like a tidal wave.

My own entitlement demonstrated itself in my being a Yankees fan in a Red Sox world. But the Red Sox don't win, I said to myself. And I, as a winner, wanted to associate myself with winners. I had to keep this allegiance quiet, of course, but I could rejoice secretly, savoring the victories of my heroes in the city-state south of Boston before I went to sleep at night. And at fourteen or so, champagne was beyond the range of my purse and imagination. But I remembered the time we were visiting in New York. My Dad took me to Yankee Stadium. We had seats in the third base mezzanine – a shaded view of the green garden where men cavorted and baseballs flew in and out of the sun like Icarus. The monuments to Ruth, Gehrig, and Huggins sat in deep left center. The great grated facade loomed like a portcullis above the action and the Court House shone in marble splendor, conferring a legal sanction to the Yankees and their triumphs. But most of all, in those days, was Joe D. He stood calmly in center, behind Gomez or Ruffing, ready to gallop after anything hit to that vast lawn known as outfield. And you wouldn't realize how far the ball had been hit until you glanced at the runner already at second as the ball settled into Joe's glove. Routine. No one ever saw him dive for a ball. Ted Williams? A great hitter, with eyes that could count the seams on a curve ball as it slid toward the plate, and wrists that could snatch the ball from the catcher's glove and still pull it to right. But DiMaggio was DiMaggio. Joe, that is. And, when the ball was not in play, few eyes in the Stadium were not watching him.

"You what?"

"I made a straight-in approach."

"I'll have to file some sort of report."

"Of course."

This was not an officer falling back on bureaucracy or trying to cover his ass. It was someone trying to concoct a narrative that would satisfy his superiors and perhaps pacify the lads whose aircraft I had totaled without compromising his mission.

I noticed that my hands were trembling. Beer was splashing onto the back of my right hand, scrubbed almost clean of blood. It was the delayed reaction I had not experienced in more than fifty years.

"Can you say that the pilot was killed in the crash?"

"But if you are correct, Dave died of a gunshot wound."

"Must have hit him in the back as we took off."

"We will say that a single body was found in the aircraft. We will say that the identity of the person is being withheld until proper notification of family is made."

"Okay. What do we do now?"

"We cannot just barge up to Breva's Rancho Montanoso. As you did. We don't have enough."

"Obviously, neither did I. I will follow the rules of engagement from now on."

That meant that I was not to engage at all.

"Please do. Had you remained in captivity up there, I could not have done a thing to help you. You would not have compromised our operation, but some people would not have been happy with you."

True. A long list of people would have been very unhappy with me.

All people praise our civilian leadership of the armed forces. It prevents the military dictatorships that characterize so many of the third world countries. But it depends on which civilian is Commander in Chief at any given moment. I think that only Eisenhower could have ended the Korean conflict without evoking an outcry of "softness" on communism, even "treason!" And, of course, leadership of the CIA has been uneven. Dulles lied to Kennedy about the Bay of Pigs. A rabble of fifteen hundred was going to defeat a well-equipped army, even Castro's army? And then the ideologue Woolsey, who could only claim incompetence in the face of Aldrich Ames' selling out of our entire Soviet operation. And, before that, the demented Casey, brain-dead even before his brain was invaded by multiplying cells of malignancy. And the ambition-crazed Tenet, who thought it was a wondrous thing to be in the same ovality with little Bush. And, worse, an absolute hack like Porter Goss, utterly incapable of understanding how intelligence works and how it goes wrong. So that good leadership – Admiral Turner, Judge Webster, Gates – was often helpless in the face of a corrupt culture that blended stupidity with arrogant certainty. And now Penetta has to buy into that culture to establish "credibility." They'll play him like a Stradivarius.

I got out when the FBI refused to go along with our torture program. I wanted no part of it, either. You get good intelligence by establishing contacts and mining them for information. The memo that Bush waved away about Bin Laden's determination to attack within the U.S. was the result of a painstaking effort within the most difficult of contexts – the Muslim shadow-world that is almost impenetrable for even its co-religionists. But we got it right. We also knew – and warned – that the hijacking of airplanes and their use against selected targets was a possibility. And little Ms. Rice, she sat on her tuffet. She had been warned of precisely that prospect. It was not, as they said, the greatest intelligence failure since the Trojan Horse or Pearl Harbor. It was a failure of leadership. And somehow that was forgotten in the shock of 9/11. It took Katrina to make the point.

We had awakened from naps after sandwiches and wine in the Alfonso cafe.

"At times," she said, "I feel like Mersault in the Camus book – totally detached, like a face in a Macy's parade floating above Fifth Avenue. And, at other times, I am angry, enraged – the poverty, the children who are all hungry eyes, the killing."

This was a young person talking of her inconsistency. It was an awareness of what the bi-polarity of early efforts at maturity – the swing between extremes. She made love like a Maenad. That was her escape from the chilly aloofness that she could discern in herself.

"You've done a lot of reading," I said.

"Unis – the UN School. The Manhattan campus had a great after-school elective in photography. Then Hunter. They pile on the books."

83

"Long walk."

"From the UN, yes, it would be. We lived on 52ed. The number six train ran from 51st right up to 68th. Easy commute. I was basically interested in photography, though. New York cries out for black and white photos."

"Why black and white?"

"It is not really a colorful city. Valencia has its fireworks. Barcelona has its Gaudi. Paris has vistas. Kansas City in the spring has its fountains and flowers. Rome has Salvi and Bernini. But New York is shadows. And, of course, in black and white you get a depth field. Color stops your eye at the first bright place in the frame."

"This work?"

"If it calls for a photographer. It pays well. Supports my habit. A lot of travel. And I just do as I am told – take pictures of what people want to see. Point and click."

"You're really a New Yorker, though?"

"No. Not like the people who move there and become New Yorkers – completely jealous of their possession of the city. I hung out mostly with UN kids. I met some kids from Hunter High School when I went over there for some classes. But the UN kids are cosmopolitan in ways New Yorkers never can be. New Yorkers are among the most provincial people I've ever met."

"But you worked as a photographer?"

"Free lance. I supported myself by doing translations."

"For Mexican prizefighters?"

She looked at me.

"When a Mexicans is fighting, HBO or Showtime has a translator in the corner to tell us gringos what the trainer is telling him to do. 'He say, "jab more."' 'He say, "the other guy tired."' Profound stuff like that."

"I'll look into it when I get home," she said, laughing. "A whole new career field. You like boxing?"

"I did. I boxed."

I pointed to a white scar on my nose that for some reason the sun never touched.

"And I saw Joe Louis at the end of his career. His last knockout of Lee Savold at the old Garden. My parents were visiting friends on Park Avenue. I saw Ray Robinson in his prime. He did manifest the sweet science, as Leibling called it. Left jab, right to the body, left hook to the head. You didn't see the punches until the other guy's head suddenly pivoted to the left and his knees became an unsolved problem in number theory."

I had been giving her a massage. My hands grew young against the smoothness of her back.

She rolled over and pulled me close.

"I am enjoying my older man phase."

I was not deceiving myself. Or so I kept telling myself. This was a few moments in an exotic foreign city, amid the fume of spring blossoms and the aphrodisiac of a slight whiff of danger. That erased the age difference. But only temporarily. What I was doing – quite consciously (but very secretly) was reimagining my wild fling with Anne so many years before. Why should that be so significant – given the several lush episodes between then and now? Because, with Anne, my world was pre-responsible, almost unconscious. I had no financial fears. I was totally free. She was absolutely uninhibited and I extrapolated 'woman' from her. I assumed that many more like her awaited me in the eternal springtime ahead. Those were moments before my frontal cortex enlarged to accommodate being broke and women who yielded with cooling reservations, and fear of unwanted pregnancy and fear of death. Anne had been an ontogenetic recapitulation of phylogeny that only a privileged few could enjoy. And, of course, I did not know that at the time. I had been living before the fall. But old fools are supposed to know better.

And – I knew it – I was using Maria to revisit those moments. I don't think she would have minded that much. She was taking this less seriously than I was.

"Time to head up to the bullring," I said, rolling off the bed and standing.

"Will it be any good today?"

"Should be. Get a couple of photos of Ponce and Juli."

"I will. Extra curricular."

The game is close. The halfback from Cambridge makes his cut, but I have the angle on him. I close in, aiming for his fly, from which he cannot fake. I notice that my cleats are suddenly grinding dirt. I fall, my shoulder pads clattering around me like the armor of an unhorsed knight. The halfback from Cambridge dances past, untouched under the hangtime of a halfmoon, and unmolested toward the stripes of the promised land riding out from the shadow of the goalposts. In those days, they put the football field down on top of the baseball diamond. I have failed to pick up the slow curve of the pitcher's mound, over which I have tripped – accompanied by the delighted laughter of five thousand people barking to a crescendo as I pick myself up and prepare to try to block their extra point.

Do people feel that they are living in the wrong time? I believe that I should have lived in a pagan world, one with a fluidity and a lack of doctrine that our world lacks. It is not just the restrictions of religion, but the way everything is codified. I, as a member of the upper middle class, had mastered the codes automatically. But still, I was bound by them. In pagan times, I might have met Helen of Troy. I might have seen Icarus fall from between his wings into the Mediterranean, the two wings waving back and forth and shedding feathers like wisps of cumulous as they followed him down. I might have met Heracles, and Theseus, and Achilles. I might have meant the Cumae, who forgot to ask for youth along with the years she requested in that cloud of seed. I might have seen the figure heads of the Trojan ships drop to the sea and become mermaids, who would swim on to harass the Greek galleys trying to get back down the Aegean. I might have seen that horse pushed by a thousand backs through the opening of the wall. Would I have warned the Trojans? It may be a creed outworn, as the poet says, but I would have breathed a sky still exploring the meaning of the stars. Actually, I was doing that, here in the lush springtime of Southern Spain.

"Did you ever meet Cheney?"

"Oh yes."

"What did you think of him?"

"A very dangerous man. Powerful, but ignorant. Like Rumsfeld, Cheney thought he knew more than any one in the room."

"But don't we need strong leaders?"

"Yes. But Cheney was a bully. And that is never strength. He oversaw a number of our briefings for Congress. Just having him there, glowering, created an intimidating atmosphere. Those people are politicians, after all, and their main concern is never the public good."

"No?"

"It's getting elected. They asked few questions when Cheney was there. Questions might suggest doubt, and they were afraid of expressing doubt and getting blasted. Cheney could kill a career with a word or two. And he did."

Maria was lovely and very intelligent, but like most people her age, naive. That was refreshing, I suppose, compared to my cynicism.

"Let me explain," I said. "Cheney was infuriated when Nixon drained so much authority from the Presidency during the Watergate thing. Now what happens psychologically to someone that angry?"

"He tends to overreact."

"He does indeed. Cheney became Nixon – the Nixon who would make up for his errors, the Nixon who would restore the 'unitary executive' he had shattered, the Nixon who only physically had gestured from that helicopter that day. So – naturally – Cheney, like Nixon when challenged, hit on illegality as the only way to combat jihadism. We needed a target. Cheney decided that we could not attack North Korea, or Egypt, or Saudi Arabia, but that we could attack Saddam. An easy target. And guess who decided to disband the Iraqi Army?"

"Cheney?"

"The order filtered down from his assistant, Addington, though no one has traced it back to the office of Vice President. They blame Bremmer, of course, but it was not his decision to make. And it insured that a well-armed and well-trained resistance would spring up immediately. The decision would have seemed intentional if it had not been the product of sheer incompetence."

"So you're saying that strong leadership..."

"Has to be intelligent leadership. Almost everyone panicked after 9/11. But our fallback position was the Constitution. That's what it's there for – emergencies. Like the assassination of Kennedy. That's why Spain is in danger."

"It has a constitution, though."

"Yes, but if the U.S. Constitution can be so easily overridden in an emergency – and 9/11 did occur – think of how frail the Spanish Constitution will be. Think of how easy it was for Bush to get most of the telecoms to break the law for him and do all of that illegal surveillance."

"I'm not sure. Isn't there the possibility of enlightened leadership?"

"Plato's philosopher king? Leadership can only emerge within contexts and can be effective only within controlled environments – oversight, checks and balances. Look at what bad leadership does. Over half of the people in the U.S. believe that torture under certain circumstances is okay. They've been sold that by '24' and by Cheney. They think it gets results. It gets confessions. And the bastards don't realize that 9/11 was the result of a revenge culture. They wanted to get back at us for perceived injustice. Bush said, 'They hate us for our freedoms.' Talk about a radical misreading of motive. And Bush used the word 'crusade' early on before someone told him to shut up. So we invade Iraq and kill a lot of people. We torture prisoners and take photographs of that degradation. We incite revenge."

"You are angry about it, aren't you."

"I am. You work for most of your life for things you believe in and the shadow of Richard Nixon suddenly starts calling the shots. Yes, it is anger making."

"I guess I've been around the UN too long."

And I could understand that. Civility. Debate. Powerful countries – whether the Soviet Union early on or the U.S. later – ignoring resolutions and going their own way. Corruption. Nepotism. If one observed that environment, one could develop a yearning for decisive leadership. And Cheney, no doubt, had been acting in response to that climate. He knew what he wanted to do and sought lip-service in support of his already formulated conclusions.

"Let's open a bottle of wine," she said.

"I will calm down. Wine usually exacerbates the mood I'm in when I take my first sip."

"I'll change the subject."

"That is a good idea."

I had given up my cover as a correspondent de los toros, but I went dutifully to the corrida the next day. The security issue was still very much alive. The King was there and acknowledged the many eyes turned toward him. One set of eyes might well have been planning a shot to punctuate the next afternoon.

Ponce was elegant as was his wont, cool and fluid with the left wrist, pulling the bull past his body as if it were a cloud. Juli was spectacular, as was his wont, seeming to design his passes extemporaneously, creating a primal dance with his bulls that hearkened back to Cretan festivals alive only in ancient carvings. But the star was Juan Padilla, a little man from Jerez with the heart of a lion. He placed his sticks brilliantly – Juli no longer essays the banderillas – and faced off against a cathedral of a bull from the ranch of Marques de Domecq. He did a heart-wrenching faena and was assured of dos orejas – two ears – from the demanding and discriminating Sevilliano crowd if he killed well. But how could he? The bull's head was still high and the bull's shoulders came up to Padilla's. He lined up for the volapie – the run in for the kill – making sure that the bull's eyes were on the muleta -- the small cape. He sighted down the sword to the spot between the bull's shoulder blades where he wished to drive the blade – and went in like a destroyer against a dreadnought at Jutland. He was suddenly on the bull's right horn and then in the air. The man is dead, I thought. I glanced at the sword. It was in to the hilt. Pedilla landed on the crushed stone. Dead, I thought. His trophies will be posthumous. He rose. His beautiful green and gold traje de luces was covered with blood. I will watch him die, I thought. But it was the bull that dropped, first to its knees for a final look around the Plaza, and then to its side, its legs splayed stiffly outward. It was the bull's blood on Padilla. The Plaza was full of handkerchiefs and rhythmic shouts of "Torero!"

And we tried to induce the judge to give him un rabo -- a tail -- in addition to the dos orejas. But this was Sevilla and no one could recall the award of a tail here since the days of local favorite, Paco Camino. What Padilla had added to the remarkable skill of Ponce and Juli was a gutsiness that brought my stomach to my throat. I had not had that sensation since seeing Cordobes in Tijuana some forty years ago.

The three matadors were carried al hombros – on shoulders – though the main gate of La Maestranza. No greater honor exists in the world of the toros. And even outside the arena people were looking at each other and speaking in exclamation points at the beginning and the end of their sentences, coming down from exaltation and sharing it with their fellows. For a moment, we were a community of souls.

What I noticed was that the old feeling had returned. It is called aficion. It is like being in love. It is a response from the depths that can't really be described. But I recognized at the moment that it returned that I had lost it. I suppose that an art historian is at first inspired by a love of art. But the more he learns in pursuit of that love the less fierce that love can become. He knows the material, but the enjoyment is in the knowing, in the clinical expertise. That is what had happened to me. I could see, for example, how Jose Thomas dictated the next pass with a flick of the wrist at the end of the previous pass that brought the bull around again. But it was observation without passion. Padilla had pulled me out of that, or had pulled something out of me. I had not expected that.

"I got Padilla," Maria said, pressing through the throng toward me.

"You should do a book when you get back."

"I may. Who knows?"

"I've built up a thirst."

"El Cairo?"

That was a restaurant on a side street nearby with a bar on the second floor and abundant tapas. And it was to there we wended through the still-ecstatic people.

I had not expected my aficion to return. But I had not expected my libido to flow back from the deepsea caves into which it had withdrawn. Not all the surprises that life provided here at the end of it were nasty.

X.

He heard the warning voice torn away
in the wind. What youth heeds a wiser word?
He may have felt the heat against his neck,
the trickle of wax along his spine. But he
rose higher. This so new! So far above
the wrinkled blue below! He felt the sway
of wings back and forth. No seaside bird
had come this close. Did he perceive a speck
of feather rising past the apogee,
the wings above him as his body dove
through their fragile grip that sunny day?

Sean Malley,
Labyrinths

My hand-held computer, which did give a GPS reading to whoever was monitoring me, had to be telling that agent that I was somewhere other than where I was. Of course, it could be that no one was paying any attention to what my alter ego was transmitting. A ghost was up there in the hills, telling people of his presence or, like many a ghost, frustrated that no one could see him, angry that he had ceased to exist except as an isolated consciousness that could communicate only with itself.

One of my problems – one that has plagued me throughout the many years – is that I do not wait for other people's reactions to decide how I feel about something. Right and wrong, black and white come instantly into view on my evaluative screen. I do not always take the narcissists' way out. What do other people think? What do the polls say? I am a misfit. When the Leviathan was sailing for the last time out of New York Harbor to sail off to be scrapped in Scotland, WBZ broadcast an elegiac farewell. "Now the great ship is passing an incoming freighter. The incoming vessel sends a mournful signal to the Leviathan, a final greeting, as the huge ship, now sadly tattered and forlorn after years of disuse, makes a last passage toward the open seas for a one-way voyage to the scrap heap."

I wept.

It was not like, ""It's burst into flames! It's burst into flames and is falling. It's crashing!" or "Schmeling is down! Schmeling is down! The men are in the ring." Herb Morrison and Clem McCarthy conveyed excitement, whether horrified or anticipated, not slow, elegiac inevitability. They did not create a person of a ship, a ship that knew somehow that it was going to be a ship no more.

But I react quickly and I do not mask my reaction. That is one reason why I was fairly early relegated to a desk job – it was not just my mythical analytical ability. The CIA tries to find places for "its own," and that habit can result in the retention of incompetents – or traitors. Or misfits like me.

I don't claim that I can't be fooled, though. I try to be a gimlet-eyed realist, but that is often a pose adopted so that people around me will make that inference. That is another way that narcissists operate – assuming an expression, a posture, a gait that says something that may be half-true, may have been true at some past time – the ex-athlete now suffering from all those injuries – or that was never true. I don't fool myself, but I can be fooled myself.

A long time ago, a variety of grimy arenas dotted the New York City area – St. Nick's, Sunnyside, and Laurel Gardens, in Newark. One night, when I was visiting my cousins in South Orange, N.J., they and I went to Laurel Gardens to watch wrestling. Wrestling had become briefly popular on television, with Dennis James narrating the fakery with wry charm. And it was well done that night. A huge Negro named Zimba Parker beat up handsome Billy Darnell, Linda's brother. Parker fouled Billy repeatedly and left him helpless and half-conscious along the ropes. It was an elimination format, and when Billy was counted out, the next opponent, a French-Canadian named Maurice LaChappelle leaped over the ring post and lashed Zimba Parker around the ring with a series of judo chops. Sweet revenge. Zimba crumbled, black skin losing definition like obsidian melting away before the fury of virtue, LaChappelle went over to assist the still-dazed Billy Darnell, kneeling by the ropes. And, at 14, I believed all of it. It was wonderful!

I don't always know what triggers memory in me. Smell, yes, as Proust suggests. But, for me, it is usually a combination of tiredness and radical sensory stimulus. And I was tired. The trip had wiped me out. And Andalusia had been hit by a thunderstorm the likes of which – if it ever hit New England – would have erased the grid for a week. I could see the clouds building up over the Plaza as the rage rumbled down from Extremadora. Maria, thank heavens, had not come this afternoon. She was in her room studying the photos she'd taken, looking closely for any evidence that anyone – other than those whom we had already identified as security -- was paying more attention to the royal box than to the swirling drama on the crushed stone of the bullring.

I had planned to take a nap, then call her for dinner later on.

But the storm came. We huddled in the damp murkiness under the stands, pushed together in a space not meant for anything but passing through. It smelled of bodies and wet clothes. I finally said the hell with it and walked back to the hotel. The sky was alive with lightning outlining the vivid musculature of clouds and, every so often, showing an angry, cartoon face in them. The River seethed and hissed as if aflow with scalding water. The street streamed with a brown rush full of the soil of despoiled gardens. I squished up to the desk for my key and shrugged.

"Hace lluvia," I said to Pepe.

"Un poco," he said, laughing.

I toweled down and took a hot shower, but I could not rinse the thick scent of that underground from my pores.

I lay down and listened to seethe of storm moving back and forth in the trees below my window.

But I did not sleep. I was very suddenly in the back seat of that T-6 right after we had been hit. Cochran was slumped forward in the front cockpit. The sharp smell of an electrical fire came back at me as I pulled the stick in my cockpit back with both hands. Cochran slid to his right side, pushing the stick to the left.

"Captain Cochran!" I called. "You okay?"

Obviously not.

Some smoke was beginning to unfold from the front cockpit as I pushed the stick to the right with both hands to bring the wings level.

Cochran had let me fly the plane, of course, but not once we got close to the enemy lines. Now we were over them.

I pushed the stick to the left toward our positions. Cochran lurched to the left and the aircraft slid into a steep bank. Again, I forced the stick back. By now, smoke was flipping back into my face. It was no longer white, but had turned a greasy black.

I could see Seoul, a brown smudge on the horizon, to my right. Our field, then, was straight ahead.

"Reddog Control, this is six eight niner."

"Six eight niner. Reddog."

"Reddog, six niner. Pilot wounded. Request permission to land."

"Six niner. What is your current position? Over."

"Reddog. Six niner about ten miles out, north."

"Six niner. Understand. Cleared for runway 27. Call in on final. Over."

"Six niner. Have ambulance standing by."

"Six niner. Wilco."

"Six niner. And crash equipment. Aircraft is on fire."

"Six niner. Wilco."

Easy for you to say, I thought, you lucky son of a bitch. But I could think of nothing more to say. I was alone again.

"Aircraft in vicinity of Adjunct Field number two. Emergency in progress. Use number one if necessary. Otherwise, fly clear of traffic pattern."

Now the smoke was thick. I could not see Cochran's head in front of me. I pulled the canopy back, aware that I might fan the fire, but also aware that I was not breathing very well.

The engine, though, that sturdy radial, kept turning over. Now, I could hear flames licking at something. What could burn? The back of the front instrument panel. That must be where the black pitchy smoke was coming from. Would I lose the instruments I had in front of me? The one I needed was air speed. About 110 knots before I landed. Less and I'd spin in. More and I'd overshoot and bank into the pile of rocks that had been removed to build the field. I knew that from watching Cochran land the plane. But he kept the needle glued to the panel. I watched it wobble back and forth through the smoke.

On prior missions, after I had called in coordinates for whatever blur of movement that caught my eye on the northern mountainside, I would relax. The relaxation meant that someone else was in charge. But that was a dangerous indulgence. At this moment, with Captain Cochran lolling back and forth in the front cockpit, I heard a voice telling me to lean back and watch what happens. This is not you. You are watching a film. And I had seen all those films, with Wayne, and Payne, and Van Johnson, flying intrepidly through smoke and flack and enemy tracers. It became an easy substitution. Just watch. Just another film.

No, I said. I can't just watch. I had to pull myself away from that lulling voice, physically yank my mind back into that cockpit, where I was not a spectator but someone about to die.

I stuck my head out. The air was cold against the sides of my goggles. But there it was. Runway 27 etched in mud between two hangers that looked like giant half-buried garbage cans on one side, and rows of tents on the other.

Gear down and the nose came up. I forced it down again. I put down some flaps and the nose came up again. I pushed the stick forward with both hands. Then it dropped sharply as Cochran fell against the stick in the front cockpit. I pulled it back just before I banged down, going much too fast, rose again in an ungainly stall, then bounced again. I hit the brakes and ground looped, one wing flying up and pushing me against the side of the cockpit. I could hear Cochran bang against the side of the front cockpit. But we were stopped.

I got out and climbed up the left wing. Damn! Cochran was dead, his mouth sagging wordlessly in front of his microphone.

The firetruck crunched up.

"Fire's out," I said.

They pulled Cochran out and put him in the ambulance, but it was a going-through-the-motions process, no doubt outlined step-by-step in some manual. They flashed the light, but they did not bother with a siren on the way to the big damp tent that was the base infirmary.

I got a ride back in the base commander's staff car. I felt a stinging in my right hand. My glove was burned off. I had not noticed it until now. I reached for the pack of Luckies in the left pocket of my flightsuit and reconsidered. I needed no more smoke in my lungs just now. I remembered then that I had forgotten to call in on final.

"Bad luck, Winthrop," Major Carswell, the assistant base commander said. "You did a good job. You should have someone look at that hand."

I peeled the remains of my thin leather glove from the hand. Some skin came with it.

"Unguintine," I said.

"Purple heart," he said. "And maybe something more than that."

It was more than that. In unpopular wars, they hold medals out like boxes of popcorn. It doesn't help. Cochran got a Purple Heart too. And more than that.

I was walking around the room, not aware of where I was. I opened the doors to the tiny balcony that overlooked a wild sea of palm trees, and stood in the rain. It washed the sweat from me. I was in Spain again, watching a great storm rumble down the river to quench itself against the Mediterranean.

Maria and I had planned to go out to dinner. I hoped that she'd be willing to put that off and settle for room service and a bottle of Parxet Chardonnay or Freixenet Reserva Real. Or both. I had built up a thirst. I would start without her with one of the bottles of Torres Coronas from the restocked mini-bar.

Into vacancies come questions. My most vulnerable time arrives when I lurk between dream and wakefulness, and consider the latter while trying to recall the former. We humans must have an agenda, a list of things to do each day, a way of pulling ourselves from sleep to obligation. Without that little list that scribbles itself on the tabula raza of consciousness at dawn, we are lost. I am, at least. I think of Anne, of course. We loved before the expulsion, before intimidating angels with molten swords blocked the way back, before the gate forever slammed with a great iron clunk upon its flowering vines and fruit trees. I understand that. But I think of her to dispel other thoughts. These thoughts do not dwell on the evil I may have done. Yes, past moments do exist where I "followed orders."

That does, believe it or not, buffer guilt. I say to myself, I could not have known better at the time. What troubles me are the moments when I behaved as an automaton. Chief Justice Rehnquist once asked, when a man had been wrongfully sent to the death house, "But did the law work properly in this case?" In other words, guilt or innocence was irrelevant to the proper process of some abstraction. That was Platonism run amuck. The law could function like an elegant machine. But it tended to chew the people up within the precision of its rhythms. The times that most troubled me about myself were the times when I was the functionary in Kafka or Camus, or at Treblinka or Belsen, or in my own Company when the "selected out" button was pushed, and I acquiesced. The genius of any government is to inoculate the mid-level practitioners who direct the killing, and who sometimes do the killing. I don't believe that many can resist the process. It is the avenue to promotion, reward. If the powers-that-be say it's okay, it must be. It permits us to warm our chilly souls in the bask of approval. It is the treacherous process of narcissism. And, having succumbed to it too often, it is the shadow that mocks me when I awake. And so I daydream of Anne and of the innocents we were back then even as we delectated in what the mores of the times would have called sin. Sin, hell! It was the joy itself.

I was just old enough to have caught the edge of the world before it became attached to War II. And my primary memory of that time seemed to be Fred and Ginger movies, Eleanor Powell, and Myrna Loy. But those trips to the lost Atlantis of black and white film occurred much later on. I could seem to remember the originals in their times, but that was a deception. Looking at that deep art-deco world and listening to the songs was a retroactive construction of a consciousness that had not yet come alive during the amnesia of childhood. I did remember the Andrews Sisters singing the "Hut Sut Song." My primary memory, though, was of the World's Fair of 1939/40. The Trylon and Perisphere dominated the landscape and long lines wended up white walkways to enter the globe that had been sent on pillars in the Flushing swamp. The air was murky with the ground's recent past. You entered a hushed zone of shadows and sat in a comfortable chair in a line of chairs that moved within the darkened space around you. But in front of you opened up a wonderful world of alabaster cities, green fields, silver trains swallowing monorails as they sped from place to place, aircraft settling gracefully through the smokeless atmosphere. And behind, a voice told you what you were seeing. But a tyke could not both look and listen. I leaned forward and took in this wonderland. A kid who likes alternative universes had to love what he was seeing and to want to live there, or at least to have these toys. When you got out, blinking in the particle-laden sunlight, you received a button. "I have seen the future." I thought it was true. Time lasted longer back then and I held that future in view until December, 1941, when the subject was changed.

Thus musing and almost asleep again, an expected tap on the door roused me. Maria!

XI.

The darkness after moonrise, as the snow
rides out from under tree, is stark, colder
by way of emphasis then even when zero is low
in the mouth of Mercury. The light is bolder.
No moving shadow challenges its slow
control of a frozen moment growing older.

Perry Mulholland,
Landscape

I was so tired that I wanted to put my hands down and say, "no mas, no mas." The other guy – a light heavyweight from Brown with hair all over his body – was much better than I. And he was pounding me – jabs, hooks, straight rights, uppercuts. It wasn't the pounding, though. It was just the exhaustion. Get me out of here! Then the bell rang. I said nothing as I slumped on my stool. But as the bell rang again, I stood up and put my gloves up under my chin and walked out into that bright zone where I was getting pounded. But it wasn't bad. My second wind had arrived from some distant seacoast within my finite geographical space. I finished and even landed a good straight right hand.

"Good fight," the kid from Brown said. "You're tough."

I never considered myself tough, though. I did believe in second winds.

No. It was Contreras. I assumed that he was coming to tell me what arrangements he had made for moving me and Maria to another site.

"I came to tell you that your photographer is missing."

"Missing?" I said, as if not knowing what that might mean.

"Yes. She has not been in the hotel since early this afternoon."

He looked at me and shook his head.

Was he suggesting that I should have guarded Maria more effectively? No. And she had established enough independence from me during the week to let me know that she neither needed nor desired a watchdog. Contreras was telling me that he did not approve my crazy freelancing. And it did seem mad in retrospect for me to have invaded the Breva domain single-handedly. In retrospect, hell. It seemed crazy at the time. But I was being warned.

I motioned toward a chair. He shook his head.

"What about Maria?" I asked.

"We will be looking for her."

But not too hard. Like me, she was a minor player in all of this.

And, this time, I knew that I could not do a damned thing.

I did, though, go to the corrida the next afternoon. I was still infused with a sense of mission, even if my own role had been deleted. And, I was hoping that Maria might turn up in the callejon, camera in hand.

Something niggled at me as I sat there. When I can't remember something immediately, I relax, think of something else, and then – most of the time – it comes to me. What was it?

Maria had showed me the photographs she'd taken from the callejon. They showed the various sectors that Diego had told me about, the places where observation of the arena was being conducted. There were several people inside La Maestranza, of course, who would seem to be intent on the corrida, but whose binos would be scanning a selected segment of the arena. Diego had a man in the Giralda, the high tower that overlooked the squat buildings along the river, and one on the only rooftop overlooking the Plaza, an apartment building just beyond the Sol section -- the cheap seats, where you stared into the sun that bisected the arena at five pm.

I had looked at Maria's photos. They checked out. I could see the operatives in their locations within the Plaza. They were in civilian clothes, but they had the same standard issue binos that would have been unnoticeable had I not been looking for them.

Maria had shifted from place to place in the callejon so that each time she took a photo it looked as if she were taking a picture of bull and matador. But something was wrong.

"Of course, our men in the Giralda and on that rooftop will be out of sight."

I looked at the photo of the Giralda. I could see no one there. But who ever was there could have seen Maria taking his picture. I looked at the photo of the adjacent rooftop. Yes! – I could see him. Had Diego changed the drill?

I grabbed my cellphone. It was dead. How could that be? It was new and I had checked the batteries yesterday before leaving the Alfonso. Or had it been the day before?

I swore aloud, several recognitions hitting me at once.

I thought of trying to get to the royal box. No. I'd be arrested before I could issue a plausible warning.

The plaza outside the bullring held only a few pedestrians, some vendors leaning against their stands awaiting the wash of outgoing spectators, and a single cop.

I flashed my identification at him.

"Call Contreras, Policia National. Tell him the sniper is on the roof behind the Plaza de Toros. Immediatemente!"

Who was I to make such a request? He was on his phone immediately. Contreras could dispatch whoever was closest to the roof. I was going there myself. I began to circle the Plaza de Toros, ran into a stinking cul de sac against the wall where they keep the bulls, circled back, and got to Adriano, which went down the north side of the Plaza.

The elevator was stuck on 5, the top floor, so up the service stairs I went. I got to the steps that led to the roof and paused. What now? I was out of breath and the backs of my calves were rigid with pain. I had surprise on my side. I laughed and began going up the rickety steps that led to the shed on top of the roof. Would the shooter have anyone guarding his back? Probably not. Snipers moved all by themselves.

I reached for my Glock. Damn! It was gone. I had not heard it fall behind me.

I pushed open the rough wooden door – gently, gently – and stepped out on the gravely roof. Yes, crouched over his Winchester and adjusting his scope was a man on one knee, his elbows under the rifle and tucked tightly into his gut.

Had he swung the rifle at me and fired I was a dead man. But he reached behind him for his pistol and I managed to dive on top of him before he got it out. His head banged against the concrete wall from which he had been acquiring his target. His eyes were glazed with the edges of unconsciousness, but he was strong and desperate. I could feel his barrel chest and rock-hard biceps beneath his shirt. He pushed me back with both hands and chopped at my forehead with his right fist. I saw many colors – not stars – just a brightly lit passageway into pain. And then I heard a pop.

The man sagged to his right and took his weight with him to the roof. I lay there, trying to come back up through the layers of hurt toward an ability to see again. And a willingness – unconsciousness would be a blessing!

"Senor, are you all right?"

"I will be."

It was one of Contreras men. I could see the lion and serpent on his shoulder as he rolled the would-be assassin over with a booted foot.

My shirt was shredded, and the roof had delivered a load of gravel to my back. I had a head ache just beginning to curl in from my reptile brain. Concussion. The sun slanted across the roof, touching the dead man's eyes with glitter.

"Scott. You all right?"

Contreras strode across the roof toward where I was sitting.

"Sure. Give me a hand."

"I got your call and dispatched Phillipe immediately. The elevator was jammed."

"I know. Phillipe is a good shot."

He nodded.

"We've picked up a couple of others. I doubt that they will lead us to Breva. He could have, probably."

He nodded at the dead man, who seemed to be shriveling beneath the stare of those open eyes. The sun had left them.

But I knew who could lead us to Breva.

As Contreras pulled me up, I heard a roar from below. I looked over the lip of the building. A sector of about thirty degrees of La Maestranza showed from there. In the royal box, Juan Carlos was watching the invisible matador and toro below.

"I called his security detail," Contreras said. "I could not get through."

He shrugged. One more detail that had become snarled in competing jurisdictions and bureaucracy. And I had not asked about it. Nor had I checked my cellphone before I left the hotel that day. Little things mean a lot, as Kitty Kallen told us years ago. They can get people killed. I did not feel old as I fought off a mild attack of vertigo. I was old.

"Con permisso."

Phillipe brushed the gravel from my back.

"Do you want a doctor?" Contreras asked.

I was oozing blood in several places and feeling that thick dampness that such effusions cause. Good sportshirt from Paul Stuart ruined.

"No. I'm okay. Can you give me a lift back to the Alfonso?"

"You Americans!" he said, smiling.

What he meant was that this time he was happy that I had taken independent action. He was happier than I was. A few scrapes didn't bother me. But what I had found out during the past half-hour made me very angry. My anger was directed primarily at myself, and that is an anger that I do not handle well.

I sipped from a flask of tequila that I'd had in my back pocket and forgotten about until I got into Contreras' unmarked Mercedes. Maria's Fiat was idling under the canopy of the hotel as I climbed from the car.

I remembered something she had said.

"The UN? My father gave his life to it. Of course, it was kind to him. But it is an irrelevancy, posing for its picture next to the East River. I think it took his life from him."

Those who despised the UN could come from the far left, of course. And the far right.

She had made an amateur's mistake. When an aircraft loses power at low altitude, you have no choice but to take it straight in. The airfield from which you have just departed and to which you turn with hope is an impossible goal. Even the great British ace of WWI, McCudden, made that mistake. And, when you are on the run, you don't go back to where you have been. Someone will find you there. You leave your things behind. Yet, there was Marie's car – a rented Fiat convertible – purring under the canopy in front of the Alfonso Trece and ready to leap forward along the road north to Carmona. She had come back for her things, figuring that I would not make it back this soon. I should still be at the corrida, or pressed among the panicky throng that had heard that gunshot. I had her. They had used the lowest-tech technique of all on me. No fool like an old one. She had been on temporary leave from Frederico Breva. His lover? Probably. That would account for the strange sense I had at Rancho Montanoso of being evaluated by him. It meant that he did not complete agree with his use of her.

I was tired and maybe a little drunk from the tequila. The latter condition was so standard these days that I couldn't be sure. Pepe must have grown accustomed to my wild appearance. This time I was disheveled and still shedding gravel as he gave me my key without comment. The door to her room was ajar. I pushed it open. It was dark, except for the light coming from the bathroom.

As I looked at her, I went back, way back, to a moment in New York. The shadows crafted by the light in the bathroom created a set of strange angles and partial perceptions. She looked at me from above her tan leather suitcase strewn with luminous garments. Her eyes seemed to pick up light from them, and the lucid skin above her cheekbones shone. The rest of her melted away. The eyes signaled acceptance. Perhaps she thought I still had that Glock compact tucked in at the base of my spine. But it was not Maria there. The scent of an open bag – leather and fresh laundry and cologne – took me back. I was packing on the last morning that I had seen Anne. She was looking at me without saying anything. Nothing to say, of course, but regret lingering, particularly since we were still simmering with each other's bodies.

"Drive carefully," she had said, as if that made any difference. It was something to say, a way of saying something. Yes, that she still cared, even it that was no longer enough. The love affair had crashed into its own future, which meant that it had to end because it had no future.

Maria's car was idling under the canopy at the hotel's entrance.

I circled my right hand through the shadows.

She zipped up the bag. She would probably drive north to the ranch outside of Carmona and from there to who knew where?

"Drive carefully," I said.

I expected that she would follow my advice.

EPILOGUE:

I was in Ben Maclin's office again, overlooking the parkland in Langley that would provide sniper practice should anyone try to sneak into the building through a bugged environment posing as bucolic woodland.

I gave a very guarded account of my recent visit. As I rendered my brief narration, the events seemed very far away, distant memories. That was partly because of their intensity and partly because I had not had time to re-experience them, to make sense of them, and thus to consign them to that specific time and place known as the past. But the memory of Maria was still intense – her scent, the shape of her body in my hands, the smooth fuzz at the base of her spine, the soft wordlessness of her voice. Even the more recent trip back, amid the cocoon of a Virgin Atlantic Upper Class cubicle, seemed more remote.

"Come, come, Scottie! You are being much too modest."

Let him think that. Let him believe that my circumspection was a habit ingrained by the years, even if I were being debriefed by the Deputy Director. I had deceived no one but myself. I had played a game of youth, had embraced a final fragment of narcissism. And yet, for all of that, I did not lacerate myself. Why? I believed that something good had ignited itself between Maria and me. Was that just a last vestige of self-deception? If so, so be it.

"The Spanish did a very good job," I said. "They were highly professional."

"And we aren't."

"I did not say that."

"They feel that you did a very good job," he said, handing me a thin, velvet covered box.

"Open it."

Inside was an ornate chain with a flared Maltese cross attached. A card said "La Cruz de Carlos III." A certificate was enclosed, signed by Juan Carlos I of Spain. Under his signature were two words. "Estoy agradecido." I am grateful.

"I can't wait to wear it."

"And there's more."

He handed me a letter from the Policia National. I looked at the bottom. It was signed by Brigadier Hernan de Rando.

"We wish to thank you for your recent service to our homeland.

"Your skill and initiative helped us to prevent a terrible event. Something that did not happen can be a cause for celebration even if the world is blessedly free of the knowledge of it. We know and we appreciate your significant contribution to our efforts.

"It will be of interest to you to know that we received information regarding caches of weapons, training sites, recruitment lists, training manuals, and outlines of further planned terrorist activities that have permitted us to make significant arrests and to disarm and blunt the organization involved in the conspiracy that you helped to foil.

"It will interest you to know that the informant, who remained anonymous and whose identity was not uncovered, credited you with the encouragement of the divulging of this treasury of information. We conjecture that that person wanted you to know as much.

"Brigadier Contreras joins me in sending you felicitations and hopes that you will return again to Spain, this time to enjoy a role strictly as un aficionado de los toros."

"Was Breva on the list?" I asked.

"What list?"

"Just tell me."

"No."

So Breva would start again from scratch. All victories are incomplete.

I hope that the guy who had tried to warn me and who had probably left the way open for our escape had also escaped. He was probably too low on the hierarchy to know much or to do much, but he had helped. Such people do exist. The Turks set up a system that killed Armenians with a bureaucratic efficiency that the Nazis could envy. We – the CIA, I mean – trained the Savak, the Shah's brutal secret police. Treblinka and My Lai do happen and leaders are shot down in theaters and train stations and plazas in Dallas. But people who would do things differently do exist. I believe that the man who had guarded my door merely absented himself at a crucial time and permitted something positive to occur during his absence. Most people do nothing.

Had Maria intended for me to see the photograph of the man on the roof? I would assume so. And then she must have heard of my rendezvous with the assassin. And given further information to Contreras in one of her moodswings toward conscientiousness. Perhaps she had seen through her allegiance to the power-princip. I was putting it all in the best light. They had had someone on the inside all right! I had been infiltrated. They had known what they were doing. Had they intended to aim a specific woman at me – one who reminded me of Anne? No. They were good, but they weren't that good. I had fallen in love with the ghost of a woman I had loved once. No statute of limitations exists for first love. Because first times have nothing to compare themselves with, the rest is often an effort to get back there to that incomparable moment. And I had behaved like a man in love. I had been that blind, that stupid, that happy. I had been the ghost of my former self. I hoped that Breva would not find out who had given all that information to the Policia. He wouldn't. She had not given Contreras the link that would have doomed Breva. And her.

"Who was the informant?" Ben asked.

I was ready for that question.

"I assume that Dave Remington got word to the National Police before he was killed. He would have wanted me to know that. I suspected him, as I told you, of being one of them. We did not have a chance to discuss any of that."

"Yes. That makes sense. He would have known a lot of the details. And he would not want you to have thought ill of him, had anything happened."

"As it did."

Thanks, Dave. And Maria thanks you too.

I kept looking for that book of photos that I had encouraged Maria to produce. What came one day was a large manila envelope with no return address on it and an indecipherable post mark. It had been sent by Royal Mail. Great Britain. In it were superb black and white photos, full of contrast, of shadows trembling with the echo of the bells of the Giralda nearby, of the matadors we had seen as they killed their bulls. Forty six large photos in all. Fandi, Paloma Linares, El Cid, Ponce, Juli, Puerto, Amador, Juan Avila, Jose Thomas, and three of Padilla, in color – one as the horn probed for his gut as he rose with the bull's upward thrust, another of him lying breathless on the bright crushed stone of the ring, and the third of him covered in fresh blood standing over his 600 kilo bull. It was a rare collection, particularly so in that it brought back and sharpened each of those intense moments for me. She was really good. When she said she had "got" something, it was the truth.

She had quoted Dorothea Lange to the effect that "a camera is a tool for learning how to see without a camera." Maria's photographs allowed me to see again – almost with motion – what I had seen once without a camera. She had published her book.

I looked inside the envelope, even shook it. No note. But she had said thanks.

I realized then that I had expected that.

FULL CIRCLE

A time there was when
it was enough.
But that was way back then.
And now? – well, that's just tough.

Benjamin Mellon,
"Countdown."

After I put down the phone, bleakness set in. Predictable. I felt like the Hemingway character who tries to think of something good. I can't, he replies to himself. What is it about time? It sharpens regret. It italicizes our mistakes. It erases the times – and they must have existed, right? – when all seemed good with the world and with the tiny person striding along under God's clear blue sky.

Time exists so that things don't happen all at once. That's good. A smashing collision of events and objects, everything flying together with the shearing of metal and the bright punctuation of flame in the suddenly chaotic traffic pattern would not be good. But that is what my memory was doing to me. Of course, it took only the brief message I'd just received to trigger the conflation of all bad things into a sequence of

115

past events riding above single tone of gray. And it was a tone – if not a voice, certainly a subtext.

I stood in the kitchen – that's where the phone is – for long, gray minutes. Traffic pattern. Yes, I had reverted to that metaphor. You are on downwind. The aircraft in front of you turns from base to final. That first ice-laced bottle of San Marcos or Kirin already invades the anticipation evolving from the desiccation created by the O2 that has flowed into the nose, mouth, and sinuses from the mask. The mask is now slimy with moisture and it smells like bad breath. The need to stand and stretch cries out from the bones and sinews that have been strapped into this killing machine for these long hours. And then the runway opens up, long and lovely, like a spreading of legs, as you ease back and hold the aircraft off until it ceases to fly. Or, as you approach your home base, you hear the reassuring voice from some zone beneath the storm, "On glide path. On center line." He can see you on those two radar scopes even if you cannot. Or, as you slide down final in the silence of the fog, the twin indicators of the ILS dial constantly tell you how to correct with tiny flicks of stick and rudder to maintain your alignment with that desired length of welcoming, tire-scarred concrete. Or the GPS visualizes the runway for you as if the sun were shining. The runway gets closer, wider, longer and becomes a pathway home.

I had thought at first, hell, it will be impossible for me to go out there. And then I thought, hell, it will be impossible for me not to go out there.

Paul had been my wingman. It did not matter how many years it had been since I had seen him. I had been among the first people his wife had called.

Outside, the leaves were suddenly active, turning their pale side upward. Then it was raining again. That summer voice muttered of all past years. Yesterday, the heat had come in with the zap of exhaustion that hits me every summer. But today, it was raining again. That's what it is, I said, light-deprivation depression. Without light, you see only bad things. The rains might go. Queen Anne and Goldenrod would vie for sovereignty in the mad hubris that wildflowers know, and Hydrangeas would explode their medallions into the light. Around them, heat would be supreme. That is, if it stopped raining.

Those who have not been there may mock us, or utter some formula like "Thanks for your service," but the bonding does occur. And it lasts. It holds for a lifetime, in proportion to the intensity of the experience.

The 105 was huge for a fighter plane. Those of us who had flown the nimble 86 resented this ponderous aircraft. But priorities changed. Our leaders decided that the way to attack the Soviet Union was to refuel at altitude over the Bosporus, descend to TV-antenna altitude and zip in to a pre-selected initial point. We would then pull an Immelmann – a turn at the top of a loop – and fly back home. Meanwhile, according to a calculation programmed into a black box, a "shape" would release from the bottom of our aircraft, describe a parabola, then descend toward the target. Children would be on their way to school, holding books in leather straps, and skipping unconsciously, some chatting to friends, others to invisible companions. Women would have begun to shop, looking at the fish staring back open-eyed on top of banks of ice in the markets, encountering the fresh-baked scents on the swing of the bakery door, saying good morning to their neighbors, hoping for a tidbit of gossip as they bought their lamb chops. Men in fedoras would be on their stolid way to work in the streetcars, grinding the bright rails and whistling at intersections. Old men, many with ancient medals drooping from their wrinkled suits, would be sitting in the coolness of the shadowy park reading newspapers expertly folded so as to fit two age-spotted hands held close to the eyes.

Some might hear the distant scratch of the jet engine against the rose of the southern sky. Some might even discern the shadow that the shape made on the snow of the western mountain. None would sense the instant flash that obliterated them and their city.

The 105 was designed to replace the 84F for this mission. Both were sturdy, stable aircraft, capable, like all Republic planes, of taking plenty of battle damage. They flew well at low altitudes, but were no match for the Mig-15 or the Mig-17 when they reached altitude. But that did not matter. Once they reached altitude at the end of their climb, their target would be dust and ashes.

Priorities change. The Soviet Union became a remote threat. It was the installations in Hanoi and Haiphong that concerned us in the late-1960s. The 105 was designated to attack these targets. The Soviet SA-2 missile became the countermeasure.

We lost half of our 105s over North Vietnam, including mine.

We flew the D model of the 421st Tactical Fighter Squadron from the Royal Thai base at Khorat, across Laos and curled around the mountain north of Hanoi – "Thud Ridge." We then descended for our run.

In spite of the sudden jolt and the brightness that penetrated my visor, I thought -- My aircraft had survived the nearmiss of a SAM detonation. I still had power and control. But then, through the slickness of the oxygen mask came the unmistakable stench of fire. Burning water. An electrical fire. That meant that the wires that gave me my instrumentation were sizzling into uselessness. Or, more vitally, that the systems that fed fuel from my tanks to my engine were about to fail. Or, more immediately, that the aircraft itself was about to disintegrate. I would probably survive an ejection – severe back injuries were fairly common – but I'd become a POW. No chance for a successful extraction via a CH 5 this close to the capitol of North Vietnam. They'd try, of course, and probably be shot down.

All of this went through my mind in a milli-second as I climbed out from my target.

"Number one. You okay?"

"Negative, two. On fire."

"Okay, one. I'll take a look."

I looked to my left. Paul came along side, then dipped his wing and slid beneath my aircraft.

"One. Damage on the fuselage just aft of the wings. Something's leaking. Thin mist of vapor."

"Hydraulic fluid."

"I think so, One. Probably."

That meant that the stick was about to become a dead weight in my hand.

All the while, I was turning to the right, toward Laos.

"Bill! Bandits! Nine o'clock low. Four of them."

I was not about to turn and try to engage the aircraft that had no doubt scrambled from the base just below Hanoi. They would be under radio control, according to Russian doctrine. They tended to be tethered to that voice on the ground. That gave us some flexibility.

"Two. Dive!"

We dove.

I was still at combat power, so the aircraft picked up speed and went through the mach. Paul stayed on my wing.

The bandits, climbing, could not gain the airspeed they needed to catch up.

I had to bleed off some airspeed before I ejected. I deployed my speed brakes and pulled up.

"Two. I'm punching out. Report my position and head on home. Your fuel will be critical."

"Negative, one. I'll see you down."

"Two. Go home. And stay clear."

The canopy came off with a shriek. I did feel myself compress as the explosion sent my seat into the atmosphere. My neck and pelvis seemed to collide somewhere along my backbone.

The chute opened automatically and I felt that sense of rising upward that anyone who's ever done it will report. But I would have delayed opening the chute had I had the choice, because I was dangling helplessly at about two thousand feet. That's one of the problems of fully-automatic systems. They work, but they also remove some options. The rising sensation was not accompanied by exaltation. The jungle heat came up as if from a cauldron of some foul and boiling broth. Cool it with a baboon's blood. And two shadows swept toward me from the right.

"Get that pilot," the voice had told them.

They didn't have to hit me with their 37 mm cannon. The open chute was an easier target.

I waited. I could not do a damned thing. Sitting duck. I had a .45 strapped to my right leg. Sure, I'd reach down and shoot at these bastards! A last act of futile defiance, a la Frank Luke, the World War I balloon-buster, who had fought with his pistol and been killed rather than be captured by the Germans..

But the two Migs broke left, switched on their afterburners, and left a wavy shimmer of vapor as they flew south toward Cambodia before they got a shot off. And then I saw Paul's 105 pulling a tight right turn and firing a couple of cannot shots after the disappearing 17s.

"Now. Go home, Paul," I ordered into the swampy air. Time for me to try to land without busting anything. Perhaps I would land on one of the thousand elephants of Laos.

The last thing I saw before I invaded the canopy of trees feet first was my 105 sending a bright ball of superfluous heat into a superheated noon.

When I was finally in the helicopter and angling back toward Thailand, I noticed that my left hand was burned. The glove had curled away from heat that had been coming up through the throttle assembly. I had not felt any pain. Adrenalin had been flowing, I guess, or some other automatic analgesic, and certainly my consciousness had been focused on more immediate factors than the need for Unguintine. So I have a Purple Heart tucked in next to my Air Medal. I also have a scar on top of my left hand.

"What did you do to your hand?"

"That is an etching of the Mekong Delta. I had it done in Laos."

That usually brings shocked incomprehension.

"See. There's the River," I say, pointing at a line that undulates through the scar, like a reverse life-line.

It can be an attention getter, almost as good as walking a brilliant red setter on a co-ed campus.

"What's his name?"

"Casey. What's yours?"

II.

The great clock in the square began to toll.
I have made it! he exalted.
And then he heard the carriage pulling up.
outside his door, on the street below.
He looked down. The horses' heads
were plumed in black. The bell rolled on.

                    Martin DeTrane,
                    "The Midnight Hour."

I had been born in 1944, product of a leave my father had been granted in late 1943, before going overseas. The tide had turned in 1944. Both empires were shrinking. Their cities were ravaged. Their good pilots were dead. Hitler's rockets rose, and dropped down upon London, but it was a desperate final action. Japan's kamikazes tumbled into our warships off of Okinawa, but it was too little, too late. The Saint Louis Browns won a pennant.

My dreams had changed recently. I did not remember them specifically, but they found me observing, not acting. I was no longer the central player in some narrative that found me among friends of childhood whose names I only recalled in dreams, as I searched for the keys for the car I needed to go somewhere, or realized that what I wanted was back in a room in a hotel in some nightmare city whose grid of streets led me into unfamiliar and menacing neighborhoods. I no longer dreamed of being in the alienating space of a cockpit whose instruments were telling me all the wrong things – low on airspeed, fuel warning light blinking red at the intersection of life and flameout. But now I was an onlooker. I suppose that translated into a gradual detachment from life itself. Dreams usually tell me where I am, and where I am not. In the case of the recurring USAF experiences, of course, waking up was only a partial solution. It took a while for the sweat to cool, the heart to fit itself again to the ribcage, and the eyes to agree that it was just darkness, nothing more, that was coming at me.

"United to LAX, United Express to MVC."

"MVC?"

"Mountainview. That's Amerigo's airport. You really want to go there in August?"

"No choice."

I was going to one of the hottest and most ozone-replete cities in the world, held in the hollow at the bottom of Empire County. In August.

"I don't imagine I'll be able to see the mountains."

The Tenderfoot Range would be layered in the smog that hugs the San Marcos Valley for ten months out of each year.

I eased into my first class aisle seat. 2-B. Or not to be. My travel agent had upgraded me on an emergency basis, bless her heart, and I tongued a Bloody Mary as the rest of the aircraft filled up. I smiled at the occasional child who passed by at eye level.

I thought of what Karla had said.

"It was unexpected."

I repeated my question.

"It was unexpected."

It was the way she had said it – don't ask me anything more. Fear?

Did she think her phone was tapped? Some paranoia brought on by Paul's unexpected death? Had he been murdered? I would find out.

I was happy to be leaving my own corner of the universe.

I had just been fired again. And this time, I assumed, for the last time.

This was not the financial disaster it would have been for most men. I was not married. I had just begun to draw social security. I already had a retirement pension that paid me a couple of thousand a month. And I had taken my small nestegg out of a dot-com fund in early 2000 and put it in treasuries.

But I had enjoyed my job. And I suppose that is one reason I got fired. In the dour and Calvinistic northeast, one is not supposed to enjoy work, just do it. What good are people if they don't complain about their work?

The stewardess reminded me of someone. Her lips. The luminous tone of her skin. Something. Who? Oh yes! I should have forgotten her long ago.

We live in a republic, we are told, but tyrannies abound from sea to shining sea, smaller satrapies gated and closed within the illusion of freedom.

After I got off active duty, I went into teaching. I went back to my old prepschool, Oster Academy. They needed a lacrosse coach, a squash coach, and a history teacher – in that order – and they preferred their own. I had been Vice President of the Fifth Form. That meant, in theory, that I was a "team player."

The game, though, had changed since I had been an old boy. Back then, Oster was a "prepschool" prepschool, meaning that it attempted to emulate controlled environments like Choate or Deerfield. In such places, some eight attendance checks were made and turned in every day, seven grueling days a week, from breakfast to lights out. The game, of course, for the boys was to defeat the system by breaking one of many, many rules, one by one. But it was mostly harmless activity – sneaking food out of the dining hall for a latenight snack, stealing the aluminum pitchers and trying to ferment grape juice, pulling on an occasional cigarette (for smokers, Deerfield included an isolated shack with ten thousand empty Camel and Lucky packs thumbtacked to its walls. At Choate, smoking was an offense warranting expulsion). Such activity did encourage the breaking of rules, but many of these young men would go on to Yale and then to Wall Street, so they were mastering the rudiments of their craft at these expensive, superbly-groomed sanctuaries. Rebellion could manifest itself simply in wearing a foul and greasy tie and daring an exhausted master to challenge it.

But, for me, it was a start on a teaching career. You did learn to teach against that friction of adolescent resentment. I had no illusions about my being, as Newton Vanders, the Headmaster, said, "a shining example to these boys. Someone who has been to war and returned with his head held high." I could begin graduate school in the summers and, with GI money, afford to get at least an MA, then perhaps teach at a community college or catch on as an adjunct at a four year institution.

What had changed, though, was that Oster Academy had become ideological by the early 1970s. The war ground on, but opposition to it had faded to bitter alienation. No longer did the protesters believe that they could change a thing. The great movement toward civil rights had been diverted into the anti-war movement and both noble causes had withered. Some thought that the diversion was intentional. Paranoia was easily come by in those days. But what Headmaster Newton Vanders decided was that his school would become all that the 1960s had not been.

Vanders had black hair and very dark eyes that flashed challenges from the chiseled chalk of a face that had become amphibious out of the right gene pool.

"We are a place of good manners," he said during one of his Sunday sermons, his eyes glinting over the rows of sullen boys and attendance-taking masters. "We are a place where, if I may say so, breeding matters. You come from fine families..." He could say so, of course. Who would rise to challenge him? The boys did come from wealth, and Oster specialized in celebrity sons. Famous stars sent their sons there. And some of the families were fine. Others, though, had shipped their inconvenient little boys off to be raised by foster parents in an elegant and suffocating environment. And those little boys knew it. Oster Academy may have sat high on a hill above a wretched mill town, but some of Oster's inhabitants were exiles from other hillsides.

"We do not tolerate the excesses of our recent history," Vanders continued, "the violent confrontations, the vulgarity of Woodstock, the wretched so-called music, the denigration of the institutions which our founding fathers bequeathed unto us..."

And so on. The counter-culture was an obscene stain the tinct of which Oster would not absorb. I agreed with him about the music, but Vanders did not mention Vietnam. Those who inveighed against the response to Vietnam, which was, after all, "the culture," never probed the source of that discontent.

And so I found myself quite unwillingly to be the emblem of Vanders' crusade. He himself had served heroically as a staff officer in D.C. during the final years of WWII, but had gotten a Legion of Merit that he displayed proudly above his desk in the Headmaster's Study.

Many old-grads glanced angrily at their institutions and complained of their "politicalization." They did not recognize that their schools had always been political, invisibly so, mindlessly turning out functionaries for the perceived status quo. Under pressure, of course, those schools might train an occasional minority student to perform within the established dispensation. They would congratulate themselves on their open mindedness. When Vanders was asked in the 1960s whether he thought Oster should integrate, he said, "Oh yes. We are looking for the right one." He found the elegant, Swiss educated son of an African ambassador to the United Nations. But when SDS chapters began to spring up on college campuses and young people started spelling their country with a "K," the old grads looked as if they'd been swallowing Ivory Soap. The 56/100 % that was not pure.

Now, Vanders was courting them – and their sons.

I cannot stay here long, I thought to myself. I was proud to have served in uniform. I prized the pilot's wings above the left pocket of my uniform jacket. I certainly had doubts about the cause. I admired Muhammad Ali's "I ain't got no quarrel with them Vietcong." I did not want to be taken as an embodiment of all that was good about the cold war run amuck. I was like many of my generation beginning to see through the lies we had been told. I was in the process of deciding whether I'd go along with those lies, or resist them. And couldn't I just be a civilian for awhile? No. That option is not available when one begins to think.

I needn't have worried.

"Spring Promenade" approached – and don't let anyone catch you calling it "Prom"! Or, having gotten past that danger, pronouncing it 'aid' and not 'odd.' I wanted to take the weekend off and travel across to New Jersey to see some friends, but, inevitably, was assigned to the "Promenade Patrol." That meant that I had to pop up here and there unexpectedly to make sure that no immorality was being conducted in the shadows trembling out from the strings of Maurice Wriston and his Foxy Trotters as they quavered along through current songs like "Doe, a deer, a female dear" and, daringly, "Yesterday, all my troubles seemed so far away," along with old favorites from the Gay Nineties. It would be a final wafting of melody before spring break began the next weekend.

My old tux no longer fit and had holes in it besides. I could rent one, of course, but I wore a uniform instead – summertans just right for April, with medals. In a fit of foolish pride, I had purchased miniatures at the PX at McGuire. I had been tempted to get a Mexican Border Campaign medal to commemorate my six months training stint at Laredo, but restrained myself.

And so I arrived, half laughing at myself, half fulfilling Vanders' platonic conception of me. I enjoyed it, and the dates from the girls' schools of New England were breathtakingly gorgeous, even if their smiles revealed the occasional set of braces.

I was leaving, that is, slipping out, on Saturday evening – "Some Enchanted Evening," I was being told as the soft air brushed moonlight across the lawn that led to where my car was parked. Because my dormitory had been taken over by the visiting young ladies, along with my apartment, of course, I was staying at the Haven Inn down near the Parkway.

As "Younger than Springtime" faded to the star-illumined blossoms, I could not help but hear the ragged sound of stomach contents being ejected into some nearby shrubbery. We used to call it barfing.

A young woman stood helplessly beside the ill young man.

I recognized him.

"Ted Barker."

He raised his head briefly, eyes brimming, and nodded.

"Something he ate," said the girl.

"No doubt."

"Are you the police?" she asked.

I laughed at that.

"In a sense. Ted!"

He spat and raised his head.

"What house are you in?"

"Grantley, sir."

"All right. Go back to Grantley. Clean yourself up. Go to bed. If I am asked, I will say that you became ill and that I told you to go to your house and go to bed. Understand?"

"But..."

"Just do it. I will escort this young lady back to wherever she is staying. Go!"

I pitied the rhododendrons from which I turned.

"You, young lady. What house were you assigned to?"

"I think it's called Christopher."

"Okay. Come with me."

"But the night is young, officer!"

"It got old very quickly."

"At least..."

Her shoulders gleamed in the shift of moon. She put her hands to them as a small wind rose. I took off my uniform jacket and placed it around her shoulders.

"At least what? Come on, let's go."

"I am nineteen!"

"That is good. Ted was not about to be nailed for nailing jail bait."

"Let's just go out for a beer. I mean it. The night is young. I don't want to go back and stare at the fucking walls."

She displayed a very promising pout.

"You may not be jailbait, but you are too young to drink in this state," I said, unintentionally rhyming. "Now, let's go!"

But I had, unwittingly, begun to negotiate.

"I mean, we just grab a cold sixpack of Bud."

The moon rose a couple more notches on its pulley. We had moved away from the stricken bushes. From Goldenrod Pond a half a mile below us the scent of ice melting and of spring rising rode up the hillside.

"What is this one?" she asked, fingering one of my medals.

"That," I said, leaning down, "is a Purple Heart."

"Umm! I'm impressed!"

"What is your name?"

"Jeanine Babcock. Like the song."

"I'm Bill Chambers. You are not supposed to drink during this weekend."

"Maybe Ted wasn't. I didn't sign anything."

But I had, not physically, but indelibly.

"Okay. But let's make it Rolling Rock."

"Suits me."

Was I being a fool? Oh yes. But it had been a long grind through winter term and into these delicious moments of early spring. Let he who has not been keeping one step ahead of the diabolical little boys for these many months condemn me. And it had been a long time since I had ridden forth on such adventures. I did not want to stare at the fucking walls, either.

Back at the Haven Inn, Rolling Rock disappeared. Then Jeanine's lovely rose gown disappeared into wisps like western clouds at sunset along the beige rug of my room.

And the young lady was a virtuoso, a savant in sexuality. She dictated everything and had absolute control of everything until – heaven be blessed for it! – she lost control completely. For a week, I trotted in my cleats up to my small apartment from lacrosse practice to shower there. The etchings on my back could not be attributed to some terrible itch I'd had.

"I think you have something to tell me."

"What would you like to hear?"

Vanders looked disappointed.

"Bill, Bill, we invite these young ladies to our school and what happens?"

"I have no idea."

"Ah, but you do."

"Has there been a complaint?"

"That is not the point."

That was a relief!

"I would say it is, Headmaster. Why have you called me here?"

"Reliable reports tell me that you returned one of our guests this past weekend back to her residence at a very late hour. A very early hour, I should say."

"True. Her date had become ill."

"And you took her home?"

"I escorted her back to Christopher House, yes."

"At three a.m.?"

"As you said, it was late."

"We have you buying a six pack at the Henderson Street 7/11 at ten thirty. That is a man in a white shirt, black tie, and uniform trousers."

"Could have been a waiter from Bleu Cheese."

He glared at me. He had so enjoyed his detective work – and I was mocking it.

I had better not enrage him, I thought.

"I am of legal drinking age," I said.

"We have a witness saying that a young woman was with you – in your car – at that time."

"Again – what is this meeting all about?"

Vanders' feigned patience, stretched very thin, snapped.

"You know damned well, Chambers!"

His eyes glittered nakedly for an instant.

I did, of course. I had done an inexcusable thing. I had gotten laid. And, of course, he was right. I should not have touched the delectable Jeanine. But then I had known that at the time.

"Again, Headmaster, I ask you whether a complaint of some sort has been lodged."

I was pretty sure that Jeanine had not complained.

He knew that and calmed himself down with breathing exercises.

"In a case like this, I lodge the complaint for the young person."

"In loco parentis."

"Precisely."

"But if the young lady is of legal age?"

"Not to drink, she isn't."

"Not to purchase alcohol, perhaps."

"You are being difficult."

"Not at all. I am trying to isolate whatever the problem is."

Actually, I was calculating the chore of moving out of my modest digs suddenly and grabbing some kind of summer job. I'd have a headstart in that market, since school would not be out for another month.

Had it been worth visiting those brief and passionate moments of Lilac Time?

Hell yes.

"Your contract will be terminated..."

He paused, as if wrestling with a profound dilemma.

"At the end of the current term."

"June?"

"I have to think of the school. You have classes. You have the lacrosse team. I can't leave them in the lurch, even if you could."

Now he was accusing me of irresponsible actions that I had not committed.

Hypocrite. He was pushing me more deeply into the wrong, of course, but he should have just fired me on the spot. I probably should have quit on the spot. Inconvenience compromises conviction. I had just learned my own lesson from Newton Vanders.

"What official record is there of any of this?" I asked.

"This matter is being handled informally."

He could fire me if he wanted to for no reason at all, but I'd at least be able to get a recommendation from Laurence Bentley, head of the History Department.

It had been time for me to leave. I flipped a salute at Vanders' Legion of Merit. It was a decoration I had not achieved. I thought of dropping a line to Jeanine Babcock of Locust Valley, who was going to Vassar in the fall, but thought better of it. I had left her with nothing to complain about. I would leave it at that. My back resembled the trenches and barbed wire stitched across the Western Front in 1917, but it would heal.

Yes, it was the attractive pout below eyes that told of a smile on the way.

"Another bloody mary, sir?"

"Yes. Thanks, Jeanine."

She looked at me and smiled. No accounting for some passengers!

III.

"He'll be fine once he learns to keep his hand out of his shirt."

> Casey Stengel, when asked about his new outfielder, Danny Napoleon.

I still muse about power. I have seldom had any. Or, if I have had it, I have not recognized it. I automatically translated it into responsibility. What is it about power than is so corrupting? Lord Acton would say that the corruption is automatic if the power is absolute. But I think it is more subtle than that. It is a corollary of the Peter Principle: those who have risen to great heights – as they perceive them – enjoy the perks but know somewhere that they don't deserve them. They are King Lears. They want the name and all the addition but their own humanity shrivels within them. Their careers are spent in defending against the possibility that someone might find out who they really are. That's what Shakespeare's play is all about. It is about the very brief life of Lear – from his abdication of his throne, through his discovery that they lied (he is not "everything"), to his discovery of his "child, Cordelia," to his recognition that she is dead. "Look there." It does not take long. And we will resist any version of that process for ourselves.

Fred Herman was a frightened little man masquerading as a tough, decision-making executive. If he only had a chin!

My course in World War Two was radically popular.

I did concentrate on battles, as opposed to underlying trends and tendencies – building up to the confrontations via the personalities of the generals – Field Marshall von Paulis waiting for permission from Hitler to break out of the salient at Stalingrad, or Marshall Zhukov anticipating the German plan to attack at Kursk, or George Patton wheeling three divisions facing east to a move north toward Bastogne, or Japanese General Kuribayashi deciding to fight from underground on Iwo Jima. I looked at the equipment at their command and built away from the battles by examining the results – not just what did happen but what could not. After the Battle of Britain, for example, Operation Sea Lion could not be embarked because the Germans could not control the air above their invasion. After Stalingrad, Operation Barbarossa was doomed, although Kursk was probably just as significant, because after Kursk the German retreat began and never stopped. But I pointed out that Barbarossa had already doomed itself by beginning a month later than scheduled, by Herman Goering's decision not to build long-range aircraft, and by the assumption that winter gear would not be needed. Operation Barbarosa supposedly invoked a German warrior slumbering beneath a mountain. But it also summoned the sleeping giant of the Soviet Union. All those soldiers! And they would prevail, in spite of Stalin's killing off most of his good generals in the late 1930s. Iwo Jima told us what we already knew – that the attack on Japan proper would be incredibly costly. And I explored some of the imponderables. What if Hitler continues attacking the RAF, instead of diverting his aircraft to London after a meaningless raid by the British on Berlin? The RAF is probably out of the war. What if Admiral Halsey and his five carriers had been in Pearl Harbor that morning? We have lost the war. What happens if Japan refuses to surrender after the Nagasaki bomb? We have no more a-bombs left.

But what the students really liked was my weaving into the larger pattern personal stories – the diary of a French soldier describing the Stuka attacks on the Maginot Line in 1940. "It was not just the bombs," he said, "it was the screaming siren that signaled their arrival, as if death were a gendarme grabbing me by the collar, just doing his job." And the words of a submariner under attack: "We could hear the scrape of the depth charges against the hull. I know that had I seen fear in the eyes of any of the faces around me, I would have started screaming. I tried to keep the fear from my own eyes, but it must have been there. Yet my shipmates did not scream." The experience of a German pilot baling out over England: "I tumbled out into the air, through alternating visions of blue sky and green land, splintering like many colors in a kaleidoscope. I reached to pull my rip cord but all my fingers grasped was my flightsuit. Had I lost my parachute? With a great effort of will, I looked to my left. The steel handle had ridden up on my left shoulder. I threw my right arm across my body and pulled it and felt the bundle unload at my back. As I seemed to rise again, I realized that the war was over for me. I knew that I would survive until it was over for everyone. Victory and defeat meant nothing to me as I floated down toward a field. I would live. My first thought was that I must get word to my parents in Kiel. I was still alive and surprised at the breath that was calming down as I descended. I would survive, but I wondered whether my parents would. This one was not like other wars." An American soldier at the Battle of the Bulge in early winter 1944: "I dove into a shell hole. The air splintered around me, but I was aware that it was very cold here. I might not be hit by anything in-coming, but I might freeze to death. And something stank. I looked around, then realized that it was me."

Every battle, then, had an eyewitness account from both sides, except Iwo Jima. There, the enemy fought to the death and the few prisoners were mute. For Hiroshima, I had to rely on John Hersey – the imprint of a victim etched in black upon a wall. A Rorschach that meant only death. The eyes of those who participated in the battles saw very little of the battle and the mind behind those eyes had no way of understanding what the outcome of the battle might mean. Crane gets that right in *The Red Badge of Courage.* They were all meaningless pieces finally adding up to a meaning that many of them did not live to appreciate – or hate. As a staff officer on the Western Front asked in 1917, after leaving his neatly pinpricked maps back at hq and actually going up to the churned-up mud of the front, "We sent men to fight in *this?*"

I notice that those who oppose whatever progress may be or who resist effective performance take to repeating the same complaint, as if by reiteration it becomes the truth. Health care is socialism. Illegal immigrants are using up all our money. Obama is not an American citizen.

"And," Fred said, "you are guilty of lowering academic standards,"

He paused, steepling his fingers in front of disapproving lips, as if he understood what academic standards might be.

With a hundred students in the WW II class and two other smaller classes, I had told the larger class that if anyone told me that he or she had done the reading, I would give them a pass. For anything more, a paper would be required. I knew that ninety per cent of the students would write the paper. The *Gridley Grinder* – the student newspaper -- had already leveled the charge about academic standards.

But I was hardly offering the "free pass" they accused me of giving.

I laughed.

"I have a course of just over one hundred students with no assistance at all and you accuse me of lowering academic standards? Most institutions would have sections of this course – four or five of them -- led by junior people. And those junior people would be reading the papers."

"We are not most institutions."

"True enough."

He gave me a sharp look with an upward furrow of his pale brow. One could agree with Fred and still insult him.

I had been a good athlete. He would have thought a jock strap was something with which you covered your nose in the winter.

I had been an officer. I exuded not just arrogance, but a sureness of purpose that resonated with competence. I was good at what I did, and I knew it.

Even more fatally as far as Fred was concerned, I did enjoy my work. I strode to class with the alacrity of an Ariel. Fred lugged a bulging briefcase home at night, looking like Willy Loman. Naturally, he refused to delegate authority. To do so would be, in his mind, to give up power. So, like so many, he was a prisoner of his own power. And like most masochists, he pulsed sadistic energies into the system.

His petit-bourgeoisie mentality life included a stickthin wife with angry button eyes. She, no doubt, saw him as presidential material, not as the ultimate example of the Peter Principle.

I liked to dress – perhaps a subtle glen-plaid jacket and gray slacks, button down shirt, silk tie with little repeated emblems – cable cars, wasps, squash racquets – and a silk handkerchief carelessly slid into the pocket of the sportcoat. Class was a social occasion for me, and I gave it the respect I thought it deserved. My colleagues often showed up looking like chicken farmers who had rushed from their harvesting of eggs to the inconvenient interruption of a class. As some of them had. But Fred would have gotten it all wrong had he tried to wear anything but staid polyester. He must hate the fact that he did not even know how to look like a Republican.

For Fred that day, the lapel of my navy blue blazer sported a tiny green gold pin with two red eyes issued by the Irvin Air Chute Company, emblematic of my membership in the Caterpillar Club, whose members had ejected from aircraft and returned with the d-ring – the metal slot that pulls the ripcord – in their hands. I had tucked mine inside my flight suit but took credit anyway.

And I had written a controversial book about military spending and the forces that drove it, which were seldom linked to national security. Other than rhetorically, that is. The Gridley board was made up of right wing investment bankers who had not had the privilege of serving in uniform, but who would fight to the death for someone else's right to die in one of their misbegotten wars.

My most recent book, though, was probably what created the iceberg into which I was heading at full speed. The CIA has been the target of plenty of exposes, of course. I placed them in the category of those groups that "know better," that are superior to the laws and the way a document like the Constitution hinders their "nimbleness," as they call it, organizations that posture as lonely defenders of the public good. The Klan, for example. "Our very way of life is at risk!" I suggested that the CIA mentality had actually invaded the executive branch itself. The CIA, after all, acts with impunity. True, Richard Helms got a suspended sentence in 1977 for lying to Congress about Nixon's instructions to knock off Allende, and contractor David Passaro got eight years for beating an Afghani detainee to death with a flashlight. But in most cases, they get away with their crimes. Unfortunately, their immunity reinforces their sense of infallibility. If they make mistakes, those errors are in the service of a higher cause and therefore excusable. "We don't torture," said the little man with the flag in his lapel. And even if no one believes him, it makes no difference. He goes on torturing. My book pointed out that to abuse prisoners who come from a revenge culture like that of Iraq or Afghanistan was to bring upon our troops a response that far outweighed any advantage that Cheney claimed for "enhanced interrogation."

Needless to say, the patriots were offended.

That Fred hated me was true. That the reasons he hated me were manifold was also true. That he could admit those reasons, though, would be to reveal to himself who he was. And that he would never do. As a behavioral psychologist, that which disturbed his own shallow psyche was unavailable to him. He would have had to admit that Freud's theory of repression was valid. He could not afford to pay any attention to the man behind the curtain. Helpless as a child, Fred made sure that the adults around him now were rendered equally helpless by his incompetence.

"Times like these..." he began, toying with the cellophane wrapper of one of his plastic-tipped cigars.

"Oh," I said, interrupting him with the simulation of a eureka moment, "it's an economic decision. Yes, I understand."

He looked relieved. I had given him the answer.

"You could say that."

"Tell you what. I'll teach the course for half of what my contract says. That will free up money for other instructional costs."

His white face turned even blanker.

"We could not allow that."

"Why not? I'd sign the new contract. It would be perfectly legal."

"It would set a bad example."

"Yes. It probably would. But what example do you set when you fire a popular teacher who takes on half of the departmental load every term and who has the publications that support his work in the classroom. How many others at Grinder can make that claim?"

"That is not the point."

"You have not made a point, Fred. Other than that I am getting canned for no reason that you can articulate. You said it was for economic reasons. I've said I'll work for half of what my contract gives me. It is already on the bottom of the assistant professor listing."

He could say nothing to that, of course, because it was true. I could identify my own salary when I saw it.

But that's what they did – the "they" who called the shots in places small and big. They declared an emergency. They had already selected the heads that would roll as a result of the "Mayday!" they had shouted to the moon. In times like these... They sent Squadristris or Brownshirts to break up meetings. They sent their opponents, jobless, out onto the streets. And then they could deal with the dangers of loitering, requesting large items from the municipal budget to address the problem. It was a process. And it worked. It often seemed like the reasonable thing to do. And, when it did not, those who did not believe they were threatened, remained silent. Fred very effectively imposed that silence. He would have made a good Eichmann.

And, yes, I thought, I have health care through the VA. I'd make it.

Perhaps needless to say, I did not commiserate with Fred, even if he had never been a member of the club on the hilltop where the birch trees bent along the acorn-laden pathways, where we would sit over imported beer after tennis, thick towels savoring the sweet sweat of exercise, Jack Purcells stained with brickdust, where, after a dance to the quicksilver medleys of Lester Lanin or Ben Cutler, we would go to smaller parties to which invitations were whispered at the bar between sets until the dawn turned the east to a lemon pie and where a demure brunette in a pale blue gown might raise the gown sufficiently so that its primary evidence was the gentle rasp of taffeta in rhythm to the unspoken music of pleasure. He had not enjoyed the automatic deference that one received because one was "a member." Fred had not known such joys.

"Think about it," I said, rising. I did not offer to shake hands with him.

And I think that I invited the anger of the "manner born" contingent simply by sneering at all of that I had been born to. Oh, yes, with a slight admixture of yearning. It is a lost world and where ignorance-is-bliss can be a happy place. And one is always young there on the playing fields of Eton. Unconsciousness has its rewards.

So I had left him frustrated and dissatisfied. Something about that did not go well, he would think. But I had gained only the satisfaction of defeating this puny little man who held all the power. He had the satisfaction of having fired me.

A significant finger of my left hand, above the decorative map of the Mekong Delta, contains a jagged white scar. It was stepped on once somewhere near a dusty line-of-scrimmage and bled like fury. A few years ago, it throbbed occasionally. I mentioned that to my doctor, an expert on athletic injuries.

"When it throbs," he advised me, "elevate it."

I discovered that it only throbbed when I passed the Gridley administration building. I trusted that the High Dean, in vacant or in pensive mood and having nothing else to do, was staring out his window as I drove by.

No one, after all, enjoys being sneered upon.

I could almost smell the sour mood coming up at me from California. Summer schools had been shut down. Good young teachers had been fired. Gated communities were half-built. Foreclosed homes sat in front of stagnating pools breeding mosquitoes where once the gin-and-tonics had rippled in frosty glasses. The homeless huddled beneath bridges. The unemployed held signs saying "Three young children, Please help."

The once-fertile valley that had provided a quarter of the world's grapes, tomatoes, onions, and melons was drying up in drought. The state was billions of dollars in the red.

The little jet landed at Mountainview and taxied past a row of F-16s, with CALANG markings. The Viper.

Times have changed, I mused. The aircraft had a huge bubble canopy, birdproof, they said, and certainly great for visibility. Of course, a lot of what we used to do with our eyes was now done with a headsup display. The stick was side-mounted. I would never have been able to accommodate to that placement. The aircraft had a fly-by-wire capability, meaning that any slight adjustment that the pilot wanted to make was transmitted to the control surfaces. That was a good idea, considering the plane's mach-2 capability and the 9-gs it could pull in a turn, but I think I would have preferred the old hydraulic system. Perhaps that is because I understood it. "It flies you," pilots said of the F-16. No thanks. I do not like to cede control.

"Home of the 142nd Fighter Squadron," said the sign on the hanger.

Within the tide of exhaustion that flowed as the trip neared its end, I recalled watching my 105 explode. At the time, before I lost sight of the sky in the sudden jungle twilight, I thought, yes, I got out in time. I meant to. That is what procedures are for. You go through them automatically and, if you have time to think about the process later, that means that the procedures have worked. The book is there for a purpose, as Captain Queeg says. I think that most pilots would agree with me that we rationalize emergencies. You are trained. You identify the problem. You snap through a sequence that has been hardwired into your thick skull, and it works. Often, the fact that it has worked is the first thing you think of after identifying the problem. The interim has been automatic.

I am not sure that pilots would also agree with me about what how the process works beyond the physical. The millisecond of my acceptance of the disintegrating aircraft extended in one of those quirky ways that time has into something longer, into a dream that went on and on, a dream in which I could not get out of that burning aircraft. The dream does not go away when I wake up. And, its proximity, lurking just over the horizons of consciousness, makes me reluctant to go to sleep at night. I would guess that ex-fighter pilots don't talk about that kind of thing too much as they move their hands through imaginary altitudes.

IV.

I should not have tried to turn, but when I came
to a moment in the road from which I could
not see ahead, I grew afraid. I could
not breathe. Was that because I could not see?
Or had the robbery of eyes and breath
occurred at once? I turned. And then a voice
said "No!" I realized then that I was dead.
Of course I could not breathe! But worse than that,
I understood as well that I was damned.

Anon.,
The Lost Play,
Mephisto

I was sweating by the time I wrestled my bag into the trunk
of the rental car. I looked again at the map they'd given me.
I started the car, turned the air up to MAX, and followed the
Exit signs out of the airport compound.

The house was a neat white stucco structure in a middle
class neighborhood of similar houses north of the city. Nothing
ostentatious. As the United Express Embraer 170 had banked
for its final approach, we had passed over a community to
the west, punctuated by the unnatural blue of swimming
pools. That's where the rich people lived. I did not see pool
maintenance trucks lining West Grove Avenue.

I had known that Paul had gotten married. He had even
sent me an invitation. I had sent him a copy of one of my

books, suitably inscribed and the inevitable note telling him that, if he came east...

But my own marriage had long since broken up, leaving an enraged ex-wife and a maddened little girl behind. So I was cynical about the institution itself and profoundly guilty for having betrayed my child. Some things are irretrievable, and we all can't write "In Memoriam."

I had also known that Paul's wife was younger than he and that they had had a daughter somewhere along the way.

But I was not prepared for either of them.

"Yes, Mr. Chambers – Doctor Chambers, I mean -- come in."

She was tall, with lustrous black hair, high cheekbones, and luminous skin. Her eyes held a depth of intelligence that suggested more fathoms than I could contemplate. She wore a white shirt, enticingly sculpted, and jeans over long legs. She was at that very attractive moment of a woman's late thirties, still taut of body and clear of face.

Laurie had the same flashing dark eyes and skin of delicate light brown. Seven or eight.

"Are you eight years old, Laurie?"

"No. Seven. But I will be eight in September."

"I knew you were at least close to being eight. What's your dog's name?"

She held out a white, stuffed dog, worn with hugging.

"This is Spot."

"Drink, Dr. Chambers?" Karla asked.

"Please, I'm Bill. If you'll join me. Beer if you have it."

"Si. Hay Corona."

"Bien!" I said.

"You speak Spanish?"

"Un poco. Bastante para mendigar una cerveza. Dos anos en la escuela superior. Muchos anos pasado."

She laughed.

"You must be Paul's age."

"He was a year younger. Born in '45. By the time the bomb exploded and the death camps were discovered, I was already saying, 'Mama.'"

"One problem I wanted to ask you about," she said. "Be right back."

I thought to myself, Paul would have done this for me – gone east, tried to help out – and I wanted to be asked. How seldom, I thought, do people want to be asked to help? Or – perhaps they are disappointed that they aren't asked more often. Who was I to judge? But for Paul. For Karla.

The living room was cool – a whirl of air conditioning sounded deep beneath the rug – and bright with colorful reproductions – Frida Kalho, Orozco and scenes from Mexico, highlands under the mountain that is the goddess of rain. I sat on the couch. Karla set my beer glass down on a coaster and sat in a chair to my left. She was holding the bottle from which she had poured my beer and took a swallow. Laurie stood to her right and stared at me, holding Spot on her shoulder. Spot considered me from a single, button eye.

"I can't access Paul's business account. That's where most of the money was."

"Needs his signature?"

"His and mine. I've got the paper work under way, but..."

"They are giving you a hard time."

"They are putting us through a bureaucratic process designed to take as long as possible. The bank manager could sign a waver easily enough."

"You are being singled out."

"Oh, yes. Welcome to the Inland Empire. A couple of years ago, an LAPD sergeant was cuffed and 'proned' in his own front yard in Riverside. African-American, of course."

I took out my wallet and counted some bills out on the coffee table in front of me.

"Here's a hundred and fifty. So you can get groceries."

"I'll pay you back as soon as..."

"Sure. Meanwhile, I'll use one of my credit cards and get more cash."

"Mine is a debit card. They put a hold on it."

"You don't worry about the money right now, Karla. Paul was my friend."

"And you are his."

I looked at the painting by Frida Kahlo. It showed a hummingbird hovering below those intimidating black brows. "I hope the ending is joyful," she had said, the day before she died. "And I hope never to return." But you have, Frida.

"The ceremony is at the airport. The ANG hanger."

I must have looked puzzled.

"Paul and I did not belong to a church, " Karla said. "I wouldn't ask St. Angelica's even if we had gone there. I was a Catholic once upon a time. Paul was an Air Police officer in the ANG unit."

"He didn't fly?"

"He flew their trainer. Just to get his hours in. He retired. But he said that the fighter pilot was obsolete."

"I think he's right. One air-to-air kill during the entire Iraqi operation. Drones and missiles are the future. I understand that the guys who operate the drones from some remote bunker actually get Air Medals."

"Paul was happy to retire from the reserves. He hated our foreign policy. He felt like a hypocrite when he put on his uniform. But they needed an Air Police officer and it fit in with his law degree. He enjoyed it."

The Guard compound west of the airport had a few permanent personnel, but was largely deserted when we pulled up to the hanger where the ceremony would be held. It was a fenced-in zone with restricted entry and an Air Police presence. The AP patrol cars roamed randomly around, although nothing more than an occasional speedlimit violation was likely to occur. It can be difficult to keep a powerful car under 25 mph.

A small group, mostly men from Paul's guard unit, huddled in a corner of the huge and echoing hanger.

I wanted to hold Laurie, or say something to her as the service went on. What did she make of "the resurrection and the life"? She just knew that all that had been mortal of her father – the laughter, the gentle instruction, the hugs – was closed up on that box under that flag and that when the flag had been folded and handed to her mother it brought with it nothing of her father.

I thought of the last time I had seen Paul.

I had done some routine things for awhile after my escape from the capacious reaches of the jungle. I filled in as adjutant, merely signing the forms that a knowledgeable master sergeant slid into my inbox. My left hand was anointed and lightly bandaged every morning and I could not wear the tight leather gloves demanded by the legerdemain of the cockpit. And I had flown the requisite number of missions, so no one was bugging me about returning to flying status. I never did return to flying status.

Paul and I flew back to Travis together, a long lumbering ride. We wore our ribbons. He had gotten a DFC for his defense of my vulnerable ass hanging from that chute. My adventure had earned me a Bronze Star with "V" attachment. It was automatic for an escape and evasion. I had also gotten my Purple Heart, which, though down on the list of my decorations, was the one I prized. True, it had been gained involuntarily, but it proved that I had "been there," even if "there" was an unidentified vacancy above the rot of the jungle where my left hand smoldered unnoticeably for a few moments before I punched out.

Paul and I parted at Travis, with promises that we would get together soon and frequently. Of course. But that never happened.

Before I lugged my dufflebag across the tarmac toward the C 130 that would waft me with the jetstream to McGuire AFB, Paul snapped me a salute. He then pointed his right index finger at me.

"See you!"

I returned his salute and said, "Roger that!"

And as I thought of it, I understood that such pledges seem still redeemable while the other person lives. When the other person dies, the word "never" hardens into the terminal date inside the closed parenthesis. And you try to think of something else.

As the ceremony ended, I took a look at the crowd. Yes, it was almost exclusively military.

I turned to Karla.

"No. My family disapproved. It didn't matter what I wanted. I was marrying down. It's a wonder I haven't gotten any 'good riddance' messages."

A white man, large and deeply tanned, came up to us.

"Sorry, Mrs. Palmer. He was a good man. And he had guts."

"Thank you. Chester Longley, this is Bill Chambers, a friend of Paul's from the Air Force."

His grip was strong.

"Mr. Palmer helped several of my workers," he said. "People can scream all they want about illegals, but they are human beings with very good values, and they sweat under this godawful sun for their wages. I could not bring in my several crops without migrant workers."

"Viva Cesar Chavez," I said.

"Yes. And Paul Palmer, too," he said.

I went over to the sergeant who had led the squad of bearers, all wearing the Air Police armband and with a nametag in place.

"Valdes."

"Yes sir."

I held out my hand.

"Bill Chambers. Paul and I served together in Vietnam. I can't tell you how much it means to a veteran like me to see you guys here."

He took my hand.

"We respected Major Palmer, sir. And liked him."

I shook my head.

"Still hard to believe."

He took a quick scan of the room over my shoulders.

"I know some of the deputies sir."

"And?"

"The Police Department made a surveillance tape of the arrest."

"But he died in custody of the Sheriff."

"That's right. But they said he was falling-down-drunk."

At that point, the chaplain, a Captain came up.

"Valdes, we are ready to go to the cemetery."

Later, I sat with Karla in her living room as dusk took a long ride westward over the Pacific.

She took my left hand in her right hand and looked down with concern.

I did not retail my Mekong Delta joke.

"It looks like lightning in a summer sky," she said.

"That's what it was."

I told her the story.

"Paul never mentioned it. Just that you were a good friend."

"You know, Karla, we don't say much about what happened."

My left hand was still in her right hand.

Oh, oh! It happened. We were suddenly enclosed in a zone of shared energy, a cocoon of resonance, a trembly place like that created by a machine – a computer – of whose sound one is unaware until you listen.

"I think..."

"Let's be careful," I said. "Some things to sort out."

"True."

But she kept my hand in hers and we enjoyed whatever it was we were transmitting to each other. Whatever else might happen, at that moment, each of us remembered Paul whom we had buried an hour ago.

V.

The street was empty.
Rain glittered at the edges.
Music came from somewhere.
Black and white.
Somber chords.
"The End" rose like a placard
over the long and luminous street.
Stark letters.
White on black.

Vance McWay,
"Old Film."

"No," Karla said. "He was driving back from a meeting with the Chicano Association. He may have had the proverbial couple of beers. He seldom had more than that."

"Did he call you?"

"Yes. Told me he'd been arrested. Told me not to worry. He said the breathalyzer didn't budge."

"They gave him a breathalyzer?"

"That's what he said. Why?"

"He probably exaggerated on the results, assuming he knew them. But he did know how much he'd had to drink. They claimed he was falling-down-drunk."

"Not true. I have never seen him even close to that."

"Did you get a lawyer?'

She shrugged.

"I am one, of course. I never passed the California bar. I was going to..."

She smiled.

"Laurie arrived. Who needed one more lawyer in the family? I talked to one. He told me to forget it. He said that suing would not bring Paul back. That was true enough, as if that were the point."

"He was really saying..."

"That suing the Sheriff of Empire County would be a) useless and b)..."

She paused, a bleak look in eyes that were looking at nothing.

"Suicide." I said.

"Yes. Dangerous. They hire Latinos. They even have a black cop on the police force, but this is what they call a 'conservative' community."

"Meaning anti-gay, anti-abortion."

"Anti-immigration. Racist as the deep south in the 1940s."

"The cops or the Sheriff?"

"Both. The cops are just casual racists. The Sheriff, Duclos, is worse. He tried a number of gambits. He cracked down on prostitution a few years back. Not too popular with the conservative movers and shakers who were the clients. Then he decided to go after drunk drivers. He had patrol cars trailing drivers who were leaving the parking lots of bars – mostly dives, not high-toned hotels – at one o'clock on Sunday morning. That did not make him popular with the rednecks, and it's an elected office. So then he went after the immigrant farm workers. Bingo! Suddenly he was Lou Dobbs' hero!"

"Oh yes. I knew I'd heard of him somewhere. I can't stand Dobbs. What an arrogant prick. Glad he's gone."

"Paul had always been a target, of course."

"Not just paranoid?"

"Oh no. A black man. Automatically a threat. An educated black man. An educated black man who was an officer in an elite branch of the service."

"And he refused to go to the back of the bus."

"Like Jackie. Yes. But he began to champion the migrant workers. Even the documented workers were getting harassed, rousted, arrested on the inevitable disorderly conduct rap. And Paul went to court with them."

"I flew with Paul. He was not a careless person."

Some people think that fighter pilots are reckless daredevils in leather jackets and silk scarves driving in the prop wash, laughing over a whiskey after a treacherous mission. Not so. Or, if it is, the daredevil dies young. Most of us are meticulous. As we preflight our aircraft, we know that what we detect or fail to discover can kill us. Every step is set down in order. And we follow each step in order. Our driving, for example, is usually precise, punctuated by turn signals and constant swiveling of the head. I do get nervous, even angry, at drivers who drive too close to the back of my car. That's often where danger is for the fighter pilot. And for the driver. Someone too close inhibits a driver's ability to make the right decision in an emergency.

"No," she said. "He was very careful. But he said that the people he represented were a lot more vulnerable than he was."

Little did he know!

"What was he doing that pissed them off so much?"

"Besides being black? Let's face it, California does have an immigration problem. They need the workers to bring in the crops, of course, but recent estimates peg the cost at ten billion a year. You can imagine how that goes down in a state that is cutting its teachers from already overcrowded schools. It comes to $1200 a household. People seeing that say, it's a mortgage payment, or its six months of car payments, or it's a year's worth of beer, whatever. It strikes a nerve. And they claim that fifteen per cent of school children are the children of illegals."

"So they crack down, as Duclos is doing."

"Right. They get deportation orders. Now what Paul was doing..."

She paused, her voice losing its way in her use of the past tense.

"Sorry. He was working on what they call cancellation of removal."

"Trying to keep them here."

"Yes. A lot of factors go into it. How long the worker has been here? Does he have a family here? Were any of his children born here? Did the worker serve in the US military and get an honorable discharge? Paul even worked on getting some general discharges upgraded to honorable. Does he own property or run a business? What is his employment and its value to the community? If he has a criminal record, has he been rehabilitated? What is his character?"

Obviously, she had worked on this with Paul, no doubt providing expert advice as well as linguistic fluency.

"That's a lot."

"It is. And it is not easy to get the documentation. It takes a couple of weeks just to get an authentic copy of a service record. And some growers are very reluctant to give character references for fear of being considered friendly to illegals and thus encouraging the wrath of Sheriff Duclos. Most of the farms are within his jurisdiction and you do not want to piss off the Sheriff."

"What does he do?"

"He has a thousand ways of harassing people. He'll spot a car outside a roadhouse, check on whose it is, and do a routine stop a block away. It can be very targeted and still perfectly legal. And no one raises a peep if he harasses a Mexican. The others are too scared to say a word."

"They'll be deported."

"Yes. For example, a worker pays money to some scammer who promises to get him a green card. Of course, that card does not materialize. But the victim doesn't dare complain. He is already illegal. Paul was working on several cases like that."

"What happens to those cases?"

She shrugged.

"You think anyone around here is going to pursue them? Now?"

The main headquarters of the Amerigo PD was on Seguro Boulevard, about a mile below the Residence Inn, where I was luxuriously ensconced in an "extended stay" suite. When I had been asked whether I wanted one over the phone, I had said "affirmative" for some reason. Fourteen extra bucks a day.

I believed that I had to get that arrest tape. It would show the standard, roadside evaluation, and it would show whether or not Paul was falling-down-drunk as the Sheriff had apparently claimed. If the claim were accurate, I'd go home.

"Hi, Sergeant. I'm Captain Chambers, Air Force."

I held out my photo id, hoping that Sergeant Lopez would not notice that I had aged a bit since the daguerreotype had been recorded.

"What can I do for you, Captain."

"Checking on survivor benefits, Sergeant. For..."

I pretended to look at a notebook I'd just purchased at a drug store.

"A Major Paul Palmer."

"So?"

"Apparently died in custody."

"You want the Sheriff's Department. Two blocks over on Arbole Verde."

"Actually, sergeant, I want to look at the tape you made of his arrest on..."

157

Again, a glace at the notebook.

"6 6 10."

"We'd need written authorization."

"I can get that sent. Priority e-mail. But I've got a case up in Fresno this afternoon."

He hesitated. Then, he picked up the phone.

"Lieutenant. Guy here from the Air Force. Wants to look at Palmer's arrest record."

"Just the tape," I said, recognizing that I'd be happy to get the record as well.

He put the phone down.

"Lieutenant's office. Second door on your right," the Sergeant said, pointing with his left thumb.

I could not believe my luck.

"Lieutenant Bascombe. I'm Captain Chambers, USAF."

"So I understand. Have a seat, Captain."

He was an African-American, about forty. Very wide of shoulder.

"Football," I said. "Number fifty four."

He raised his eyebrows and smiled.

"Good to be remembered."

"I am glad, sir, that I never tried to go over the middle on you."

He had played for the 49ers during their Joe Montana years.

"So am I," he said. "What's this about Palmer's record?"

"Just routine, Lieutenant. Survivor's benefits."

"Why should that be an issue? Retired from the reserves."

"From the National Guard."

"Difference?"

"Some National Guard duty does not qualify."

"What's his arrest have to do with that?"

"It doesn't. I was just making a clarification."

He stared at me for a moment.

"What I would like to see, Lieutenant, is the tape your department made when he was arrested."

He laughed.

"You are not here about survivor benefits, are you."

It was a statement.

"No, sir."

"Look, Chambers, I think you are stepping out on thin ice. You sure as hell are overage in grade. If I were you I would honor Palmer's memory, give your condolences to his wife, and take the next plane to LAX. I mean now."

"Why do you say that?"

He looked at the door behind me.

"I am a token officer, Chambers. We had a bad incident two years ago. A couple of my brothers were stopped by this department. One was beaten. The arrest tape disappeared somehow. But the stink that got raised by the State forced the City to adopt a code of standards and, by way of showing that they got it, insisted on a black officer in the chain of command. But if you think..."

"I don't. But I would like to look at that tape."

"I won't be able to do a damned thing for you. Or for Mrs. Palmer. She is a nice lady. And I liked Palmer, too. He was a pretty good cop too."

"I'd like to see the tape."

He took out a form, checked in several boxes, scribbled a note in a blank space, signed it, and handed it to me.

"Down the hall. Left at the stairwell. Basement. Sergeant Logan."

"Thanks."

"Look, goddammit, Chambers, be careful, will you? I don't think you realize where you are."

The tape was grainy, pulsing, the figures seeming to get larger and smaller in the intermittent light from the cruiser.

Yes, that was Paul. Tall, a little more stooped than I remembered. Hell, it had been thirty years or more! He was actually laughing, as if he knew that this was a setup. He performed the demanded actions with grace and, if I read him accurately, with scorn. Touch my nose? Do it all the time. Walk a straight line? I do that too, so as not to bounce off the walls. The tape would not support absolute sobriety, of course, but it would refute any assertions of "falling down" drunkenness.

"PBT?" I asked, hardly daring to hope that I'd get it.

"Just a moment, sir."

And there it was. Preliminary Breath Test: 0.01.

With the notation: "No evidence of hyperventilation."

Hyperventilation immediately prior to breathing into the balloon could lower the reading.

But the reading argued a couple of beers at most.

"Can you make me a copy of this, Sergeant Logan?"

He looked at me as if to say, You know better.

"No can do, sir."

I did not press my luck.

"Laurie is actually Loren. Named after Paul's father, Lorenzo. A great man who labored all his life so his son could go to college."

"He must have been proud."

"He didn't live long enough."

It was late. I'd had half a bottle of wine. The shadows grew from the single lamp on the table beside the couch. We were in a delicious lull. I would either get up and go back to my hotel or we would drift into her bedroom, take off our clothes, and probably just fall asleep with some part of our bodies touching.

But as I looked at her, dark hair and that depth of eyes, the shadows playing at the planes of her face, in the chair across from me, I drifted into a kind of dream.

Carol. Many years ago.

We had been at the rathskeller at Muller's in Livesley Center and I'd driven her back to the street outside the quadrangle on which her dorm fronted. I had come back a little early – that is, with a half hour before curfew. I parked a hundred yards beyond the entrance.

We necked in the front seat of my Pontiac.

"Let's get in the back seat."

"No! If anyone comes along, I'll be thrown out of school."

"No one's going to come along," I said. "And we'll keep watching," I continued, refuting my confidence.

She paused and looked at the empty sidewalk.

"All right."

Proust is right about scent and its instant recall into the past. But shadows have a more pervasive capacity. And the hold of the memory they bring lingers. Scent insists on an instant almost physical return to a past moment. Shadows last longer and invite a narrative into their suggestive length.

Carol raised her dress and slid down on top of me. I could not see a thing except her face, rocking in the touch of the distant streetlight as she scanned the sidewalk behind my car.

"Anyone coming?"

"No."

"Then, come here."

Our bodies were linked in a pleasant rhythm. She bent her head forward and completed the transaction.

Nobody else came.

"Thinking?" Maria asked. "You are looking at something."

Yes, as the Bergman's said, "When you knew that it was over, you were suddenly aware that the autumn leaves were turning to the color of her hair."

"At the past," I said. "The distant past."

"That's all there is," she said.

We marched back from the flightline. It was Friday and our spirits were high. The weekend opened vastly before us. 0600 hours Monday morning was a lifetime away. We fell out. Paul was ahead of me, walking back to our barracks.

"Hey, Paul. Wait up."

He did.

"Going into town tonight?"

"You kidding?"

We were fighting a war, however thinly premised on the Gulf of Tonkin Resolution. Civil rights and voting rights laws had been passed. But we were at a base in southern Georgia, along the stretch of our fair land that runs through Florida's Panhandle, and on into Mississippi and Louisiana.

"Sorry," I said.

"That's okay. I have been told, very informally, you understand, to be careful when leaving the base. I have also been told – and I believe it – that this is the most racist section of the country."

"Okay. Let's go over to the O Club for steaks."

"No. You want to go into town."

"Look, Paul, I could go in to the Stateline Hotel, have a couple of beers, pick up a local lovely, and a dose of clap or a colony of crabs."

And even then, my own safety was not assured. We were young, educated, making good money, and drove big, new cars. The local lads resented us. I did not blame them. I, who had lived the privileged life, still had a touch, a feeling of the resentments that that privilege could breed. We often came out of the local VFW, which welcomed our patronage, to find our tires flattened.

"We'll both be safer at the Club." I said. "And we can walk,"

"And help each other walk back," he said, laughing.

And, after that, I did not go into Retriny Corners very often.

I had gone on to do the usual liberal thing. I wrote letters. I expressed the proper sentiments. I even taught a course at Gridley on African-American history and literature. It had been requested by some very good students of various shades of pigmentation. It occurred just before the field of African-American Studies suddenly burgeoned. The course was very popular with the students. Wright, Baldwin, Ellison, Clever, Malcolm. The primary criterion was to find a large enough room in which to give the course. But the administration and my colleagues hated it. "Litrachu cum sociology," sneered one outraged little fellow, a scion of tidewater aristocracy. He had tenure. I never did achieve that promised land.

But Paul?

He had been living his beliefs, not just professing them.

And, although I thought that I was doing the right thing by teaching my course in the face of typical academic hostility, I was doing more than professing my beliefs right now.

It was natural that I would remember those few years in the USAF. My own memory is, I suppose, like a card sorter. Push the right button and all those cards with the unspindled and unfolded surfaces flip into the right slot. An ancient metaphor from the days when the brain was being compared to a computer. But now, everyone twitters apparently, bringing absolute triviality to articulation. Some things are best forgotten. Some things should be forgotten – the observed details of combat that you cannot notice because you must focus on a few essential actions or die, the look on a daughter's face when you say goodbye and know that it is goodbye. But what happens to minds that deny the richness of memory by pulling everything into a brief memo? We become the ultimate narcissists, not just imitating the behavior of others but claiming that our own behavior is significant. We become surfaces. Reflective surfaces in the sense of mirrors, not of thought. We no longer think.

I was rubbing some oil into the base of Karla's spine. The dry, virtual desert atmosphere was good in some ways. But it did dry the skin.

I had asked her whether she had met Paul in law school.

"Not exactly in law school," she said. "But almost. Paul came to my school to discuss immigrant problems, particularly their interface with the legal system and social services. It's a particular issue with children – school, medicine. Arnold has gone back and forth on it, first advocating a wall between San Diego and Tijuana, then calling that idea something out of the stone age. Fifty percent of our county work force is from Mexico or deeper in Central America. And they are uneducated. Bad times haven't helped, of course. They are not coming as fast as they once did, some are even going home, but many are still here. God – it's a problem and Paul did not claim to have any solutions. He did give us some case histories to vivify the issue. Anyway, I liked him, of course. I waited for him after his talk with some inane question or other."

"Good for you. You picked him up."

"Yes, but he picked me up, too. Very consensual. He was looking for an administrative assistant, someone to help him with his caseload, a kind of social worker really. He had not considered hiring another lawyer and, of course, no one in Amerigo was about to take that job. He mentioned it to me. His Spanish was good. Mine was better. I was finishing my third year, so I jumped on it.

"Needless to say..."

"Needless to say," she replied, rolling over and smiling, but looking up at the shadows of a past that, however recent, was just as irretrievable as any day before yesterday.

I thought of a line in a poem I'd read in prep school.

"I cheer a dead man's sweetheart. Never ask me whose!"

VI.

"Hell, this dying isn't much."

Errol Flynn

We were free as kids to go where we wanted. We were boys. Sexual predation was not an issue in our isolated enclave. We did have to scrub behind our ears lest we grow weeds there, or crabgrass, but we were seldom admonished.

One day, my older brother Ben and I got a ride in a rickety old truck that belonged to Jack Johnson Sides, who did landscaping for a neighbor. We stood in the back, leaning against the splintery boards and went all the way to Madison and back. It was a wonderful adventure, driving along those old roads in the wind under the oak and elm and past the elegant homes of that part of New Jersey, brick, colonial, and pseudo-Tudor astride their cashmere lawns.

We should have lied about it, of course, but we stood silent as we were admonished for our recklessness. Ben was ten years older than I. He bore the brunt of it. He should have had better sense. Yes. We would simply select another version of recklessness next time.

Ben was killed in Korea, an eighteen year old infantry man lugging an M-1. I could have selected the "single surviving son" option and avoided the military altogether.

My father had been in the Army, of course, and looked back on those four years as the best years of his life. He did not say so, of course. So he approved my decision to go to OCS. My mother? What can mothers say?

I often wonder whether I made the right decision. Fighter pilots know what Hamlet is talking about when he speaks of infinite space and bad dreams. But I know I did the right thing when I talk to a fellow veteran at the VA or merely pause to chat, as he comes down the aisle at the super market, wearing a veteran of this or that war baseball cap. I don't know whether other people notice, but we do communicate, across lines of age, education, and, yes, class as well.

An older guy stands in front of me in the line to get plates. I see from his paper work that he is applying for a Purple Heart decal.

"Where were you hit?"

"Italian campaign."

"Wow," I say, "that was an awful campaign."

"Weren't none of 'em much good," he replies.

I nod. For a moment, I feel authentic.

I did not have much time to think, to pull back and see myself and the pattern. That, of course, was somewhat by design. The right-wing is a minority, really a splinter group. But they have virtually paralyzed the governing majority and sneered at it for being unable to deliver. And they have the money. I was in the middle of what was happening – a fascist takeover. Of only one city? Perhaps, but it was a start for those whining about the decline of America, its humiliation as Obama apologized, or as Bill Clinton legitimized the little Kim Jong Il, whom little George had called a "pygmy," an act of supreme projection. They expressed their grievances by calling for unity, purity, and energy, a parody of the old Ballantine Ale commercials. They stood for a return to national pride. They polarized and then capitalized on the fissures they engendered. And, of course, Obama was trying to lead from the center, striving to be bipartisan. You can't lead from the center. You just open the center up for the likes of a cynical prick like Boehner. But those who cheered as Karl Rove's permanent majority shriveled like a leaf blown from a November oak tree were complacent. The best lack all conviction. My fellow historian, Robert Paxton, had identified the phases. Bush's encouragement of telecom companies to break the law quite consciously was a signal. Duclos' control of his domain was a fact. And, of course, it had majority support where he lived and the approval of an irresponsible egotist like Lou Dobbs. But I could not pull back and consider it in my book-lined study. They had killed Paul. My own life was at stake. Karla's. Laurie's. I had a sudden shuddering sense of how the Jews must have felt in Berlin after Kristallnacht on 9 November, '38. A spontaneous uprising, of course, like the recent Tea Parties that just happened to happen and the enraged confrontations at heath care forums. If they could, the Jews got out. If they did not, they would die. And their families with them. How many fathers woke up to that bleak certainty at some uncounted hour of the early morning? And the bastards even accused Obama of being a fascist. Angry words, even without substance, can come alive.

In the center of Amerigo is El Parque Nuevo, hardly new, where the Rio de Los Remedios has carved the gentle swirl of a basin and where the city has been held away. One gets a sense of non-invasion there among the ancient oak and the bougainvillea running down the river bank toward the gentle counter-clockwise swirl of the pool.

And it was there that Karla, Laurie and I went one afternoon.

"We might as well be sides of beef living in air conditioning all the time," Karla had said.

We walked, Laurie between us but refusing to make it a threesome by taking my hand. She clung to Karla's. That was okay. She remembered other times.

I did push her on the swings and she assisted with the pull of her slender arms, but she did not shriek with enjoyment at the outward voyage. She was a sober child, still processing what had happened. But she had no language for that, and neither Karla nor I could provide the words.

Still, it was a restorative interlude. The heat of the baking city seemed to hold back from the park as the wind rode the river's surface from the north. It was like another world.

As we walked back to my rental, Karla nodded to her right.

Yes, a sheriff's cruiser was parked along the street near my car. We could not see the eyes inside, but we could feel them see us.

Sheriff Duclos was a cliche. You expect a burly swaggerer with a cartridge belt straining at his pot belly and an intimidating leer clearing the way in front of his arrogant progress. But all Duclos had was the pot belly and the sneer. He was about five four, with bandy legs that turned his walk into a waddle. But he had gained power and that made him feel ten feet tall. He wore two guns – the old-fashioned Smith and Wesson .38s – and that doubled the intimidation factor. He was the cliche in miniature.

He was leaning against a cruiser as I came out into the furnace of early afternoon from the A.P.D.

"Mr. Chambers. Got a minute?"

It was not a question.

He expected that I knew who he was.

"Sure. But how about a cooler climate?"

"Okay. My office."

That's when I noticed the waddle.

We walked the two blocks across town to the Empire County Sheriff's Department. We went down Segundo Avenue, past the side of the building. It had no windows on the first floor, barred windows on the second floor. Duclos did not have to point at them. What would it be like to be behind those bars in August?

The P.D. headquarters had been a dusty, used space echoing cigarette smoke and sweat. An occasional window unit may have rearranged the heat, but the place was hot, oppressive, a stale zone where losers are brought, booked, and then turned over to the Sheriff. The P.D., Karla had told me, had only a holding cell.

Duclos' domain was a palace. I followed him past the metal detector and through the vast doors that swung open on the command of an alert deputy seated to the left of the entrance. The driver in the cruiser must have alerted someone that Duclos was on his way. I don't think everyone got the open sesame treatment. The a/c hit me right away, chilling the sweat on my back and predicting a cold that would slither amoeba-like into my sinuses. I used to get them in the summers, climbing from a superheated, JP-4 saturated concrete strip into an aircraft that would start throwing iceballs from its a/c by the time I got to 10 000 feet.

The floor was stone, with a shiny shield etched in marble on the center of the entrance foyer. "EMPIRE" it said. A set of steps led to a long desk of polished wood. Deputies scurried to and fro, but paused and came to semi-attention as the Sheriff waddled past.

"Is the second floor air conditioned?" I asked.

"Cool air rises," Duclos said, laughing at his cruel joke.

His office, down a hallway at the rear of the building, was huge and surprisingly Spartan. I expected myriad framed photographs of Duclos with Dobbs, George Bush, Charlton Heston, Bill O'Reilly, et al. But there were none. Of course, any photographs would have made him look like the shrimp he is. Even the little creep from Yale is taller.

He did have some plaques on either side of his desk and some framed award certificates. But the man had not surrounded himself with the usual narcissistic significations. He was powerful. He knew it. He did not have to pretend to be, like a Bush, a Himmler, a Bull Connor.

"You from New England," he said, leaning back in his swivel chair and fingering his pot belly with contentment.

"Right," I said.

"My grandfather was from there. Biddeford. Worked in the mills. Came out here during the war. We stayed."

Yes, the name told me. French Canadian. They had infested the college town where I taught, loud with guttural French and a pseudo-patriotism that obliterated nuance with cries of 'treason!' Their sons had died in Vietnam while the students of Gridley College had enjoyed exemptions until the spring of '68. I did not savor the smugness of privilege, but I disliked even more the unexamined but shrilly articulated assumptions of the mill worker population, now absorbing whatever bottom-feeder jobs there were in the old mill towns of Maine and Massachusetts and still existing in their three story firetraps.

And, of course, Duclos knew that it was a matter of class. It was not a matter of skin or ethnicity, but of education. Educated people tended to "do nuance," as G. W. notoriously refused to do. For Duclos and his ilk the Constitution was an impediment to the exercise of arbitrary power – as it had been meant to be. What he was telling me now was, Yes, you've had the advantages and the education. I can tell by your face and by the way you talk. But I, Paul Duclos, grandson of a millworker from Biddeford, have you by the balls.

"You know, Chambers, we are in a state of siege here in Empire County and in California itself. I can only do what I can do. I can't declare martial law, but within my charter, I can act to control what I can control. All law enforcement is local, or it does not exist at all. My men and I put our lives on the line day in and day out."

He had just outlined the myth of his identity. His speech had a rehearsed quality. He had uttered it, replete with all the little humble pauses, in front of the Kiwanis, the Rotary, the

CNN audience out there in the sweeping reach of television-land. He was another of the many for whom the law was an encumbrance, an impediment between him and what needed to be done.

I looked at him, just a trace of exasperation in my face. I could not say, Spare me the sanctimony.

He reached to his right and picked up a folder.

"In my hand is a copy of Palmer's file."

"Including his initial arrest?"

He held his left hand up as if signaling a car to stop at an intersection.

"From the time that he was remanded to the custody of the Sheriff's Department. It is not a happy story. You people wonder why we keep a hand on the arm of a prisoner, even if he is in handcuffs?"

"I'll bite."

"It is to preclude exactly what happened. The deputy has been reprimanded, by the way. And that letter is here, with the name blacked out. But Palmer wrested himself free, lost his balance, and subsequently tumbled down a flight of steps."

I would bet that those very words were in the report.

"And," he continued, "that is consistent with the Coroner's report that is also here."

And, of course, the County Coroner was a department under the Sheriff. The report could not, of course, say whether Paul was assisted in his loss of balance.

"I am going to give you a copy of this report. I am hoping that it will answer any questions you may have."

He was also hoping that I would not pursue any legal action against his Department. Sheriff is an elected office, and Duclos needed at least marginal minority support from the thirty percent Chicano and the ten percent African-American population to make it. A lawsuit would inevitably bring up the issue of racism in the Sheriff's office. Vague allegations no doubt helped him with the right-wing whites, but direct accusations would divert energy from his anti-immigrant campaign. He was hoping that I would just go away.

"I am going a little beyond my authority here," he continued. "But I am a servant of the people. You were a friend of Palmer's, and I don't want you to leave our city harboring any ill will."

He had mastered the cliches and, at some level, believed them. He was the selfless public servant laboring on in the face of the indifference, ignorance, and downright hostility of the population he protected. It was the way many cops thought of themselves. I prefer the cynical ones who knew better.

"I have, as I said, edited out certain details for the protection of our own procedures and personnel. You will see that the report contains no hint of illegal activity on our part. And it is the complete report. I have signed an affidavit to that effect and had it notarized."

By giving me the record, Duclos set up a pattern of cooperation that he could use later, if he needed it.

He reached forward and brushed a hand against a telecom modem by the side of his computer screen, as if brushing off a speck of dust.

So he had recorded our conversation so far and just switched the mechanism off.

"Now that you have the record, Mr. Chambers, I suggest that you leave this jurisdiction. and perhaps take the little Mexican lady and that poor child with you. I don't think they would want to live here any longer."

I had just been told that I should go and that they had better not stick around either.

I took the folder in my left hand, as if agreeing with the agenda he had set out.

I had, after a lifetime, mastered the rudiments of self-control. I could still flare into roadrage, but if I prepared myself, I could simulate calmness. Duclos was one of those authority figures who dared someone to get angry at him.

Then the victim became the criminal. It was the technique of bad cops.

"Anything else?"

"Let's just say that forty eight hours should be enough."

But forty eight hours were not enough.

I had met with Duclos in the morning. When I got back to my room after lunch, my phone was blinking.

"Lieutenant Bascombe, please," I said to the Sergeant. "Mr. Chambers returning his call."

"Stay there," he said. "I'll meet you in the lobby."

I had browsed through Duclos' report, of course. It contained no surprises.

"Prisoner was intoxicated when turned over to Sheriff's Department. He had to be assisted by two Deputies, one on either side."

The photographs that had been taken at the Police Station and appended to the report – one frontal, one profile – gave no evidence of drunkenness. Paul's eyes were clear, if contemptuous. Perhaps I was just reading that attitude back into the event. No one was holding him up, though, and that was before he arrived at the Sheriff's office.

"While prisoner was being escorted to incarceration on the second floor of the Sheriff's Department, he wrested himself loose of the two Deputies on either side of him and attempted to flee back down the stairs. In doing so, he fell. Having his hands restrained behind his back, he suffered massive head injuries. Efforts to revive him were unsuccessful. A doctor was summoned. Prisoner was pronounced dead at 2335 hours. Subsequent autopsy confirmed that death resulted from trauma to the cranial area, resulting in fatal damage to the frontal cortex."

That, of course made a lot of sense. A prisoner being escorted up a staircase in a secure building makes an effort at escape. I could hardly ask why they had not used the elevator. And the report contained no reference to toxicology findings. Of course not. Any such evidence would refute the Sheriff's case at its heart. The breathalyzer had remained in the P.D. files, as had the taped record of the arrest.

Memory is tricky. I am seldom sure what triggers the revisiting of episodes and people I would have thought safely buried in some long-rusted set of synapses in that vast planetarium lodged within my skull. Something about Duclos...

Yes. Paul and I, he a first lieutenant and I a captain had been having a beer at the O Club on base. Singha. More than one. We'd been on a long mission and our throats were dry.

But the bartender, an old master sergeant waiting out his few months until retirement, served the beers with obvious reluctance and a palpable sneer as he said "sir."

I had seen the paperwork on him. It was a question of a couple of months for his twenty five years. That meant that he had begun his service just before the armed forces integrated under Harry Truman. That must have been a shock to many of them.

I was tired and still jumpy. The major who had debriefed me had seemed skeptical about my report. I put my ass on the line only to be doubted by a staff officer about the secondary explosions I had reported. That meant that we probably had hit a store of ammunition or rockets. He had signed off with obvious reluctance. And now this surly sergeant.

"You having a problem, Sarge?" I said as he removed the empties from the moist bar.

He looked at me with a flippant expression, but said nothing.

"Leave it alone, Bill," Paul said.

"Two more," I said. "Over at that table."

I pointed at an empty table behind me.

We carried our glasses over there. The full bottles were delivered and set very deliberately in front of us without a word.

"Look, Bill, I've gotten much worse, believe me. I have learned not to make a fight of it unless the stakes are worth it."

"Still, that bastard..."

"He brought us our beers. He resented the hell out of doing so, I grant. But he's probably a cracker who doesn't just hate Niggers, but me particularly. He has to salute me."

"Right. And he probably hates all officers. The sewage treatment plant is the officers' swimming pool."

"Right. West Point was bad. I had to be twice as good. And I had to keep my mouth shut."

"Still..."

"Look, Bill, it's a fact of life. You know, Jackie showed us how to do it. He played harder than anyone else. Maybe he had to, but he took what he might have said and transferred it to his feet and hands. I loved the way he put that bat way back and lashed at the ball."

His eyes looked at that sequence in the shadows for a moment.

"But you..."

"I only saw him in newsreels, but you could tell. His dynamism translated."

He laughed.

"Not in living color. Black and white."

"I wish..." I began.

"I have not gotten rid of my sense of justice, Bill, but there is a time and a place for trying to do something about it. We have to get through this..."

"You do. I have been removed from flying status. I'm just biding my time, like our friendly barkeep there."

"Okay. I do, then."

VII.

One dark morning in the middle of the night,
two dead boys got up to fight.
Back to back they faced each other.
They drew their knives and shot each other.
A deaf policeman heard the noise,
and came to rescue the two dead boys.

Anon. Late Nineteenth Century.

I saw an Amerigo PD cruiser pull past the main entrance and go around to the back of the Marriott. Bascombe entered from a side entrance.

He motioned me into a deserted shadow of the lobby out of sight of the registration desk.

We sat in leather chairs that faced each other across a low table.

"Duclos knows that you saw the arrest tape."

"And read the PBT report."

"You did? Didn't know that."

"Both of them refute his report."

"So he is not going to let you leave Amerigo."

"What can he do?"

"If you try, he'll issue a fugitive warrant."

"How can he do that?"

"He'll think of something. Wanted for questioning. Whatever."

"Doesn't he need a judge?"

"He has a judge."

"Okay. Can you escort me out of the County?"

"No. Duclos has jurisdiction over every community – and every road – around the City of Amerigo. We can't even follow a suspect in hot pursuit. We have to turn it over to Duclos half a mile either side of the city limits."

"So I'm in a trap."

"Yes. You and Mrs. Palmer. And their kid."

"Jesus!"

"He can't do much while you are here."

"But, Lieutenant, I can't do anything at all if I stay here."

"I know. It stinks. Thought I'd let you know. Got to get back to work."

"Do you know anyone in the State AG's office?"

"What good would that do? You'd have to file a complaint. It would take weeks to even get it read. And Duclos has friends in all places, high and low, in Sacramento. You'd be buying trouble."

Could I purchase any more than I had now?

"Thanks for... the warning."

I had almost said, Thanks for nothing.

I had come out here for Paul's sake. Futile gesture, I know, but we do make them. Now I had put his wife and child in danger. And my own ass as well.

In retrospect, I could see that it had been inevitable. We elect a black man on a great tide of hope. And, when the tide recedes a bit instead of raising all boats, out come the racists from the stink of the mudflats. The Republicans would deny any such motive, of course, and perhaps have been unable to access it within their own sour souls. I don't think that Iago, the rationalist, is capable of discovering the racial-sexual core of his hatred of Othello. That black ram holding the luminous white skin of Desdemona! I won't let that happen! he screams behind his calm facade. And so now the right-wing is determined to destroy Obama's presidency. And they may succeed. Who thought that electing a black man would resolve our racial problems? Never. Those problems have been exacerbated. Don't underestimate the hatred that lurks in the heart of white Amerika. And don't underestimate the ability of a minority to block all action and paralyze government. The Brownshirts did it.

Combat veterans will tell you that they often get a very cold feeling along the spine just in advance of something happening. It is a developed reflex, I think, and may also be a trace of an ancient survival technique, acquired before our ancestors recognized that they had been endowed with an encumbrance called reason. A fighter pilot knows to attack, if he can, from the lower right of an enemy. The natural tendency of the person being attacked is to turn to the left, away from the larger mass of muscle. And in that instinct, a fatal shot can be fired.

It was dark in the room and the remnants of a falling moon drifted through the curtains. Long slants of silver shadow trembled in the undervoice of the air conditioner.

But it was not the airconditioner that gave me this ice along the spine.

The television set reflected the room in black and white. And beside it stood Paul Palmer, in his flightsuit as I had remembered him. The flightsuit absorbed what light there was, except for the luminous letters on the leather name patch on the left front. His eyes came at me as if from behind a mask.

"Paul, I'll do my best," I said.

But he continued to glare at me.

"I'll take care of them," I said.

Whatever had been there wove itself back into the fabric of light and shadow.

I got up and raided the mini-bar for a Dewars. The icicle that had been my spine became my spine again.

I realized that I had already made that vow before he had asked.

"Rest, rest, perturbed spirit," I said to the empty mini-bottle of Dewars.

Some elements inhere in every emergency. First is communication. If you can tell someone that you are experiencing an emergency you can get help. It can be advice from a flight leader or just an "I'll be right there." You've articulated your fear to a sympathetic ear. That helps get it out of your own system. Emergencies are compounded, obviously, when no help is at hand. There's that other voice telling you that it is not your ass hanging here in this burning aircraft. Relax and see what happens. It's just a film. Second, you interact with the situation, assessing and rejecting options. You need more power. But the engine may be on fire, so to feed fuel into flame is to encourage an explosion. Since fuel is already going back into the engine, you may want to stop-cock the throttle. But that means that you have to set up the optimum airspeed for a glide. And to glide for any distance you need altitude. A flamed-out 105 sank like a dead shark. This kind of quick analysis – it takes a second or two – may lead the pilot to opt for ejection. But you may be over enemy territory. Enemy territory sends a strange feeling upward to the base of one's spine from its ridges and trees. And so on. The third point of course is that an emergency is a process. It calls for the right response or set of responses in an absolute sequence.

She was a beautiful woman, of course, but what I noticed about her was her voice. Its low melody was reassuring, even when it expressed doubt, fear. Somehow, as I listened to the voice, I knew we'd get out of this. Just the self-deception that comes with falling in love?

"What should I do?"

"I'm not sure," I said.

It was nine pm. Laurie was asleep.

"You are sure your phone is tapped?"

"Yes. Whirring noises. Sometimes a click just after I dial a number. No heavy breathing, but if I asked for help..."

"They'd trump something up."

"Yes. The restraints on a police state are really frail when you think about it. I think most communities would be appalled at Duclos. Not reelect him. But he gets on Lou Dobbs. People are so proud!"

"Chester Longley?"

"If we could get to him. But we are surrounded."

"'Where'd all them Injuns come from?' as General Custer asked."

And at this point I knew that Karla, Laurie, and I had better get the hell out of there. ASAP. Duclos knew that I could refute his report.

"I am going to try to get out of here and get some help."

"Where will you go?"

"I don't know. Once I am out of here I can find someone. I'll contact the DA or the State Police."

"Will that do any good?"

"Look, Karla, all I want to do is to get you and Laurie out of here. The hell with any notion of seeing justice done."

"As the lawyer I contacted said to me. But you could just leave."

"No! You can't leave now. What would Paul think of me if I just took off. What would you think of me?"

"Duclos wanted me to sign a statement stipulating that I would pursue no legal action against the Empire County Sheriff's Department."

"I doubt that he'd accept that now. I have complicated the case."

"What will he do?" she asked.

"He's thinking. Probably checking on how to make the charges against me stick. If he does, I am neutralized."

"Then I could sign the agreement."

"Probably. He'd let you leave."

"And you'd go to jail," she said.

"Probably."

I stopped at an Exxon station, then drove my rental car to the airport.

I had been offered an upgrade when I arrived for an extra ten dollars a day but had declined.

"I'd like to take you up on that upgrade."

I placed the keys to my rental on the counter.

"This one is in Hertz slot number eleven."

"Fuel?"

"I filled it up two miles ago."

"Let me see what I have available, sir. Please come back in fifteen minutes."

Then I made my mistake. That is, if it was a mistake. I had begun to wonder whether anything I did, right or wrong, made any difference. I had visions of James Chaney, Michael Schwerner, and Andrew Goodwin being let out of that jail in Mississippi into the wilds of Neshoba County after sunset and then tracked down on that lonely road, headlights probing the nowhere ahead.

I went across to the neon splash of bar and ordered a scotch and water. Did I need some Dutch courage? Hell yes. I was, as always, probing the moment ahead. Usually, the sequence involves nothing that threatens me. But you never really get used to the moments that are coming back at you with danger. And the process probably gets more difficult as you get older. The oblivion of youth is unavailable. The analgesic that shallow consciousness sluices through the brain has long since dried up. I was afraid and cursed myself for that fear.

I got the big car within a mile of the Memnos County line. I might have tried to outrun a pursuing cruiser, but, ahead, I saw the blinking blue lights of a road block, replicated from the throb of the overcast. A signal for the end of the world, the place where the ancient maps depicted a drop into oblivion where the jaws of dragons waited.

"Routine check, sir."

I had my driver's license, of course, and handed the Deputy a bunch of paper work from the glove compartment of the rental.

"Will you please step from the car, sir."

I know that any resistance, verbal or physical, brings on a stronger counter response.

"I detect alcohol on your breath, sir."

It might have been anything else. Erratic driving. It could have been speeding, of course. Radar results are easy to doctor.

The event was being taped. I was a star at last!

"Please place your hands behind your back."

And so, cuffed and strapped into the back seat of a cruiser, I arrived at Duclos' ministry of justice.

The building had been built well. The a/c did not reach the cells on the second floor.

I was soon down in the cool swing of air on the first floor.

"I don't enjoy being called out in the middle of the night for this kind of thing," he said.

I had been recuffed, this time with my hands in front of me – no doubt by the book – and taken down to Duclos' vast chamber.

It was 2100, hardly the witching hour.

I did not enjoy being hauled in to his domain either, but that was beside the point. He knew that I had seen the surveillance tape and, probably that I knew the results of the breathalyzer test. He had actually given me the evidence that my own investigation refuted – his Official Report. He must be furious with himself.

And She a Shade

"You have become a problem, Mr. Chambers."

"In what way, Sheriff?"

"I have to spell it out? You are challenging my authority as Sheriff of Empire County."

"That's not true."

"But it is, Mr. Chambers. You have illegally represented yourself to obtain information that is confidential. That is a violation of State Law 1001, section five, paragraph C. Furthermore, your breathalyzer test is borderline."

"Which side of the border?"

"Enough for a driving to endanger. I could hold you on my authority, pending the posting of bond."

But he wouldn't. And my illegal obtaining of information was a misdemeanor, at best. That information tended to flow freely enough in most jurisdictions, particularly since it was often incorporated into further legal action. A good lawyer would get the case against me dismissed in ten minutes. Duclos was smart enough to know that he was in a weak position legally. He would not push things until he had to.

"But your lady friend is outside, squawking about habeas corpus and other mumbo jumbo. So I am releasing you with the provision that you not leave this jurisdiction until I have checked to see whether the DA wants to do anything on violation of State Law 1001."

The sweat had crystallized on my back, but my hands were still slick. I did not give Duclos the satisfaction of seeing me rub my wrists after the cuffs were removed.

"I got a call from the PD," Karla said, as she pulled from a parking spot across from the County Sheriff's office.

"They didn't give me a phone call."

"'Minor traffic violation,' they said."

"Meaning I could have rotted in that sweatbox."

"Duclos knew he was on shaky ground."

"We'll still be watched."

"Look behind you."

A County Sheriff cruiser glided along behind us.

"Where's Laurie?"

"I asked a neighbor to come over."

We were trapped. Duclos was not about to let me leave his jurisdiction. He would do his best to have me locked up on the misdemeanor charge. If I tried to get away I'd be picked up as a fugitive from justice. We might both have to sign some sort of agreement to get the hell out of Empire County. If necessary, I would do so. But I doubted that it would be that easy. Duclos had told me that my looking at the P.D. evidence was, in his eyes, much more than a misdemeanor. He was not sure what I might accomplish if I found a sympathetic person in authority beyond his domain.

It was Saturday night. No use trying to find anyone in the State AG's office. They'd be around the pool at or home after a round at the club on the recently sprinkled greens, wondering what the State was going to do about its water shortage.

"At least we've got some beer in the fridge," I said. "I have built up one of those thirsts again."

I noticed that I was grateful for the small favors that the gods of the invisible mountains were granting me.

VIII.

I am about to go on stage.
I have forgotten my part.
All eyes are upon me.
A great blank zone known as audience
expands in front of me.
"Oh what a rogue and peasant slave
am I!" I say. Is that the right play?

Stanley Woodsum,
"Amnesia."

I had the procedures for this one in my head. But like some emergencies – an airstart at low altitude, for example – this one had to go right every step of the way or fail. And the results of failure... you could not think of that outcome and succeed.

Duclos would learn of our plans at some point. I had to hope that it was later rather than sooner. I had to hope that, while he had sealed the borders of his principality, he had left some space for movement within it. If he found out what I was trying to do after my first move, it would be close. I had filed the Air Guard area in my mind as a place that Duclos could not reach. At least not without some official sanction.

And that filing for future reference combined with my crazy idea. I had spoken briefly to Longley before Paul's service He, too, was a pilot.

Karla had called from a pay phone near the Park.

Her call had been to Chester Longley. Was his Cessena still at Mountainview Field?

Could we borrow it? It was an emergency.

Not exactly like borrowing a car.

Karla got back to watch over Laurie. I went to the same payphone and called Master Sergeant Valdes of the California Guard Air Police. He was not on duty.

"Please contact him, Airman. This is Captain Chambers. We are on our way there. Ask him whether he can keep two people inside his station for a half-hour? Yes, civilians. It is an emergency."

It was. An emergency partly of my own making, true. And too many things could go wrong.

But Valdes met us at the gate.

"Should be a half hour," I said. "Delay Duclos if he shows up. And keep these two in your custody whatever else may happen."

I drove to General Aviation, being very careful. I know one thing about emergencies. It is often what you don't anticipate that trips you up. I had all the steps figured out. But between the steps? You cannot rush. Emergencies have their own time scheme.

I approached the circular desk in the lobby of General Aviation. A young Latino – Jesus said his nametag – looked up.

"Mr. Longley call?"

"You Mr. Chambers? Please sign here, sir."

He handed me the keys.

I did thank the god of visual flight rules. He did not ask to see my pilot's license. My instrument card was about forty years old and it was stamped "Jet Only" on the back.

"Plane is # three in the line to your left, Mr. Chambers. Fueled up."

I detached the guywires under each wing, climbed in, and muttered to myself for a while about fuel mixture, carb heat, and prop setting. I checked the control surfaces for free movement and taxied out of line to the left, where the fenced-in Guard area was.

Karla and Laurie came out from the gate, accompanied by Valdes.

I opened the door on the right side.

"Thanks, Sergeant. I owe you more than one!"

"Duclos is looking for you," he said.

"I'm sure he is."

Karla had put Laurie in the back seat and strapped her in.

"Karla, strap in and close the door."

I taxied toward the active runway.

"Mountainview Tower, Cessena 172. Request permission for departure."

"172. Tower. Cleared for runway niner. Wind from the southeast at 10 knots. Visibility two miles, four thousand feet."

As I lined up and gave the aircraft full throttle, Tower came on again.

"172. Tower. Abort takeoff. Return to General Aviation Terminal."

"Tower, last transmission garbled."

Duclos, realizing what I was trying to do, had contacted the control tower right after it had given me my clearance. It's all in the timing.

I pulled the plane from the concrete and began a right hand turn toward the north, toward Fresno.

"172. Tower. Return to Mountainview immediately."

As I looked past Karla, I saw a chopper tilt its way toward me from the field. Duclos.

"Tower. 172. Unable to read you. One by five."

We'd be about even in airspeed. The wind would not be a factor. But, fortunately, the clouds were lower than the last report had called them. Storm must be coming in. So I was soon surrounded by whispers of cloud and then buffeted by a thick blanket of gray. Soft-looking clouds are deceptive. They are like rocks. I kept the nose of the little plane just above the artificial horizon and then leveled off to build up my airspeed.

"Wow!" Karla said. "Honey. Did you enjoy the takeoff?" she called back to Laurie.

"What happened to the ground?" she asked.

"Still there," I said. Hard as a rock, I said to myself.

I hoped that Fresno was not socked in.

Let's see. I fumbled with the thick book between the two front seats.

"113.4," I said, clicking in the omni setting.

I was only ten degrees off course.

If the chopper knew that I was aiming for Fresno, he'd be there waiting for me.

Longley had said that he'd have the Compton County Sheriff meet me there. But I had to get down first, and the chopper would have someone with an M-16 aboard trying to make sure that I fell into a grove of pecan trees. He'd have all the maneuverability as I came down final. And then he would disappear into the night.

"San Francisco Approach Control. Cessena 172. Enroute. Will call for landing instructions when five miles out."

"Cessena. San Francisco Traffic. Did you file a flight plan?'

"172. Negative. VFR."

"172. Current heading and altitude?"

All of this, of course, was to get Duclos to fly to San Francisco or to have someone there ready to arrest us after we landed. We'd be hauled back to Empire County on a fugitive warrant without a chance to object. Duclos had no doubt had one of his judges sign it by now.

"We aren't going to San Francisco are we," Karla said. It was not a question.

"No. I may contact Fresno when we get closer. Just trying to throw Duclos off our trail."

She reached across and touched my right arm.

What I hoped to do was to land at Chandler, to the west of Fresno. If Duclos did not fall for my feint, he'd probably be looking for me at FYI, the commercial airport to the northeast. If Longley had gotten through, the Sheriff would be waiting for me at the terminal at Chandler. I had learned that, in emergencies, we do depend on people we do not know.

I descended gradually, hoping that I would be in the clear at one thousand feet. I did not dare go lower.

Yes, the rotating beacon to my left brushed against the lowering clouds. I banked toward the field and leveled off. To my right, up there at FYI, I saw a black chopper settling toward the tarmac. We had ten minutes. Maybe a little more. By time I touched down pistol shots of rain were pelting the glitter of the runway.

But we did not need the ten minutes.

I could tell that the airport was ready for us when I received taxi instructions and was guided to a parking space in the spatter of rain by the two illuminated batons of an attendant. Good, I thought, they'll take care of Longley's aircraft.

I had the strange feeling that I had had a dream in which I climbed over a wall and made it to the other side, which was where I wanted to be. Dreams seldom put me where I wanted to be. The brief experience with altitude in a motorized boxkite had felt good. That was in retrospect, of course. The rain felt good as it rinsed the sweat from my face.

The Sheriff was there, just inside the old art-deco Fresno terminal that had served the city until the new airport had been built in the 50s. We huddled through the big glass doors like three wet hens.

"Chambers?"

He was tall and whip-thin, probably ex-military, with the appraising glint in his eye that characterizes platoon leaders and peace officers.

"I am supposed to serve a fugitive warrant on you."

"I'm sure you are."

"But I have a twenty four hour zone of discretion."

"That's good. Sheriff, this is Mrs. Palmer and her daughter, Laurie."

The Sheriff nodded.

"I knew Major Palmer. Hi Laurie. What's the name of your dog?'

"He's called Spot. He's a little wet right now."

"Welcome to Fresno, Spot. All right. We are going to escort you to the commercial field. United Express to San Francisco. United to Boston. Whatever you do, do not go outside airport security. I could only get first class on the red eye, but on an emergency basis…"

"It won't break the bank," I said. "And Laurie missed her nap."

"Ever been to Boston?" I asked Karla.

"No."

"Ever read *Make Way for Ducklings* to Laurie?"

She nodded.

"Matter of fact…"

"We'll go there. Public Gardens."

"Let's go," the Sheriff said, turning and beginning to walk toward the parking lot at other end of the terminal.

And so we did.

As we followed, Laurie reached up and took my hand.

Epilogue.

Duclos lost his next election. Murmurs of legal action against him apparently helped defeat him. He is a traffic control officer in Mirable County. I hope that means that he directs traffic at some carbon-laden intersection. The City of Amerigo is still strongly anti-immigrant and was still singled out for praise by Lou Dobbs until he left television. Bascombe is Deputy Chief of Police, perhaps still a token. Karla and I were married that winter. She, Laurie, and I live in a pleasant white frame house on a quiet street only two miles and two traffic lights from Sudbury College, where I teach history. Karla plans to take the Massachusetts bar exam next spring. Laurie's dog, Spot, has completely dried out from the soaking he got on the evening of our escape. He still has that all-seeing eye.

Sometimes all you get to do is try to pick up the pieces. And a lot of people don't even get the chance to do that.

fin

ONE MORE CHANCE

The king will force me, then, to treason? I have
No choice. Unless I be a traitor to
Myself. I am a traitor either way.

Oliver Medway,
Worchester's Rebellion (1597).

At last, after a damp and drizzly July, August had arrived in the fullness of its heat. It was a time to plug in fans and to hoist the old air-conditioner into the open window of my bedroom.

Nothing was going to happen. I had no trips planned. Labor Day was a distant place beyond which, yes, classes would begin again and all of the excited bustle of students arriving, syllabi being disseminated, attendance being taken would absorb a week or so. And I, Harry Marston, Associate Professor of History at Stimson College, Hollyhock, Maine, had not grown so cynical that I did not enjoy that process. The books might be heavy, but as soon as I told the students to consider them part of their weight training program, that problem translated itself into just another happy prospect for privileged youth.

I had a few more articles to read and the notes for my piece on Heydrich to complete. Had he been assassinated to invite the retaliation that would then reignite Czech resistance? My answer was a tentative yes. The Reichprotektor had been doing too good a job in pacifying an occupied country. I had a couple of items to translate and incorporate into my bibliography, but the heat argued that that very minor task could wait. It would give me something to think about doing, maybe on Thursday.

An index of my inactivity was that I actually wrote a poem.

> Queen Anne reigned over August heat,
> tall, imperious, scarcely deigning to cast
> a shadow across the grasses swimming past
> the long afternoon of summer, a mere heartbeat
> of tracery, as if the source were high
> enough to be invisible. Today,
> the shriveled blossom is hunched into a gray
> skeleton of fist, soon to lie
> beneath the crystal alphabet of storm,
> a hieroglyph like seeds in April sown.
> Dry and brittle is the word, the form
> of law outside the window, a life of one's own
> that allows a moment to flourish in the warm
> days of summer like a flower and to be cut down

I had been reminded of the sampler my parents had had over their fireplace in Little Mountain. Needle point. Something about man coming up and being cut down like a flower. It had been created without Emily Dickinson's irony by Emily Whitfield, South Bloomfield, New Jersey, 1843. I wrote the poem, shrugged my shoulders, and contemplated an afternoon nap.

I thought of mortality, of course. We college professors have too much time on our hands. Not all of us can fill our days running errands for our tubby wives, as does Josh King, a teacher of Spanish, who checks out of his office every morning at about 0930 to begin to gather groceries and other necessities like aspirin and foot pads for his more-than-ample spouse, Gertrude, whose garments are crafted by Omar the Tentmaker.

I was driving home after grabbing a few things from the store, listening to old songs on a station that played them. Frank Sinatra's rollicking version of "The Sunshine of Your Smile," an ancient song that Tommy Dorsey had resurrected in 1940 came on. Yes, he had a sweet and effortless voice back then. But I was cut off by an idiot driving a Jeep station wagon. In the resultant swearing and finger-jabbing, I failed to listen to the song. Had that episode taken three minutes off my life? Perhaps. But at least I did not have to return, a laden paper sack in each arm, to the likes of Gertrude. Verily, her cup runneth other.

I got home and put the groceries away.
Then the phone rang.

The call exacerbated my self-loathing. Yes, I was a coward. I could not hide behind my effort to authenticate the memo from Churchill's bunker under Downing Street. "PM suggests assassination will infuriate Adolph, excite strong countermeasures."

Assassination could only point at Heydrich. That's who they were talking about. And certainly Adolph became upset. He eradicated Lidice and Lezaky, erased them from the tiny points they occupied on the map. Adolph was also angry at Heydrich for riding around in an open Mercedes, flaunting his authority, inviting an attack.

But my carefully constructed case – and it did depend too much on the historian's "it is probable" qualification – seemed irrelevant now.

I had not stood up. Like many, I was too damned comfortable. I had tenure, a good health plan, a pleasant way of life on the right side of the tracks where I had always lived, about five hundred ties of silk, a generator that went on automatically when my local power company blacked things out in bewilderment at the storm that came as a surprise only to it, and a fridge full of Heineken. I had grown up in a home of Turkish rugs and huddled masses of photographs by Bachrach in silver frames on top of the Chickering. I had learned to resist the automatic assumptions that such a background invited. Or so I told myself.

But I had not stood up. Some of us saw that the tactics of the far-right in their effort to bring down Obama were akin to those of the Brown Shirts, the thugs that Hitler dispatched to disrupt meetings in the 1930s and, ultimately, to bring government to its knees. And we deplored those actions. They were only superficially like the protests of the 1960s. Then, the government had refused to listen to reasonable objections to its policies. The government merely escalated efforts that were already not working. In the present instance, Obama had asked for response. He got rage and mindless opposition from the sour shoepolished Boehner , the cherubic idiot, chinless McConnell, and the drug-addled tub Limbaugh. One would have thought that Obama had threatened to take away their assault rifles. Where we went wrong was in assuming that because the right-wing had no leader – no Fuhrer – they posed no threat. Who would harangue the klieg-lighted masses? Newt Gingrich? Both David Patraeus and Colin Powell turned down overtures to become the leader of this furious band. But the genius of anarchy is that it requires no leader. By definition. The other inevitability is that, once anarchy instills enough terror in a given population, someone will take over.

And Dick Cheney did so.

And I, in my comfort, had remained silent. Oh, I was not the only one. But to point at other cravens does not absolve one of his own cowardice. I had thought better of myself. Now I lived a coward in my own esteem. Sure, the right-wing had ravaged the population with terror, backing up its "Mayday!" with arrests and the simultaneous suspension of habeas corpus. They cited Lincoln, of course. But I had remained silent. And silence implies consent.

And now Cheney was modestly calling himself "Acting President of the United States." He promised a new election once the situation had stabilized. But, of course, stability was in the eye of the beholder.

And of all the people in the world, she had called me.

"You are the only one who can help me."

Nonsense, I thought, but then I realized that she was right.

"I'll do what I can."

You don't bat away the hand clinging to the lifeboat do you? Maybe you do. Some of the occupants of the Titanic's lifeboats said that they would return into the waters reaching toward them with frantic shouts "when things thinned down a bit."

I came over the hill. I had several thoughts, almost simultaneously.

The first was, turn around! Go back!

The second was a line from Dante, as he viewed the mere vestibule to Hell.

"I had not thought death had undone so many."

Hell -- that had been in the fourteenth century. Death had still been an apprentice, though the plague was providing a steep learning curve.

Below me in the valley, hemmed in by the shrug of two stony mountains was a vast city of canvas. Tent upon tent huddled within a wall that touched the foothills and circled below a distant lake. In front of the wall, down the hill I was descending, was a large, half-painted wooden building with a parking lot to the right. To the left was a dirt landing strip with a windsock sagging at its eastern edge. A couple of small aircraft were tethered to the tarmac.

I still fought against the impulse just to turn around and head home. I would pretend that this had been some fleeting nightmare.

Instead, I pulled past the sign and through the outer gate. I expected "Arbeit macht frei," but what the sign said was "Pine Mountain Correctional Facility."

My god! What have we done? What are we correcting here? Where will the inhabitants of the tents go in December? It was beyond Holden's question about the ducks in Central Park. The heat inside the tents must be intolerable, but the winter?

I parked and walked up the concrete steps of the administration building.

I faced a long counter. A man behind it looked at me.

"Photo-id."

I produced my VA card.

"I need a driver's license."

"This is a federally-issued photo-id."

"I need a driver's license."

I produced one.

"Business?"

"Here. Visitor."

"Relative?"

"Family friend."

"Name?"

"Alex Chamberlain."

He brought a clipboard from under the counter and scanned a list clipped to it.

"Alex?"

"Alexandra."

He flipped a sheet over on his clipboard.

"Okay. Over there."

He pointed at a row of chairs along the wall.

I waited while a fan behind the counter distributed the hot air and dust.

And I waited. The game, of course, was to be forced to approach the counter and ask what the delay was. But that might block the process completely.

"For Chamberlain?"

I stood.

"Follow me."

I followed a guard around the end of the counter, through a door into the still and heated outside, through a metal detector, and down a dirt path to a small tent. It had gathered heat all day and was stifling.

The place did trigger allusions to grim literature. Abandon hope, all ye who enter here.

I was told to sit on one side of a long set of tables. Two or three people, on either side of the table were talking in murmurs nearby. Those on the far side of the table wore orange jumpsuits.

Alex appeared at the other side of the tent. No mistaking her. The orange jumpsuit sculpted itself unmistakably around a body that could encourage long moribund clocks to tick again. I regained my own breathing as she approached. Her skin was the dusty gold that I recalled, a face that had absorbed sun and wind. I noticed a few white lines chiseled at either side of her eyes. The eyes were the profound blue of a Crater Lake. A wisp of silver touched her blonde hair at the temples. The room quivered as she walked through it, and the guards stiffened at their posts, their eyes following her progress to the prisoners' side of the table.

And the voice. Had I forgotten? Smoky. Half-mocking. Suggesting that little was to be taken seriously.

"Hi Harry. Thanks for coming."

Even here, the voice suggested that this was a joke. The voice said that all things are transitory, therefore not to be accepted as definitive, or even important. Alex had grown up in the rugged spaces of Yorkshire and had never wanted to escape the out of doors. This encampment of the damned must seem like civilization to her.

She sat down and held out her hand.

In it and then in mine was a folded piece of paper.

"Get word to them, if you can. They may not know..."

"What a place."

"They were caught short," she said. "The prisons are full of drug dealers and illegal aliens."

That meant that the newly rounded-up "suspects" had been herded into these tented compounds, like refugees in some African principality.

"And they haven't processed us all yet."

"How'd you get a call to me?"

"A friend had a cell phone they missed. I couldn't believe that you were at the same number."

"I haven't moved. I can't believe that you remembered the number. Have you been processed?"

"I have a number."

"How can I get you out?"

"I'm not sure. I had to let someone know where I was first. Those others..."

She nodded toward the paper which I had slid into my pocket.

"... have been disappeared."

"Can a lawyer...?"

"I don't know. That's what those other people are talking about, I'd guess. Habeas Corpus. Of course, I'm on an extended green card. Still, Habeas Corpus goes back to Magna Carta."

"British Embassy?"

"It might be worth a try. But I think they'd go along with this program. We are still your poodle. The P M supports the war on terror without asking any questions."

"Okay. I'll see what I can do."

"I knew you would. Of all the people I have ever known, you are the one who still had a sense of outrage."

"I still do."

But I lied. I had done nothing. What had happened to the young man with the sense of outrage? He had grown old. The ridges of stomach muscle had slipped into the slouch in front of the computer. The mind had been rinsed away by the universal solvent, another beer.

II.

When tyrants kill their enemies, they find
Them rising, hydra-headed, from the grave.
A tyrant multiplies his foes, for he
Can never kill enough of them to stay
The teeming womb that brings revenge to birth.

Raphael Buttery,
A Chronicle History of Richard II (1591).

I reentered the administration building, but took only two or three steps.

"Will you come with us, sir."

Two big guys on either shoulder. I long ago learned that any resistance to so-called law enforcement elicits greater force.

"Sure."

We turned right down a hallway. The Exit sign of the administration building glowed enticingly to my left. A thousand miles away.

We entered a sterile cubicle.

One of the men closed the door and indicated a chair against the far wall.

"Sit down."

The man stood a few feet from me. The other stood at parade-rest near the door.

"We have reason to believe that the prisoner you visited passed you information."

If I denied that and they searched me – and they would – they'd find the list. Then I would have committed a really bad offense.

"Yes. I was given a list of people to notify about their friends' imprisonment."

"Imprisonment?"

"Incarceration. Whatever you want to call it."

"I want that list."

"Look, these people have a right to let others know where they are."

"I will ask one more time. Give me the list."

I handed it over.

"Call Captain Nelson," the man said to his companion.

The other man said something into a hand-held device.

We waited.

At a single bang on the door, the other man opened it.

A slight man in a gray uniform with an HLSP patch on the left pocket and cloth captain's bars sew to his shoulders entered. I read his face. He was that little man, savoring his first taste of being an officer, of having power.

"Sir," said the man holding the list. "Here it is."

Captain Nelson of the Homeland Security Police scanned the list. I felt sorry for the people whose names were there. They faced whatever further punishment would be meted out. By asking for help they had gotten themselves in a worse fix.

"Alright, Cooper. Good. Put this man in a holding cell for the time being."

I wondered how long the time being would be.

I could tell time by the way light shifted across the far side of the wall. The bars moved like the projection of a playpen. On dark nights, of course, time would move elsewhere, and the stars would show like icicles beyond the bars. Would I be here that long? I could hear the voice that came unbidden. What's the use? And I lay down. I dreamed of my mother. She had believed fiercely in me, because, I think, her own goals and abilities had been diverted into conventional housewifery. Had she been a man... Of course that had made things difficult for me in all kinds of ways. Living out someone else's life in the next generation? How many have had to do that? But now, her voice saying, You can do it, merely came back at me in silent echoes from this barren room. Do what? Despair is physical. It weighs inside and escapes in sighs. Do what?

The door scraped open. I assigned the noise to my dream, then woke up.

One of the guards who had arrested me entered.

"You have been assigned a number."

"What is it?"

"You do not need to know. We will process you formally sometime next week."

I was part of a backlog, but at least I would escape into the camp's general population. As I had waited in the cell, I transferred the cash in my wallet to a pants pocket. Before I was escorted to my assigned tent, they took my wallet, keys, a couple of pens, and my loose change. But currency might come in handy in prison. And, I thought, I can take mental notes on the Foucauldian thesis of how a society is reflected in its methods of incarceration.

What society had done, of course, was to condition us to the process. We take our shoes off at airports, and shuffle like peasants through detectors that object to belt buckles, under the eyes of uniformed persons who can, if they wish, make us miss our flights. Children go to schools that are militarized, uniformed cops in the hallways, drug tests administered randomly, a Boy Scout knife cause for handcuffing and incarceration. We are the criminals, and we accept this designation automatically.

But this onslaught had come suddenly, and even in a society conditioned to the quantification of everything, they were having trouble catching up. Within this bureaucratic delay might be a chance at resistance. Escape?

And Alex found me there amid this welter of confused and dispossessed people. In tent number seventeen, row nine, block four. Treblinka probably had the same precise grids.

"Sorry," she said.

"No. They'd probably have nailed me anyway. They just had an excuse. But they didn't want me going out to find legal help for you or any of your friends. That process complicates things for them."

"Yes. They are operating on the principle that people will be too afraid to do anything, but..."

"They must realize how thin a line they are treading. How long can the 'National Emergency' they've declared be maintained? Scalia and Thomas will go along, Alito. Roberts, of course, but even a fool like Kennedy must see through what they are doing."

"So they'll block any legal action if they can."

"Sure. National security justifies all actions in its defense."

"But if it hadn't been for that list..." she said.

"Nothing we can do about it now, Alex. Look, I saw a couple of aircraft on a field on the way in."

"Yes. They fly in Homeland Security people, and out again."

"How do you know that?"

She paused.

"One of the guards told me."

"Is there a way to get to one of those aircraft?"

She thought.

"Yes. But it would be tough."

"For me, true, but I am in decent shape, believe it or not. Tennis."

"I forgot! You were a pilot, weren't you."

It was a statement.

"It's a long shot, but worth a try. Let's keep our eye on the weather."

The concept of prisons – at least of this one – is to produce monotony. It is not active punishment. It is certainly not rehabilitation. It is not reeducation. And they did not make the laughable claim that we had any useful intelligence to divulge. We were meant to become lobotomized by boredom. Foucault would have discovered in our vast camp a reflection of the surrounding society. Here it was absolute conformity, from diet to clothes, a logical consequence of the narcissism of our great land, where people who had never had anything to do with the military bought Hummers and put yellow ribbons on them, where men affected Cheney's side-of-the-mouth snarl and women Lynne's very proper appeal to a Rinso-white past. The projection of that quiet desperation, of course, was the celebrity culture that could actually launch one of its own to the presidency. Clinton, of course, but Skull and Bones had intervened in horror at that enormity. And the inevitable did occur: Obama of rhetoric without conviction.

For me, the excitement of finding Alex again was proof against ennui. We saw each other now and then when our meals schedule coincided in the vast and musty mess tent. But our encounters were maddeningly brief and exasperatingly public. And I got the same feeling I'd had before as relationships failed – that the paucity of our meetings was partly her doing.

I wonder whether other men – women – have the same fleeting fantasy as they encounter a former lover, someone who was once the shining center of their emotional cosmos. That is that somehow it had worked out, that the relationship had continued into the years beyond the final goodbye. The corollary, of course, is that it could continue now, as if no one had happened since, as if time that had furrowed a few wrinkles on fading faces had erased them. I don't feel my own until the mirror does it for me. Alex! The limitless possibilities I felt once returned again. Gone were the moments when I'd say, over the phone, "At least I can hear you breathing. I know where you are." Gone was the bitterness of the other invitations that a beyond-a-dream body had accepted.

III.

The blinded monster threw the many stones
Into the sea. Ulysses mocked, as waves
Encroached upon his boat. The blind throw rocks,
But seldom damage what they cannot see.

Marcus St. Olive,
Westward, the Winds! (1602).

A hurricane swept up the coast, resculpting the shoreline of the Carolinas, churning Cape Cod into shingles, and spinning toward the Maritimes. It would bring heavy rain and booming cannonades and brisk electricity to our camp. People were slinging ropes over the canvas and pounding spikes into the ground. But I doubted that any of that would do any good. Canvas is made for sails.

"Won't it be dangerous?" Alex asked.

"Sure," I said. "But it's our best chance. Everyone will be busy."

"Yes. The guards will just batten down in the administration building."

"Let's hope so. Let's see that key again."

She looked around, then slipped a key from her pocket into my hand.

I looked down at my palm.

"Yes. This is for the Cessena. You sure he is not setting us up?"

"Yes."

And she was probably right. The guard, Kenneth, would be in trouble if our escape plan came out. Prisons, I thought, are strange places. Life goes on in thwarted ways. Kenneth had fallen for Alex. I had not asked her what she had done to get that key. But children had been delivered at Auschwitz to become newborn ash. Children were born at Rikers, their mother's legs in chains. I understood Alex's reluctance to begin again with me.

"And we can bring Marianne?"

Marianne was Alex's friend, a pale young woman with a faint reddish complexion under the pallor, like a winter rose. I kept thinking of her as Rose.

"Can she make it over the fence?"

"It's you I'm worried about."

That was not a putdown. It was a motivational speech.

Fortunately, the fence was just that – a wooden fence about eight feet high. No razor wire. No electricity. Lights probed the fence randomly at night. This place had been thrown together. And its location argued that there was no place to escape to from here.

This was a wild night, wind making the rain visible as it lashed across this city of the damned and tugged at stakes and sent damp canvas airborne. The unmoored tents looked like hands without arms groping for darkness. And – finding it.

"One at a time!" I shouted, watching the lights raise the level rain like a duel of many sabers.

I went first. I got a foot on the cross-beam and hauled myself up, thanking all the gods for the old pair of work gloves Alex had scrounged up for me. I got both hands on the rough board edges at the top of the fence and pulled myself over. I did a tuck and roll on the other side – training from all those years ago – and waited. A light from one of the towers probed through a crack in the boards. Instinctively, I crouched down as a splintery sliver of light crossed my face.

We went through a woods one by one along a narrow path. A thunder crack exploded directly overhead and the entire forest filled with bright, white light. Dante's Wood of Suicides, I thought. I was still getting my breathing under control. A brief sprint, a quick climb and I had become breathless. Tension. No one who has not engaged in competitive sports recognizes how tension can drain your energy. You have to make it work for you. I had once. But I had already used up whatever sparse supply had been given to me this night. Beyond that final surge waited exhaustion.

We came out behind a hanger.

Damn, I thought -- if they've put the aircraft in the hanger...

But they hadn't. The hanger held an old DC-3. I could see its proud, high nose through a window. The smaller craft, tethered to the tarmac, trembled in the wind.

Damn! It will be a crosswind takeoff. I was glad Marianne had come, slender as s he was. We would need her weight.

"Okay. Alex," I shouted into a rain hitting my teeth. "Be ready to release the right wing when I tell you to. Then run like hell for the aircraft. Marianne, get in the back seat."

I released the control surfaces, removed the pitot-tube cover, and climbed in. I pulled the key from my pocket and mumbled about carb-mixture, fuel settings, and throttle. The little plane wanted to flip over in the wind. I waited for the storm to take a deep breath. I waved to Alex. She released the guy wire and hustled around to the door on the right side. The aircraft almost tipped over when she climbed in.

"Strap in," I shouted as I released the brakes.

The aircraft shuddered forward. It trembled, trying to pull itself apart. As I lifted it off it went over on its right wing. I threw left rudder and lowered the nose. It staggered ahead. But the mountains were right in front of us.

I glanced at the fuel gauge. Thank heavens – the tank was three quarters full. I could keep the aircraft throttled-up as I tried for altitude.

Then I made a decision.

I had planned to climb over the mountains to the west and set down close to the Canadian border. We would then try to get across.

What I did though was to turn north. The wind pushed us like a lost oak leaf in November toward the lake above the camp. At some point that became Canada. I would send a radar signal to a dozen different eyes once I contacted the Air Defense Identification Zone or whatever surveillance they had along the border. The last time I had had to worry about that sort of thing the Rio Grande had been the electronic barrier.

"Wow!" Alex said. "How fast are we going?"

The flight had smoothed out, the rain in luminous lines ahead of us, as if we were flying into a time-lapse photograph. The camp was to our right, shaking like a pack of angry animals.

"Just under the mach," I said.

"Are we going to Canada?"

"No. That would set off too many bells. I'm going to turn over the lake. Fly along the river for a while. The mountain is too high."

Marianne leaned forward.

"Good job! I can't believe it!"

"Still have to find a place to set down," I said.

"The river is on our side," Alex said.

"Our side? In a geographical sense, yes," I said.

"Better be soon," she said.

"Right. They'll have an all points out on us quickly enough."

"Thank God for the storm," Marianne said.

"Yes," I said, but I said to myself, I had better find a north south runway. I do not want to try to land this tiny boxkite in a fifty mile crosswind.

We sped over the lake. I began a left turn, knowing that I'd be blown northward as I turned. It looked as if were about to fly into the mountain until we eased over the river. I kept the left wing low as we slid past the mountain's edge. The rain rattled against the fragile craft like hail.

And there, illuminated by a sudden expansion of molten light was a town by the riverside. I blinked and checked my altimeter. Visibility wasn't bad at one thousand feet. And there, beyond the town was a rotating beacon. Now – which way did the runway run?

"West Run Junction," Alex said. "It's where the river twists around and runs west for a couple of miles."

"Yeah," I said, "Frost wrote a poem about it."

And I have come to epitomize that poem, I thought, banking to the left and feeling the fragile craft shudder into an uncoordinated lurch. I was that in humans that opposes the way most people are going. But the wind was stronger than any azimuth. And the aircraft was not a comfortable place. I could feel us at the end of the very slender thread that held us between aerodynamics and an uncoordinated tumble. Alex and Marianne must have felt something in their stomachs. Pilots don't get airsick, but I feared for my passengers.

But, there west of West Run, illuminated in spasms of lightning, was the runway. I thought for a moment how good it was not to have to worry about the length of it, as I'd had to do in the heavy fighter-bombers that demanded a high touchdown speed and a long tense roll after landing, waiting, waiting until the airspeed dropped to a point where you could tap the brakes.

As it was, we seemed almost stationary – though banged around by the wind – as we descended.

"Over the fence," I said.

But as I rounded out, wings level, a nasty crosscurrent tipped us to an eighty degree right bank. Not an attitude approved for landing. Just when you think you have it made! I kicked rudder and moved the mushy yoke. The aircraft stalled, but touched down on both gears. Superb professional skill and ninety per cent luck.

I taxied into the shelter of hanger wall. The aircraft still wanted to become airborne in the gusts wheeling around the open space of the landing field.

"Now what?" Marianne asked.

"We change," Alex said.

I tied the aircraft down by its left wing. It was not mine, but I still respected it and what it had done for us. I had asked more of it than the manufacturer specified. Thank you, Wichita!

Alex carried the big bundle, wrapped in a brown paper bag, toward the hanger door, followed by Marianne.

I waited, figuring we'd have to change in the cramped cabin of the little plane.

But the door opened. Trusting folks here in West Bend Junction!

"Ken's stuff will be a little big for you," Alex said.

"No doubt."

But it was serviceable – a cotton shirt washed almost to transparency, a pair of jeans that were very tight around the waist if two inches too long at the inseam, and a nondescript brown jacket that I rolled up at the sleeves. I had not asked for a bespoke suit from Tripler, nor for something from off the rack at Chipp or Ben Silver.

But – now what? It was a good question. The storm pounded the corrugated metal of the hanger roof, a marching beat of snare drums without a melody. We stood under the dim lights that had been on when we entered the building.

"I don't think anyone will believe that we flew here," I said.

I wouldn't, I said to myself.

"Won't they miss the plane?" Marianne asked.

"Let's hope they think it blew away," I said.

"They were busy finding a place to hide," Alex said.

"And we had better do that," I said.

"Be back," Marianne said.

She started toward one of the rooms along the hanger wall.

"There's a bridge about a mile northwest of here," Alex said.

"You know the area?"

"A tad. We did an Outward Bound course on the river a few years ago."

"How far is the border?"

"Ten miles. Small border crossing at St. Benedict's."

"Look!" Marianne cried.

She was walking toward us. In her arms she held dark green slickers and hats.

"Where'd they come from?"

"A locker next to the woman's room."

"We can send a check later," Alex said.

"Okay. Let's get this stuff on. Then, let's get as close to the border as we can."

"The river isn't the border?" Marianne asked.

"Not here," Alex said. "Only from Lake Ontario to Montreal."

"Can't we cross tonight?" Marianne asked.

"Maybe," I said. "But we have to make sure we have a good place to cross. We really should do some recon first."

"Right," Alex said. "We'll find a good place to cross. We don't want to get picked up at this stage of the game."

"And remember," I said, "any cars out in this storm will be emergency vehicles. We'll have to be very careful on the road."

By the time we crossed the bridge, one by one as the others crouched at one side of the bridge, below the concrete posts put up by the WPA in the thirties, and then at the other end, plenty of emergency vehicles were undulating their menace through the valley. We had had to dodge from the highway and huddle into our slickers in ditches and behind trees.

"Must have sent out the alarm," Marianne said.

"Let's get off the highway," Alex said. "There's a dirt road down to the left."

The rain was scouring the road down to stones and pebbles and it was tricky going.

By this time, of course, our feet were soaked and the night had turned cool.

"Wait!" said Alex, who was leading the way.

She peered ahead.

"House. No lights. May be deserted."

"Maybe no electricity," I said, glancing up into the weave of rain but seeing no wires.

"Let me look at the path," Alex said. "That will tell us. Come with me for another hundred yards. Then wait."

Alex went ahead. I lost sight of her until I saw her on the porch of the house. She turned and waved us forward.

"No one's been here for months," she said.

Marianne and I waded through golden rod and queen anne's lace. I pushed hard on the front door. It opened grudgingly against the warped floorboards of the hallway.

Alex flicked her small flashlight around. Staircase straight ahead. Living room to the left. A few pieces of rickety furniture. Stone fireplace.

"Be it ever so humble," I said.

"Do we dare light a fire?" Marianne asked.

Alex took a match from a waterproof pack, lit one, and held it into the fireplace.

"Flue's open," she said.

"Don't want to start a chimney fire," I said.

"Of course not," Alex said, "but with this rain..."

I grabbed some newspaper by the side of the fireplace wadded it up – "Senator Ted Kennedy Dead at 77" – built a small house of kindling and put a big log on top.

"Nicely," Alex said, lighting the paper.

And soon our faces were vibrating in the ebb and flow of the flames.

Marianne without a word or a hint of inhibition took off all of her clothes and turned around and around in the warmth.

"Does feel good after that cold shower," she said.

Small breasts, but neat and well proportioned, good shoulders, a trim but full underneath, where it counts in a woman, and, as viewed in their natural habitat, slender legs, with thin ropes of muscle. Very pleasant to watch as she pulled the firelight over her body as if it were liquid, particularly since she did not seem to mind being watched, so I didn't have to pretend not to be watching.

Alex unwrapped some hardboiled eggs.

"Don't know how Kenneth smuggled these out, but..."

She also had small bottles of water.

"There is a stream in the back. We can always refill," she said.

"If we want to get wet again," said Marianne.

I had stripped to my shorts. I was interested primarily in getting my shoes dry. But I was also afraid that they might shrivel up like burnt bacon. I could see myself running barefoot over the stony border. I prayed for pineneedles.

"I'll go," Alex said. "Drink up. We have to stay hydrated."

It is hard to describe sound. Perhaps it is just I. I could not be a Proust, riding a theme from a fictional musician through his memory as if it were a stallion called Libido. Nor could I be a music critic. But Alex's voice tended to mock not just convention but her own assumptions. Bix. You hear a stultifying, on-the-beat arrangement of "Love Nest" by Whiteman's orchestra. It lovingly embraces the song's cliches. "Like a dove's nest, down on the farm." Then, suddenly, sixteen bars of Bix, playing against the beat, laughing at the song by arriving at the notes with the indirection of sheer virtuosity. I know what the damned note is, but listen to what I can do with this cornet until I remind you of the melody. You are suddenly aware of the symbiosis of instrument and player in a simultaneous revelation that derives from the bell and that arrives at the ear. Alex's voice.

We found some ancient mattresses upstairs and hauled them down to the fireplace. They had not turned moldy, in fact had a crisp, bleachy scent, no doubt impregnated by generations of sheets.

Marianne put on a couple of items of clothing and curled up next to me.

"Body warmth," she said. "Basic survival technique."

As it might well have been. I was asleep in the wash of childhood memories no doubt invited by the scent of bleach.

I woke up to see a blue light pulsing at the ceiling.

"Quick!" I whispered. "Cops outside."

We pulled on half-dry clothes, reluctant in their dampness to let toes and fingers slide past, and fled out the back door into the woods.

"They'll be waiting for backup," I said.

And, as I finished speaking, we heard sirens looping great wheels of sound through the dripping woods. We made it across the stream on a bridge of flat stones and turned north. The storm was passing, gray lumps of clouds beginning to take shape as the sick light of dawn slid in from our right. The clouds began to look like headless bodies. Good, I thought. Menacing, but they can't see us.

"Border ahead," Alex said.

We saw a cleared space about one hundred yards wide, grass and wildflowers and the stumps of pine trees.

Behind us, the sirens had stopped.

They had been replaced by the yapping of dogs.

"Let's go!" I said.

Alex chugged, her powerful body driving into the soggy turf. Marianne glided, a graceful lilt to her stride. I was surprised, because she had seemed gangly and awkward. I could make these style judgments since I was puffing in the rear. I could still run as I had run, but only in the occasional dream.

We arrived in a zone of scrubby pine and birch trees torn like ancient manuscripts.

"They'll pick us up on the other side of the stream," Alex said.

"Don't they have to stop at the border?" Marianne asked.

I was groaning involuntarily and breathing hard.

"No." I said, between deep breaths. "Hot pursuit. Lawless zone."

"Right," Alex said. "Unorganized territory on one side. They operate on the basis of informal agreements between state cops, local sheriffs, game wardens, and border patrol. We have to keep going."

"Nearest town?" I asked.

"Saint Nym. About three miles. If we can get to a phone..."

We set out. We finally got to the top of a hill. I was out of breath and the backs of my legs were cramping. If I kept going...

"There it is," Alex said. Below us, in a valley, curled along a small serpent of stream, now green in the rise of day, was the town.

I stopped and sat down.

"We'd be better off on the far side," Alex said.

"Okay," I said. "Help me up."

We made our way along the small hill to the west of town. It was fairly easy going, since hunters had carved many paths there as they sought deer and bear, muskrat and squirrel.

But we reached a point where I could go no further.

"Okay," Alex said. "I am going down to make a call. They'll have a call in to the Mounties, but they'll be looking for three people. If I am not back..."

"Just come back," I said.

IV.

We flee, my lord, because we are afraid.
But fled-from fears beget a further fear,
And take from us our selves.

But not our heads.

Oh yes, my lord, that would remove our fears.
A fear without a head is not a fear.

Barnaby Coppersmith,
Malcolm, Earl of Cumberland (1604).

The sun had risen. It seemed to drive the final scud of storm northward. Alex disappeared down a path. Marianne and I settled into a leafy glade.

"You okay?" she asked.

"My calves. Got painful back there."

"Yet you kept going."

"My options?"

"Giving up."

"Not an option."

"Damn shirt is still damp."

She took it off and put it down in a patch of sun.

She considered it for a moment, its red and green plaid shining in the sun, and doffed her jeans. She stretched them out carefully in the tremble of brightness.

"Let me get at those legs and lower back. Take your pants off."

"Happily."

She kneaded my calves and pressed hard against my lower spine.

"Great legs," she said.

"Yours?" I mumbled.

"Yours."

"Once upon a long time ago."

I rolled over. She came into my arms and kissed me hungrily.

A longer time for her, I thought, than for me. Because she is younger. Time moves in divers ways with different people as we pursue our seven ages.

She was wearing panties, but they were easily slid aside.

"Basic survival technique," she whispered between heavy breaths.

"You are so strong," she said.

I did not feel that strong. I laughed.

"No. I mean it. Alex is a pro. She's great. I latched on to her right away in the camp because I knew she had so much to offer. But you are the leader."

"No."

"Oh yes. Alex may be in front, but you are the one pushing us. How were we to fly that airplane?"

She did have a point. I had not had time to review the flight, but it came back to me in a gestaltian glimpse. We had been mad even to attempt it. As with any dangerous mission, I had made a series of small decisions. Had any one of them been wrong... But that was the benefit of certain kinds of experience. Training becomes instinct. And, when you have a chance to look back, you know you did some things right. That overhead at deuce in the third set with the sun directly in your eyes.

"It's a sequence," I said. "We need her survival skills now. By the way, who is she calling?"

"Kenneth."

"Think so?"

"Know so."

So that had been the plan. I adjusted to it. I had been in love with her once. Her voice had brought all of that back in a sudden flow of memory and desire that I would have thought long gone like those tubers blossoming in some lost April. But her deal with Kenneth erased all of that – for her, at least.

"She...ah...?" I began to ask.

"I don't think so. But what is it about necessity and bedfellows?"

"And Alex is a loyal person. That element is more important to her than just her feelings."

"Oh yes. Look at me."

"But there, her feelings and loyalty line up," I said.

"She's wise that way." Marianne said.

"I hope she brings us some food."

I am wise enough not to believe in seamlessness. It never works. You slide into a new relationship as escape, not destination, and you crash and burn. Suddenly. The descent is never gradual. I would have said that Alex was forgotten. No so. Just repressed. And that means that she had come back powerfully into my consciousness in the past week. You believe that an entire segment of your life has been partitioned off. It was there, yes, but it has no relevance to the present moment. Nor is available, except in the random corridors of a dream that closes down with the click of consciousness. But then I heard Alex's voice again.

Yes, I liked Marianne. Very much. I liked the way she moved. Sinuous, long muscles seeming awkward only when they waited for their motive. Yes, I had fallen in love with her as I observed the certainty of her stride. The achieve of, the mastery, as the poet says. And her voice always had a question in it. What was the answer? It was never easy, but the process of responding opened up into her joy and sense of humor. Her voice was an invitation to relationship. And I did like the way her body moved over mine and mine over hers. It was like one of those days in June that pull shoots of joy unbidden out of a cloud-covered soul.

We sat on the hillside within a bowl of stars.

I was hungry. But as we sat there in the mild wind, I felt good. We were out from the fences and away from the sour smell of wet canvas. You are trying too hard, I said to myself. Thinking freedom. True. But on the other hand, I felt a new kind of freedom. We never should have tried to escape in an airplane during a storm. Desperation. We never should have made it. Luck. But we had come this far. I had contributed my segment of the journey. Now, it was up to Alex to lead and Marianne to pull. And push. I could do nothing about that process. I could actually relax and follow the dictates of these two splendid women. Not exactly Buddhism, but a pleasant loss of control, a fall through space without a bottom, therefore no fear of falling. Fear of falling comes from the fact of a surface below and from a perception of the line that connects you to that hard and waiting place. But letting go was one of the best things I could do this side of annihilation.

A new beginning. No. Beginnings were elsewhere. Beginnings were children going to school again, believing that something good might happen. Believing that something good would happen. How soon before they realized that things did not work out. It had taken me a lifetime.

Marianne guessed my mood.

"Didn't you enjoy camping out when you were a boy?"

"No. I was a Boy Scout, but only because it was expected of me. If I had been born in a previous generation in Berlin, I would have been Hitler Youth."

"That is a dark way to look at it."

"No. It's a way of saying that most of what I have done has been modeled on someone else's conception, not mine. It's narcissism."

"Isn't everything then?"

"No. You have to be privileged to be a narcissist. You need the opportunity to copy what you consider to be successful behavior. Sure, that process does occur in the ghetto."

"But..."

"I wouldn't consider survival in that category. Natural selection. Sorry, I cut you off."

"I think you are too hard on yourself."

"You don't know me."

"No, but I do know that you are coming down from that plane ride. It may not have been a high..."

"It was. More than that."

"That's what I mean. You don't just walk away from an event like that. I mean you don't just put your feet on the ground."

"No. You don't."

"The sine wave dips down below the line."

"Assuming there's a line. Yes, it does."

"You..." I began.

"I know what you are going to say."

"You do?"

"Yes. I haven't had much experience."

True. I had been about to say that she seemed almost to be a virgin.

"Right?" she asked.

"Close enough."

"I had a boyfriend. We were both virgins when we met. We learned together for a while. Then he was killed."

I reached out and touched her hand.

"So. I haven't wanted to take the chance since then."

"I understand."

I suppose that I did. To have that commitment suddenly just yanked away. I could also have understood had she become wildly promiscuous.

"Until now," she said.

"Didn't anyone know you were in that camp?"

"I don't know. I disappeared quickly. My father had abandoned us and then he disowned me for good measure. I had protested the invasion of Iraq. He was a patriot."

"Military?"

"No. Like Cheney, he had other obligations. I went with Charlie for a couple of years. In school. UMaine Farmington. He was in the National Guard. For the extra money and the educational benefits he'd get if he went on active duty. He did."

"Go on active duty."

"Yes. Killed when a bomb blew up his vehicle."

"Sorry, Marianne."

She nodded and looked down.

"How'd they happen to send you to that camp?"

"I continued to protest the war. Asked them what Charlie had died for. They could not tell me."

"But they resented your asking."

"Oh yes."

"But they didn't put Cindy Sheehan away."

"No. Too high-profile. But there were several other wives and girlfriends back there."

"A double crime. Kill your man. Imprison you when you protest."

"That is the way it works these days."

She looked up, staring bleakly at a sky that glanced bleakly back for a moment, then went on to larger concerns.

"Funny thing is," she said. "I did not mind the camp. Alex was a great companion, and I never really lived anywhere."

"You didn't?"

"College dorm. I had lived with my mother and her boyfriends."

"Doesn't sound..."

"It wasn't. I had to threaten one of them with a knife. Said I would cut off his you-know-what if he came near me."

"Did you tell your mother?"

"She would not have believed me."

And then she had met Charlie. And then she had placed all her trust and all her expectations in Charlie. And then Charlie came back in a box, wrapped in a flag courtesy of your federal government.

"Anyway, Charlie's parents supported my stand, but I couldn't get word to them. Alex was going to try. Charlie's father is a lawyer. He might have been able to do something."

"And the list was confiscated."

"Yes. Kind of strange. No body knowing where you are."

"I do."

"Where the hell is Alex?" I asked.

It had grown cold in the night– not freezing -- and we slumbered within the cocoon of each other's body heat until the chilly dew of dawn awakened us.

"Suppose she got picked up?" Marianne asked, shivering into her sweater.

"Who knows? All she had to do was make a call."

"That can be difficult. Don't forget that she was calling that damned camp, which by then would have been on emergency status."

"Right. They would have monitored all incoming calls."

"They do anyway."

"And she was going to get food. I'll go in."

"Let's wait a while."

"Hell, Marianne, we'll starve."

"You have any money?"

"Yes."

"But they won't take American money any more."

"I'll tell them not to discount it. They'll accept a ten per cent markup."

"Let's go together."

"No. If I get caught, I get caught. But I'll be back."

"Will you come with us, please."

It was framed as a question, but it was rhetorical.

"All right, Sergeant. Take him to the station, hold him, and notify their HSD."

Their HSD – U.S. Homeland Security.

"You can ride up front, Mr. Marston," the Sergeant said. Watkins said his name tag. I had not identified myself, yet he knew my name.

I had slipped down into town to get some food. Mistake! The unmarked car had been right at the entrance to the little market. I hoped that Marianne and Alex would go on without me. At least they still had a chance.

"I haven't been booked?"

"Not yet. The station is out on Route 17."

"So I don't exist."

"Officially?"

He laughed.

"You will only begin to exist in about a half hour."

He pulled over at a small restaurant.

"But let's get something to eat first."

We did.

"You know, Mr. Marston, we are supposed to cooperate with your people."

"My people?"

"Government. Extradition, that sort of thing."

"My people. Sure."

"But we have our own sense of right and wrong. You people to the south – eh? – are always talking about independence and that sort of thing."

He pronounced "about" "abut," as if the preposition refuted its object.

"But we really believe in it. I don't think anyone really understands what has happened to you since the World Trade Center attacks."

"I do."

"Sorry. Yes. You do."

I had had a burger and fries and coffee. My stomach would pay for it later. Right now, I was ready for a nap.

"I am going to stay here for another cup of coffee," Watkins said. "Across the road is a trail. I suggest that you go out into the parking lot and get some air. You will need it."

I did.

I could only hope that Alex and Marianne had waited for me. How long had it been? I started up the trail. Our camp site would be slightly to the west. My nap would have to wait. I held my eyes open against the pressure of exhaustion.

I did not exist officially, but the strain in my calves as I climbed reminded me that I still clung to an existential identity. That was all I had. No. My first tossing out of a lifeline from the free-float of alienation had been to – Marianne! She was what pulled up over the pineneedles, roots, and stones of a trail that thinned as it rose up the side of the hill. Rose, I thought. My nickname for her. I remembered that I had dreamed of her last night. She had placed a smooth hand on my shoulder and said, "Come with me into the garden."

The garden was a clearing overlooking Saint Nym.

The campsite was clear. The fire had been put out, the ashes scattered, the zone covered with a branch.

Alex and Marianne sat next to a small pack that held our rain gear and whatever Alex had been able to get in town.

"Let's go, Harry," Alex said. "We are meeting Kenneth two miles from here this afternoon."

"I have to sit down first."

"How are your legs?" Marianne said.

"Getting stronger."

"Did you eat anything?"

"Believe it or not, yes. Sorry I could not bring you anything."

"We're okay," Marianne said. "Alex brought some trail rations."

"Let's go!" Alex said. "They will be looking for us."

"They've found us," I said.

"You mean...?" Alex asked.

"I escaped."

"Escaped?" Marianne asked.

"For the time being," I said. "The report will say that I was sighted near St. Nym. They have to do that much."

"Then, let's go," Alex said.

"The time being. That's all the time there is," Marianne said.

"For us? Yes. But at least we realize it," I said.

V.

My mind tells me I have become as bad
As this person on whom I work revenge.
I tumble headlong into the same evil.
I rose too high upon this parapet.
And now, I fall. I see the ground below,
The earth that I become in falling there.

Guido de Franz,
The Cornwall Tragedy (1599).

Finally, we linked up with Kenneth. He had a big Dodge pickup with a comfortable back seat and Canadian plates.

"I've got an international driver's license," he said. "Needed it for my job."

Alex leaned toward me from the back seat.

"Is that awful man still there?" she asked.

"Which one?"

"The dean who dithered around about my program."

He had done more than that. He had made the decision that doomed our relationship. Or, more accurately, he had made the non-decision.

Peter Herman.

Stimson College, where I had taught until my disappearance, was one of those little places with an institutional Napoleon Complex. What it had in common with, say, Swarthmore or Amherst, was its small size and its preference for brick buildings being pulled apart by the roots of ivy. But it would mention those colleges among those "with which we like to compare ourselves." But Stimson was the only outfit doing the comparing. Its genius was to appoint harmless incompetents to administrative positions. That way, the status quo was maintained and giving from a Republican alumni rose every year in proportion to the institution's unchanging character. Peter Herman, though, was not just incompetent. He was destructive, a hater, a snide overreacher who actually believed that he deserved his status. He did not seem to recognize that all of his efforts went into justifying his position. Or, if he recognized who he was, he spent some of his energy denying that knowledge.

"The guy is really pathetic," I said. "One could almost feel sorry for him."

"Like Nixon."

"Nixon actually accomplished some things before he collided with his paranoia. Yes. Almost. Pete actually thought he was in line to become President of Stimson."

"That self-deluded?"

"With little Bush as the precedent, yes. His wife was furious when she found out he'd been passed over. Of course he was never really considered, but he had fantasized himself on to the short list. And now he had to go home to confront the angry buttons of the little woman's eyes as she hissed at him from his shoulder, dampening the polyester. At least he's taller than she is."

When Emory Beamer became President of Stimson College, he set in motion events that would affect me profoundly. I could not foresee that future history. Only The Spinner of the Years had detected the events to come. Beamer was a "conservative scholar," meaning that the truth was always "somewhere in the middle." His magnum opus on Sir Phillip Sidney could ignore with absolute obliteration that Sidney had been a poet of note. Beamer was within the tradition of the very conservative Stimson family that had made its money in New York but that believed that education occurred in Massachusetts. And Stimson College had been founded when Maine of spiny trees and quartzy rocks was still part of Massachusetts. So when the Governing Boards sought a President, Emory Beamer, historian, Rhodes Scholar, sodden alcoholic, addict of "General Hospital" and man incapable of innovation, except for a transition from b/w to living colour (as he had learned to spell it at Oxford) in choice of personal television, was selected. And Emory Beamer, needing strength at his shoulder, chose Peter Herman, aka Herman Munster, as his Dean.

Herman lacked only the mortician's blood-draining valve to be type cast. But finding the office above him powerless, he wielded power, and found the office above him incapable of responding to his abuses. Herman built a satrapy composed of those who told him he was doing a great job and were rewarded. All others were punished. Needless to say, the faculty atrophied. Those of us who believed that travel to professional meetings from this isolated outpost was essential to our development had to fight for minimum travel money. Stimson, like the bed of John Donne and his lover, was the center of the universe and deserving of the unruly sun's absolute attention. Why travel to Washington or London? What could be there that Stimson did not provide?

But somewhere at the bottom of his psyche below the grandiosity of his consciousness, the trembling naked fool that he was must have laughed at him. He was a behavioral psychologist, a failed failure, who could not account for any depth of psyche. But he must have known deep down that he was not what his consciousness told him he was. It was a message that his wife gave him every morning as she sent him off to work. He carried a load of inadequacy down the sidewalk with him as he trudged to his elegant office. He shed that inadequacy as he entered the building and began to receive deferential nods and murmured good mornings during his progress. Only a few people like me exacerbated that inward mocking and he paid me back. Punishment after all – the electric shock when one pecks at the wrong button – is known to work in the lab.

I once came back on a Saturday from a conference that ended, for whatever reasons, at Saturday noon. I had papers to grade. Herman stiffed me on the air fare which would have been less, I admit, had I included a Saturday night stayover. I had delivered the keynote address for this conference, but ended up paying for most of it myself. I thought that a behavioral psychologist should at least have mastered the art of positive reinforcement. He had, of course. It was just that I had not lined up to kiss his ass and thus was not to be rewarded. I had pecked at the wrong button.

"Why do Stimson administrators walk so slowly?" I asked a class once.

They weren't about to touch that one.

"Because they are holding their pants at knee level while their rear ends scan the horizon for a smooch."

But okay. He was an annoyance. An easy subject for satire. I had not believed that he could become a destructive agent. I underestimated him.

Alex had been an Outward Bound instructor. She specialized in canoeing and cross country skiing.

Outward Bound had proposed a program for Stimson. A weekend during Freshman Orientation and a one week Spring Vacation option. It would have been very popular with the Stimson students, many of whom were there because of the nearby ski resorts. Alex would lead the program. And, I assumed, since we were already living together in an apartment near campus, that we would get married.

I got a note from Mrs. Pond, the Dean's Secretary, to make an appointment with her to see him.

I did not look forward to this meeting. Herman gave me the creeps. He was a sour man with a downturned right side of mouth. His attitude suggested that he resented wasting time on anything when he had so many more important things to do. That signaled a man who had nothing better to do and nothing else to do. And so he hated his job. But that hatred engendered his only enjoyment, which was using his job to punish those he was supposed to serve. But I could endure a few minutes with him if he had good news to deliver. The proposal had been carefully crafted and represented a valuable addition to Stimson's offerings.

"I'm afraid I have bad news."

"Bad news?"

I was more afraid of the bad news than he affected to be.

"Yes. The Outward Bound proposal has been turned down."

"How can that be?"

"It does not fit with the long term goals of the institution."

"Why not?"

"I am not going to debate the issue. The Committee of Five was unanimous."

"But surely you have a reason. The proposal was put together with the goals of the College in mind. The program itself is carefully planned and would be conducted by experts."

"That was one of the problems."

"What was?"

"The credentials of the director."

"She's got years of experience in all phases of Outward Bound."

"But no college degree."

"It's not required for Outward Bound."

"It is for Stimson."

"That was never stipulated. You permitted the proposal to go forward."

"We did not recognize the problem at first."

"Hell. The first thing anyone does is check credentials. Alex's are superb. And the recommendations of so many people plus the evaluations of the programs she's conducted speak for themselves. We could have gotten someone with a degree to head the program had that been a stated requirement."

"We?"

The son-of-a-bitch was having it both ways. He should not even be delivering this word to me. But Alex was not officially part of the Stimson staff. And, at the same time, Herman was playing organizational games with me. I was certainly not part of the Outward Bound organization.

"Outward Bound."

"I suggest you do so."

The program had needed approval last week so that the staff could be assembled, sites and permission to use them obtained, where necessary. Approval now would have meant a rush. The delay attendant upon finding another leader with credentials that would meet whatever Stimson's criteria might be would mean cancellation.

His thin smile told me that he knew that. It was all he could do. He could encourage nothing new into being. He could not summon creativity from within his vast emptiness. But he could block things, stop things in their tracks. It was the politics of childhood. You cannot be an adult, but you sure as hell can screw with their plans and activities.

Alex had had to move to Vermont and was often away from her base for two weeks at a time. Our relationship did not survive. Naturally enough, she met a fellow instructor who shared her love of cold and danger and of sex.

I found out when Alex responded to my jealous question with "Why would I do that?" When you get an answer like that you can be sure that the respondent did do that and is possibly wondering why. Or wondering why not, as the case may be. A simple yes or no would have sufficed, even if it were a lie.

But I did not blame Alex. Active evil does exist in the world. Nazi Germany. Stalin's Soviet Union. Bush's White House. But passive evil also exists. I think it is more prevalent and certainly more insidious. Herman epitomized it. Caesar says of Cassius that such as he are never at heart's ease while they behold a greater than themselves. Herman swam in an ocean of mediocrity. The others around him tended to be persons of very modest accomplishment who when they banded together rewarded each other. It is the tendency that gives poetry awards to the likes of Mark Strand, Mary Oliver, and Charles Simic. But Herman made sure that he defeated any initiative that might challenge students and any faculty member who might exceed Stimson's low-to-middling standards. And Herman had been elevated so that he could represent a tendency reflected in society. Don't try to be someone you are not. Good advice, but it keeps people from moving beyond the stereotypic frameworks that society constructs for them. They are Jacques' man, fulfilling a prescribed pattern from infancy to oblivion. And so the mass of men and particularly the mass of women become underachievers and are haunted all their lives by the sense that they could have been more. But they are not supposed to be and they obey. Most people have mediocrity thrust upon them and they accept it. They live in Dilbert's world, having been conditioned to believe that no other world exists. And that is a passive evil. It may deny many the chance to fail. They can feed on insects in the swamp of mediocrity. But it denies almost everyone the opportunity to be great. I was hardly great, but I was better than Herman. And he knew it.

What gets me is the assumption of superiority that the vicious office holders take. Herman came to believe that he was "holding the place together" during the sodden years of Emory Beamer's reign. And his myth of identity made himself worthy of the higher office when Emory was driven from it. A stooped, inarticulate, snarling, plastic-tipped cigar smoking, polyester jacketed hack who was already viewed with wonder by his fellow deans from the small New England colleges when he attended this or that academic meeting. He wore the Great Seal of Office in a golden chain around his neck as he shuffled along in front of the academic procession at graduation and other solemn convocations. We all deceive ourselves, no doubt, as we render ourselves into another dawn, believing there will be meaning there as it unfolds, but Herman's kidding of himself was profound.

And I had thumbed my nose at him, arrogantly oblivious to the consequences, which had also been profound.

You play the role set down for you. I was in London once, years ago, and went to a modern recreation of a medieval Crucifixion play, originally produced by the Nail-makers Guild. It was in a tiny theater that permitted spectators to mingle with the action. We all gathered around one of Christ's miracles – the healing of a blind man. And when Pilate asked us what we wished done with Christ, we all shouted "Crucify Him!" We were only incidentally doing God's bidding by fulfilling the prophecy.

I had played the role set down for me. But limits did exist. Peter Herman established those limits. But he was also the executioner of the piece.

VI.

Yet stand with us, dear friends. This battle won,
We'll celebrate our victory with cups
That overflow, and go to war no more.

Reginald Moorland,
Edward, Black Prince of Wales (1599).

We were at eight thousand feet. I unclipped my oxygen mask and brushed my face with my leather glove. The mask created a slimy zone across the mouth. Good to get rid of it, even if the air inside the cockpit smelled of the deep sweat of armpits and exhaust from my flight leader's aircraft. I made a slight adjustment of throttle to ease back to the wing of Major Crawdon's ship. We would descend over the border and come in at two thousand feet over the base, go in-trail, pull a tight turn known as a pitch, throw out speed brakes, landing gear and flaps, then touch down just as the low fuel light began to blink red signals into the twilight of the cockpit. Good to be homeward bound! I could taste that first beer already!

I had watched the lead ship, tipping a thin ice-trail from its tail pipe into the blinding blue altitude. Air behaves like a liquid. We could be fish. The lead ship held an austere beauty, even here as earth's close hold turned everything gray, like that of a shark skimming the fathoms that its search controlled.

"Number two! Break left!"

I snapped the stick to the left, added some throttle, and watched a missile slide under my ship. It exploded in front of me, sending my aircraft up and to the left as if it were a kite that has suddenly snapped loose from its string in a storm. Fortunately, I had my visor down against the smear of sunset over Laos, so I was blinded only momentarily. My artificial horizon told me that I was riding at an angle of sixty degrees upward and about twenty degrees to the left. I continued a roll downward to the left and added more throttle. But adding throttle produced no response. I pushed the nose down to bring my airspeed up to three fifty knots.

"Number two. You okay?"

"Affirmative, one. But I've flamed out."

"Understand. Do not attempt airstart."

"Right, one."

If my engine were damaged, an airstart might blow me up. I'd be sending JP-4 back into a waiting fire.

I put down ten degrees of flaps and assumed a two hundred knot glide.

Seven thousand feet.

The smell of burning wrinkled at my nostrils. No smoke. Just the dull brown undertone of wires burning. Not a cause for throat-stopping panic. But it did induce a quiver of worry. What systems was I about to lose?

"Number two. Can you make Pathum Chai?"

Pathum Chai was an emergency field just over the border. How far? Ten miles? If more...

"Number one. Sure. No sweat."

Major Crawdon, throttled back, had tucked in on my right wing.

"It'll be a stretch."

"Yeah. But it's an east west runway. I can make it straight in."

"If you cannot, eject."

As they say, you can't stretch a glide. If I ejected, I'll be down in the jungle. Tigers would take note and begin to pad toward the smell of a sweaty fighter pilot. In the jungles of the day, stripes would glide sinuously over the sleek muscles that linked the legs to the body. Velvet nostrils would expand with the scent of their prey. I could feel the .45 strapped to my right leg.

"Two. I'm low on petrol. Gotta hustle. Stay at Pathum Chai. I'll send a chopper for you."

"Wilco, One. Any smoke?"

"A thin trail from the tail pipe. No flames."

That was reassuring. My spine was chilly, believing itself to be leaning against a burning aircraft that might at any instant disintegrate into metallic fragments with a touch of bone inside. It was a burning aircraft, but some fires are worse than others. I assumed from the smell that I had an electrical fire. That was better than, say, sniffing the draining off of hydraulic fluid. If my hydraulics went, the controls would go as well.

"See you back at base, Two."

"Rog, One. Save me a cold one."

Maybe he would see me back at base. A number of things had to happen first. And I had to try to be part of that process, rather than just an observer. Something in me wanted desperately just to lean back and see what was going to happen.

Crawley turned on the burners and climbed. If he flamed out, he'd have the altitude he needed to make it back to Sarabari.

The jungle reached for me. I thought I could smell the murky shadows cast by that vast expanse of green.

But there, beyond it was the runway, long and lovely, riding a luminous trail of sunset in my direction.

"Pathum Chai. Air Force Six Seven Niner."

"Sever Niner. Pathum Chai."

"Deadstick approach. On final. Three miles out."

"Seven Niner. Understand. Aircraft in Pathum Chai area, emergency in progress, stay clear of traffic pattern."

I reached a point where I would have to eject if I were going to do so. Could I make the runway?

You can't stretch a glide. You can't stretch a glide.

Fortunately, I didn't have to.

The aircraft settled on its two main gears. Helluva landing! I could pretend that I was just showing off, but it was a combination of luck and the knowledge that it had to be good. I had no throttle to take me around again. And, if I had had an engine going for me, I had no fuel either.

The tower had been efficient, but I had not requested crash equipment. I clipped my ejection seat safety pin in and exited the smoldering ship with dispatch. By the time a fire truck ambled up toward the aircraft, the blatting of a chopper was beating at the leaves of the jungle to the west. One of the first things I'd do when I got back was to throw out my flightsuit, maybe even burn it. It stank of smoke and fear, of the moment when the leaf fire suddenly twists its foul smoke into your face and of the swamp that has accepted burlap bags of living cats into its depth over too many years. I did not want to go back during some Proustian moment to those long moments of emergency.

The issue for those of us in the military was not danger, but fear of danger. Once, early on in training, my T-34 developed a runaway prop. Even after I had reduced the rpms, the damned thing kept rotating at the max. I did what the book said to do. I raised the nose to put a load on the prop. And it worked! The rpm indicator fell into normal range. That proved to me that procedures work. Flying, then, was easy enough, even though that was where emergencies could happen, even though that's where the danger was. But you had something to do. It was the time in between that was the problem.

That one exception to most of my life -- The USAF. I'd had to act. That is one reason – not the only one – why so many men look back upon their military experience as the most significant years of their lives. They had had to act. Or die. Their friends died. And that is the other reason – the friends that died.

VII.

If it were only to love, this life were one of ease.
But when that love is lost, the dark of night
Affords no sleep, nor any balm for pain.

Rogelio Latimer,
The Virgin's Lament (1595).

"You were married?"

"Once."

What happened?"

"Unfortunately, I met Alex."

Marianne nodded.

"Or, fortunately," I said.

"You don't have to explain Alex. I've seen people fall in love with her at fifteen feet. But tell me about the others."

"The important ones."

"Yes."

We were in a motel along a barren stretch of a secondary highway well west of Toronto. Alex and Ken were getting supplies. Tomorrow we would search for a place to stay. Ken figured that it was more dangerous being on the road than camping out for awhile.

But I enjoyed being alone with Marianne. I poured the last of the wine into the two plastic cups.

"The others? Other than Alex?"

"Yes. I understand about her."

"The stuff of which legends are made. Two others. Fran and Naomi."

"Only two?"

"A lot of footnotes."

"Fran?"

"Fran. I don't know how rare it is, but it was the first time for both of us. It was painful for her at the beginning. A couple of times. Then we were insatiable, exploring what we had discovered, doing it wherever and whenever we could, often on the spur of the moment, when the chance suddenly presented itself, often in dangerous circumstances where we could have been discovered by the chance opening of a door, the random entering of a room.

"Naomi was married to a fellow faculty member. Taught chemistry. She had dark skin, almost gray, but it was a pearl-gray, luminous. And it was thick. When I massaged her, I could touch the layer of muscle underneath riding on top of the depth of bone. She said once, in recounting one of our meetings, 'And then you gave me a back rub that I felt for a week.' We had a very sensuous relationship."

"But Fran was first?"

"Fran. She and I were Episcopalians. We loved what we were doing, but our religious orientation conditioned our coupling. We suffered bouts of guilt during the brief letdowns after we made love. Half an hour or so. And she loved me the jock, the fast halfback, the doubles player who excelled from the ad court. I could hear her voice over all the others at football games. And I always played my best tennis when she was looking on. I do not understand why one person being there should make a difference, but it did. I never played as well after we broke up. I have to grant that I enjoyed possessing her. I enjoyed being able to put my hand where I wanted to, without resistance. With acceptance, even joy. She loved it when I touched her. And I loved it when she initiated the action. One Friday, I showed up at her house in Larchmont. We necked on a couch. It got really passionate. Her mother was due back at any minute, but suddenly she pushed me away, stood up and raised her dress. We were interrupted a few minutes later, of course and I had a hell of a time getting it back into my pants .

"The danger was part of it, of course, and the shadows of my room at Hadley, romantic in the way that half-light reveals and conceals. The luminous body

"I could still visualize the concentration – her eyes seeming to look back upon some event in the distant past – as she fitted me to her dimension – and then their widening with surprise as she slid down on top of me, as if it were always a first time. Most of our love-making was like that -- in the back seat of a car, on a couch in the living room when parents were away for an hour, she astride me on a chair in the basement when we would be "watching television" after coming back from a party or a dance. It was quick, delicious, stolen. Not much cuddling. Only occasionally slowly delineated and luxurious interludes. Yes, when we had time within a locked room and a door to be knocked upon only by Room Service, we shed our clothes and romped delightedly. She was wonderful about taking off her clothes."

"Why'd you break up?"

"The thought of getting married scared the hell out of me."

"But you did."

"Oh yes. I paid for Fran. A stern rebuke – like the counterpoint of a Haydn viola section striking back at the sweep of the melody. My wife refused to take her clothes off. I was naked, she in a demure slip. I felt like fallen Adam trying to get at an Eve who was still abiding in the garden. I don't know about most men, but I think that's the area where they'd have trouble. Don't they expect that women know something? I did. I had extrapolated from Fran. And I had gotten it wrong."

" First times have nothing to compare themselves with."

"Until they do. And I paid for it."

"And that was your exile from Eden?"

"Yes. Don't know now what happened to me, but she was introverted, mysterious, and I fell. It was a strange case of going in the opposite direction. From sheer hedonism...."

"But that was bound to happen."

"Yes. A quest for something different. I got it. She turned out to be a prude. Found some pictures of Fran in my desk and threw them out. And, of course, I couldn't ask 'what happened to those pictures?' She called Fran, 'Fat Fran.'"

"Jealous."

"Oh yes, and punishing me for a relationship I'd had before I met her."

"Children?"

"Yes. Unfortunately. But fortunately, because I love them. That kept the damned marriage going far beyond its lifespan."

"And made things worse?"

"Yes. My oldest was twelve when we finally parted. Destroyed her. And, of course, she blamed me."

"Could you have worked things out?"

"No. The alienation was so complete, and there had never been a good time. But amusingly we had one last fling after the divorce. She always got horny just before her period. And one day, she invited me over for dinner with the girls. I read to Sally while Margaret went upstairs and took a shower. She had instructed me with a significant glance not to leave. The girls went to bed. Margaret brought a blanket and a pillow and put them on the living room floor. She took off her robe. Yes, I had prevailed on the clothes thing after five years of her Sharia, but the fight and the resentment had not been worth it. 'I'm not that kind of girl,' she had protested. But that night she was. I did something I'd never done before – she usually plastered herself with spermicide, glop – but not that night. And she went wild."

"Too late."

"Yes. Though, in retrospect..."

"You regret it."

"Giving up my children? Yes. I always will. I often figure out alternative scenarios for them, better, of course..."

"Had you been...?"

"No. Five years of virtual celibacy had driven me crazy. I began a passionate affair with the wife of a colleague. Naomi."

"Dangerous."

"Oh, yes."

"And I could expect no sympathy for starting an affair. After all – where did the children come from? I couldn't say 'from a woman in slip and bra cinched firmly to her prim little chest.' I would always be the erring male."

"So Naomi was inevitable?"

"Seems so. Her love had a metaphysical quality. Our love-making was profound – not like the wild passion that Fran and I had shared – deep, as if we were exploring a new identity that we created when our bodies joined. I enjoyed not just her body and my response to it but something in my selfhood that I could feel, physically, when I was making love with her. And she seemed to understand me in some wordless way – not like the usual husband's claim for his mistress – and seemed to need that understanding, to prize it, to sense who she was in surrounding me with her imagination. Hell, it can't be described. We were two people living within an energy system that we created and shared. Two doomed people.

"Naomi was a return to the danger and the shadows -- I did not fantasize though She was vivid and passionate. Married and with two children. She'd never been properly fucked. She realized that the first time. I overheard her whisper to herself, 'So this is what it is like!' She was Jewish. We felt no guilt. Quite the opposite. The sacrament was in the act itself and it was a transformation into momentary immortality. And she hated the crew-cut jock. She saw the intellectual in me (miracle of eyesight!). Her husband was a dull and inarticulate guy. And, if Christianity is based on longing for something, our relationship was based on having found it. She was an emotionally settled person, in spite of the passion she suddenly discovered with me. And I did not discover it. I knew it by then. I shared it with her. It became ours. At first I thought it was body types."

"Similar?"

"Yes. Dark hair. Dark eyes. Ample boobs."

"Me?"

"I learned then that it wasn't superficial similarities that counted."

"Soul."

"Yes. Imagination. The ability to imagine the universal in the particular. Fran and Naomi gave me that, though the universal was different."

"How so?"

"Woman. Physical, superb woman. Sheer physicality. And spirit. A physical, superb woman, yes, but who saw something with her eyes that wasn't there, but was. Hell, D.H. Lawrence describes it better than I can. But sadly and in retrospect, I realized that Fran was not what women are..."

"Fran was who Fran was."

At some point it the past I would have been bragging. But this was a way of letting Marianne understand me – I was holding nothing back, particularly her inferences, whatever they might be. She had asked me. My story might be a way of entering her story. I felt that that was what she wanted. She wasn't sure. She wasn't sure how our histories could be twinned. It was Frost's poem, in which the two go over what the other has already passed. I felt warm and comfortable talking to her. And, for me, it was exorcism.

"Why didn't Naomi last?"

"Families. The hold of her family on her was stronger than our passion. And that was powerful. Too much would have had to be destroyed. It would have destroyed us very quickly.

We knew it was too late. We also knew that who we were when we met defined who we were together. None of this 'if only we had met sooner' nonsense. We meet different people at different times, and perhaps we insist on the relationship at some unperceived level of selfishness."

"No. It may be a level of need. It is not necessarily selfish. Why do you describe things in terms of religion?"

"Those were the terms I was growing out of at the time."

"How would you describe our relationship?"

"I don't have to."

"Good."

"It is."

"Yes."

But then I said too much, as I sometimes do.

"It just is. It is its own metaphor."

"Metaphor?"

"Yes. Two unlike elements – you and me, male and female, hard and soft – as the poet says, conferring to resolve the paradox of need and resolution."

"Who is the poet?"

"Me."

"Then you couldn't have had me in mind."

"I was generalizing. I had yet to discover the specific example."

She laughed.

"Words, words, words," I said. "Come here. Let me try to prove it to you."

Marianne had been interested. No trace of jealousy. She was as easy with the women who had made up my past as she was in doffing her clothes when they were wet and chilly. Remarkable woman!

We didn't have to talk about it any more.

And now the leaves were showing the color that lay under summer's green. Trees don't change color. They lose the green of spring. Larks were no longer telling the sunset to pause along its western edge and pour gold upon its exit. A thunderstorm rode over us. We passed a field filled with corn stalks. They wove back and forth like a mad section of violins. This was the north. It would be cold. But in that zero lay freedom. No Homeland Security Patrols rounding up the minor citizens whose disappearance would scare the shit out of the rest. And no identity except the one I held within this tiny group. Ken. Alex. And Marianne. I thought that it should be scary. Should be. But it was good. I had nothing but who I was. All that I was not – the credit cards and the photo ids with which one navigated that other world did not apply. I had nothing. Except myself. And Marianne. And so we drove west by northwest, deeper away from the artificial identities that it takes a lifetime to create. Spring would wander in, naked, cold, still shivering, still dazed. But we would be here, surrounded by its chilly entrance. The poetry, if there were any, would be of austere skies and brittle blossoms, if there were any.

"I remember one game," I said that afternoon in the echoless motel. "Fran was there. I could hear her calling my name. I ran a sweep around right end, got a block and had one man to beat. He had the angle on me. I faked inside and went toward the sideline. One of my teammates was chugging down the field. As I faked, the other guy squared up for the tackle. My teammate wiped him out. I kept on going. It looked as if it had been planned that way."

"Hadn't it?"

"A fake is supposed to set up a block, sure. But I didn't know my teammate was there. And I lost track of Fran's voice. I think that was the only time."

"Until..."

"Yes. Until I lost track of it completely."

VIII.

You have neglected me of late, my lord.

I have. I pray you pardon me. My mind
has swarmed with other thoughts. And what is dear
to me, I have forgot. Forgive me, please.

With all my heart, my lord. With all my heart.
Benjamin Culterry,
The Wounds of Love (1609).

"Harry, what is it?"

I could see Marianne in front of me. But she was the dream. The reality was my nightmare.

I had survived. I had walked smiling from the world's great snare uncaught. I had not known then that the terror was still ahead. Of course, I had never before emerged into Marianne's concerned gaze. My poor wife had been frightened and took to sleeping in the guest room. I had been afraid to go to sleep at night, knowing what might be waiting there for me. Drunk to bed got me four sodden hours and then sleeplessness until just before it was time to get up. Then, perversely, I'd drop off again.

I'd been knocked out, of course, playing football, boxing. It was like falling down through a pain that is signaled by a splintering sequence of lights. I thought, as I fell, like some disaster at an amusement park – the ferris wheel breaking free from its central spoke and rolling down a steep hill, or the merry-go-round leaping out of its circle and becoming a crack-the-whip, as, all the while, the organ pumped out "Let Me Call You Sweetheart" or "Ain't We Got Fun" to the snorting of wild wooden horses. Morphine was softer – a floating through a cloud of feathers into a sweetness deeper than pain. Going to sleep with Marianne next to me became easy. I knew I'd dream and that she would be with me in those dreams. Just there. And when I woke up and rolled over, she would be there too.

But, every so often, the sweat would be heavier and would not dry in the fires of a nightmare.

At times I had been barely able to put my arm out and slide my chute from the rack. Barely able to step from the flight shack into damp dawn, bringing day in as only a lighter shade of gray. Procedures did their work, of course, as they were designed to do. I went through a variety of checks and steps, stuffing safety pins with their bright red ribbons into the leg pockets of my flightsuit, checking the tires and the fuel. I became an automaton. That process permitted me to put myself inside it. No space existed there for the human being. But the imagination lived on underneath. And it would take its revenge. It became so automatic that, one day, after pre-flighting the aircraft, reading back an instrument clearance, starting up, taking off with another plane on my wing, I woke up at ten thousand feet. Until then, I had been sound asleep.

I thought of slumber. The shallow zone I was inhabiting now was the result of a backrub Marianne had given me. It was a place below the surface of pain where the kneading could be enjoyed. I was dough without the responsibility of becoming bread. This was a level of non-thought, where a vocalized or realized "Ah!" was language enough. This was not post-coital slumber, where the specific excitement diffuses into a general pleasurable lassitude through all veins, tendons, and synapses as the rest of the body absorbs the enjoyment of a specific part. Nor was it the ride of morphine, which I had had, where a major agony melts and one falls toward a soft and nonexperienced landing. I understand drug addiction, I thought to myself as I went under. Of course the waking up would come – the hard side of drug addiction. But now, I was floating without fear of sinking, or of waking up. Or of dreaming.

"I had leave coming up," Ken said. "And I had applied for it through all the proper channels and in plenty of time. As it was, they almost froze all the leaves. I had to pull seniority. Luckily they'd just sent us some more men to handle the influx."

"I take it that you never really bought into the system," I said.

He gave a bitter bark of laughter.

"I had it made. At least I thought I did."

The women were napping in the back seat of the truck.

"I grew up in a small town. Ruston Mills. It's a town that's all on the bottom of the hill. And all on the wrong side of the tracks. A few of kids went to college. And there weren't many rich kids. Lawyer's son. Son of the Ford dealer. Son of the Caterpillar franchise owner. But I played football. And I was good. I could block. I could catch the ball. I had a realistic hope of playing on Sundays."

"So you got a scholarship?"

"Free ride. And I suddenly got interested in the books. I was going to major in history."

"What happened?"

"Tore up my knee."

"And you lost your scholarship."

"Right. I could not put together a package that would keep me there."

"Your knee?"

"No chance. So I went into what they call security."

"A growth industry."

"Yeah. It's a dead end. And it is depressing. I am not a sadist."

"Nor a masochist."

"A lot of the guys are really sick."

"Not a pleasant work environment."

"And it is so damned boring. Routine. How do people do that all their lives? Same rounds. Same checks. Most of the people anonymous prisoners in orange suits."

He glanced into the back seat.

He lowered his voice.

"But then I met Alex."

I did understand. I also guessed that Alex had not told him about her past relationship with me. At least, not more than that I had been a friend. Okay. I would keep it that way. This man had saved us. Was saving us. And, as I listened to him, I realized that he was an intelligent young man. My own education had been assured and financed. I had put up with the two-a-days of football practice, too, but retreated to an elegant fraternity house in the evenings and a dark and well-stocked bar on Saturdays after games. And then upstairs to the dark and well-stocked Fran. I had hit the books back then with a mild curiosity that had developed into real interest in time. I had vowed that if I survived the military, I'd make up for my desultory adolescence. This man had suddenly been bitten by the learning bug. And that process had been interrupted, probably for good.

"How's your knee now?"

"Okay. I just couldn't cut."

"I know. You shuffle around and turn and the ball hits you in the nose."

"Right. You played?"

"Not tight end," I said, laughing.

"Halfback."

"What area of history are you interested in?" I asked.

"Sounds too easy – but twentieth century."

"No. It does not sound too easy. That it is recent only makes it more complicated, more debatable, more full of analysis. When we get settled, Ted, we'll get you on a reading program. Some books I want to look at too."

"You mean it?"

"Of course. We'll have to find a decent library. I have to try to keep myself up-to-date. I was interrupted too."

The only dangerous portion of my recent travels had been that mad flight to West Run Junction. And that was their strategy, of course – the great "they" who control us. They lull us, so that any unusual action becomes dangerous. And therefore we do nothing. With an all-volunteer military, most of the guys don't even have to undergo the humbling experience of boot camp. For those born to the right parents on the accepted side of the tracks, it is all very easy, as long as they keep quiet. If it moves salute it.

We trended deeper into Canada. North and west, along roads that thinned to needles through woods and across vast farmlands.

"Further we go," Ken said, "better off we are. These people don't give a shit what the U.S. is doing. And the government hates what the U.S. is doing."

"Still..." I said.

"We'll fix you up with an identity card."

"Money?"

"We'll all get work of some sort. Enough to live on. Once we find a place."

We stayed at small, independent motels, four to a room. The rooms all had double beds. Alex didn't give a damn. She'd been on so many Outward Bound expeditions.

"You've seen me this way," she said to me one day as she pranced out of the bathroom after a shower.

True, but I had not seen her on top of Ken, her mouth half open as she twisted her pelvis with a rhythm that I remembered all too well.

Marianne was utterly unconcerned about her nakedness or sexual activity or her laughter after it, which was spoke of sheer delight.

Kenneth was diffident at first – not shy, he was a jock who had taken plenty of showers in the communal setting of the locker room, but reluctant to share Alex with anyone, even vicariously. But he got used to it.

The economy of our accommodations helped us bond as four people who, literally, had nothing to hide from each other.

And, as we got further away from the U.S., I felt my own tensions fading. Just living there under the Bush/Cheney tyranny, the Obama rhetoric, and the Cheney interregnum had made me an angry man with a desire riding just below the surface to punch someone. I had not noticed that until it was gone and I was no longer clenching my fists.

I thought of home, of course, but it was a distant place, in miles as well as years. It was a pseudo-Tudor house in Little Mountain, a place of which I knew every nook and cranny. I could recall getting up on Christmas morning and finding the space under the tree suddenly filled with presents: steam shovels on which a little boy could sit, where he could manipulate the shovel and dump it out – having filled it with marbles – into the back of a truck, and Lionel train sets, including a little house from which a switch man would emerge with a red lantern in hand everytime the train passed his location. The lantern waved as the motion of the little man carried him out and in again. Of course I expected such presents. I had no sense that other boys did not get them – the elegant cap pistols, the aircraft attached to a pole that swung around like the lead-in to an RKO Radio Picture, slender English bikes with hand-brakes and gearshifts, and boxed sets of elegant soldiers preparing for the changing of the guard at Buckingham Palace. These were aspects of my expectations as a privileged little boy and they materialized in memory as I left that world behind forever. And, of course, as I grew up in that house, I learned to use it in other ways. I knew where my father kept his Scotch. Did he ever notice how watery good eight-year-old Catto's could be? And I knew the zones in which Fran and I could couple quickly and quietly, with little chance of discovery. The play room where the ancient DuMont still sent its dead-fish gleam outward was the best place of course, although one night I feared that the taffeta rhythm of Fran's gown would rouse the soundest sleepers of the house. What could I have said it was – the scuffling of rats in the rafters?

"Think we'll ever go back?" Marianne asked.

It made me realize how young she was.

"Physically? Maybe."

"But not..."

"Not in whatever other ways there are. Except in memory."

"Some more than others!" she said, laughing.

That meant me.

"Yes, but right now with you is good. Whatever little I may have learned tells me that much."

"I know. And I learn a lot from you."

"You do?"

"Oh yes."

"I must do something when I'm not even trying."

"Trying gets in the way."

"Anyway," I said, "sooner or later the pendulum will swing and they will issue an amnesty."

"Why? They don't do it for people who peddle a couple of ounces of grass."

"That's true."

"Where did it all go wrong?" Alex asked.

"The country has always flirted with fascism," I said. "The Bund before WW II. McCarthy. The invasion of Iraq was a turning point. All those Hummers. All those yellow ribbons."

"As long as someone else was doing the dying," Marianne said.

"Yes," I said. "Heroism by proxy. It's easy that way. But I think specifically it was when Obama refused to do anything about the thugs who authorized all the loopholes in our laws and international agreements. Suddenly, we were torturing, but calling it something else. Suddenly, we were yanking people off this or that street and sending them, cuffed and blindfolded off to some secret place. And all of that was fiercely defended by the fools who screamed 'National Security!' But when those guys – Yoo, Addington, little Dicky Perle, Cheney, and the smirky creep from Yale – realized that they had gotten away with it, that they would not be punished 'for just doing their jobs,' they realized that they could do anything they damn well pleased, say anything – including threatening the life of the president – disrupt public meetings, create anarchy by blocking the legislative process."

"And throw us all in the hoosegow. I love that word. Hoosegow."

Alex's voice sounded as if she were swallowing an exotic fruit.

"And they were right," Ken said.

Ken pulled over as the blue light pulsed behind us.

The officer, in a fur-edged cap, black jacket with gold chevrons and black trousers with a blue stripe emerged from his patrol car, walked up to Ken's window, and asked for his license and registration.

He examined them and, still holding them in his left hand, looked at us – at me in the front seat next to Ken, and at the women in back.

"All right," he said, handing the documents back to Ken. "This is just a caution. There is an all points out in a neighboring province for two couples traveling in an extended cab pickup like yours. I advise you to be careful."

"We will be. Thank you, sergeant," Ken said.

"Wow," I said, as we drove off. "They do not want to pick us up."

"No, but the watertight compartment between provinces won't hold. He was telling us," Ken said, "that if we continue to travel together we will be picked up."

"And extradited?" Alex asked.

"Once they pick us up, yes. The official process begins."

"We'd better..." I began.

"Not travel together," Ken completed the sentence. "And I'll see what I can do about unloading this truck. Something smaller. Maybe get a little money in the transaction. We only need something that runs."

"And starts in cold weather."

"Up here," he said, "they don't have anything else."

It was good not to be the leader any more. Good, at least, not to be the biggest strongest male at any rate. I gratefully ceded that position to Ken. My own responsibilities were becoming more specific. Marianne.

And, amid the leisure of the days, as we paused to figure out where we would try to settle down, I had a chance to write of poem. This one, very specifically, for Marianne.

> And when my eyes roll sightless, after all
> that they have loved, and every unseen star
> reflects in the empty glitter that saw before
> it had the sight of you, and loved the call
> returning from your eyes, and knew to read
> the silence in which the words that can't be said
> were spoken with the pressure of a spread
> of fingers into mine, and the whirl of love that you
> breathed out and in like oceans, and the roar
> of my own ears, and the tremble through and
> through,

that great last wave crashing on the shore,
recall my love, when my eyes fall, just who
it was they saw when they could see no more,
and wished an after life of deja vu.

I would share that with her at some moment when we
both needed it.

We were now among the stony outcroppings of the land
north of Thunder Bay, moving away from the warming
influence of Lake Superior and into winter.

"Almost all English speaking," Ken said. "Time to stay
put for a while."

"And get some money," Alex said.

We had spent most of the cash that the internment camp
had neglected to take from me. Ken had brought what he
could, but just buying gas and food had used most of that
up.

Alex's skills would be instantly transferable to whatever
outdoor programs the small city of Laurant Mountain offered.
And those programs did not ask many questions. They were
staffed by enthusiastic vagabonds of which she was one.
Marianne was a musician. Piano and, as she proudly told me,
harpsichord.

"Any market for a harpsichordist?" I asked her.

"Not much. But churches need piano players. And I'll pick
up lessons from there."

"What the hell am I going to do?" I asked of the empty
atmosphere.

"They'll be a market for tutors," Ken said. "A lot of these
kids want to go to college and need to pass their entrance
exams. They have a test on English language proficiency for
foreign students and there are a lot of them in the area. You
could set up shop right away. The exams will be coming up
before Christmas I think."

"I suppose," I said. "I can use my credentials without having to go through some formal process."

"And I," Ken said, "will join the local police force."

"Won't they check?"

"I think I can get some recommendations without blowing my cover. I won't mention my most recent assignment. But they need cops up here."

"You want to be a cop?" Alex asked.

"Yes. I will enjoy it. If I can't be a history teacher, I want to be a cop."

"We'll do some history in the meantime," I said.

Someday someone will publish a study on the relationship between delayed stress syndrome and paranormal experiences. I am sure that the vividness of my bad dreams, the gripping reality of past moments I do not wish to revisit, has conditioned me to other possibilities.

I woke up. Marianne has asleep beside me, the covers having slid down in a rumple toward the bump of her rear end. I reached over and pulled them up.

And there in the space between the bed and the window beyond, in a wash of moonlight, was my mother.

I was awake.

I said nothing.

Nor did she.

She gave me a fierce look – one I remembered from life.

"I will," I whispered. "I will."

She had been angry at me for my treatment of women, particularly of Fran, whom she had loved as the daughter she never had. She was telling me to take care of Marianne.

"I will."

Our ancient ancestors, having raised their knuckles from the mud, began to dream. Perhaps they always had dreamed. The bright and often brutal images of their lives must have transformed themselves into a vivid dream life, mostly nightmares. But at some point, as the cortex developed, they could develop a theory about dreams. The dreams meant that people that they thought were dead were still alive. "I saw him! He spoke to me!" And that primitive belief was still one of the most valid interpretations of dreams. Those people are still alive. And they can speak to us without a word.

The moon slid behind a cloud and soon sleet was slicing like a clicking of finger nails at the old window that looked southward toward the lost land of the past. Marianne stirred beside me as if she had heard my one-sided conversation with my mother, as if it had been her dream.

I was at a disadvantage. Because of my advantages, I had always known who I was within a comfortable and inherited structure. WASPville. It was full of old Turkish rugs, Atwater Kent radios that had been gutted and turned into liquor cabinets, group portraits of blonde children surrounding a Dalmatian, and good schools of one syllable – Taft, Kent, Choate. At least expensive schools. Silk ties. Cotton shirts. Wool jackets. No thread of polyester. Had I been born Giovanni Pignatore, I would have had Ellis Island in my background and a sense of how to move as an existential, even hunted, human being as opposed to someone who existed within all the sanctions and continuities of privilege. I had no instinct for survival, no sense that people wouldn't accept me, smile, and say "thank you, sir" when I held out a tip. In reality, I was nobody in that artificial world. I felt like someone with these three.

"No," I said.

"No what?" she asked.

The expression on Marianne's face as I came through the door of our hostelry, The Easy Inn, from a six-pack run had posed a question with slightly furrowed brows creasing the smooth gleam of her forehead. What sort of mood is he in? How best can I respond to him?

"Be who you are," I said. "That's who I love. We can negotiate the smaller points."

She smiled.

"I have been raised to meet expectations."

"We all have. Conditioning and reinforcement. You meet my expectations. But only when you meet your own."

She came into my arms. We did not have to negotiate the moment.

"I put down a $300 security deposit," Ken said. "And am having a cord and a half of firewood delivered."

"By springtime, it will be the lost chord," Marianne said.

And we'd be broke. Ken had had to spend most of the money he had brought exchanging the Dodge for a Subaru wagon. It was a trade down, but the negotiations were expensive because the transaction was illegal and the paperwork complicated.

The house would have been called ramshackle once upon a time. But as we stood there for a moment, under a gray and closing sky beginning to etch stick-thin trees into its background, the house seemed to reach out to us with tendrils of welcome. Of course, that was our hope coming back at us, but this was not Poe's House of Usher or Shirley Jackson's Hill House. Whoever had lived here once upon a time had been happy here.

"Bit dilapidated," Alex said.

"No," I said, "that means that it has lost its stones."

She looked at me and laughed.

The day was ending. The sun came out from under a ledge of clouds far the west and sent a sudden, golden slant across the miles. A quirk of the northern latitudes.

A prophecy?

"I love it!" Marianne said, running up the steps to the front porch and disappearing inside.

It was a large frame house floating in a sea of weeds and fallen leaves. It did have a few missing shingles and a couple of loose shutters, but the roof looked as if it had been replaced only a few years ago and it was clean and scrubbed inside.

"Any beds?" I asked.

"First things first," Alex said, laughing.

"Yes. I value my naps. I see we have some chairs, a dining room table, a couple of rugs that still have a faint design in them, and..."

I waved my arm at the great stone fireplace in the living room.

"The kitchen is great," Marianne said, returning to the living room. "Original linoleum on the floor. A big old fridge, a gas stove, plenty of cabinet space, and a pantry!"

"I wondered," I said, "why I've had a sense of relief lately. Like waking up without a hangover. But you know what it is?"

I moved my fingers in the air in front of me.

"No internet," Marianne said.

"It's great," I said. "Getting rid of an addiction. Like quitting cigarettes."

"Good none of us smoke. I'm out of money," Ken said.

"Tell you what, Ken," I said. "I've got a few bucks left. Let's go down to the store we passed a mile back and get some food. And some wine. We have a celebration in the offing."

"Sufficient unto the day," Marianne said.

"It will be your last hundred bucks, won't it?" Ken asked.

"Just about."

"You'll have to learn to say 'a but,'" Alex said. "I have another fifty."

"Rainy day," I said.

"It won't have to rain very hard," Alex said.

"Get some toilet paper," Marianne said.

By the time Ken and I got back with a couple of sacks of groceries, several six packs of Labatts Export and a bottle of good red wine, the night clouds had taken over and a cold rain had begun to fillet the darkness. As we sloshed into the driveway the rain gave way to a crystal twisting of snow.

But the light above the side porch was on and Alex had constructed a fire that told stories of home and trembled with the ghosts of those whose faces had risen and fallen on the pulse of the flames, a fire that warmed those who lived here now.

I had snuck in a half dozen roses, which I arranged artistically in an old tea pot that I found on a shelf in the living room. To them I attached a message.

The moon danced across the easy elegance of the pretty-in-pink carefree wonder (in my favorite outfit – her birthday suit!) as the dark lady behind a fragrant cloud in the black magic of a starry night gathered around a moondance gave way to a new dawn and marmalade skies above lovers lane and, from there, a whisper of sheer bliss. A rose by any other name would be Marianne. Love to you, my sunshine.

Ken and I stood by the fire, letting it drain the chill from our spines. Alex and Marianne chirped merrily in the kitchen as they removed food from the sacks and began our first celebratory meal in our new home. I heard the cork thump out of the bottle of red wine.

It was a beginning. And an ending.

fin

READY ON THE RIGHT

Note:
I am indebted to Jack Broughton's excellent *Thud Ridge* (Crecy: Manchester, G.B., 2006) for some of the details of the F-105 missions in Vietnam.

I.

An old song bounced around in my head. That was hardly unusual. Old songs in my head seemed to be the only music I was hearing these days. The lyrics and melodies arrived immediately after the dream, whatever it had been, retreated to the planetarium of the nighttime imagination. The songs were transition. Getting those little pigs to the rug. Wondering whether the hot water in the shower would last long enough for me to rinse the soap from my flesh. I could recall having gotten the coffee maker ready for the next day. Or was I remembering what I had done yesterday and forgetting what I had not done the night before? I would usually realize that, whatever my dreams may have been only seconds ago, they had not awakened me in a panicky sweat. I was no longer afraid to go to sleep at night.

The song was "Spring Will Be a Little Late This Year." Frank Loesser. End of WW II. The problem was that spring was early.

With a gentle pressure of a sixty degree day sliding in from the southwest – this in early March! – I had fallen into ancient lassitudes. Memory was pushing up like those tubers the poet mentions from soil softening for seed. Desire, abandoned in January, was rising like sap in the maples. Desire for what, though? No specific woman. They all lay back there in my long ago youth when they had permitted me to get laid on the regular basis that I had taken for granted back then. Back when. Now it was generalized, except when a very specific memory – a word, a gesture, the sound of a voice responding with a wordless vowel, the luminous flex of a naked back rising along its shadowy vertebrae from bed at dawn – punctuated my own unheard groans as I rose from a chair or sat down in it again. Groans had replaced the young man's sigh. The thoughts of youth may be long, long thoughts, but the joy of youth is that you aren't thinking at all.

I was thus musing and loafing into the early spring – and giving excuses to my puritan ancestral brain which was still demanding some measurable productivity from me – when the phone rang.

Ancient technology, I thought – not e-mail or texting – a telephone. All alone by the telephone. Irving Berlin could write that lyric almost a hundred years ago. I heard my cornet on the answering machine. Two bars of 'Oh Where, Oh Were, Has My Little Dog Gone?" then my voice saying, "Your little dog is not here." That defeated ninety per cent of callers. But this time I heard a voice.

"If this is Harry Chambers, this is Mim Hunter, Charlie's wife."

I picked up.

"Mim. Harry. Hi."

I had not met her. We had vowed to keep in touch, we four, but time and distance had eroded that promise. I knew that Charlie had married a younger woman, one of his students, and I had sent him a card congratulating him. I knew where that lucky dog had gone.

"Harry. Bad news, I'm afraid. Charlie died yesterday."

"Damn! How?"

"Car crash."

"Car crash? He was a great driver."

"I know. Went off the road and rolled down a hill. Mountain."

"Heart?"

"They say no."

"Mim. I'm so damned sorry."

"I know. You are the last."

The last. The four of us had met at Vance, gone through T-37s and T-38s together and, though luck and some pulling of strings, along with some reluctance, had flown the 105, the Thud, in Vietnam. The reluctance had been from Charlie and me who balked at becoming bomber pilots. But it was that kind of war, not Camels against Tri-Wingers or 51s fighting 109s or 86s squaring off against Mig 15s. The fighter had become a bomber.

"Harry. I have a problem."

"What?"

"Charlie and I had a joint account."

"And they won't let you touch it."

"Right. I ... ah... can't ask my parents..."

"What's the nearest airport when I can rent a car? Charlotte?"

"Greenville. But..."

"Your address?"

"Thirty three Crestview, but..."

"I can't be there before the banks close."

"No. I'm okay right now. Just..."

"Make me a reservation at the nearest motel."

"That would be Campus Corners on Merritt Avenue."

"Hold it on your card."

"I don't have one."

"Use Charlie's number then. They won't know the difference for a couple of days. I'll put it on mine when I get there. I'll see you in about four or five hours."

I made a call to General Aviation in Portland and another to my neighbor, on whose machine I left a message.

"Fill the tips and have a power cart ready for about 1400 hours."

"Ben. Got to go away on short notice. You've got Toby for a couple of days. I'll call you when I know when I'll be back. Thanks."

I gave Toby, my brilliant Irish Setter, a tousle under the chin, where he likes it, and a Milkbone on the porch.

"Back soon, Toby. Ben is in charge now."

And he understood. Toby made the shift from master to master effortlessly, just as long as there was one.

And, as I pointed the old Volvo south, I thought about those years.

The military has a way of pulling guys together. The main element is that they are in this together. That is about the only thing that gets anyone through training. Or at least so I think. I can't imagine a loner making it, though some must. Joe was a graduate of the Citadel, but for all of that, had a great sense of humor and only the impeccable posture that spoke of four years of standing at attention. Bob was an easy-going, mildly cynical guy from Westchester County and Williams College. Plenty of money. He didn't have to be here. Charlie was from Indianapolis and Indiana University and had been Big Ten singles champion in tennis. And I had dropped out of college with just enough credits to qualify for officer training and flight school. It was warm body time. Vietnam was beginning to exhaust the supply of body bags.

And so when we first showed up at the BOQ, each of us a newly-minted second lieutenant, we found ourselves sweating in the hallways of the second floor as we lugged our trunks into our rooms, showering in the steamy room in the center of the building, and heading over to the O-Club for a steak and several beers and air conditioning. We became a group. Nothing official, but it was accepted. We'd do what we could for each other from now on. We had no idea, of course, what that would be, but we did know that this flying training was not going to be, as they used to say, a piece of cake.

I had been the youngest by a couple of years. Now I was the last one left.

It was tricky. We did not want to engage the Migs flying out of Phuc Yen with all our ordinance hanging. They would force us to dump it in the jungle. Our mission was to hit selected targets, not trees and vines and exotic birds. During WW II, the Me 109s would leap into action from Holland and come up against bomber formations heading deep into Germany. The fighters accompanying the bombers would have to jettison their auxiliary fuel tanks. That cancelled their escort mission. But if we hugged the lee side of Thud Ridge – the mountains north of Hanoi that pointed directly toward the city and the port of Haiphong – we usually avoided contact with enemy aircraft on the way in.

If we flew too low, small arms zeroed in on us. We couldn't juke once we were on our bomb run. If we flew just above whatever cloud cover their might be, a SAM might tear out of the overcast and detonate before we had a choice of final words. So we would slide along Thud Ridge, sometimes a hard spiny backbone of rock, but usually half-concealed in mist – dive at 45 degrees, release our bombs and pull out with afterburners engaged. Back to Thailand, if we were lucky. We might have to play tag with some Migs along the way, but the 105 cleaned up was equal to the Mig. The problem was that by that time in our mission we would be low on JP-4. We could not hang around for dog-fights.

Most of us were not fighting the war we wanted to fight. That would have been WW II. We were not the 'greatest generation.' Nor were we Gertrude Stein's 'lost generation.' We were a small group of professionals trying to fight under rules of engagement that made us targets and for two corrupt regimes – one in Saigon and one in Washington. I, at least, existed in a kind of existential limbo, a non-zone from which whatever my humanity might be was totally alienated. The experience made me believe in the concept of soul. I had none while flying in Vietnam. I could sense its absence, even if at other times, I have never been able to detect its presence. I was Yeats' Irish Airman. I did not hate the enemy, even if he shot at me. It was his homeland. And I did not love those I guarded. I never knew what or who we were guarding. I recall a poster with LBJ's picture on it. 'This is the face you are saving.'

But we were the Four Mouseketeers, until one afternoon when I was intrail behind Bob, who had led us in and was pulling out. I hit the burner and pulled out behind him. His aircraft emitted a black poof and then became a flash against a gray sky. I had my visor down, but even then I had to blink away the luminous stain that had briefly spread across the sky. The explosion made no sound. None that reached me anyway. I broke right and felt fragments tap against my left wing. It was like driving through a burning house.

"Three and four, join up, orbiting right at 16 angels back to the Ridge," I said, having become flight leader.

There was nothing else to say.

Joe's ending was equally flashy. He was flying an F-5 during an advanced gunnery program at Nellis. Air to Ground. He flew his aircraft into the target. Target fixation, they call it. Rapture of the desert. Nothing left of him except the perfect score they would post for him on the chart in the flightshack.

And now, I was the last one left.

I could see my bird waiting as I pulled into General Aviation in Portland. Plenty of parking. People must have cut down on their flying in these trying times.

"Hi Mac," I said as I approached the counter on the left of the waiting room.

"Mr. Chambers. Your T-Bird is all set, sir."

"I'd better file IFR," I said. "That way I can fly above the weather they're having south of here."

"Yes sir. They are calling heavy storms from Baltimore to Atlanta."

I filed PMW to GSP. At 32 000 feet I could look down at the clouds dumping tons of snow on creatures there below. And no SAMs would be breaking through the clouds to try to blow me into bits of aluminum and rubber, flesh and bone.

I slung my duffle in the back seat and pulled the seat belt between the bag and the strap.

I still could not get used to climbing into a jet aircraft without fitting my chute into the hollow space in the ejection seat. But this version of the Tango Three Three had been totally refitted. The Martin Bakers had been replaced by luxurious leather seats – maybe even Corinthian, for all I knew. Only the front cockpit had a throttle and instrumentation -- the old-fashioned kind: altimeter, airspeed, vertical speed, needle and ball, and artificial horizon – and a stick, with the trim tabs under the right thumb. So this was no longer a trainer. But then I never took anyone else up with me.

When this aircraft had become available at CFB Mountain View, in Ontario, a couple of years ago, I had jumped on it.

"Another of Harry's toys," I could hear my ex-wife sneer, though I had not told her of this one. She resented my success after all those lean years of alimony and child support, when I'd had little to send, though it was pretty much all I had in those days.

I needed an outside source of power to get the turbo on the rebuilt Allison J-35 spinning. The unit was standing by as I began my preflight, mostly checking fuel in the tiptanks, making sure the wings were level (if one hydraulic strut was too high or too low the bird was difficult to taxi), looking at the inflation of the tires, and pulling out the various safety pins that kept the landing gear from folding up on the ground. As I reclimbed the ladder to the front cockpit, a man from Northeast Aviation came trotting out to run the power unit, remove the steel ladder from the side of the aircraft, and pull the chocks.

I taxied out, using the brakes at the top of the rudder pedals, and was cleared onto the runway. I held the brakes while I ran the power up. Newton's laws were still inviolable when an aircraft like this one is slow to develop any speed at all and get to the point where Bernoulli's Principle can lift the aircraft from the surly bonds of concrete. My knees! The pain radiated up to the base of my ancient spine.

"Cleared to roll, 687."

"Wilco. Thanks."

And I was on my way down the coast. I'd call Stevens Aviation at GSP to arrange for parking, refueling, and a car rental.

Now I could lean back and enjoy the flight in this stable, straight winged version of our first operational jet, still flying these sixty five years or so after Kelly Johnson's first test flight of the XP 80.

The coast with its silver cities opened up below me, but began to slide under cloud as I climbed toward my cruising altitude. It would probably be ILS into Greenville-Spartanburg, but that would be fun. I had not performed an instrument approach in a long time.

II.

Why had I acted so precipitately? "They say," she had said. The great "They" – who was doing the saying? That did not sound right to me. And – I had heard fear in her voice under those two syllables, more than that occasioned by the inconvenience of an unavailable bank account. And, of course, I could not ask why. I knew well enough that phones could be tapped.

The landing at Greenville/Spartanburg was easy enough. Just fly toward the two bars in the omni-screen. Crosswind and lashing rain, I kept the wing low once I spotted the runway, and got hit with a gust as I leveled off and rounded out. The straight wings and the empty tiptanks gave that wind a lot to lift. I kicked rudder and managed to touch down on the two main gear. Last thing I need, I thought, is a hard landing here in potentially enemy territory.

But I was met by a "Follow Me" truck which led me down the taxi strip, then came alongside and signaled me to stop.

I cracked the canopy.

"Shut her down there. We have a place in the hanger for you. We'll tow you in."

Now that was service! I'd pay for it, but so what? I could afford it. I even got an umbrella held over my head as I stepped from the hanger to my rental.

I drove the generic mid-size down the gusty road from Greenville, as rain filleted the clouds, past Brandon Mills, where Joe Jackson had lived and died, past the malls and car dealerships of Eagleville, and into the piney hills and

275

spiny mountains where nestled Valley Junction and Valley University, once a military school, now a football power that regularly sent semi-educated linemen to the NFL.

"You want to teach there?" I had asked Charlie, in one of our last conversations.

"A job. Have you any idea what academe is like these days? And the history department is not bad."

I drove deeper into an alien environment of roadside shacks and superbly maintained churches. Caesar was either being neglected down here, or Caesar lived in the white-columned, red-brick buildings of Evangelical Pentecostal Southern Deep-Fried Unreformed Baptist congregations. The shacks were probably leaking this evening. The churches were not.

And, after my redcarpet treatment at the airport, I became increasingly tense as I drove. Were people following too closely behind? That is something that ex-fighter pilots respond to with anxiety. No. What was it? Not just a reaction to a tricky landing. I had enjoyed that. Yes – it was like flying over enemy territory. You got a strange resonance from below. It was not just that people were throwing all kinds of nasty things at you, but that the very trees and bushes vibrated with hostility. Laugh those of you who have never had the experience.

And my situational awareness heightened with my tension. Nowadays, when 20/50 is eyesight good enough for a pilot and where guys sit in front of a radar screen and manipulate drones toward targets thousands of miles away, the pilot is a systems-manager. We were too, but we had to use our eyes. We had to see what was coming at us and, were it another aircraft, we had better damned well see him first. And some pilots no longer know how to fly. The pilot in a fatal USAir crash near Pittsburg a few years ago did exactly the wrong thing and executed a fraction of a split-s before his aircraft disintegrated against the ground. And, in the recent Buffalo commuter crash, the pilot responded to a stall warning by pulling back on the yoke. The proper technique is stick forward and opposite rudder against the direction of a likely spin. And the first officer compounded the problem by pulling up the flaps, canceling what little lift was left in those quivering wings.

As I drove on, I could not identify any specific source of danger, but I felt that this territory was threatening. And the threat was coming not just from below, but was all around me. Icarus, like most fighter pilots, felt his death coming from out of the sun. Just another old war movie.

As I listened to the whisk of the tires and stared at miles of pine trees and opulent churches between, I mused. I wonder whether others have been able to train themselves to wake up before the damned nightmare really takes over. I finally did manage to do that. It took time and a recurring dream. The dream was based on an actual event.

I was taking off from Don Muang one morning when the aircraft directly in front of me exploded. The first thing one might do in a case like that would be to pull back on the stick and try to fly over the fire. But I was just short of takeoff speed. So I held it down when every impulse was pleading with my right arm to pull back on the stick. I could feel the canopy in front of my face beginning to melt when I finally did yank the aircraft off of the ground and pulled my gear up. I staggered over the fire, held steady at about fifty feet to gain air speed, and finally began to climb. I looked back. A firetruck was rolling down a taxiway toward a burning squid of smoke on the runway, with just a trace of bone, and dead and pissed-off fighter pilot inside. Had I tried to pull up, of course, I would have become part of that mess. The problem was that, in my dream, I did.

I finally trained myself to wake up as the aircraft in front of me exploded. That saved me from the nightmare. It also meant a mostly sleepless night. I'd fall into a deep sleep again just before it was time to get up. But, at the time, that all seemed preferable to being in just another old war movie.

And, I thought to myself, you are not prone to daydreaming behind the wheel of a moving vehicle. Even if it's about nightmares. Focus!

I checked into Campus Corners and put the room on my credit card. But, I thought, I have inadvertently created a link between me and Mim Hunter. Was I being paranoid? Hell, yes. The clerk was sullen, a pasty-faced kid trying to grow a moustache and only calling attention to his failure. It was as if I were "one of them northern agitators sent here to stir up trouble." Perhaps I was.

I did not ask directions to Crestview, but consulted a map in the motel lobby. It was a relatively new development, to the right of a steep hillside, a couple of miles from the University. It consisted of homes that fell well below the level of elegance you would get in Rye, Darien, Gates Mills, La Due, or Far Hills, but homes of the well-heeled persons who taught and administered and coached a major sport at Valley State. I drove past the house, a modest white colonial with columns, turned around and parked two houses below Thirty three. I moved from there up the sidewalk under thick shadows drifting from oak trees.

Mim peeked out from the front door, then closed it and removed the chain.

"Sorry about Charlie," I said.

"Me too. Come on in."

The living room was on the left of the front hall. Mim indicated a chair.

"Want a drink?"

"I'm okay."

"You didn't have to come all the way here."

The light was dim, but I could see that Mim was a beauty, a classic brunette reminiscent of the early 40s movie stars. Vivien Leigh. Hedy Lamarr. Loretta Young. She was perhaps just over the edge of forty. But her face was pale, and dark circles formed half-moons under her eyes. Her mouth was sullen, as if she were angry with me.

"I did, though. Charlie was our leader."

"That's why you came?"

"No."

"Then why?"

I had a sudden thought. Mim was young. Her perception of the military had been conditioned by the post-Vietnam era, by the transition away from the draft to an anonymous all-volunteer force. My own perceptions had been formed by nostalgic echoes of WW II. The war had been terrible, as war is, but we had been fighting Nazi Germany and the atrocity-prone Japs. Gentlemen of Nippon, I mean. Serving in the military was at best questionable to her generation. She was, of course, a member of the me generation and could not have helped but pick up some of that self-centered ethic.

My God! She thinks I've come down here to get laid!

"You answered that question when you came to the door. It was chained. You bolted it again after I came in."

"I'm alone here, until I can find a place to go to."

"I grant that. But you are also scared."

"What business is that of yours?"

"Mim. I know we've never met, but Charlie..."

"So it's male bonding?" she said, sneering.

"Call it what you will. We relied on each other. It was more than, say, playing on a football team. We flew high performance air craft. We had to make quick decisions that dictated what happened to the rest of us. Life or death."

"And you lost Bob."

"Yes. And there wasn't a damned thing any of us could have done about it."

"I'm going to pour myself a Scotch. You sure you don't want one?"

"I'll join you. Ice, please. No water."

Mim was full of resentment. Or resentments. The air was thick with her anger and I felt it in the pit of my stomach. Not the least of them was probably that she was, for the moment, trapped right here, without resort to a bank account or a credit card.

She returned from the bar on one side of the fireplace and handed me my drink.

"The war didn't do any of us any good," I said.

"How well I know."

"I had nightmares – worse than that – flashbacks for years."

"So did Charlie. He'd wake up in a sweat shouting 'break left!' 'break right!' It would take me a half-hour to calm him down and get him to remember where he was."

"You didn't have children?"

"We were going to. Then he didn't get tenure at Monadnock. He searched for a year and this job came up."

"I didn't know it had been that bad."

"It took a year. They took him here because his book had just come out. And they needed someone in contemporary American history."

"And he got tenure."

"Yes. It was a fight. But the history department was for him. Teaching was great, insofar as they can measure something like that. And the book was very well-reviewed."

I had seen a review in the New York *Times* and had written Charlie to congratulate him.

"On F.D.R. and the entrance into WW II."

"Yes. The liberals thought it was balanced. The conservatives thought it indicted F.D.R. for manipulating us into war. After all these years, they still hate him. But, anyway, to answer your question, no, we did not get around to having children. We were too busy scrambling. I was a hostess at a restaurant for a couple of years before we came to this..."

She waved the back of her right hand dismissively.

"And then he started getting into trouble for his so-called liberal views. He wrote a long piece about No Child Left Behind for *The Nation*, arguing that the law was designed to destroy public education and encourage charter schools and other forms of privatization."

"They didn't like that down here?"

She rolled her eyes.

"They thought that the destruction of public education was a good idea. And they teach at a public university! Like people on Medicare complaining about a government takeover of health care. But the real issue was that an ex-combat type is supposed to be a patriot. He wrote another long piece for *New York Review* suggesting that the primary beneficiary of our invasion of Iraq was Iran."

"Isn't that obvious?"

"Harry. You are in the northwest corner of South Carolina. Redneck territory. Once a Klan stronghold. The administration of Valley State is solidly right-wing Republican. Can you imagine how they responded to Obama's election?"

"And, of course, none of those guys had ever served in the military."

"The administrators? They had other priorities. Sure, the town has some veterans. Mostly Vietnam. Charlie knew them. The last WW II vets are in nursing homes."

"Why are you afraid?"

"More?'

"A touch. I'll get it. You?"

"Sure."

I poured more scotch into her glass, the ice cubes now looking like ancient windowpanes.

I filled my glass half full and sat down.

"Because I think Charlie was murdered," she said.

III.

"Rusty?"

"That's me."

The owner of Rusty's Body Shop and Tow was a visualization of his trade. His hair was the color of the underside of a not-so-old Subaru.

"I'm Harry Chambers. I was a friend of Charlie Hunter's. Flew with him. I understand you pulled his car up from the bottom of Warlock Mountain."

"Yeah."

"I had a couple of questions I wanted to ask you."

Rusty moved his head toward the back of the garage and turned in that direction. I followed.

I had counted out five one hundred dollar bills on the coffee table in Mim's living room.

"No rush in paying me back."

"As soon as I can get the bank..."

"Would you like me to come with you and see them?"

"No."

This was absolute.

"I'm sorry. What I mean is that the banker is one of the Born Again types who infest this place. If he saw you, he'd resist as much as he could, draw all kinds of wrong conclusions, and who knows what else."

"Okay. What bank is it?"

"Bank of America."

Of course. Virtually a local.

"Except when it chooses not to be," she said.

"Mim. I will make a call. General Roberts, whom we four knew once upon a time, is on the board. I won't do anything that would complicate things."

For the first time, she showed a spark of some vital energy beneath the dark exterior.

"Great! I'd appreciate it. I want to get out of here. Sell the house, of course. This is the first place we've ever owned. But just get out of here for now."

"Where?"

"Haven't even thought of that yet."

"Where did they take Charlie's car?"

"His car?"

"His car."

"Why do you ask?"

"If, as you suspect..."

"Yes. His car could have been tampered with. I thought they might have drugged him. Too damned convenient that he was killed that way. It was an ancient Mercedes. He took care of it. It should have been in perfect condition. Rusty's Towing Service. State road 23."

Rusty walked over to a fence that cast about ten feet of shadow into a yard filled with old cars that, at some point, someone had probably planned to get back on the road again. Now they were a collective time capsule for space explorers two thousand years from now, to whom they would be as primitive as would be the chariots that attacked Troy to us.

"No thanks," I said, as he held a pack of Lucky Filters toward me.

"Not that there's no smoking in there," he said. "Just that there's too much vapor in the atmosphere."

So, he was taking his smoke-break.

"Look, mister, anyone finds out I talked to you..."

"Don't worry."

"Well, I do, but what happened is wrong."

"How so?"

"Doc Hunter took care of that car like it was like a newborn babe. Old Mercedes. Brakes were fixed."

"Fixed?"

"Most of the fluid was drained. He'd get positive response until he really needed them, then..."

"How could anyone know when he'd need them?"

"Couldn't, unless someone knew which way he'd be going. He'd stop at a stop sign on Clerwood Avenue. He'd stop for the light on the turn to Valley Highway. He'd go up the hill and then hit the steep downgrade that heads toward the turn halfway down."

I remembered that turn just from the one time I had gone down that hill.

"No brakes."

He pushed a pillar of smoke out and nodded.

"He'd pull the gearshift into Park," I said.

"He did. Car swerved to the right and rolled through the fence at the turn."

"Damn! Who...?"

"Told you what likely happened to the car. That's all."

He put his cigarette out between thumb and forefinger, stripped the cigarette, rubbed his fingers together, and flipped it toward a 1955 Ford convertible, once maroon, now the color of dried mud. The exposed seats had popped open and looked like bloated fists.

"You were in the Army," I said.

"Once upon a time. Why I am telling you this. He was a veteran too. Amazing how few of us there are anymore."

Fewer and fewer, I thought.

"Thanks," I said, holding a twenty dollar bill toward him.

"That's okay, mister. We were both there, Charlie and me. He used to stand me to a beer or two at the VFW."

As I drove away, I thought of Charlie at the VFW. Officer. Captain. Ph. D. But I understood. The VFW would be combat veterans, mostly grunts, mostly Vietnam types. If you were with them, you knew where you were. Almost anywhere else was enemy territory.

I visited Mim again the next evening.

"Thanks," she said. "The bank was obsequious in its apologies."

"I assume our old pal gave them a call."

"They didn't say. I didn't ask."

I had noticed a room beyond the living room, a pine paneled den.

"May I?" I asked, pointed in that direction.

"Of course."

She followed me.

Yes, in glass cases between shelves of books, were Charlie's trophies. Silver platters and cups and a lot of golden tennis players on top of marble pedestals. And, yes, there was the one I was looking for.

I opened the case and pulled out one of those players, hitting an overhead it seemed on top of a marble base.

"Command Doubles Champion, 1970. Lt. Charles Emory Hunter."

"I have one of these," I said.

"You do! Oh!" Mim said. "Look!"

She pointed at a photo, black and white, of two smiling and sweaty guys, holding right armsful of racquets and clasping their trophies.

"I knew you looked familiar."

We'd played the match in prairie heat against a couple of wily veterans from Randolph. They were older than we were, but they'd played together for years and moved before we even hit a shot to the place where the shot was going. They watched our racquets. And if we changed a stroke in midswing the ball usually went into the net or over the baseline.

Charlie was the best player on the court, but this was doubles. A good doubles team can negate a good singles player easily enough except when he serves. Hit to the weaker player. After a while, he will know that he is letting his partner down. His game will disintegrate. I had a good backhand return of service, a chip that would force an opponent coming up to hit a low volley or a half-volley that permitted us to get to the net. Usually, the stronger player played the ad-court, but my backhand return of service found me over there.

It was a struggle. They were pounding me. We were up 5-4 in the third set. It was hot. The hard surface held the heat close, with no breeze to waft it through the fence. I was in great shape, but exhausted by this time. I hadn't played competitive tennis since I'd been on the second doubles team at Hadley and that meant that I had to readjust to the tension attendant upon playing in a match. It takes some energy just to get used to competition again. And those who have experienced even playing in their club tournaments know what I mean. My throat was dry, my right elbow frail. My feet were on burning coals.

But Charlie and I played well together. He held serve. He poached expertly. We played as a team. I realized that this match marked the beginning of the kind of confidence we'd have in each other later on, when we flew a few feet away from each other, responding with minute adjustments of stick and throttle to the nuances of high speed combat. This match was our Playing Fields of Eton. But if I had to hold serve in the next game it would be our Waterloo as well.

The guy serving, a lean, skinny man who looked like Don Maynard, had a nasty semi-twist serve, an old-fashioned doubles serve that bounced high to my backhand. I could chip it back, but it was a defensive return and it drove me out of the court. He began to wait for it so that he could hit a forehand down the middle, which Charley had to cover with his backhand. That tended to set them up nicely to take control of the rally.

We had a chance to break service for the match. And, I figured, we had better. With my serve coming up, the sun would be driving through the prairie dust into my eyes as I tossed the ball up. I'd be lucky not to double fault to the backhand side. Hold serve? I doubted it. These thoughts crossed my mind as I prepared to return at 30-40. Match point.

So I said the hell with it. I rolled my grip around to flatten out my stroke, stepped into the serve before it had a chance at that high bounce, and swung. This was that every-once-in-a-while. My return streaked between the two sun-burned old men across the net and made a lovely skid-mark well inside the baseline.

"Nice shot!" Charley said, laughing. "If you can hit a backhand like that..."

Why don't you hit it all the time?

"I can't," I said.

"Good match," said the other guys. And it had been. I found out later that they had been Command champions several times and USAF champions only a few years before. I am glad I hadn't known until later.

"Like yesterday," I said, looking at the photo. "Some things still seem so close in time."

"I know," Mim said.

The VFW was on a highway out of town – my perception was that all roads here seemed to be going out of town. Valley Junction, home to a long-ago railroad, was blighted by the usual clutter of selfserve gas stations, fast food drivethroughs, and cheap motels among the thousand wires hanging from the poles on the state roads running out of town like metastasis. The main street was a boarded-up wasteland of abandoned stores, broken neon, empty parking slots, and fading signs suggesting that the hope with which those new businesses – the grocery, the men's shop, and the drug store -- had opened had departed at least a decade or so ago. The University had spawned few of the amenities that one would find in Champagne-Urbana, Cambridge, or Princeton. Among the pines, after the dismal stretch and greasy stink of a series of Quik Lubes, Tastee Burgers, and A-1 Used Cars, and, it seemed, a colony of grossly obese women wandering within this wilderness, the VFW came up on my right. It was a frame structure with a bunch of down-at-the-rim pickups in front. I thought for a moment that I was back at Rusty's Body Shop and Tow.

The building had a front hallway along which ran a row of one-armed bandits, a big dancefloor through a door to the left, and a bar through a door to the right.

I blinked the late afternoon sun from my eyes and went into the bar. Already, several men bent over it, while a few others sat at the small tables against the far wall. The men all wore baseball caps and all seemed to be so skinny that a shadow would be a hard throw. It was quiet. A thin blanket of smoke undulated under the low ceiling.

I slid onto a barstool, took out my wallet, and fished out my VA card.

I held it up to the bartender, a big guy with a veiny nose and a boulder-like paunch.

"Sure, pal. What'll you have?

"Anything on draft?"

"R. J. Rockers and Thomas Creek Ale."

"Rockers, please," I said, assuming that was a beer.

It was. I glanced around, hoping to spot Rusty, the guy I'd talked to the day before.

Luck was with me. He was at one of the tables about fifteen feet from me.

I held a very tentative hand up and gave it a wave. He gave me a hard stare in return. Okay. It had been worth a try. And I had realized what a futile try it would be even as I had entered the building. But I did not know where to begin. And I did not want to just leave. I was the last one left and that fact imparted certain responsibilities. But what could I do?

I turned back to the bar and jiggled my empty glass.

"Good beer," I said.

"They make a good beer down here," the bartender said. "Didn't used to."

Someone leaned toward the bar over the stool next to me.

"I gotta be cautious," he said without turning his head.

Rusty.

"Guy I want you to meet. But not right here. Meet me at my place in half an hour."

"Yeah, two more, Walter," he said to the bartender.

Rusty's was north of town. The place was closed, but I entered his office, the walls covered with old license plates and ancient calendars with drawings of girls with impossibly long legs dangling from their one-piece bathing suits.

"This here is Billy Phelps. Sorry, don't recall your name."

"I'm Harry Chambers," I said, grasping the calloused hand of a sad-eyed man with a long, stringy, white beard. The face said Vietnam.

"Thought Billy might have something to tell you."

"I work over at the University," Billy said. "Custodial. I clean at night in the Rivers Building, where all the administration offices are. Those guys with the fancy degrees don't pay much attention to a guy pushing a mop. But sometimes they meet at night. I'd say secret meetings, at least nothing to do with whatever the University is doing when it ain't football season."

He pulled a pack of Camels from his shirt pocket and held it out to me.

"No thanks, Billy. I kicked the habit."

"I've done that about fifty times," he said, laughing and lighting up with a snort of blue smoke.

"Anyways, Rusty here tells me you were a friend of Doc Hunter's. Now he was not like the rest of them. Maybe it's because he was in the service. And I heard his name a couple of times. It was not spoken in a kindly way."

"Do you know who?"

"Sure. Dr. Devaney. He's head of the history department. And Dean Whittler. He's head of humanities, or something like that."

"You say, 'not in a kindly way'?"

"It sounded like 'got to get rid of him.' I did hear, 'he's a trouble-maker.'"

"I guess that 'got to get rid of him' could have meant fire him," I said.

"Sure. But if I understand it, they couldn't just fire him."

"He had tenure."

"Right. Whatever that means – like belonging to a union, I guess – you can't just can a guy like that."

"You're right, Billy. They'd have to have a good reason and it would involve a process."

"A trial?" Billy asked.

"Like that. A hearing at least."

"Court Martial," Rusty said.

"Yeah. Like that," I said. "How long ago did you hear these guys talking?"

"Late last month."

"Did you hear anything else?"

"No. As I say I was cleaning. They told me to turn off the waxer. Funny, that's how I heard them talking."

"Do you know the reason for the meetings?"

"Yeah. Something called Stand for America."

"I am the resurrection and the life, saith the Lord."

The words came suddenly, as if the Lord were speaking over the organ prelude and the Anglican service, with its stately poetic cadence began.

The Episcopal Church was one of the smaller ones in town, a pseudo-Tudor structure near the University with beams encased in mortar. It looked like no other church in the area. The morning light slanted in, purple and red from the stained glass. The storm that had consumed the sky above the eastern seaboard a few days ago had dispersed into wispy, fair-weather clouds.

The contingent from the University sat in the front center section of the church. At least I assumed that is who they were, dressed in sober suits and ties or somber suits and blouses. Others, the women in plain almost workaday dresses and the men in shirts and with baseball caps doffed, sat in the pews on the left or right of the two aisles. The social and educational distinctions were made clear just by the unofficial but tacit seating chart.

A polished wooden coffin covered with a blanket of flowers sat just in front of the steps leading up to the altar.

Mim sat with two women friends in a front pew. I sat toward the rear in the center. I saw Rusty and Bill and I spotted Devaney from Mim's description. Yes, a portly, red-faced man in a vested suit that merely called attention to his paunch and the strain of the buttons of the vest to keep it contained. His wife was a tiny birdlike woman who pecked at the hymnal as if the notes were so many seeds. I did not see Dean Whittler.

"Should I invite Devaney back to the house?" Mim had asked me.

"Yeah. I may have a chance to talk to him."

"That means he'll have to go to the burial as well."

"Yes. But he can't very well say no, can he."

"And he won't. He knows that Charley liked good Scotch."

And so, after Charley was buried amid the waft of blossoming dogwood and cherry trees on a beautiful hillside overlooking the Little Palmetto River, under the final plaintive note of "Taps" – which was the only military touch that Mim had permitted --the small group that had come out to the graveyard drove back to Crestview.

"Yes, sir," I said, responding to Devaney's question. "Charley and I flew together in Vietnam."

"I hear he was a great pilot."

"The best. Of course, it's easier in combat."

"It is?"

"Sure. So many things you can't do anything about. We were always afraid we'd get killed in a training accident. Most pilots do. Routine. That would be very frustrating in a posthumous sort of way. Our flightmate, Joe, was killed on a practice gunnery run in Nevada. Combat is not relaxing, don't get me wrong, but you don't sweat the small stuff. You embrace a version of fatalism."

"Stoicism."

"No. You do try to extricate yourself from an emergency. Stoics don't believe in ejection seats."

He looked at me with surprise. A former fighter pilot who was also a philosopher?

"Of course," I continued, taking advantage of this sudden opening, "I did not share Charley's politics."

"Oh?" he said neutrally.

"I'm afraid I'm one of those old-fashioned patriots you read about. I know how that must sound to a university professor like yourself."

"You believe that we are all liberals?"

A woman Mim had hired came by with some hot cheese on toast and we each munched for a moment. I saw Mim talking to Rusty. Bless her heart, she had asked him to come. And, bless his heart, he had.

"I guess," I said, treading carefully. "I mean you hear of, say, history departments being full of card-carrying New Dealers."

"Don't believe all you hear."

"Gotta be getting along."

It was Rusty.

"You stayin' long?"

"No, Rusty. I'll be leaving soon myself. Got Charley buried. Not much else to do here."

We shook hands. He nodded at Devaney and turned away.

I waited. If I seemed too eager to pursue this conversation, Devaney would see right through me. He might be a drunk, but he was no fool.

I reached past him and grabbed the bottle of Black Label and poured myself a refill.

"More?" I asked.

He held his glass out and rattled the ice cubes.

"Please."

"What is your area in history?"

"Early American. I wrote my dissertation on Hamilton."

"Great man. What would have happened to us had he not set up the federal banking system?"

Again, surprise.

"Yes, and he was the last of the aristocrats. He also favored federal intervention in favor of business."

"Me too. That concept is making a comeback. Though I'm not an expert like you. I don't find the doctrine of separation of state and church in the Constitution."

"No. That comes from that scoundrel Jefferson."

"I'm wondering, Dr. Devaney. I live an isolated life in a lot of ways. Is there any sort of formal opposition being formed? I don't mean the Republicans, or the Tea Partiers, or the militias. I mean something with intellectual weight along the lines of ..."

"A political action committee?"

"I guess, as opposed to a thinktank like American Enterprise."

"Yes. Ginni Thomas has formed Liberty Central."

"Clarence's wife."

"That's right. We are having her down here next month to speak."

"The history department?"

"No. Smaller group. We call it Stand Up for America."

"Good for you. I'm sorry I'm headed north in a day or two."

"I suppose it would be all right," he said to himself.

"What would?"

"Sorry. I tend to talk to myself."

I understood. I had seen his pecky little wife.

"But, look," he said. "I must be cautious. Still, I suppose it would be all right. Would you like to sit in on a meeting? As my guest? Just to observe? I think we think along the same lines and your service to your country speaks volumes. I did not have the privilege..."

"Don't apologize. It's not for everybody."

Vietnam was mostly for poor kids who did not have any protection against the draft or a few like me who had a couple years of college and thus could qualify for OCS. And the professional soldiers. Westmoreland. Devaney had obviously not been in any of those groups. Other priorities, but I did not condemn anyone who had opted out of that war.

"But, yes," I said, before the invitation could be retracted. "I would be honored."

IV.

I remembered only a fraction of the dream. I was looking out a window. A very threatening man stood there. I did not dare go outside. I looked out again and a pudgy man was standing there. He asked someone out of camera range where he could leave a present for me. The threat had dissolved within the dream. But Mim was also there. I had been waiting for her while looking out the window.

Okay, fella, I said to myself upon awakening. She is beautiful. But ignore that. Ignore the fact that her beauty has invaded your dreams. You have other things to do. The song that accompanied these thoughts was "Begin the Beguine." Delay the beguine, I said to myself. Delay? No. Cancel it.

The part of the campus to which Devaney had directed me was virtually dark. I did find the Stetson Administration Building, though, a new spick and span brick edifice with white columns in front. This opulence squandered on clerks made me suspect the validity of dear old Valley U. Its reputation and its reality seemed to coincide.

I went up through minimal lighting to the second floor, to the Hasbie Room, at which, fortunately, Devaney had already arrived.

Devaney introduced me to Dean Whittler.

He was a tall, stooped man, very thin. But what I noticed most about him was that he seemed to have to force his head up from his concave chest. When he did, his dark eyes were hostile between the sharp bone of his nose. He looked like an angry bird of prey. I noticed that his apparent hostility was not just directed at me. I would have hated to hear him laugh. I seldom take an instant dislike to anyone, but I did to him. And his nasal complaint of a voice only deepened my own hostility. No wonder he had been Charlie's enemy. I had no trouble assigning that role to Whittler. He would have hated a successful teacher who also had a couple of medals, a beautiful wife, a heralded book, and a progressive mindset.

Devaney turned to the long table, where eight men sat. All wore suits and ties. I thought that I might be at a Secret Service briefing or an FBI seminar.

"I bring a friend, who is sympathetic to our cause. Former Air Force Captain Harry Chambers."

"Weren't you a friend of Hunter's?" Whittler asked, bringing his head up toward me as he sat down at the head of the table. It was a strange, contradictory rhythm, as if two parts of his body were resisting each other.

"Yes, sir, I was. But we did not share the same political positions."

A couple of sour chuckles came from the men at the table.

"I should hope not," the Dean said. "Well, sit over there."

He waved a backhand at a row of chairs by the side of the room.

"That is, until we go into executive session."

Devaney looked at me, a hint of apology in his eyes.

"All right. Has Mrs. Thomas been contacted?"

"Yes, Dean," said one of the men. "She's given us a couple of dates when she will be available."

"Good."

"The problem is that she wants $150 000 to speak."

"What?"

"That's right."

"Damn! Well then, we won't have her speak. We will have her come to tell us about organizing a Liberty Center."

"It's called Liberty Central."

"Whatever it is. She would not be enough of a draw for us to get close to $150 000. We'll pay air fare and put her up at the Dobbs Campus Center. Luxury suite."

"I still think we should have invited Sarah Palin," said one of the men.

"We discussed that," Whittler replied testily. "We do not want to call too much attention to ourselves at this point. And that is all she does."

"She brings people."

"Yes. But with Mrs. Thomas we are talking about a vote on the Supreme Court. Roe v. Wade. Prayer in schools. Second Amendment. I remind you that we are working behind the scenes to protect what we believe in. We are not going to follow that broad from the North Pole over a waterfall."

Just then a high whine pierced through the room.

"Dammit!" Whittler screeched. "Tell that man to turn off that infernal machine!"

A man rose from the table and went out into the hallway. The machine stopped. The man returned.

"All right. Get back to Mrs. Thomas, Peter. Stress the Liberty Center aspect and our interest in it. If she's serious about it, she'll come. And, Ralph, contact the groups at State and Saint Malcolm's. We will want to meet in July or August. Any weekend as of now. Oh yeah, and Southern Military Academy too."

"Will do," said a man to Whittler's right, jotting on a notepad.

"Now, we are going in to executive session."

I got up.

"Thank you, gentlemen. Inspiring," I said. "And best of luck in your endeavors."

I walked out and passed Bill Phelps, pushing one of those giant, janitorial mops down the hallway. I gave him a quick nod, no more than a great man of the university would bestow on a serf.

I got an amused smile back from within the wilderness of his white beard.

I doffed my jacket and tie, tossed them in the back of my rental, and popped a "V U" baseball cap on my head.

"Hey, Walter. Rockers draft, please."

I had had a couple of beers by the time Billy Phelps came in.

He slid in next to me at the bar without acknowledging my presence.

"Buy you a beer?"

"Don't see why not," he said.

"Pitcher of Rockers, please, Walter. And a glass for this gentleman."

The place was relatively deserted, so Billy and I wandered over to a small table at the end of the room, with no one on either side of us.

"Wish I'd recorded it," Billy said, rubbing his hand down his beard after his first deep swallow.

"What'd they say?"

"That's why I wish I'd recorded it. I couldn't make much out of it."

"Let's figure it out."

"Okay." He shrugged as if to signal the impossibility of my suggestion.

"Boils down to this. Do we want to be effective? Are we effective if we just act. Or do we have to let the world know about it. They fought back and forth about that like two dogs fighting over a juicy bone. Whittler said no, and I think it was left at that."

"I have a hunch."

"What's that?" he asked.

"Okay. Let's assume they knocked Charlie off and made it look like an accident. They get rid of a perceived enemy. Right?"

"Sure."

"But, if it looks like an accident, they don't get any credit. After some awful bombing, some organization usually claims credit. Right?"

"Yeah. IRA. Al Queda."

"And why do they do that."

"Show their power."

"Exactly. We can hit anywhere, any time. That makes people afraid. Fear is the great political tool in our democracy these days, and has been for most of history."

"So, if they make it look like an accident..."

"Right. People may be afraid of brake failure in an old Mercedes but not of Stand Up for America."

"The idea is, we can get you too," he said.

"Right. So you overheard a philosophical argument."

"Well, they didn't reach any agreement."

"From what I saw, Whittler seems to control that group. I think they'll stay undercover for a while. They are still organizing."

"By the way, Mr. Chambers..."

"Harry," I said, pointing at myself. "We are both veterans. No rank in here."

"Okay, Harry. One guy who was there was Ralph Blanchard. He owns the foreign car dealership in Eagleville."

"And he sells Mercedes."

"Yeah. Thought you'd like the connection."

"Billy, it's beginning to add up. But, the question is, what the hell do we do about it?"

"Can't just let it rest."

"No. But we can't take the next step without really thinking about it. Oh, is the local banker a member of the group? I was only introduced to Whittler."

"Spence Winesap? Yeah. I've seen him there. Don't think he was there tonight, though."

Bill had placed me in a room next to the Hasbie Room. It was actually a closet and it stank of dried mops and pine-scented cleaning compound. But the sound from the Hasbie Room came in through a vent in the wall. Neither room would be disturbing to the other in the academic scheme of things, unless the mops got loose.

And I could picture some of the people there. Two, at least – Devaney with his husky, Scotch-inflected tonality, wise and cautious, and Whittler, whose voice fell just short of dog-whistle range, a whine of venom and complaint.

I heard the minutes of the meeting I had attended. The minutes ended with "The Committee then moved into executive session." Damn! A financial report. The latter revealed that the primary funding for the group came from Blanchard's foreign car dealership in Eagleville. The Treasurer, I assumed, was Winesap, the local banker. It was a voice that spoke from the subtext of superior knowledge deigning to show patience for mere mortals.

"I think that we have to move, as we discussed last time in executive session."

That was Whittler.

"Shouldn't we go into executive session?" someone asked.

"Not necessary," Whittler said. "Unless someone has any objections. We know what we are talking about here."

"No," Devaney said. "We have already thrown caution to the winds. Had it not been that Chief Dobler called it an accident..."

"Quiet!" Whittler cut in. "Of course it was an accident. That is official. We can't let any questions arise on that score."

"But that is precisely what this friend of his is doing," said the voice I assumed to be Winesap's. He had come down from Olympus. He was afraid. I suppose that even bankers can know fear.

"Yes," said Whittler, "and that is precisely why we have to do something about him."

"Scare him," Devaney said.

"He's like Hunter, I'm afraid," said another voice.

"Yes. I don't think he'll scare," Whittler said. "Don't forget, Hunter's wife is involved too."

Several voices mumbled in agreement.

"He is a threat to us," Whittler said.

"But surely not as much as Hunter was," Devaney said.

"No," Whittler agreed. "Had that report he wrote gotten out..."

"We don't know what was in it," Devaney said.

"We know that it existed. We know he did a lot of research. We know he knew enough to blow us out of the water. Name names. Outline our agenda."

Now I knew that they had killed Charley. And now I knew why. I wanted to burst out of that stinking closet and into that stinking room. But I stayed still and took my breath in snippets.

I prayed for a motion to adjourn, but could not introduce that myself.

This group was forming under cover of the Tea Partiers. The latter have a legitimate grievance – they are getting ripped off -- but they have been worked up to attack the wrong targets. Stand Up for America knew who the beneficiaries of recent policy were. None of these people was wealthy from a big city standpoint, but down here they were the carriage trade, the bankers, auto dealers, farm equipment sellers, and the fatcats who sponged up the big salaries at the local university. And they promoted the exchange of wealth that had been occurring steadily since Reagan. Tax cuts! Trickle down. The Tea Partiers were pissed off, but they did not recognize who was pissing on them. Even Obama cooperated with the real agenda, via Wall Street and the pharmaceuticals. But a black man as President! That awakened all the dormant rage living deep in the American psyche. It did not matter whether Obama were facilitating the shoveling of wealth into the wagons of the already wealthy. He was black!

When James Meredith set foot on the Ole Miss campus that night in 1963, the seethe of outrage surprised even the local cops. What he was doing was treading on "Ole Miss" – the name the slaves gave to the wife of the plantation owner. It was an archetypal rape that aroused the deepest racist response. Miscegenation! Violation! Obama was producing the same result.

These guys might have been Tea Partiers with a Valley U degree, even a Ph. D. in a couple of cases. But they were murderous thugs.

Michael Sandel says something about a society's failure to punish crime. Insofar as we don't punish crime, we encourage it. With Bush, Cheney, Rumsfeld, Addington, Wolfowitz, and Dickie Pearle running around free. others are licensed to shout racial slurs, spit on elected representatives, and murder those who might expose them. This particular group yearned for the vicious control that Lynch Law had given their great grandfathers. And they might regain that lost world. They had the power. They had the money. And, as it has always been, money is power these days.

Finally, I slipped out of the building, smelling like an old mop. I wondered how they had sniffed me out so easily. Devaney. His seeming reluctance to have me at that meeting had covered for his suspicions. And Whittler must have realized immediately that I represented a threat. I'm glad I had found out. I was definitely in enemy territory. The problem was that, while I could easily evade and escape, I had to stick around.

"Mim. Did Charley keep backup files for his work?"

"I'm sure he did. But that would have been at the University."

"Has anyone... ah... cleaned out his office yet?"

"I got a lot of boxes – books and papers yesterday. In the garage."

"Let's look."

It was sad, leafing through the work of a brilliant man who would do no more. And so much of what he had written remained unpublished! It was yesterday.

Mim left abruptly. I did not blame her.

I did not find anything resembling an expose of Stand for America. I might have been wrong in believing that such a piece existed. But it must have! They would have killed him just because he disagreed with them. They did kill him, didn't they? Suddenly I had no reinforcing sense that even that was true.

"Damn!" I said, coming back into Mim's kitchen.

"I could have someone check his computer."

"Okay," I said.

The next morning I got a call at my motel.

"You remember meeting Michael Howe?" Mim asked.

"Yes. After the funeral. Guy with glasses."

He was a slight man with glasses so thick that talking to him was like an undersea experience. That is why I remembered him.

"I had him check Charley's computer. All deleted."

"I wonder whether that is SOP in a case like this."

"That doesn't matter now."

"I guess not."

"What were you looking for?"

"I think Charley wrote something about Stand for America, detailed, carefully researched. It they killed him…"

"If?"

"We don't have anything we can take to a judge. But, that would have been why."

And, of course, motive is not something that you could take to a judge either.

It did look like a dead end.

I had had time to hit the last number I'd called on my cell phone – what would that have been? – as the car forced me off the road. I skidded on some gravel and almost rolled over. But I did not go into the woods. I tossed the cell phone under the front seat just before a couple of guys with .45s approached my car.

"Okay. Out of the car!"

The voice carried the semi-professional toughness of a former cop. Probably one of the security personnel from Spence Winesap's bank or a watchman at the Eagleville Foreign Cars Depot.

I was turned around, patted down, and blindfolded.

"Jim. You take his car. Park it in front of his motel room."

"Yes sir!"

I had been coming back from the VFW, through a lonely stretch of pines a mile or so from the beginning of the greasy spoon and grease-job strip, when I'd been stopped.

The segment of SERE that I had taken at Fairchild AFB, in Washington state, had a section called "What to do after capture." It still assumed capture by a military authority and was still predicated on capture by the Chinese. It went back to Korea, of course, and it may well have been a rare instance of fighting the next war before it starts, but it had not envisioned jihadists or simple kidnap. We were still told to retain our parachutes, which made splendid temporary shelters and also great signals to friendly searchers if spread out over desert or rock. They were not as good in jungle, but could be used to barter with neutral tribesmen. We were told, of course, to preserve our body moisture.

Right now, I was sweating, but I could not instruct my pores to cease and desist.

I could listen. We were still on pavement. The car was quiet. No new car smell, but it was obviously an excellent vehicle. The doors had clunked with solidity when closed. Ah yes – a Mercedes!

I was wedged in the back seat between the two security types. The one on my right reeked of cigarette smoke.

The car slowed and turned on to a rougher road. The tires ground in gravel and small stones. We dipped in an out of potholes. We were going up.

The car stopped.

I was led up some steps into a house, sat down in a wooden chair, and tied firmly to it, arms around the back of the chair, ankles tied to each of the front legs. I flexed my right arm – my tennis arm – as the rope surrounded it, but the guy had seen that before. He gave the bicep a judo chop and deflated its intention.

Then all three men left. I could tell that I was alone.

Good – that meant that they had not decided what to do with me. Someone must be holding out on just killing me. Or – they were setting up a plan to make my death look accidental. So – I had time. A few hours. Or, like a man condemned, until dawn.

I began to work on the ropes. They would not budge.

V.

"I think he was murdered."

That told me why I had come. But it was more than that. I had settled into a comfortable life. The world was crumbling around me, but I had money enough and could take the trips I wanted to take. Mostly to Spain, to Sevilla, to stay in the Alfonso Trece for the April feria and wander up the edge of the Guadalqivir to La Maestranza and watch the bulls and the matadors in their afternoon ballet of blood and death.

And I finally had the time to sit down and read Shakespeare. Not for a course, just for the sheer wonder of it.

But I realized that I had become another passive observer – if I were observing anything – of the meaningless flow. Kids hid their ears under Walkmans and stared at the tv or computer screens. Bankers behaved as if they had done everyone a favor in having us save them. The adolescent fever of self-indulgence and recklessness had migrated up to adults. Or, this of crop adults had dragged adolescence with them as they aged. Ronald Reagan. Little Bush. Bill Clinton, for that matter. And I had become one of them even while congratulating myself on not being like that. I did it my way, I said to myself, strokingly and soothingly. But I was just as solipsistic as the next person. Nothing exists unless I see it, feel it, taste it. I had become a self-indulgent slob.

The only thing I had accomplished was to discover that wonderful vein of music running under the garbage dump of stuff written since the 1960s (with few exceptions). And that had put me in touch with a culture in which wit and talent had been part of most people's lives. And it had not been a phony nostalgia. I had also become aware of poverty, lynch law, and a weekly dose of executions. But I also watched Turner Classic Movies.

But Mim's call had made me remember another time in my life, when I'd been responsible for more than my own sorry ass, and where others had been responsible for me. How far I had drifted from those few intense years! It had begun with my marriage. I had still been in the service and had fallen for the first good looking woman I had seen after getting back from 'Nam. Mistake. And that, I think, is when my selfishness began. But I did not revisit the years of that marriage. And that unwillingness, too, was a form of self-indulgence.

And now I was feeling the bristles of rope dig into my wrists as I wrestled against myself.

I had determined early on that our mission in Vietnam was not just futile but probably criminal. The guys in uniform did not deserve the blame, though they were easy targets according to the apocryphal stories that emerged. It was Rusk the ideologue, determined not to commit a Munich, who equated the rice-growing peninsula of the 1960s to the industrialized Europe of the 1930s, who made the mistake. The better analogy was our ally, Yugoslavia, just below the Soviet Union. And it was McNamara who quantified the war. I saw a cartoon after he died of his headstone facing the Vietnam memorial: "Final Review."

So I got out of USAF, went back to Hadley for a desultory couple of years, during which I played tennis and squash and hung out at the VFW over in Fairview. They didn't resent officers, once you got to know them. I had found the fraternity scene intolerable. Only a few years from being a frat boy, I discovered that they promoted sexism, racism, and alcoholism. I found that I had unlearned racism in the military. Sexism would take a while. And alcoholism could bide its time.

I also worked on the college radio station, WHAD. Only someone who has done that can appreciate how much fun it is to be behind a live mike, operating the big board, actually spinning records on the turntable, and doing what research you can from liner notes. I got hooked. And since WHAD had a bunch of old records – 78s – and not much else, that's what I played. And I got hooked on them as well. The big bands were big because they did not have the kind of amplification we can generate these days. So they relied on reinforcement of the melodies, counterpoint, virtuoso instrumental solos, and a mike for the girl or boy singer. It was a different sound than the noise we have come to accept, and the songs themselves were often remarkable. You had Gershwin's "They Can't Take that Away from Me," Berlin's "Let's Face the Music and Dance," Porter's "I Concentrate on You," Rogers and Hart's "Where or When," Mercer's "Laura," and so on. But then I don't have to convince anyone who has been there.

To continue as a disc jockey, though, was not easy. I found a few gigs with stations willing to play those old songs. By that time, I had an incredible record collection, including some 78s that had never been translated to a more modern mode. I would apologize for the sandstorm from which the music seemed to be emerging, but I'd say, "You can't hear that version of the song anywhere but right here." The old Decca records were particularly scratchy. Okey sometimes played as if they'd been cut yesterday.

And I made the mistake of getting married. Several years of being told that I "should get a real job" did that one in. I was just unwilling to sacrifice something I really enjoyed for whatever else I could be doing. A pilot? No thanks. Just a few years of military aviation had cured me of that itch.

And then, as I approached 60 – ye gods! where had the time gone? – I had become successful and restless as hell.

One thing my success had activated was my sense of failure. I had leisure and money enough to expand into that free time. What everyone wants, of course. But I thought of my dreams – the ones I have at night – and how inventive their scenarios were, how fluid, how full of characters I had not thought of in decades, how changeable in the locale, foreground and background, and in the faces speaking to me. These were mine and far more imaginative than anything I could summon up from the frontal cortex. In dreams I fell away from the specificity of day, its gradually leaning light or its gray monotony of March sky, and tumbled into a temporal eternity – the time made up of every fragment of my own life, from every sip of coffee or Scotch to every cough, smile, unintended fart, tear or streak of sweat. All that came forward and became the fabric of these remarkable narratives. My ex-wife was an ardent lover there, not a prune-lipped prude – yes, wish fulfillment was a factor, but often the scenario was beyond my control. Yet it was mine. And that loss of control was the release of my genius in several senses, my pagan soul and my creative core. That had gradually replaced the helplessness of being strapped into the cockpit of a flaming aircraft, unable to eject, waiting the moment just beyond – when the plane exploded – and then being unable to wake up into the relief of the "it was only a dream" moment. The sweat was real and the terror continued. We were in a dangerous game, but something in us did not want to die. And that something was more basic than the rational awareness that death was a possible result of what we were doing. I say "we." I was not alone in having these experiences at some uncounted hour of the early morning in a world at peace. But we did think we would die in those dreams. And the sense of death was strongest just when we woke up.

I thought of Prospero in Shakespeare's play. It isn't the concept of revenge that he has to give up. He's thought all that out. He doesn't realize that until he sheds sudden tears when he observes Gonzalo's weeping. But what he gives up – and this decision is not easy – is the dream world. His magic has been able to summon into shape and vocalization. Pagan gods perform for him and drama occurs within those performances. Cupid surrenders his nasty purpose even as the masque swirls around him, even as personified rainbows speak words as many-colored messengers. But that is a dangerous world. It invites usurpation, from Antonio early and Caliban late. You cannot live in that dream. So he gives up for his petty dukedom and its larger future and for the inevitable grave awaiting him. It is an allegory of growing up – from the imaginative child who cannot differentiate between the stories of the night and the adventures of the day to the mature, punctual, responsible adult. The latter may have made necessary transitions, of course, or suffer the scorn of Caesar. "He is a dreamer, let us leave him." But he has also surrendered his soul. But he or she cannot keep that soul and stay alive against the demands of the diurnal world. That is the tyranny to which we are born and to which – in almost all instances – we surrender.

And the ropes were tight and painful. The pain now clenched in from my shoulders to my collar bone to my neck. In frustration, I yanked up on the rope. Frustration, carefully observed, can lead to a way out of it. The ropes were tied around the back of a frame chair. As I yanked, the upper part of the chair moved. What good would it do me to get it loose? I'd find out. I pulled the top of the chair out at some cost to my wrists. I could feel the warm blood seeping from the burning sting into the bristles of the rope. My legs were tied to the bottom part of the chair, which refused to budge as I tugged. I was able to bounce my way across the room to a brass bed with low posts at the end. I got my arms up high enough to place the chair back over one of the posts.

Here goes! Ow! The chair shattered, wrenching my shoulders. But the ropes that had been strung through the rungs of the chair were looser. Thumbs that could not get leverage to push or purchase to pull finally worked the ropes loose. The security guards had not been Boy Scouts.

I shook my arms, flexed my shoulders, and worked on the ropes around my ankles.

Now what?

I knew I'd be cold, but I took off my polo shirt, put my light jacket back on and went outside. It was a starlit night. The stars would leave frost on these hills by morning. I walked down a path in back, turned so that I could still see the shack, and tossed my shirt further down the path. I then retraced my steps and started down the dirt road. Fortunately, its ruts picked up the light of the rising half-moon. I walked carefully, not wanting to sprain an ankle or break a shinbone at this stage of things. My wrists and ankles smarted in the chilly air where the bristles had rubbed them raw.

The road led south down the hillside. The highway led east back to town. I'd go that way, unless my pals in the Mercedes picked me up first.

I hid from a couple of cars that went whizzing by, but one, a Toyota pickup, was driving slowly, as if looking for someone.

I'd take a chance. I flagged it down.

"Get in!"

A woman! She had the gravel churning before I slammed the door closed.

"I'm Molly Howe. Michael, my husband, was a colleague of Charlie Hunter's."

She was a lean, ropy woman with a gaunt face and high cheekbones over which the skin stretched tightly.

"How'd you know...?"

"Mim called. She had a call from Rusty Tarbell."

I'd gotten that one message off from my cell phone, before I slipped it under the seat. It must have been to Rusty's shop. He must have figured where they were taking me from the GPS coordinates.

"How'd he know where I'd be?"

"He knew that Blanchard had a hunting lodge up in the hills. He guessed that that is where they'd take you. He said that if you got away, you'd get back to the highway rather than take off through the woods. 'Follow known routes, if you can, in the direction of your lines.'"

What the Manual said.

"Yeah. They would have tracked me down in the woods. Dogs. I threw my polo shirt down the path on the other side of the shack."

"And bears too," she said.

"Probably cougars, too, I suppose. I like the outdoors when I can look at it through a window. Why isn't Michael here?"

"Scared shitless. Who can blame him?"

"But you..."

"I'm in real estate. Look, Michael is a good man. But he's a fucking professor! They are a timid lot. He worshipped Charley. Veteran who had the guts to stand up to the bullies. He wasn't afraid."

"Maybe he should have been."

"Maybe, but that wouldn't have been Charley."

The heat in the car felt good. I was beginning to get drowsy.

"No. That wouldn't have been Charley," I said, yawning.

But then I suddenly woke up.

"Look, Mim...?"

"We're going to pick her up. She's at my place. I had her pack a few things."

"Yeah. We've got to get out of here if we can."

"I'll get anything else she needs to her when I know where. And I'll get her a fair price on her house Your rental is at my place too."

We turned on to Cougar Boulevard, the highway that led past the University on one side and Hampton Court, Bennigan's. Ruby Tuesday's, and the Varsity Inn on the other. This was the upscale side of town. The street was marked by paw prints, presumably those of cougars, giant cougars who had slipped down from the forest primeval surrounding this oasis of cheerleaders and rednecks. And veterans like Rusty and Bill.

"You're the one who developed the American Song Book?"

"Yeah."

"Great idea!"

"Turned out well."

It was a package I had put together for a bunch of fm stations. The great songs of the twenties, thirties, and forties as sung by the singers and as played by the bands of the era. It was easy to do, inexpensive, an attractive franchise for an aging demographic that had grown up with their parents' 78s, and had made me my modest fortune. Enough to buy my toys and to go where I wanted, when I wanted to go.

We turned left up a small hill and right into a new development.

"Here we are," she said, pulling into a driveway at the side of a neat brick bungalow.

VI.

As we walked up the driveway, I thought of the song I had awakened with that morning. "And the Angels Sing." It made one of the great recordings of the late 30s, with Benny Goodman, Liltin' Martha Tilton on the vocal, and Ziggy Elman, who wrote the melody, ripping off a rousing trumpet solo. It was also the epitaph of the great lyricist, Johnny Mercer, in the graveyard in Savannah. I should not be thinking of epitaphs, I thought.

Mim gave me a wordless hug as we entered the living room.

"Kid's asleep?" Molly asked.

Mim released me and sat down again on the couch.

Michael nodded in response to Molly's question. He took off his glasses and blinked, as if ridding himself of light that was too bright for him.

"Mim told me what you were looking for" he said.

"And...?"

He held up a small manila envelope.

"University has a retrieval system that an individual can call up on the 'Save' function. Not many of us use it. Charley did. For this at least."

I did not dare hope.

"Stand for America?"

"That's what the label says."

I saw Molly give her husband a look that I don't think she had bestowed on him in a long time, if ever.

Her eyes opened wide, and she breathed out.

"Is it still there?" I asked.

"No. Someone got to the file just after I did. So this is it."

"Look," I said to Michael and Molly, "you two are in danger. Just knowing about that disc. I'm am going to take it with us. And we had probably better start. I don't think they'll know that I've escaped..."

I rubbed one wrist, then the other.

"... until morning."

"Okay," Michael said, handing me the envelope.

"That is great work, Michael," Mim said.

"Mim," he said. "Charley left a lot of stuff behind. Writing, I mean. Unpublished. I have seen some of it. It's good. Somewhat reminiscent of Michael Sandel's work on justice, but grounded in American history."

"Mim," I said, suddenly nervous. "We'd better get out of here."

"I wondered, Mim," Michael asked, "if you'd mind if I went through some of that stuff, put it in order, and did an edition of Charley's writing."

"Would you?"

"Of course. He deserves that much, at least."

She looked at the disc in my hand.

"Will that be enough...?"

"To get them for Charley's murder? I doubt it."

"But if I know Charlie," Michael said, "it will be enough to show to the FBI. Those guys were deep into illegal actions against our government."

"Maybe even treason," I said. "That used to a hanging offense. Come on, Mim. They'll be looking for me pretty soon."

If they aren't already, I thought.

I wished, of course, that I were not driving a rental. Plenty of gas. Good tires. But its hydraulic steering was mushy and, of course, its transmission was automatic. I had had a stick shift in the Volvo previous to my current Volvo. Hell, you never forget to ride a bike, fly a plane, or drive a car. But I did not have any fine-tuning available, and the car chasing us was gaining. He knew the road. And I knew neither the road, which dipped and curved in unexpected ways in front of me, nor the car, which felt heavy, like an aircraft with speed brakes, landing gear, and flaps obstructing the air flow and only the throttle pressing against an un-aerodynamic drag.

I had Mim with me. Charley's wife. That was important. I had the disc, which I assumed blew the whistle loud and clear on Stand for America. That was important. I had Charley with me, on my wing, depending on what I saw in the sky, on the ground, on my radar screen and instruments.

I saw another set of lights pull up behind the car that was chasing us. And then, on a brief straightaway, the other set of lights passed the other car. Crazy driver. He had had to race the other car and swerve in front of him. Close! But then, as we entered upon a series of curves back and forth across the side of the mountain above Eagleville, the lights began to drop back. Whoever had passed the car chasing us had slowed down! The road dictated that response, of course, but I suddenly read an intention there. And, as I glanced back, I saw, along a curve in the road behind, that the intervening vehicle was a pickup. Rusty and Bill. Or Bill and Rusty. They hadn't found me. They had found the car pursing me.

The problem with the road, though, was that one could see the sweep of lights in the on-coming lane as they glided past the side of the mountain. And there were none. The car behind the pickup began to pass. I could see the pickup gain speed, but it would be no contest once they reached a slight upgrade.

The car would pass the pickup easily and leave it far behind. And the car would catch me soon enough.

"Loosen your seatbelt a little," I said to Mim.

I was going to ask her to duck in a moment, but the moment came sooner than I thought it would. I felt the air compress above the rental and heard a pop behind us.

A .45?

"Get down!"

A .45 would be notoriously difficult to aim effectively from a moving car, but if it hit anything, a tire, the gas tank, the driver, the results would be lethal.

I'd have to take that chance.

I'd wait until the pursuing vehicle was almost upon us, jam on the brakes, and hope that I'd be able to time the rear-end collision so as to stagger away from the disabled, ah yes! Mercedes behind us.

How many times had I worn a .45 as OD and on missions. I had never put the clip in, though. Now I wished I had one, clip in, safety ready to be clicked off. It would give us a chance.

As the Mercedes began to cut in front of the pickup, though, the truck lurched to the left. The car swerved to the left, corrected radically back to the right, and ripped through the cable on the side of the road. It went straight up. Its brake lights sent a red smear against the mountainside on the other side of the road before it toppled over down the mountain side. The pickup flipped his high beams on and off and began a stop-and-go turn around.

I eased off on the pedal.

"Good driving!" Mim said, straightening up, leaning over, and glancing in the rearview mirror on her side of the car.

"That other car stopped," she said.

"It was good driving," I said. "But not mine. And the other car did not exactly stop."

My own hands began to tremble as we eased down onto the strip that led through Eagleville.

"What did happen?"

"Pickup. Rusty or Bill. Drove the other car off the road."

"Down the mountain?"

"Yep."

"They'll all be killed."

"Have been."

"Whittler?"

"We can only hope. And I assume a local Mercedes dealer."

And I could hope but did not say that the car had burned sufficiently to erase any trace of the pickup's paint on the right rear fender. Some victims are more important than other victims.

"They were trying to get to us before we reached Eagleton. I don't think they've paid off enough people to allow them to conduct a high speed chase along this twenty five mph zone."

"Eagleville," she said.

"You're pretty calm," I said.

"One thing I learned from Charlie. You fighter pilots are damned good drivers."

"We certainly don't daydream behind the wheel."

"You really meant it, didn't you."

It was a statement.

"Meant what?"

"About Charlie."

"Yes. I meant it."

"I'm sorry."

"For what? You were going through a nasty experience. I can't imagine it! And this strange guy shows up. You couldn't trust people you knew. Why should you trust me?"

"Because Charlie did."

It had taken a little while for Charlie's belief to assert itself. But that lapse often exists between the time a person dies and when they begin to live again.

I reached over and put my hand on top of hers. Her other hand covered mine and soothed the tremble there.

"I never did like chase scenes," I said.

"Hungry?" I asked.

"Getting there."

"A Big Mac's up ahead. Let's grab some double cheeseburgers, fries, and a couple of Sprites. To go."

"But there's not much of a hurry now, is there?" she asked.

I did not know what might be happening behind us. I doubted that anyone had renewed the chase. But this was still enemy territory.

"No. But I never feel secure until the aircraft has reached a safe speed and I pull the landing gear up and begin to turn out of the traffic pattern."

"I'm with you," she said.

End

CONTRARY WINDS

Every man who has at last succeeded... in calling up the divinity which lies hidden in a woman's heart, is startled to find that he must obey the God he has summoned.

Henry Adams.
Esther.

I.

It had been an early spring. Those who called "global warming" a hoax were silent. Some said that the sudden propulsion of daffodils through softening soil in March did not signal a long-range trend. Others suggested that the wild winds and widespread power outages of late February were a more likely sign of climate change than any premature springtime. Wires on poles were 1935 technology and yet we clung to that mode, even if the wires did not cling to the poles or the poles to their holes in the ground. Some deniers said, If this early blossom time is global warming, I am all for it! New England winters do promote numbness of the brain.

As one who had little more to do then than observe the nuances of wind on the tops of pine trees, crystal gatherings on my long driveway, and pink buds on the beech tree outside my window, I felt the season of warmth and lengthening days as a mild ache just below the ribcage. It was much milder than it had been when, years ago, the fevers of spring would send me pacing without destination around whatever house I was living in, and outside with aimless movements seeking purpose, but finding only the ancient, archetypal yearning for what is past and will not come again, or for what had never come in the first place. What else was new? Nothing.

I was working on my study of Henry Adams' theory of history and had just glanced up from the blue borders of my computer screen toward the wild blue that arched above the twisted reach of a surviving elm tree – hoping to pluck a thought out of the blue -- when a knocking came at the door.

I had not seen her in – I couldn't count the years – but the first thing I thought was, She is still beautiful! And I did notice that the ache that circled just below the ribcage had been replaced by a hard, invisible right to the gut that replaced my breath.

"You are still beautiful!" I said, stepping away from the door. "Come in."

She smiled for a moment at my unscripted response, but the smile drew itself across a furrow of concern. She was in trouble. Why else would she come to me? But then, why *would* she come to me?

"Have a chair. Drink?"

"Scotch, if you have it."

Those were the first words she spoke.

Proust's remembrance of things past began early. I'm not sure when mine began.

When I was, in theory, growing up, memory was merely technical. Remember to get your racquet back. Remember to look both ways before you cross the street. Remember to put your mouthpiece in before you scrimmage. Those were the days before face-masks. Maybe it was: Remember to write. That meant that you were leaving someone in the past and that the rest of your life would be a series of hellos and goodbyes, each coming and going accompanied by some degree of regret or joy. Life would never be a whole again. And – at some point – you learned that most of your life had turned to memory. At this point in my life, almost every word I heard brought back a word or sentence that has been spoken to me or that I had uttered. The past was recycling itself whether I wanted it to or not.

That truth came home as I looked at Diana for the first time in a long time.

Since I had known her, Diana Gregory had gone on to become a famous investigative reporter. She had done a number of pieces for *Vanity Fair,* exposing the usual suspects – torture of prisoners by the CIA, killing of unarmed non-combatants by the Army, Cheney's active interest in the affairs of Halliburton while Vice President, Bush's off-the-record meetings with Exxon and BP to ease regulatory oversight. She had explored the strange circumstances behind Paul Wellstone's crash in that King Air, but had never been able to penetrate the final wall of silence and secrecy and thus prove who either sabotaged the aircraft per se or interfered with the signals it was receiving from ground control so that it drifted off its flight path and crashed. She had proved that it could not have been an accident. The plane was in its landing descent and configuration a couple of miles before it should have been. She had broken the story about Bush's personal involvement in getting the Bin Laden family out of the country even as other commercial flights were grounded. It had been almost the first thing he had done once he escaped from the pleasant fantasy of 'My Pet Goat.' Diana's face would have been familiar to those who watched Blitz Woolfer and Bottomline.

She looked around the room – bullfighting posters, some photos of me and flightmates – young, fit, smiling, a few who would die later that year – beermugs from Germany, tarnished tennis trophies. But I could tell that she was not seeing any of this.

Still beautiful? Yes. Dark hair, green eyes, and that certain type of body that seemed to rise from the ribcage toward a male wish to unzip the dress and pull it down – Katherine Grayson, Jane Russell, Deanna Durbin. The lilting cheekbones that bespoke money lost in the panic of 1893. But not all of that old money. The well of joyfulness bubbling below even the surface of her preoccupation. I had watched the straightest of women fall in love with her just while having a chat. Not much had changed, that is, as far as I could tell from a safe distance. But was there any safe distance from Diana Gregory?

"I've got some people coming after me, Don," she said, after a large sip of Scotch. "I've been warned."

"Who?"

"Better I not say."

Okay. I had not agreed to help her. Would I? Oh, yes.

"If you disappear?"

"I am 'on assignment' if anyone asks. Since I only appear once a week at the most, no one will question that for a while."

"Will that keep them from looking for you?"

"No – but it will reassure my friends. It will save a missing-person report, rumors. Those would complicate things."

As if things were not complicated already.

"Okay. Now what would whoever is after you expect you to do?"

"Flee the country?"

It was a question.

"These people 'mean business' as we used to say?"

"Oh yes. And they control the security apparatus – the people responsible for protecting people like me."

Yes. Local law enforcement was powerless, or thrilled to be working for higher authority. The FBI probably did not have jurisdiction. The War on Terror, in its facelessness and lack of defined hierarchy, could pick its own targets. With impunity.

"I think they would expect you to flee the country. And that's where they will be looking. Air ports. Border crossings."

"So what do I do?"

I poured some more Scotch over the click of shrinking ice-cubes in her glass and took a slug from the bottle, letting its heat melt along my throat.

"We don't flee the country. We don't mess with pass ports, customs, borders."

326

She looked at me and raised both hands, fingers beckoning as if to say, come, we don't have much time! I was still thinking.

"We go south."

And, of course, from a state that borders Canada, this seemed obvious as soon as I said it. If we did not go north, we went south. The ocean was to the east, and, to the west, was a spider's web of two-lane roads climbing mountains and more mountains into Vermont. That was an option, of course, but I did not know where we could hide out in Vermont.

"Where?"

"I'll tell you as we go."

I had been attracted to nineteenth century American literature from the first time I encountered Poe as a kid and scared myself to the marrow by reading 'The Fall of the House of Usher.' Shakespeare was great, of course, but beyond me, as I recognized early on. I could only stand back and admire. American literature was the only other period, it seemed to me, that got close to what Shakespeare was doing. Prospero has to surrender his pagan vision, in which gods and goddesses, even natural events like rainbows, waft across the clouds at his command. Prospero has to get down to earth, ultimately literally, as he knows. But the rare world he has summoned from his imagination remains in ours even as he tosses his book into the depths. And Melville made Ahab. Poe brought Madeline Usher back from the grave to summon her brother thence. Hawthorne wrote 'Rappaccini's Daughter' and 'The Artist of the Beautiful,' James had Strether wander the French countryside, creating a masterpiece as he went. Some imaginations are already darkened. Some bright visions come to confusion. But the new country challenged its writers as only our arrival to the east of Eden had done. Emily saw through it, of course. Her imagination was anchored by skepticism. And Henry Adams clung only to the dream of learning in a world no longer within the centripetal tug of a Madonna or under the totality of a sea of faith. That I chose Adams probably argued my own lack of imagination. But also, as I kid myself, it signaled my own desire to keep learning.

My interest in Adams was also occasioned by the lucidity of his writing, but even more by his personal struggle against who he was. I think that trait is inherent in who we are if we are to become anybody. That is, we battle against what we have inherited, what we assume, what society expects of us. We no doubt run, like Oedipus, into precisely who we are by being "frantic to flee," as Hopkins says, but the process is our education. The mass of men are quietly desperate, of course, because they pause along some level of their identity and accept the shallow persona that has worked so far as their own. And, of course, I had done plenty of that, until desperation forced me to do something else. But Adams, an Adams, a Quincy, a Brooks, a Boylston, descendant of presidents – one of whom, J. Q. A., he despised -- fled Boston for Lafayette Square. He looked across at the White House but he was destined, early on, never to live in it. And that was just as well, because he would have been unable to make the kinds of compromises for which he excoriates J. Q. A. – and out of that resistance he emerged to seek his education. Frost describes the process in 'West Running Brook' – the counter current "flung backward on itself." "It is from that in water that we were from." Some "strange resistance." "A backward motion toward the source." If darkness lay upon the face of the deep, the deep did move at some point. Its motion had to be against the darkness, against the stasis, just as all of us stirred once upon a time within the amniotic fluid. Our mothers felt that push and our desire to be something beyond an embryo. "A backward motion toward the source" because it gave us the impulse to move toward the end. But with a purpose, a "strange resistance" against annihilation that would come when it came.

I liked the New England obstinacy. Not Adams' virulent anti-Semitism, but the insistence that he keep asking questions, often for which the answers, if there, were being formulated as he asked. I did not approve Thoreau's anti-Irish bias, but I liked the Thoreau who could childe Emerson for being outside the bars, and the Adams who did not ride his family carriage to some complacent grave. But then, he learned early on that he could not. The old aristocracies had surrendered to the rougher energy of the frontier and he did not retreat into a lifetime of disapproving sniffing.

Adams looked back toward the Virgin of the twelfth century, who pulled adoration unto herself, even as she adored the infant in her arms. She was the unmoved center of attention, a centripetal icon of faith, when arches were rising against the medieval sun, where the sun referred stained-glass rainbows to the stony floors of churches, and Latin phrases rang upon illiterate ears, reddened within the vast chill of the cathedral. The dynamo generated power outward, driving the world toward progress and destruction. Adams manifested in his interests his own awareness of where he came from and where he was going. The world too was roaring toward destruction. Phylogeny recapitulates ontogeny. As we gained ascendancy over technology, it took command of us.

I enjoyed the Victorian spiritual crisis. Having never believed in God, I appreciated those who had experienced the loss for me. Arnold heard the grating roar of withdrawal riding out under that sea of faith. Dickinson saw an approving God overseeing the sudden death of happy flowers below. Hopkins woke up into nightmare and touched the hide of crouching darkness. Adams watched a beautiful sister die of lockjaw under the hammered bronze of a Tuscan summer and could no longer believe God to be a human. A substance, perhaps, but not a human.

But most of all, I liked his lifelong battle against who he was. He could not change his name from Cassius Marcellus Clay. I hoped that he would. like King, have come out against Vietnam because it represented the problem King was addressing, even though King was criticized by uncomprehending whites at the time for abandoning his focus on civil rights. Those were disproportionately black bodies being shipped back from the rice paddies to the U.S. Their purple hearts conveyed no rights.

I did think, now and then and always with a shudder, of having been a rifleman. Some of us who volunteered for other dangerous duty did so, I'm sure, to avoid the infantry. I recalled Hardy's description of the men in each army trying to sleep before Waterloo, as the wounds of older battles delivered aches to their joints under the "impartial" rain that fell through that night and early morning in 1815. And James Jones writes of infantrymen who, convalescing in Army hospitals, did not recognize their surviving platoon mates, so deep was the shock of combat from which they were trying to emerge.

And now I had been summoned from a study of the constant learner. Diana had interfered with my complacency just as it was becoming terminal.

And now, I could do something I had always wanted to do. Just goof off. I did not really need to write another book on Adams. Oh, I would read. That had been a given since I had been five or six and started in on O. Henry. But I would help Jud MacCray with his duties as pro at the North Hyannis Tennis Club, and that would amount to a vacation that would otherwise cost a bundle.

So before Diana and I drove south, I made a phone call.

Jud owed me a favor, probably not as big a one as I was asking in return. I would try, though, to collect on my response to a call he'd given me a few years ago. Well, more than a few. Would he remember that?

"Hey, Don," Jud had said back then, "I'm in a spot."

"What is it?"

"Jack Bascombe has torn his shoulder up. I need a partner for the Silver Racquets."

This was a doubles tournament for top flight former college players and younger club pros that could be very significant in the cutthroat competition for instructing the up and coming young prep school stars who could afford to pay for private lessons. And Jud was just starting out, with an implied promise to take over at Hyannis when the legendary Lenny Broadhead retired. But Jud would have to build his own clientele.

"I haven't exactly been playing," I said.

"Yeah, well. I'm in a spot. If I default..."

Yes, I thought, but a first round exit would be just as bad.

So I said yes.

Now, Jud was very good. He took any overhead within reach. All I had to do was return from the backhand court – that chip backhand was my strength, and it threw other teams off, since almost invariably, the best player took the add court. And, I had to hold serve. But if I slid my first serve in deep to the other sides' backhand, Jud had a chance to poach. We played well together, seldom getting caught out of position. And, since a weak shot in singles is often a winning shot in doubles – a medium-depth drive down the middle, for example – my own modest ground strokes worked well on the green composition courts of the Island Club on Long Island Sound in Rye.

We were in the midst of a tough three set match against Tyres and Rownull, two former number ones at Williams.

I was exhausted and content to have gotten to the finals, when I looked over at Jud. He was getting ready to return serve in a game we had to win. His chin was thrust out, his eyes glinted in the afternoon slant of sun.

He wants to win this thing! I thought.

I forgot how hot my feet were in their green-stained Jack Purcells.

I did remember that if we broke serve, it was Jud's serve coming up.

Yes, we could win this thing. And we did. He'd remember.

"Jud. We need a place for a little while. That cottage still there?"

"It's hardly habitable."

"Our need is great."

"I guess so."

"I'll water, brush, and roll the courts for you."

"That I do need. Our man got a job in a restaurant at the last minute. Happens all the time, of course, but I was about to put an ad in the weekly."

"I'm your man."

And it was a great way to begin June. Sun and the salty mist that typifies Cape Cod for a day or two every week. Watering the brickdust clay courts. Rolling them. Brushing them. Whisking off the lines. A few beers in the club house with a roast beef sandwich for lunch. Wine with Diana in the drafty cottage that was pleasantly cool after the warmest days. Shopping the Good Wills with Diana, her hair under a scarf, her green eyes lurking behind sunglasses. Playing myself into shape and hardening the callus on my right hand with some competitive doubles with some of the guests on Saturdays and Sundays in front of a crowd crunching celery soaked stalks with vodka and Bloody Mary mix – the crunch, crunch, the mock, mock of tennis balls against taut strings -- and with Jud's young charges during the week, cocky kids from Choate and Exeter who would be playing for Princeton and North Carolina and Yale in a few years and then in clubs in Darien, Short Hills, Merion, and Chevy Chase. After working thorough aches and pains, I got back into reasonable shape again.

Yes, but it couldn't last.

My epitaph – Yes, but...

"Don, I got a call. Someone asking questions," Jud said, his fingers laced as he leaned against the fence.

"About me?"

"No. About her."

"Not a positive development."

"Didn't sound it."

"Looks like I just got a better job in a restaurant."

"Okay. I can enlist a couple of the kids."

And so, we packed quickly and turned my old Volvo south again.

II.

I had a Light Colonel as a CO once, really good guy, who greatly admired the fact that I was a college graduate. I inspired him to invest in a thesaurus, with which he began to lard his discourse.

He called me into his office one day.

"Lieutenant, I have to introduce Major General Coleman at the change of command ceremony next Thursday. How does this sound?"

He read from a slip of paper.

"Any words of mine in eulogy would only add to the paucity of the occasion."

I paused for only a second.

"Colonel, you can't improve on that."

"Did Jud have any idea who it was?"

"No. Official sounding. Identified himself as Agent So-and-so."

"Sorry I got you into this."

I laughed.

"Yes. You see me weeping!"

I hadn't asked much about what she had been doing when not doing her career. And I didn't care. Whatever had etched a line or two into her ivory brow, it had been experience. It had been what she had not had those several years before, when our relationship had ended. More than several years. And I hadn't really been doing a damned thing – working on my second Adams book, teaching classes from time to time as an adjunct at a nearby university, grading papers. The physical life – the exercise, the surfing of a willing body, the pleasant ache of exhaustion after just-too-much tennis, just-enough love-making was something that I had consigned to the past. I hadn't known that, of course, until it came back.

"Where to?"

"It's off-season on the west coast of Florida. I made a call to a place where I've stayed in the past. Pleasant condo on Siesta Key. Air conditioned, of course. Great kitchen."

"If they know you..."

"I told Melanie – the owner – that I'd be using my pen name. To avoid publicity and autograph seekers."

"She bought that?"

"I'm paying a good weekly rate. And you are Mrs. J. Quincy Boyleston."

She laughed as we rolled down the west side of the narrow bridge over the Cape Cod Canal.

"And I call you J. Q?"

"Only in public."

"Good, I'll just call you 'You,' then."

I am always surprised that non-academics, even very intelligent non-academics, are surprised at what we know. We spend a mature lifetime studying a specific subject and we should damned well know it. And, I had either been blessed with a good memory or, along the way, had nurtured it.

"You still think about Henry Adams?"

"Oh yes. The dynamic of his book is education. His humility in light of what he knew is incredible. He kept on trying to learn, and not just surround himself with comforting mythologies."

"For example?"

"He found himself living in a late nineteenth century that was changing more rapidly than had any prior epoch. Before then, he said, 'the roads were still traveled by the horse, the ass, the camel, or the slave; the ships were still propelled by sails or oars; the lever, the spring, and the screw bounded the region of applied mechanics. Even the metals were old.'"

She looked at me in surprise. Hell, this was my specialty.

"As opposed to?" she asked.

"The dynamo. It was more than what Adams called 'a movement of inertia.' It called for a formula for acceleration, not just movement. The modern world, he said, is like 'a fish caught by a hook.' We are no longer the controller of the forces we have discovered."

"It seems that way. Oil companies not knowing how to plug the holes they make. Atomic weapons in everyone's hands."

"And their possession justified on the basis of national security."

"Or national pride."

"Yes, the celebrations in India when it got the bomb."

"It helps me understand," she said.

"What?"

"The frantic need to maintain some reassuring status quo."

"Right. The so-called conservative movement is nothing like that described by Russell Kirk, as a kind of brake on new ideas, the creation of a testing phase, refinement, debate. So-called conservatism has become completely reactionary."

"And dangerous."

"Right," I said. "They will try to stamp out those who stand in their way."

"And no one tries to stop them."

"No. People can see what happens to people like that."

"Like me," she said.

Diana had no mystery. Remarkable vitality – a fire that burned constantly on a seemingly inexhaustible supply of sensuous fuel, but no mystery. Typical extravert. And thus I could be detached, as I had been when we broke up. Another woman I had known back then had held something within her that I could never know, that she could not know herself. She had the face of Botticelli's Primavera, and the slender waft of body just coming ashore. And she had loved me. I screwed up in some way – didn't take her seriously, treated her love too casually, whatever – and she withdrew. But she took something of me with her –whatever it was that I could not discover about her – and I had a terrible time. I tried to get her back, knowing that it was futile and knowing that I was making her hate me with the effort. Before, she had just been disappointed.

I sat across from Diana, at a sidestreet restaurant in one of the Carolinas, taking in her still-vivid beauty – something that that the spirit breathed into the perfect features – but I was almost totally detached. This is someone I knew once, I thought. Could we start again? Of course. She might have reached the point she could not have attained those many years before. I was only older. It almost did not matter. It was not the urgent necessity of years ago – the urgency that could drive the goal away, like the colored circle of a beach ball bobbing on an outward wind. That we had reached this point sufficed. We were where we were and that was pleasant, and needed no adjustments, no plans for the future, if a future was to be. Was that maturity? Was that stasis? Death? No. Just a moment of calm before whatever happened would happen. I would observe that process, encouraging it by not trying to direct it.

My dreams, under the hum of various air-conditioners in the motels where we stopped on the way south, were vivid. What I remembered about one dream was that it was incredibly confident about the nooks and crannies, lights and shadows of the house in which I grew up. Something in me remembered better than my own memory. I could describe the house in detail, of course, but the dream knew better. It got the feeling of being there, of being a twelve year old in that perfect space.

I did not remember the details of the dream when I woke up at some unnamed hour of the moon, in a blanket of silver clouds, lower in the window. It was as if some inner stream of light had picked up everything that memory forgot – the details, grain of wood, the color thrown from stained glass to the wall, and more – the touch of being there alive, to be at home again in that house where I grew up. The dream knew what I'd forgotten. Time need not apply when the mind sinks to eavesdrop on what is lost. The bright, the shadow, beam and carpet where I crawled, the table top I could not reach, and words were meant to rhyme.

A space of cashmere lawns and velvet April evenings brushed by the blossoms of cherry and dogwood. Yes, a place where one could dream. That may be why I dreamed of it now. Hummingbirds quivered on invisible wings in front of the rhododendrons in front of the leaded glass windows. A Whitman's Santa smiled above the fireplace in December. It was a sad day when the tree came down, but we salvaged the tinsel, plucking it from the stiff, dead needles – an action designed to make mother believe that she was watching every penny. She had been a child of the Depression, and childhood memories never die, even if her family had survived in affluence. One saw the gaunt faces in the photographs, the one-legged men selling pencils in front of Bamberger's, the long lines of fedora-topped men hungry along the sidewalk that led to the steaming kettles of the soup kitchen.

But after the war, when supply met demand in a collision of exchange, when I was born, everyone seemed to be making money. But everyone was white and lived in a big house like ours, and played ball on the grammar school field – baseball until the leaves began to turn, football until snow – and we did mow our own lawns when we got big enough to push the old mower and even trimmed the edges, down along the cobbled gutters – and no one was Jewish, or even Catholic. It was an Episcopalian enclave where I grew up. I don't regret that totally. I learned the liturgy and later learned to understand Shakespeare's plays that way, and learned why white men like my father believed without hypocrisy that they were the ones who should lead, or, at least, should vote for the likes of Willkie, Dewey, or, as my father and mother got to do, for Dwight David Eisenhower. But the good thing was that the religion was not doctrinaire. If I left it – and I did, of course – it had not defeated my habit of asking questions. I'd never understand the Trinity, but I might grasp a few things before darkness fell. Since I did not believe in the immortality of my soul, I could leave the mystery of the Trinity behind without fear of any haunting by the Holy Ghost.

But the land of childhood was itself an impossible dream. It was Maine that I had left. Diana had asked me what I would miss about it. One thing I would miss would be the thought of getting back there, no matter where in the world I was.

Winter in Maine can be long. But I loved the contrasting seasons of New England. So did Henry Adams. I would miss my oldies station. The guy who ran had a macabre sense of humor. He had a spot in which one of his DJs talked about "lightening your burdens and gladdening your heart." Then he would play 'Gloomy Sunday,' 'Moanin' Low,' 'Brother Can You Spare a Dime?' Always a high point of my day.

II.

During flight training, we had a lecture on E and E – that's Escape and Evasion – from an old Captain who had been shot down over North Korea but who had made it back to U.N. lines in spite of a massive effort to capture him.

It was a great story, but I could sense the Captain's bitterness. He had a Silver Star, a DFC, and a bunch of lesser medals and should by this time have been at least a Light Colonel. But the twist of green and red veins in his nose betrayed the reason why he would soon retire as a mere Captain. It is not easy to retire from the USAF without having attained field grade.

At the end of his talk, he asked "How many of you are college graduates?"

About half of us proudly held up our hands.

"Very good," he said. "That will give you a better choice of dying words."

"We can't stay here,"

"Why not?" I asked.

"I mean we can't *stay*! They'll find us."

I knew that she was right. We were staying in a condo that I had rented many times before on a little cul de sac off of Midnight Pass on Siesta Key. We did our own housekeeping, which kept things very private, and snuck out for meals, Diana wearing sunglasses, a scarf, and a figure-muffling raincoat. She was indelibly present to me, but incognito to other eyes. But other eyes were tracking her, and once they discovered her link to me a few clicks would give them a vector. Sarasota – even Siesta Key – was not a good hideout.

Of course, I hated to leave this place. Comfortable in the hum of the air-conditioner, reassuring in the rise and fall of markets on CNN, pleasantly cool in the morning when I walked up to the 7/11 to pick up the *Times*, soothing in the touch of the sun and the unguents that Diana stroked to my back.

"Where to, then?"

She hesitated.

"I have a friend..."

Ah! – there was some mystery about her. I did not have to guess.

"Harry Vance. He has an island with an airport."

"Airport?"

"Landing strip."

"And?"

"He has a plane."

"Is it on U.S. turf?"

"The plane? Yes. Or if it isn't..."

"How about the island?"

"Yes. On the Gulf. Well below where the oil went."

"We don't have to worry about passports?"

"No."

Or oil.

"Okay."

"Can you still fly?"

"Sure. Of course, that depends on the equipment."

"Let's call him."

It took several tries and a couple of rebuffs, but Diana was skilled at this game. And soon Harry – whoever Harry was – was on the other end of the line.

"Can you fly a T-38?"

"Glass cockpit?"

"No. Basic instrumentation. It's been modified to incorporate a single canopy. No ejection system. And, of course, I have no ILS here. Just lights. I was going to get a GPA unit installed, but..."

"Okay."

"I'll call and have them roll out the external unit."

"Okay."

"Make it quick. There's a storm is riding up this way."

Diana accompanied me on my preflight.

"Tires look awful," she said.

The usual white filaments extended from the tread.

"If you see red," I said, "then they need changing. This wear and tear is normal. Our bags are stowed?"

"Yes."

"Then climb aboard. I'll be ready to start up in a minute."

And it was fun, having the firm touch of a high-performance jet under me again. This one trimmed up beautifully. I could fly it with two fingers.

"There's the storm."

"I see it," I said. "I don't see Piper Key, though."

A black smear was spreading from the southeast, gradually staining the sky. It looked like a reflection of the oil slick that had recently savaged the waters close to the Gulf coast. Flicks of lightning outlined the gray shoulders of clouds. The sea glittered, a mirror reflecting the sun painfully at the eyes. The surface began to spit as the wind picked up, as if drowning mouths lay just below.

Here is where a fighter pilot's eyes should pay off. In those old days, we had to do with our eyes what the instrument panel now does for the technician who stares at it.

"To the right!" she cried.

And, yes, there it was, a thin scratch of sand in a seething sea. Thank God for young eyes! Tendrils of storm were beginning to finger the key's southern shore.

"Good eyes!" I said, banking to the right.

But good eyes would do us no good at all if the storm closed over the tiny island before I could get this aircraft on the ground.

I now entered that zone that all pilots hate. On the basis of a brief glance from two thousand feet, I was descending toward what I hoped would be the runway. But a number of variables could have pushed the aircraft in one direction or another. I had no way of gauging the wind, thus no sense of which wing to lower to compensate for a crosswind. It felt as if the wind were swirling, of course, but was it shifting back and forth so as to balance its effect and let me fly a centerline that coincided with the runway?

I could not go any lower than 300 feet. If I did not see the runway by then I'd have to go around. But would I ever find Piper Cay in this storm? No. I had enough fuel to stooge around for a while. But the storm would only intensify in that time. I could flee in the direction we had come. I'd do that if I didn't get it down this time, even if we would be escaping in the direction of our enemies. By now, I guessed, they had the word out.

Passing through three hundred fifty feet.

The storm drifted in front of me. But it was thinner now, a sequencing of gray and white coming from the aircraft's right. Therefore... and there it was, to my right. The runway, two rows of lights that looked like a bridge over an empty canyon. I had one chance, and it called for dangerous flying with everything hanging – gear, 30 degrees of flaps, speed brakes. I poured in throttle, banked to the right, leveled the wings, kicked left rudder, pulled the throttle back, kicked right rudder, and rounded out. Just as I touched down, a vicious cross wind from the right tore the aircraft from the ground again like a fluttering leaf. I pushed right rudder with some right stick thrown in and touched down again. This time, I felt the aircraft relaxing into inertia. The hydraulics absorbed the weight of the aircraft on each main gear like a fighter sitting down on the stool at the end of a round and letting his shoulders droop. The nose gear came down.

I had come in at 180 knots – higher than normal landing speed, but recommended in gusty winds – so I was going too damned fast. I raised the nose again to about ten degrees to slow the aircraft, lowered it at 100 knots, and tapped the brakes.

"Hold on!" I called to Diana.

Through the intermittent weave of storm, I could see a cauldron of sea beyond the runway, headless shoulders above a surge of gray. I would overrun this landing strip and plunge into the sea, both intakes eagerly pulling in salt water. I hit the right brake. The aircraft swerved and became briefly airborne again. It trembled for a moment, trying each wing against the wind, and came down hard on both main gears. That did not do them any good, but the aircraft had slowed. I was on a road that crossed the end of the runway.

"Welcome to Piper Cay," I said. "Passengers may meet their parties at baggage claim on the lower level."

"Thought we were going to meet someone else," Diana said with a laugh.

"Ye of little faith."

Whoever it would have been for me, it definitely would have been on the lower level.

Nosewheel steering on this aircraft is not easy. It is activated by a button on the stick. I managed, though, to turn inland at the end of the runway on the road to the right and trundle down to the back end of a hanger. We still quivered in the violent breath of the storm and water sluiced down the canopy, obscuring everything but the road ahead.

"I'm going to shut her down. We are going to get wet."

"We almost got wetter," Diana said, laughing again.

I briefly recalled a time when friends of mine and I had rowed ashore at Essex during a rainstorm. Getting out of the dingy, I fell in to my waist. We arrived at the Griswold – used to damp sailors – quite wet, of course, but I was soggier than anyone could remember having seen that fall.

A man in a green rain jacket came running out of the hanger with a step ladder.

"We won't have to jump," I said, releasing the canopy lock and pulling the canopy lever back toward me.

The rain lashed into the cockpit, like heated steam from a kettle.

I leaned out and pointed with my thumb to the man with the ladder at the rear cockpit.

Diana waited for me as I climbed down. I almost slipped and fell on the top step of the ladder. Her eyes were bright with excitement, even here in the low clouds of storm. One strand of black hair was pasted across her pale brow.

I closed the canopy with the external lever and we followed the man into the back of the hanger.

"I heard you," he said, "but I couldn't see you."

"I couldn't see you either," I said.

"I'm Harry Vance," he said. He was tan, with assessing green eyes. Obviously fit. About forty.

We shook damp hands. He gave Diana a hug.

"Two squeegees," she said, laughing.

The hug lingered just a bit longer than that of two old friends or relatives. I thought, Okay. I am not about to get into some contest with this guy. Mere life at that moment was a pleasant possession, a gift from an unconcerned god of chance. A good Scotch would do for now.

I held my hands behind my back to conceal their trembling. That sometimes happens to me after an emergency, particularly a close call. I would, in retrospect, have given our odds on a safe landing at 500 to 1. But during the episode, I felt that I had no choice but to proceed as I had done. The choice would have been to turn around and run before the storm into the embrace of those who were chasing us.

"Tires are probably shot," I said.

"Hell, the aircraft is intact. I figured you might bust up more than the tires."

"How long is your runway?" I asked.

"Five thousand feet."

"It would have been easier with just a tad of headwind."

Harry looked at Diana.

"No," she said. "I had no doubt that we'd land safely."

I could see the fleeting look that passed across Harry's face.

I'm with him, Diana had said.

"Car's out here," Harry said, catching himself in a just-too-long regretful stare and pointing to the front of the hanger.

"Welcome to Piper Key!"

I refuse to worry about things that have not happened. That is, until they wake me up at night. The trembling of my hands, though, told me again that I did not have to replay that landing to know that I'd been lucky as hell.

IV.

In the window, through the woods, dawn burns the resisting shade,
and the kindling goes to flame, a danger to those within perhaps,
who turn to the light, as I roll from it, and blame the dream that
drags me to unwanted day too soon. No sleeping now, for even
desire yields to that lemon sky, cracking the way that touches the
west with the urgency of fire. Since all eyes consider flame and fear,
they do not heed the flight of gray cloud, its youth a breath away
behind the near spires of pine and further hills, a crowd of almost
human shapes that were human here, and laughed and died, and,
as children, cried out loud.

"I slept with Jack Goldsmith last night."

"What! Jesus!"

She looked at me mournfully, from swollen eyes. She hadn't slept much.

I was still enjoying the sweet memory of that inward instant on Friday night. Strangely, it helped. At least I'd done that much before Jack Goldsmith came along. Of course, 'that much' had in its way been the rubbing on the ancient lamp. The genie does not return to it.

I breathed a couple of times, in and out.

Personal jealousy aside – and I felt a stab of it – I think I understood.

"What you were saying is" – I steadied my voice -- "'I am not ready for a relationship with you.' You were saying, 'Don, I don't want total commitment at this point in my life.'"

She stared straight ahead, little light escaping from the dark circles under her eyes.

"I'd say that you are afraid of losing this relationship. That fear dictates your thinking now. Your actions last night said otherwise. And they would again."

I could get her back easily, I thought. But hers would a sudden flight to something she knew, a return to a comfortable past, motivated by fear and guilt and confusion, a sigh of relief that didn't do a damned thing about the problem. It would be nothing on which to build. It held no future.

I was doing exactly what I had to do to get her back, of course, behaving maturely and not flying into a rage. But I thought then of what would come, in a month, in a year. She would leave me. She would destroy me. And I was feeling strong at the moment, strong enough to avoid the wipe out that would come. I was for an instant in charge of inevitability. I felt as I seldom did – in command. That is, except for the difficulty I was having in breathing.

She looked at me from the right seat of my car. Her eyes were pleading.

"Look," I said. "I understand what happened last night. It's good that it did happen before we made any commitment."

She made no indication of leaving when I pulled up under the pines in front of her dorm.

I got out, walked around the back of my car, and opened the door.

During that walk, I had visions of months of uninhibited frolic, in the nude for foreplay, naked for the act itself. It was mine for the finger-snap.

"Come on. We both have other things to do today."

Reluctantly, she unfolded herself from the car, turned once to me with that silent plea that almost broke me down, then turned and walked away.

Was this cruel of me? No. It was pure self-preservation. Unless I walked away I was doomed. I was doomed anyway. But I would try to dictate the terms of surrender.

It had been on Friday night that we had become lovers at last. We'd been sleeping together for months and doing everything except, but her pelvis developed an impenetrable twist into a jagged letter when I tried for the prize. But that night, through some gyration or acceptance, or accident of posture...

"It's heaven," she said. "You're heaven!"

She was not at a loss for words, but I – having been "true" to her for a long time – arrived fairly quickly and joyously into the palm of my right hand.

I did try to get her to stay, but she rose, donned her clothes and walked back to her dorm, Beechcroft Lodge, around the corner. She knew, of course, that, if she stayed, the visitation later, at some moon-fallen moment of the early morning, would be longer. That instant of her loss of what she called "technical" virginity would have to last for a while.

But not for long.

She had a party on campus on Saturday night. I had made sure that our relationship would not interfere with the transitory joys of college days. My next date with her was for brunch on Sunday, after which she would study in the library and I would grade papers for return on Monday morning.

I had no reason to question these plans. Life had become automatic, except for the expectation now of another delicious entrance into Diana's up-to-now verboten inner sanctum. That, however, I was not going to rush. I had learned that much.

But Jack Goldsmith had cancelled my planned-upon patience.

The transition away from Diana was made easier by the emissary that she sent to me. Molly Orlander was a willowy aristocrat from Cricket Ridge on Long Island. She was an earnest young woman who was taking a course in free will, a concept that appealed to whatever the myth of her own identity might be. She also had supple fingers capable of imparting ecstasy to aching joints and muscles. Diana had once encouraged her to give my shoulders a rub one evening when the three of us were drinking wine at my place.

"You want me to take my shirt off?" I had asked Diana.

She nodded.

I think she was showing me off.

So when Molly Olander appeared at my door, I said, "I know why you have come. While you plead the case, you can also knead my shoulders."

"Oh yes, you hurt your right shoulder, didn't you."

I had done so. I was giving an instrument check ride once in an ancient trainer to a reservist struggling to stay on flying status, when the engine exploded.

"Let's get out of here!" I had shouted, jettisoning the canopy.

The antique ejection system required that I release my seatbelt and then, once the seat had whipped off behind me, that I pull the chute open via the stainless steel d-ring in front of me on the left side.

All went well until, tumbling head over heels at twelve angels, I reached for the d-ring. I felt an excruciating sting in my right shoulder that exploded toward my neck.

Furthermore, I could not locate the d-ring.

"Ow!" I said to the air rushing past. It was not listening.

I looked down to my left. The d-ring had ridden up on my left shoulder. Its bright steel bounced up and down like an antic letter on Sesame Street. It looked like an impossible distance away from the necessary tug with the right hand. It glowed into the dimensions of a nightmare.

I slid my left thumb under the strap and pulled it toward the center of my chest. Then, with another remarkable lightning strike of pain, I got my right hand around the metal. With both hands pulling outward, I deployed the chute.

Beneath the dominant pain, I could feel what was supposed to be the pleasant sensory aftermath of an ejection – the flapping of the chute unfolding from my rear end, as if I were giving birth to a great circle of silk and the sudden rise – or so it seemed – when the chute opened and pulled me from my fall. But the explosion that had popped me from the aircraft had also torn my shoulder apart and deafened my right ear, though I did not know that until later, when I found myself turning to the left to listen to voices and other articulate sound waves. The reservist landed sans scratch.

"Actually," I said to Molly, "it's the base of my spine. I whiplashed once when I hit a tackling dummy too low."

And that was true, too.

It was wild, energetic. She was a bi-polar Maenad. Her eyes seemed at times to roll back in her head, as if escaping to a primal zone of exotic foliage from which the stolid eyes of saber-toothed tigers gleamed and in which elephant graveyards were thick with ivory, like driftwood on shores. At other times, she stared at me with gigantic pupils as if I were a sudden island to a sailor on a sun-scorched raft, a beach that had to be a mirage of wave, wind, and desire. The frustrations of the relationship with Diana that had just been assuaged with our brief but elegant coupling were further relieved. It was as if I had never been deprived. Or, if I had, it suddenly did not matter, when during the wandering in the desert before arriving at the Promised Land it had mattered hugely.

One prays for rain, but not flood.

I had met Molly's boyfriend, with whom, Diana had told me disapprovingly, Molly was sleeping, and I did inquire about him. He was a polished aristocrat and somehow I did not think he'd mind that much. Still, I felt just a little bit like an interloper, a feeder in someone else's pasture.

"What about William?"

"Oh, William. I'm going to marry him."

Emphasis on the pronoun. I was, of course, ineligible for the long run, even had I been a candidate. And Molly, the young aristocrat, already had her life constructed in the compartments that would arrive as inevitably as she would at the house on Sum Sound in August.

"Can I tell her that I am at least making progress? I feel terrible!"

She did not feel terrible about cuckolding William, but of betraying Diana. Strange can be the loyalties of women! (And men).

"Molly, I don't think it's fair to tell her that you are making progress. I really love Diana, but I can't see our relationship being anything but full speed into an ice berg."

And, beside, I did not say, I am enjoying you to the point of virtual pedrocide.

"Well, I believe in free will, but I don't think I can keep sneaking out here almost every night and claim I've been at the library."

"Claim you've been somewhere else, then."

"That's not what I meant."

But she did return almost until the semester ended, as semesters must. I ended the affair just before that point, though, since it would have ended anyway, and, again, I wanted to control the agenda rather than have ex post facto regret suddenly rear its unexpected head. Then she drifted back to the gentle valleys of western Long Island, with their green private tennis courts and azure swimming pools and their hidden homes, elegance revealed only after the final turn of a dogwood and azalea lined drive. That was a trick that poor Gatsby never mastered.

V.

We did get to wear pilot's wings before we got through pilot training.

We would put them on for our classbook photograph. The photo would be cropped above the wings for the classbook, which had to be produced before the actual graduation ceremony. If, however, we were killed during training and while the classbook was still in the works, our photo would appear at the beginning of the book, with wings.

It was a tough way to earn your wings.

"Professor Wildwood, this is William van Dusen."

"Yeah, hi, William."

"I'd like to talk to you."

"Sure. I have office hours tomorrow morning. 0900 to noon."

"I'd prefer to see you at your home."

This was going to be trouble. But I could hardly deny his request.

"I'll be home today at around 1630. Four thirty. Come by for a beer."

"I'll be there."

Just what I want! A triangle, with two undergraduates as two thirds of the isosceles. Ye gods!

"Hi, William. Come on in."

He came through the entry way to my living room-kitchen, a pleasant, book and bottle filled space, with my cathedral ceiling and chandeliered study beyond.

"Nice place!" he said, ducking in for a look at my study.

"Thanks. Sam Adams?"

"Sure."

We sat at the kitchen table, across from each other with two burgeoning pilsner glasses between us.

"I have a problem."

"Okay. Shoot."

"I figured you being a friend of Diana's and knowing Molly might be able to help me."

"I'll do my best, William."

I breathed out a great sigh of relief. This was not an angry and accusing young man. He had come to me as an older confidante, a man of experience. Little did he know!

"Can I be frank?"

Or maybe not!

I took a sip of my beer.

"Of course," I said.

He took a sip of his beer.

"I know all the stuff about not going all the way with anyone until you're married. I grew up with all those warnings. Pregnancy. Aids. You know."

"Yeah."

"But Molly and I...."

"You've been going together how long?"

"Year and a half."

"And one thing has led to another."

"Right."

"Perfectly understandable. The same thing happened to me."

And a vision of Bethany Venebles – an image never far from consciousness and embedded deeper than that – floated unbidden past my sight.

"It did?"

"Yes. I assume Molly is not pregnant."

"No. We've been careful."

I hoped so!

"Okay, then..."

"She's been a little standoffish lately."

And that I could understand. She had told me that she had "made it," as she said, with William a couple of times since we had begun our liaison. I had told her that that was good for community relations.

"You don't mind?" she had asked.

"No," I had said. Her eyes had quickly cleared of a brief disappointment – had she expected me to object? – and she nodded.

"Okay."

"I assume, William, that Molly was brought up with the same sort of prohibition – the warnings..."

Diana sure had.

"Yeah."

"You may, then, be getting some of that in her attitude. Not guilt. Not regret. But a little residual carryover from her upbringing. She considers herself a 'nice girl,' as they say."

"Oh, she is!"

"I'm sure she is. So that is probably what is happening. And I can tell you from experience that it is the last subject a man can bring up with a woman. Her reluctance. It's threatening to us men and it usually leads to a disagreement if we raise the subject. So we tend to let it ride and hope the problem goes away."

"That's what I've done."

"Sure. I have a suggestion. It will sound radical."

"Okay."

"You and Molly plan – tentatively – to get married?"

"Yes. We haven't discussed details."

"Of course not. Too soon for specific plans, though I'll bet they will fall into place automatically. But it's understood, right?"

"Yes."

"Here's my suggestion. Take control. Tell her that you think you both should refrain from any further sexual activity – complete sexual activity, that is – until you are married."

His jaw dropped.

"You have to take charge here. She's already reluctant, as you say. So instead of trying to overcome that reluctance – it will only cause problems if you do – you take charge."

"I think I see what you mean."

He didn't, of course.

"Let's say she goes along with it. From what you say, she will. I can tell you what is going to happen."

"You can?"

"So you don't go all the way for a couple of weeks. You can handle that. You will be making out on a couch some late night with no one around. Get the picture?"

"I think so."

She'll pull her dress up to a convenient height and wait for you to extract an eager hardon to insert in the usual place.

I did not say that, of course.

Molly knelt amid a rumple of sheets, their blue stripes zigzagging after our tumble.

She looked at me from above the firm blossoms of recent breasts.

"William said a strange thing to me."

"What was that?"

I looked across at her from my position on my back, across the detumescence that no longer embarrassed me.

"He said he wanted to be celibate until we are married."

"What did you say?"

"I said okay."

"Good for you."

"Good for me? Since we started..."

"I know, Molly. But it is a good idea for us, too."

"It is?"

This was almost a wail.

"Yes. Not fair to either you or William. Not while you are going with him."

"I am, kinda. I mean the parties and everything."

"Of course. And you are not going to stop going to parties and things."

A sudden bleak vision opened before her. She was picking up my hint -- me or college! None of the frivolity and spilling of suds that were the reason for being for a twenty year old college girl? No, not that!

"So," I said, "I think we part. Except for being friends, of course."

"Except for being friends," she said, forlornly. There were certain advantages to living between two worlds, enjoying their fruits with none of the disadvantages.

But I had tasted the fear of discovery. And I had also begun a discrete affair with Rosemary Lafitte, a very junior assistant dean of students. We had both been on the prowl for someone unattached who wanted to stay that way.

A few weeks later, I spotted William picking his way across the icy waste of the inner quadrangle. He threw me a brief grin from above his sculptured chin and gave me a hip-high thumbs up. It had not taken long!

"What about the girl?"

"Molly?"

"Molly?"

That was a shriek.

"Oh. Diana?"

"Who is Molly for god's sake?"

"No one. Some one. Some one I used to know."

"Jesus! What about Diana?"

"We broke it off?"

"We?"

"Mutual. She met someone else."

Dammit. Rosemary had become a dean here in the rumple of sheets damp with the after-scent of love-making. I suppose that deanship ultimately seeps into the marrow, chilling it and freezing the blood in its flow. But the pity of it!

VI.

Only a little while ago, we boys worked in the summer, to support certain habits like soft drinks and movies and girls and then, of course, the inevitable piece of junk that became our first car. A friend and I mowed lawns in the summer and shoveled snow in the winter for about ten clients.

Later, once I had an actual job, I was promoted from busboy to assistant short order cook. That meant an extra eight bucks a week.

But I'd be out dancing at Rod's or Ernie's on Saturday night and my date would sniff and ask, "Do you smell French Fries?"

"No. You hungry?"

"No. It's just that I suddenly smell French Fries."

One afternoon, I shelled, half-sliced, and breaded fifty pounds of shrimp and put them in metal baking trays for that night's special.

At about two-thirty, after the rush hour at lunch had ended, I said to my boss, "Vic, I'm going out to get a haircut."

I went across the parking lot, through Woolworth's, and crossed over to the barber shop on Millburn Avenue.

I entered, noticing a certain shock of recognition.

The three barbers slowed, suddenly doing meticulous work. A chair along the wall, opposite the infinite regress of mirrors, opened for me. Visiting royalty!

One barber finally had no choice but to swivel his customer out of the chair, shake out his striped sheet and say, in what sounded like a stage whisper, "Next."

He was a strange fellow, working in quick snipping bursts and scurrying over to his sink to do breathing exercises.

Finally, he finished.

"Boy," he said, as if strangling, "You musta caught a lotta fish today!"

Then, of course, it dawned on me.

"Yeah," I said. "Fifty pounds of shrimp!"

I flipped him a quarter tip from five feet away and went back to the Wee Ivy Cottage to get ready for the dinner crowd.

"What would Adams think of today?" Diana asked me once, as we were sitting at Pallone's waiting for our pizza to arrive.

"Of course I've thought of that. Politics, he said, is 'the systematic organization of hatreds,' so he would be at home in that environment. And he would understand so-called 'global warming.'"

"He would?"

"Sure. Most science since Newton has accepted what Newton said about motion and questioned much of the rest of it. Particularly the concept of constants. The speed of light intersects the nature of time. The universe is not a finite measurable quantity, but as Hubble discovered, it is expanding. And heat is not a static entity with mass. Adams was fascinated by the second law of thermodynamics, having to do with changes in a system."

"You are getting over my head."

"No. It's easy. The German scientist, Rudolph Claussius, used an example that explains it. If a glass of water with ice in it sits in a room with a higher temperature than the ice, what happens?"

"The ice melts."

"Exactly. Entropy increases. The molecules disintegrate. Or, to put it another way, the natural process involves a dissipation of energy. That process can only go one way."

"It can?"

"Yes. It is the arrow of time. It's what links the second law to the theory of evolution. Think of it this way. Can heat transfer from something cold to something warm?"

"No."

"Right. Heat only goes one way. There's no cycle involved. No exchange of energy back and forth. That means that a perpetual motion machine is impossible."

"I see that."

"So, in time, the interaction with the environment between the system – the glass and the ice – and the room around it equalizes."

"And nothing happens."

"Exactly. And that stasis is death."

"So, if the ice caps are melting..."

"Right. Heat continues to pour into an accepting environment."

"But when the process stops."

"The earth dies of heat."

"I see that."

"That's the theory anyway. I'm not a scientist so I haven't created models that imitate the process. And other variables apply – the shift of the jet stream, the change in the Gulf Stream, maybe even oil under the surface of oceans."

"Speaking of a glass with ice cubes."

"Good idea. All that explaining makes me thirsty. And you don't have to go to university to know what you should do when you thirsity. Tony! Two more beers, please."

And, I think that Adams, who studied politics so assiduously, would have understood the manner of my getting canned by Blowditch College. The transition from the freedoms of the period of the 1970s and early 1980s to the imposition of the Political Correctness Patrol in the 1990s had been sudden, or so it seemed to me. Or, perhaps I believed that the rules did not apply to me. PC had been invented to make sure that nothing happened, after the obvious attacks on all that was holy that the counter-culture had launched in the late 60s. The fools and buffoons who ran higher education, though, were the same. Political Correctness suddenly gave them something they could understand and enforce. I had offended by screwing the occasional co-ed. A few others had protested the war at some point before it became a popular position and tended to continue their hectoring by objecting to Blowditch's radical mismanagement. We offenders against the way life should be were purged. I had a partial disability due to deafness in my right ear caused by that damned ejection that had ruined my shoulder, so I'd survive. I did wonder, though, about the other people, being expelled into a job market that had shut down entirely, except for the occasional one-year replacement and the tutoring of illiterates who had somehow been accepted into the colleges of their choice.

What rankled, though, was the manner of my firing. The bastards were good at nothing but covering their own skinny rear-ends.

I was called in to see the high dean, a stooped functionary suffering from terminal mediocrity.

I figured that the meeting had to do with my upcoming tenure hearing.

I knew something was wrong, though, when he did not invite me to join him at his conversation area, a couple of chairs around a low table heaped with professional journals – *The How to Get the Most Out of Mediocrity Monthly* – no doubt a self-help book aimed at academic administrators – *How to Terminate Without Getting Your BVDs Sued Off, The Monthly Nadir, The Polyester Quarterly*, and suchlike periodicals.

Dean Gustav von Pilchart remained behind his empty desk, a polished barrier of gleaming wood that picked up his pale hands, fluttering like featherless birds.

"I wanted to let you know that I am not convening the tenure committee."

"You aren't? Why not?"

"It's only fair to tell you that it would be a waste of your time to assemble all the necessary material, get all the references, et cetera, et cetera. And a waste of the time of busy committee members."

Oh yes, pity the busy committee members!

"Why?"

"Because I cannot make a positive recommendation in this case."

"Why the hell not?"

He frowned at my profanity, but got himself under control.

"The relative paucity of your professional record."

I had gotten a late start, of course. Five years in the military, then graduate school on the GI Bill, but the teaching was strong and my book on Adams was due that fall.

"Your own form on teaching should tell you that I have a high rating in that area."

A mistake. While he was proud of his evaluation form, it was a contradictory mess. I had attacked it when it came up for re-approval in a faculty meeting. I had told more than one class that I was ashamed to be judged by such a travesty. That got back to Pilchart, of course.

"But you don't believe in that form."

"In that you use it to make decisions on other teachers here at Blowditch and in that, as flawed as it is, it rates me higher than all but a few of my colleagues, it should be counted in my favor. Furthermore, my book..."

"Your book has not appeared as yet."

"No. But it is in press. If you knew anything about it, you would know that a scholarly book takes time. I did a complete revision as requested by the reviewer that the press had hired while still holding down a full time teaching schedule. How many other books are coming out this fall from your faculty?"

He had stiffened into a deadly sort of rigor during my comment. Deadly to me, that is. Something about being tied to a corpse crossed my mind.

"That is beside the point."

"Easy to say. That is the point."

Of course, I should not have reminded him that he knew nothing about the process which I was about to bring to a successful conclusion.

"No. All publications must be submitted before the committee meets. But it is beside the point simply because I am not making a positive recommendation."

And he would stick to that. It was the broken record technique. If I had a chance to meet the committee, of course, I might have been able to sway them. I knew that I would get strong recommendations from outside Blowditch and a good one from my department chair, who had refused to be intimidated by von Pilchart.

He pulled his bony shoulders up as the shiny polyester padding of his suit sought for support. From this intimidating posture, he stared at me.

I stood.

"You are an incompetent dipshit," I said.

His expression did not change. Perhaps he had heard that song before. Perhaps he knew as much. But it was true that he did not care. What he knew, I suppose, was that I was getting laid on a regular basis and that he was not. Such men as he do enjoy deploying their power in other ways, even if their cocks cower behind the portcullis of their zippers.

Since I had not been charged with the offense for which I was being canned, I could not mount a defense. The bastards were clever! I could have taken a junior dean named Rosemary with me, of course, but that struck me as a petty action against someone who had not really hurt me. But you can't hurt a Pilchart, a Cheney, a Rumsfeld. Having no consciences, no pain can penetrate the smug walls of their self-justification.

And She a Shade

Once during a wild blizzard, I took two huge plastic garbage bags of the peanuts used to surround fragile items while being shipped, and dragged them to the center of the Blowditch campus. I shook them into the storm. They blended perfectly with the heaps of snow piled up by wind and plough, but persisted stubbornly into the spring. I recall walking to the library in April and watching the odd peanut whipping around the corner in the wind.

But one day, as I approached my office in Lawrence Sergeant Hall, I saw my friend, Barney, with whom I watched Giants' games at the Locker Room Sports Pub on Sunday afternoon, on his knees and plucking peanuts from under the blooming rhododendrons

I felt a brief pang of guilt, until Barney looked up with a laugh, and said, "Keeps me from gettin' laid off!"

I had been unable to resist telling Diana that story. Not out of pride of accomplishment. Just that I thought someone should know.

"Oh, that was you?"

"You heard about it?"

"I was a student representative to the Public Image Committee. The Dean was furious."

"Herr von Pilchart?"

"Yes. Ripshit. He blamed it on the Betas. He was going to put them on social probation."

And he had still been furious when he banished me from the academy.

VII.

Yesterday, a bird made a leap of gold across the morning and turned out just to be a brown siskin, once it reached the hold of a cherry tree, edging the woods on the lee side of the sun. Last night, I held a board and trudged up the snowy hill, as others fled, and darkness came with me, and the land fell toward the night, leaving me alone with my inflexible sled, too late for play, as light slid past the oak, black and implacably ringed with time. Today, mist rises from boot prints in the field, as the soak of rain makes a ghost of the man who passed that way – me – yesterday in the morning's rise, awake now to a dawn sliding underneath the slate of a stiffened sky, wanting another take of dream, knowing it is too late to find that technicolor genius who created those long tracking shots and brief montage of rooms and faces that I knew along the framing of a former life, dropped even from memory, except the still scenario at the bottom of the mind.

"Think you can navigate in the 39?"

"Yes. What's up?"

Harry and Diana were pouring over a chart on the big table behind the couch that faced the shell-embedded fire place.

Could I navigate in a boat? The military had taught me an affirmative mode. Never volunteer, but always look eager. Sometimes I regretted it. But, hell, I had navigated in aircraft, using VOR only as backup. What would be different about a boat?

"I got a warning," Harry said.

"They found us?"

"May have. No use taking a chance."

I had learned to handle Harry's 39 foot Sea Ray, but, of course, hadn't taken it anywhere beyond sight of Piper Cay for fishing. You could toss a line over and catch a fish that would be sizzling succulently that evening in a frying pan in a sea of olive oil.

"Where away?"

"Small island about fifty nautical mines south west of here. Has a house. Not very fancy. A fisherman and his wife live there and take care of it for me. The 39 has been under cover so I don't thing they'll notice it's missing,"

"You mean they've looked at Piper Cay from the air?"

"Probably. We are not dealing with minor leaguers here. A storm is coming this way, so you wouldn't be spotted. But..."

"How big a storm?"

"Looks nasty. But the 39 should be able to handle it."

Yes, if I can handle the 39.

Diana smiled at me. She'd been with me in that T-38.

"Okay," I said. "I don't like the options."

"It'll be dead reckoning," Harry said. "The Garmin is out for repairs.

Okay, I had not grown up with GPS.

"I learned to navigate the old fashioned way," I said. "Compass heading corrected for the wind."

"Wind will be in your face. But she's fueled up. I'll give you a note for Enrique."

I was aware, of course, of the angry tensions ripping the Hadley campus apart while I enjoyed the golden haze of college days. I had signed up for flight training as a cadet and would get to Randolph during the summer of my year of graduation. So, I kept quiet, did my work, and figured that if I survived my four or five years in the USAF, I'd figure out what I wanted to do. It was an existential existence – though I did not know that at the time. I felt like Camus's Mersault, alienated from my immediate environment, walking through it as if it were a rehearsal for a play whose lines I did not know. I was living the recurrent nightmare of actors. I knew why, of course, but that knowledge did not alter the surrealistic quality of those few years. It was more like a dream, I would guess, than the experience of most college boys as they slide between the different habitations of uncomprehending adolescence and chronological maturity.

The quality of those years – like the shimmer that gathers around the background of a film that has had a foreground imposed upon it -- was reinforced by their having been led, in their most memorable moments, in shadows. Fraternities were horrible institutions. No "system," except insofar as it promoted alcoholism, racism, and sexism – an indoctrination that was their unstated intention. But they had the great advantage of conferring freedoms upon their members greater than those enjoyed at home, where the old rules were immediately reapplied during school vacations. And that, of course, meant the second floor of Delta Alpha Psi. Once, a tie hung over a door knob signaled "Do Not Enter." But with a relaxing of in loco parentis rules, doors could be locked with one of those old fashioned keys that had a semi-circular knob at the end.

And, in the shadows, sometimes cast by the moon, sometimes by the rise and fall of purple and green flames in the fireplace, sometimes in a sudden flash as a log would scissor apart and crash into the grate, sometimes as a crystal congregation would gather on the window sill, Bethany would move above me, mouth half open, perfect breasts at eye level, eyes wide with their effort to pick up and regenerate what light there was. The shadows, of course, enhanced the images. Once, when I had turned the big old leather couch around to face the fireplace – it must have been February in Massachusetts – she rose and stroked the radiant warmth to her body. It is an image, a moving picture, vivid to me to this day.

She liked to watch, and would lean back and stare down, through the gap between her breasts.

I had never known such intimacy, of course. We had both been virgins. Having her that close! Well, first times have nothing to compare themselves with. The comparisons waited in the future, and for me, they would forever fall short.

"What do you look at? You? Me?"

"I look at where we come together."

I assumed, later on, that visualization enhanced the physical feeling. It certainly did for me, though I had the better view.

Invariably, I put some records on the old machine in front of the room's single window. Old songs – Ella and Duke and Peggy Lee – and an occasional recent tune. That would be Elvis's "I Can't Help Falling in Love with You," or Paul McCartney's "Yesterday," or "The Windmills of Your Mind." They were an obbligato to our joining. Along with the shadows that stroked Bethany's body, I recall the lyrics rising above the minor mode of the guitar.

I can get the sights and sounds. I cannot capture her scent. I think I'd recognize it again though should I ever drift into its zone.

Not the autumn leaves, but the sky at night would turn into the color of her hair. I believe in yesterday.

After fourteen months at Randolph that included a tdy stint at Nellis for air-to-ground gunnery, I was assigned as an instructor. I expected to make a transition to the F-105 and then fly along the spiny marker of "Thud Ridge" to bomb Hanoi. Whether then didn't think I was good enough or whether the orders were a prize, I did not ask. An instructor is in a tricky position. He is always ready to say "I've got it" authoritatively when the student is about to prang, but he hesitates because the student will soon be flying solo in an F-type aircraft without another hand ready to grab the stick. You can't say, "Thanks, God, I've got it now" too often.

But it beat death in combat. That death may be cleaner and neater that than of some poor slob of a rifleman bleeding into the stench of a rice paddy, but it made the pilot no less dead. It did take care, in most instances, of the costs of cremation. But as my grandmother said, You're dead for a long time. I always think of that when I think of eternity. Always.

Suffice it that I became very familiar with the T-38. It is not like riding a bike, but most pilots of single-seat aircraft have learned how to fly the damned thing. They can't plug in George and go back to take a leak while the plane flies along all by itself. We were a hands-on generation, the last. I thought that I had walked away from flying – with my Soldier's Medal, for grabbing a loose fire extinguisher once while flying right seat in a Gooney Bird, my Commendation Medal, and my National Defense Service Medal. After five years I did not savor the stink of the oxygen mask, filled with one's own dry saliva or the biting stench of an electrical fire, or the sudden cross wind that hits an aircraft low on fuel and an exhausted pilot just when he thinks he's earned that first and second Lone Star at the club. But sometimes life circles around and meets you again where you once were. As Diana had. And, yes, I admitted, she came in tied for first with Bethany. That is, as memory worked her into that archetype of first times.

And someone else, too. I had noticed that, as I made love to Diana, I sometimes thought of Molly Orlander. Memory can be perverse.

"By the way, whatever became of your roommate? Molly something-or-other."

"Molly Orlander. Oh, she married William, of course. About the only guy she ever knew."

"About?"

"Oh, she may have had a boy friend in prep school, but once she met William, that was it."

"That's nice."

"Three kids. Two girls and a boy."

I had a quick glimpse of what might have been. No. Diana had not been ready back then. Molly was. For William, once her final pre-nuptial fling had been flung. Our choices come back at us, of course, in time, but my decision with Diana that day had been right.

VIII.

As I did so often here in this climate of wide leaves, big-winged birds, and exotic songs summoning a pre-heated dawn into being, I thought of memory per se, of driving along back Maine roads in November. November, for me, had been the month of memory and regret.

The sodden ground stretches. The leaves are gone. The pond moves westward toward the icy mouth of the river. On the hill, behind the wire, a ghost of horses grazes along a melted zone. Four of them, outlined against a wash of sky. Today, they shake the sunlight with careless grace, but sniff the salt of winter's rigid face, as crinkled water reflects a reach of gray. Today, the lives that were not led return like the invisible melting above the frozen corner, just where it disappears, or like the burn of November's leafless flame, or like the blur of a toy soldier's tumble from a table's edge, or an angel, discharged, failing the luminous ledge.

I would not be on that November road again. That fact seemed only to matter at some point just before I woke up, as I hovered between whatever dream I had been having and whatever the day was to bring. The day would bring Diana. And so would the night, just before the dream.

We were in a storm again, and, again, we could sink. Not through altitude but through fathoms. The air acts like an ocean, and Bernoulli had developed his principle with liquid. And ocean has its own slow-motion gravity. Neptune could be an angry god. Everything was a metaphor except the storm.

I throttled down, as Harry had instructed me to, as we met the storm. Head-on, as Captain MacWhirr of the Nan-Shan advises. We still bounced, at times almost becoming airborne, the props on the big Mercs whining wildly until they dug into the water again. The boat wanted to yaw to one side or the other as we ploughed into a wave again, so I corrected, even as the bow disappeared in a wild green seethe of sheer water.

Holding on to the sides of the entry way with each hand, Diana peered up at me.

"We'll be okay," I shouted. "Get below and hold on!"

Instead, she clambered up and twisted into the seat to my right, just as we rose again on an incoming comber. She held on, and as we landed, she slammed back into the seat and almost bounced out again.

"Strap in!" I shouted.

She was laughing.

Fun? I guess so. I started laughing too.

I had looked at Harry's map. We were tracking toward Hidden Cove Island, within a band of 5 to 10 degrees. I had it timed, of course – that is if were making the progress I had estimated in my flight plan. And it had been a flight plan in a couple of ways.

"Should be coming up on our right!" I shouted. "I don't want to run straight into it."

"What are you going to do?"

"Remember the map?"

"Yes."

"Run past the east shore, turn, and head into the harbor. It runs almost due north.

"And it will have plenty of water in it."

"Okay."

Yes, it sounded good.

We skinned by the island much too closely, almost getting caught in the cross current formed by the wave action against the shore. I gunned the engines through the chop. I turned slightly to the east, careful not to get any water over the starboard side of the cockpit and made a hair-raising 360 degree turn that almost found us picked up and tossed like a kiddy's boat into a fifteen foot trough. Then we were speeding along, almost at idle toward the narrow inlet that gave the island its name. I made small corrections as we rushed toward the narrow opening beyond which the water was yellow. We rose on a huge wave and were rushed into calmer water. It was like the final push you get when coming out of the tunnel of love toward where the man waits to tie you up.

"Good!" shouted Diana, laughing again, as if there had never been any doubt.

And a man was waiting for us, a sun-darkened face under a yellow rain hat.

Enrique took the line that Diana flung to him. He tied us up.

"Perfect!" Diana shouted, jumping on to the wharf.

Could I do it again? No. Blind luck had flowed beneath the keel. I would not try it again. Blind luck might fail to see us next time.

Enrique led us to the shed at the end of the splintery wharf. His own boat – a once-white fishing craft of about thirty feet – shouldered its name back and forth in the slip. "La Otra Mujer: Puerto Occulto."

I handed him Harry's note, the envelope soggy.

It was short.

"Take care of my friends. Conceal the Sea Ray."

"Any planes flying over you?" I asked.

"Not so far," he said. "I'd hear them. I even heard you a while ago coming past the island. Venga conmigo, por favor."

He led the way to a house that looked like a large shack, constructed of the discarded planks of ancient fishing boats. It seemed to have a permanent lean to the north, like a tree growing against a constant flow of wind.

But inside, it was paneled with a sweet-smelling cedar over which colorful woven blankets had been hung. So it was a quiet zone amid the echo of storm against the outside boards.

Enrique indicated a couch in front of a huge fireplace of stone and seashell. It held no fire, but it was warm and dry there, and a good place for us to lay down our dripping slickers.

"Tengo tequila," he said.

"Gracias," I said. "Dos, por favor."

Diana and I had seated ourselves when Enrique's wife came out from the kitchen that ran along the east side of the house. She was wiping her hands on her apron.

I rose and turned.

I saw Enrique give me a glint of appreciation.

He introduced us to Maria Angelica Calderon y Vega.

"Mucho gusto," I said, bowing.

She was slender, dark of eye and hair, except for a whisper of white at each temple, wearing a white apron over jeans. Very beautiful and obviously delighted to have company on this lonely strand.

"If you are hungry after your – voyage," she said. "I have red snapper and plenty of it."

"That," I said, "is one of the best offers I have had recently!"

She laughed.

"Harry says to take good care of them," Enrique said fluently, accepting the use of English for further discourse. But he had appreciated my limited Spanish, as Spanish speakers are wont to do.

"And so we will!" Maria said, turning back toward the kitchen.

"You've been very good."

"I have?"

I was certain that this was not true.

"About not asking."

"I've had enough to do."

"Yes. But you don't know why."

"I do though," I said.

"I appreciate that, but..."

"If you want to. I can live without it."

"I know. But do you recall the Hatfill case?"

Oh – so that's what she was talking about! Not her former relationship with Harry Vance.

"Let's see," I said, pretending to pause to think, but pulling my mind to the issue she was raising.

"Steven Hatfill. FBI was convinced that he was the guy who mailed the anthrax letters."

"Right."

"So you..."

"I found out that they were trying to hound him into suicide. That would be a de facto admission of guilt and they'd close their case."

"They did get someone, didn't they?"

"Yes. Bruce Ivins. He did commit suicide with pain killers. They did have a case against him, though."

"Hatfill sued the hell out of them, didn't he?"

"The FBI. The *New York Times*, some crazy professor from Vassar who had implicated him. But the point is that they tried to get him to kill himself."

"I thought Mueller was a fairly honorable man."

"He objected. But he was helpless. His resignation would have looked really bad in the good old War on Terror."

"How high did it go?"

"How high do you think it went?"

"At least as high as Ashcroft."

She put her hand above her head in a phantom salute.

"Higher."

"Cheney."

"Right. At least as high as his office. That could have been Addington. And, if my information had come out, the Bush administration would have finally had to pay for some of that criminal activity."

"So, who is after us?"

"The Democrats are helpless, as usual. They just blow off the illegal wiretapping as if it never happened. The Republicans are trying to kiss the Tea Party's ass. But these people are organized and control much of the Homeland Security apparatus. Harry knows all of that, of course, even knows some of the people involved. That's how we keep one jump ahead of them. But the even bigger story..."

And here she paused to look around as if the walls had listening devices in them or spies lurking behind secret panels.

"The bigger story is why Obama said 'Let sleeping dogs lie.' But that's not why they're after me. They don't know I know."

"'We won't revisit the past,' he said."

"Yes. And he said that for good reason. What I found out is that he was threatened, very credibly, very confidentially. And, of course, the cowards threatened his children."

"You can prove that?"

"Sure. And, of course, they got the NRA on board. I've got a Most Confidential memo from La Pierre saying there will be no talk of 'Second Amendment Solutions.'"

"Their code for political assassinations."

"Yes, as Sharron Angle said. But who will touch it?"

"David Remnick, maybe."

"Yes. I thought of that. He's done Sy Hersh and Jane Mayer."

"But you haven't reached him with this?"

"No. I didn't have time. And it does not look like I'll be able to. Get it to him, I mean."

"And you can name names?"

"Oh, yes!"

"Bigger than the Pentagon Papers."

"Oh yes!"

"But it's the former VP who is after you on the Hadfill thing? Do you know specifically who?"

"It's called the Action Wing of a big company that does a lot of security work. I'd hate to think what their Non-Action wing does.."

"The company's name starts with 'H'?"

"It might."

"And it is not Hallmark."

"Not unless they send out cards saying, 'Heard You Disappeared from Sight!'"

"What would your friend Adams think of our little island?"

"He would have enjoyed it. He visited Samoa with John La Farge and was paddled ashore by naked savages, as he called them, who were, he said, 'as little fluent in English as if they had studied at Harvard.' He was an adventurer, for all of the propriety of his background."

"He didn't think much of Harvard."

"No. As he knew most colleges teach toward the status quo. That's what keeps them in money. Think of what a fuss the alums made when in the 60s and 70s they believed that students were politicizing the institutions. Even today, most colleges don't promote much education beyond their four years, unless it is specialized training in medicine or law. And that specialization involves learning the received wisdom and serving the status quo. Adams spent his lifetime trying to learn. And he didn't attribute that impulse to Harvard."

"Blowditch College."

"Blowditch takes it to the second power."

Camus says something about a suicide's being exiled – "deprived of the memory of a lost home or the hope of a promised land." Having thought of suicide, sometimes intensely and sometimes randomly, I did recognize that the promised land at whose grape-heavy vineyards and profound lakes I had been staring for some forty of my sixty years was indeed an illusion. Or, if not, that land lay in the past and had not been recognized when I had inhabited it. Bethany had been my Eve. But I thought of my mother, not in some Oedipal way, but of her fierce will toward her own identity at an historical moment that defined her role as wife, mother, and commander of the household. The latter had found her pressing her foot on the buzzer under the green dining room table to summon one of the many maids we had engaged over the years. But there had been much more to her than that. And, I thought, I inherited her ferocity, even if it never found specific fulfillment. For me, at least. It did not dictate going out into my driveway and driving a bullet into my head. And so, I thanked her. You can go home again, if you recognize what it is that you have brought with you into exile. Promised land? This cedar lined house trembling under storm was going to be close enough. Not because I was here, but because of who was here with me.

Diana, suitably disguised under a baseball hat and a shapeless slicker, delighted in crewing for Enrique. She arrived back, crusty with salt, reeking of fish, sun-darkened and happy. I still had a couple of books -- *The Education*, *Democracy*, and four tragedies by Shakespeare – so I read, made notes on a yellow legal pad, loafed, drank beer, worked it off by body-surfing along the beach on the west side of the island, and improved my Spanish by talking with Maria.

"How did you happen to get here, and why?" I asked her one day.

"Porque? We had no choice. Enrique worked for Fidel, drove him, took him on fishing trips. Enrique was accused of smuggling. It wasn't true. We were warned and left Cuba on La Otra Mujer. He would not have been welcome in Miami, of course. The old ones with all the money they took out when

Fidel took over still have a price on a lot of heads. But he had met Harry Vance. And so..."

Two more exiles.

I went over to the beach on the west side of the tiny island. It was a shallow zone of sand between two stony points that featured five foot waves breaking over a bar about two hundred yards from shore.

I walked out until the water came to my shoulders, ducking the incoming fleece of waves already broken and treading water as the waves rose and fell beneath me. I would see one just beginning to lip its inner wall, swim toward it, then turn on my left shoulder, sending a lash of spray against the deep blue of the sky, take a couple of quick strokes and ride down the wave as it broke around my hips. I became part of the wave. It was a great ride into the oozy place where wave turned to sand and pebbles and began withdrawing. I had repeated the experience of my ancestors, the first amphibians. I usually had water in my ear until sometime in the evening when it suddenly trickled free. It made me deafer than usual, plugging my left ear and blocking what little hearing I had in my numb right ear. But my body still carried the memory of a wave crashing down with me part of the natural force. And then, although I did not explain the analogy to her, I would repeat the experience with Diana.

I would walk back up the shady, insect-humming, bird-caroling pathway to the house, have a sandwich and a couple of beers, perhaps bat out a page on the old typewriter I'd found in a closet and gotten into working condition except for that sticky 'e' that I had to reach up and disengage most of the time, and take a nap in the hammock under the awning on the porch on the east side of the house. A relaxing, untaxing routine.

IX.

We had a review on Saturday mornings at Randolph, after which we had a glorious day and a half in which to forget everything. Of course, we "flew the airplane" constantly during our free time, procedures becoming indelibly imprinted in the folds of our frontal lobes even as we ordered that otra cerveza. But it could be fun to watch Squadron B during the review. They had a kid named Clarke, "Clark with an e" when roll was called, who, when his drill master was turned away, would get egregiously out-of-step. That meant that the guys behind him would get out of step. When the drill master turned back to his charges, Clark with an e would be stepping smartly along while the rest of the group looked like drunks, staggering and stumbling home from the bar. The drill master would fire choice epithets at his misfits. Clark with an e was held up to them as an exemplar to which all cadets should aspire.

By the time I woke up, Diana and Enrique would be back. Diana would clean fish, then take a nap. I would do some writing. Harry had sent over some more books, so my mind would not atrophy even if my body were going native.

I was working on the nineteenth century crisis of faith as it reflected itself in Hawthorne's anti-transcendentalism, Emily Dickinson's skepticism about the "approving God," and Adams' helplessness as he watched his beautiful sister die as Tuscany rioted in blossoms and sensuous fumes around her agonizing death from lockjaw. This was a very different moment than that that Tennyson, Arnold, and Hopkins experienced, but it paralleled in a uniquely American way what was happening as British intellectuals encountered Darwin or as Hopkins plunged into the Dark Night of the Soul, to him a black eternity. My essay might never see any light of day itself, but that did not matter. I enjoyed the working on it, thinking about the issue, not feeling its pressure myself. And I had published and perished already.

I got up from my nap, opened another Heineken, and wandered down to the wharf along the island's tiny harbor.

Maria was standing there.

"Not back yet?" I asked.

She shook her head.

"Weather's good," I said. "They may have gone a little further south today. Enrique knows where to find the fish."

But Maria looked worried.

And, after we had walked back to the house and after another hour, I was worried too.

"Come on," I said. "We'll take the thirty nine and have a look. Engine trouble probably."

I had become "Don Donaldo" to Enrique, "Don Don" to Maria.

"Okay, Don Don, but..."

But Enrique kept his twin Chryslers fine-tuned and well oiled.

The afternoon Gulf shone like a gong of hammered bronze, but except for some distant sport fishermen, white tracings on the horizon, we saw nothing.

I cast a wary eye at the sky, but the few jet trails of the morning had flattened into a thin veil to the north.

"Let's go up to Harry's."

She nodded. We were almost there anyway.

"Okay," Harry said. "Let's not panic. Put the thirty nine under the canopy and let's take another look.

We did a search in Harry's fifty four foot Hatteras.

"We'd find something," he said, after we were back in the air-conditioned whirring of his living room.

"Even if the boat blew up. An oar. A piece of cabin. A life belt. But then, I don't think it blew up."

"They were picked up," I said.

"I think so. Bigger boat. A couple of high-powered rifles. Has to be something like that."

"Where would they go?"

"Any of a hundred places, including down to one of the Keys. Damn!"

But after taking a sip of his Scotch, Harry gave me a puzzled look.

"Kidnapping. Strange. Wouldn't fit into the way they operate."

"No? Extraordinary rendition?"

"Possible. But on the high seas? Just doesn't fit a rogue CIA operation."

"Which you think it is."

"Which I think it would be in the case of Diana. Picking her up on a street, hustling her into a car. Not going near where she lived. And nothing that amounts to an act of piracy, which this..."

"Wait a minute," I said. "Suppose..."

"I think I see where you are going."

"Exactly. They were after Enrique."

"Yeah. And they caught Diana in the net."

"In which case..."

"In which case," he said, "We go to Miami."

"Little Havana."

"It's worth a try."

Maria had been silent as Harry and I volleyed back and forth..

"I will come with you," she said.

"Not a good idea," I said.

"I know who to ask," she said.

"No!" I said. "You'd be snatched up just as they were."

I was worried about Diana, of course, but in a different way now. What would they do with her? Would they find out who she was? They would. They'd probably know right away.

"She's right," Harry said.

"I don't like it," I said.

"I have family there," she said.

"But what side are they on?"

"Family comes first in Cuba."

"And look, Don," Harry said, "the younger generation in Little Havana – for that matter those who are middle-aged – have lived here all their lives. They don't even have relatives in Cuba anymore."

"So what?"

"So this. The only fierce anti-Castro types are old men who got kicked out in the 1960s. The bankers, casino and plantation owners, import-export types, the last vestiges of the old Batista oligarchy. They may have some hired thugs, but they don't have a lot of support among the other Cuban-Americans. That means that Maria has a chance of finding some things out without being in danger herself."

She could certainly do more than I could.

"Can we bring in some muscle of our own?"

"If necessary," Harry said. "Let's find out where we are – where they are – first. I have access to a condo on the Upper East Side."

"New York?"

"No. Miami. Some of the same people live in both places, though."

And so Harry and I waited.

We worked out in the condo's health club. I was surprised. My swimming and surfing had maintained the trimming me down and tightening up that I'd achieved at Jud's tennis club. That seemed a long time ago. Oh yes, as had pleasant late night and early morning workouts with Diana. They still tingled in muscle memory.

I rat-a-tat-tatted on the light bag and threw clubbing body shots into the heavy bag, which squeaked upon its chain. I thought of perfect shots in squash – not just winners, but ones where I set up for one shot and hit another, as my opponent broke the wrong way – of the clean clip of a wooden bat on a softball (not the hollow ping of metal) as the ball fled over second base on a line, bisecting the facets of the diamond precisely, and of a first-serve in tennis, where my back came up and my wrist came forward to meet a perfect toss and my body followed as I hustled up to join my partner at the net, even the spring forward in ancient times as the boy who was "it" wandered around the side of the house and left the thick, old bark of the oaktree unprotected.

The old memories were still alive in the muscles. But, careful old boy, you are not home free. You are no longer the cocky young man who thought that Survival School at Stead was easy. Still, if I felt readier for action, even combat, than I had in many years.

I saw Maria get out of the taxi that had pulled under the palm trees far below. She leaned into the front window to pay the driver.

"She's back!" I shouted to Harry.

It was a great relief within a larger field of tension.

"They are in a safe house on Calle Fulgencio."

"For how long – do you know?"

"Apparently, they don't know themselves. They did not realize that your friend, Don Don, was a well-known person. That complicates things."

"Sure it does," Harry said. "They're in trouble no matter what they do."

"Unless they 'disappear' them both," I said.

385

"No," Maria said. "Too many people know. No hay secretos en Havanacito. Very few secrets in that community."

"But they have to do something soon," Harry said.

"Yes," Maria said. "Once upon a time they would have shot Enrique..."

She shuddered delicately and got herself under control again. Some of her reaction came, no doubt, from the tension of her just-completed under-cover mission.

"... and dumped him on the street."

"Right," Harry said. "The message that any right-wing likes to send. But these guys are old-fashioned anti-communists. Their approach is out of *To Have and Have Not*. They are stuck in the middle of the last century, or earlier. It's a vendetta culture. Nothing high tech. And they are very unimaginative. They did not know what to do when they recognized Diana."

"So?" I asked.

"They are not about to let them go. They won't know yet that Diana is on someone else's wanted list. At least I don't think so. I'd say a little recon. And, the sooner the better," Harry said.

"5063?"

Maria nodded.

"That would be on the left hand side of the street as we go south."

"Si. La izquierda."

Very sinister, I thought.

And so, in a nondescript rental, Harry and I cruised past 5063 Fulgencio. The street was teeming with what must have been a perpetual fiesta. Music, shoppers wending between markets and stalls, laughter and the high-pitched chatter of rapid-fire Spanish.

"Where the old-timers live," Harry said.

"Plenty of young people, too. This looks promising. Lot of people around."

I pulled a Yankees cap down over my brows – hated to be wearing it, of course, but it was camouflage, along with dark glasses that hid my blue eyes.

"If I can get down the alley..."

"Too risky."

"So was sending Maria down here."

Harry shook his head.

"If I can find out what floor they are on..."

Harry turned left at a light, left again into a driveway, backed out. turned right, and headed back toward 5063.

"Just that much," he said.

"We don't dare call the cops."

"No. That puts Diana at risk. No way we could hide that from the bastards who are looking for her. They probably have a contact at every p.d. in the western hemisphere. They'd..."

He did not say what "they" would do. He slowed and pulled in just beyond a fire hydrant on the crowded street.

"I may have to move."

"I won't be long."

Down the alley was an iron railing with a set of concrete steps going down to the basement. The door was open to the night breeze that wafted the street sounds toward the far wall.

I went inside.

A man staring at a newspaper looked up at me.

"Lo siento. Yo olvido mi llave," I mustered, looking helpless under my crossing N and Y.

He shrugged. Yankees fan.

I got up the stairs to the lobby, hoping that Jesus had not made a phone call to security.

Now what, paleface?

The building had twelve floors. I could see from the registry that the first three were businesses of some kind. Securities. Law offices. A dentist. That did not rule them out, but it made them less likely. The top floor was my first choice.

I took the elevator up to eleven and went up the double set of stairs in the fire exit to twelve.

I pushed the heavy door open carefully. Nothing in the carpeted hallway, but it took a right angle toward the rear of the building.

Very carefully, not knowing what I was doing or was going to do, I padded down the hallway and peeked around the corner.

And there in a chair, sat a man in a stained straw hat, reading a paperback. No weapon in sight.

Enough, I said. Back to Harry! He's probably had to move the car anyway.

You've come this far, I said – that old debating voice that had always gotten me in trouble. It hadn't happened in the Air Force because procedures allowed for no debate. But this was an emergency for which no "don't forget the dingy" or "look down and locate the d-ring" existed.

Distraction. With what?

"Hola, Pedro!"

I ducked around the corner. I could hear him coming. Would he have a chambered and cocked .38 in hand? I'd find out.

A good sucker punch demands just a bit of preparation.

"Look!"

His eyes swiveled in the direction of my left hand. His chin was wide open. My right caught him on the side of the jaw. His eyes were crossed as he hit the burgundy carpeting. No weapon in his hand.

But I noticed two more things. First, he was an old man. I hoped that I had not killed him. Second, the crack I had heard when I hit him had been in my right hand.

Ow!

I took off his belt and tied his wrists to his ankles. Face down, he'd have a hard time even shouting. Of course, I had no place to hide him, so I could only hope that no one came along. I slipped a snub-nosed .38 – his pistolero – from his jacket pocket and held it in my left hand. My left hand had been confined to a jab that was mostly from the shoulder and a toss in tennis – like placing a glass full of water on a shelf that is almost out of reach. But now it was my right hand that was out of reach.

X.

The frost on the windshield, as the car awaits the dawn, shifting around the side of the house, and the silent sound of the friction of shadow, sliding far along the layered leaves of the wood – the frost delays assumptions, and forces others in. The ice divorces the act and makes a pause where mode (the assumption of November's need for heat of hearth and hope of heart) is met by only the hissing start of fire in the grate and bleed and rattle of sleet, erasing sun. The oak are silvery purple, the beech are red, signing above the birch the measure of what has not been done.

Was there another guard inside the room? One way to find out.

I slipped the .38 into my belt, pounded on the door with my left fist, backed to the side, pulled out the .38, and waited.

At last, I heard the bolt slide free and the knob turn. Who would I find? And what? A single round from a .45 that would rip me apart as it drove me across the hall? The little .38 was a useless toy in my left hand.

Enrique. His hands were tied behind his back, so he had manipulated the door with the strong fingers of a professional fisherman.

"Diana?"

He nodded toward the living room.

She was standing, arms tied behind her back with clothes line.

I would have liked to use a knife, but I got her free, using my right hand in spite of the pain. Then, with dexterity, she freed Enrique.

"Let's get out of here!" I said.

But as we got to the door of the apartment, we heard shouting from around the corner of the hallway.

We ran the opposite way. Into a dead end.

We ducked into a service closet, shelves full of sheets, towels, and cans of disinfectant and cleaning fluid.

"Great," I said. "We've trapped ourselves."

"They know we can't have taken the elevator or the stairs," Diana said.

"Un momento," Enrique said.

He looked down toward the now empty room, then turned and whispered.

"Venga conmigo."

We ran down toward the room. The door was ajar. Enrique pulled it shut. We ran toward the elevator.

Diana pushed the "L" button. The elevator had stopped at twelve. The door slid open.

"Aqui!" Enrique said.

We went down the fire exit to nine.

Diana looked at the elevator signal – a single clock hand sliding down. It was passing six.

"Let's get to three," Enrique said.

We took to the stairwell again.

I thought of Tony Zale, who had knocked out Rocky Graziano with a left hook after breaking his left hand three rounds before. The analgesic of action. My hand was killing me.

Enrique trotted down a shadowy hallway and looked out the window toward Calle Fulgencio.

"They just came back inside," he said.

"How about the fire alarm," Diana said.

Enrique considered.

"No. They'd cover the stairs."

"Won't they anyway?" I asked.

"Not if we hurry."

We went down to the basement. The attendant was gone. The door had been locked but we opened it, went up the steps, and came out into the alley.

"You two stay," I said. "I'll look for Harry."

Timing is not everything, perhaps, but it comes close sometimes. Harry was just turning around and heading back toward 5063.

I waved a "come ahead!" to Diana and Enrique

"Jesus!" Harry said. "I was about to give you up. We're going across to the Fisher Island ferry. You three take the Hatteras. It's gassed-up. I'll call ahead right now."

"Maria?" Enrique asked.

"She's at the condo, Enrique. I'll get her and bring her across later tonight. No one is looking for her or me."

I moaned.

"Hurt your hand?" Harry asked.

"Yeah. I hit a guard."

"Back of the hand?"

"Yeah. How'd you know?"

"Classic boxer's injury. The hand bangs down into the wrist and the wrist snaps forward and breaks the hand on the way back."

"Good to know. That helps."

And it did. For me, knowing the exact cause of an injury often eased the pain.

"That and a bucket of ice," I said.

"How'd you know...?" Diana asked from the back seat.

"Maria," Harry said. "She did the advance scouting."

"Que mujer," I said. Some woman!

I turned to look at Enrique in the back seat. He nodded. Yo se. I know.

"Of course I did not know that this idiot was going to play Rambo on us," Harry said, as if still under the misapprehension that I had been caught.

"Rambo never got a scratch," I said, trying to knead the pain from my hand.

Harry pulled over for a moment, before we started across town.

He punched in a number on his cell phone and spoke for about a minute. He repeated the process twice.

"Okay," he said, turning onto the eastbound ramp. "I am going to drop you guys at the ferry for Fisher Island. The Hatteras is at the Club Marina. They know you're coming. I just told Maria to be ready to go. My Bonanza is at Opa Locka. We'll beat you there. I didn't want long phone calls, Enrique. She knows you are okay."

"They still make Bonanzas?" I asked.

"It is the longest continually made aircraft in history. Originally tested in 1945. Mine's an A 36 with an Allison 250 turboprop package."

I would have volunteered to accompany him in the right seat, except that I looked forward to a cruise with Diana. And my right hand was pulling in the rest of my concentration.

And so, on a tranquil evening on which the moon became a silversmith along the smooth surface of the Gulf, we all went back by sea and by air to Piper Cay.

In the spacious lounge of the Hatteras, with Enrique at the helm, Diana rubbed some lotion on her hands and wrists.

"Was it scary?" I asked, pulling my hand from a bucket of ice for a moment to open another Heineken.

"Not really. I knew that you'd find us."

Find them, maybe. Free them? Maybe not.

But her smile suggested that she *had* known. And I realized then what it is to have someone believe in you. The hairy landing at Piper Cay. The boatride through the storm to a little dot in the Gulf. My impulsive intrusion upon the site where Enrique and Diana had been held. None of it would have worked out without her implicit belief that it would – that I could do whatever was required. Maybe this time, the relationship had been earned.

Harry and Maria tied us up along the pier at Piper Cay.

We sat in Harry's spacious lounge, walls of light blue, doors of louvered white, Winslow Homer prints of the Bahamas under wind on the walls. Exhaustion flowed into me, to replace nervousness, excitement, fear, exhilaration.

"Cubans won't try again," Harry said. "They don't know who's been alerted."

"Nobody," I said.

"They don't know that. And I doubt the Action Wing got any word about Diana. They would have had they moved you somewhere."

"They were planning to," Enrique said. "That's why only Tomaso was there when Donaldo showed up. They were coming back for us when we ducked into that closet."

"Okay," Harry said. "Here's a plan. But only if you two approve."

Diana and I both looked at him and waited.

"Sort of like witness protection," he said. "But only for the time being."

"However long the time being may be," I said.

"We sail around to Cayman Kai and put you off at Sand Pointe. I have access to a place there right on the beach."

"British, right?" Diana asked.

"You've been there," Harry said.

"Oh yes, so I have."

I smiled at Diana. I was not about to plunge into whatever her secrets might be.

"Anyway," Harry said. "I have a berth at Kaibo Yacht Club. I put in there."

"Passports?" I asked.

"We get you new passports under new identities. We go to George Town to go through customs. I know somebody there..."

"Better than flying in," I said.

"Right," Harry said. "This way we avoid any scrutiny."

"How long?" Diana asked.

"Hard to say. I will make inquiries, very quietly, of course. If we can get the story out..."

"You can do that?"

"I think so. Just attributing 'reliable sources,' not your name."

Which story? Harry no doubt knew about Hadfill and the FBI. I assumed that that was the one he meant. The other one might come too, in time.

"If you could," I said, "that would take the pressure off Diana."

"Exactly," Harry said. "Robs her of a significant credit, though."

"But won't they come after her anyway?" I asked.

"No. The damage will have been done. If she worked for a network, they'd get her fired. But they know that retribution after the fact is counterproductive. And some people still go to jail, even big wheels."

"Bernie Madoff," I said.

"Right. But as I said, Diana loses a byline on this one."

"I'd rather live," she said.

"You do have good taste," I said.

She laughed and pointed at me.

"With the occasional exception," I said.

"So we can relax for the time being," Harry said, interrupting our foreplay. "Glass is falling. Storm coming. We'll get you back to the little island tomorrow. Then on to the Caymans."

"Why should we do anything?" Diana asked.

"Because they probably have spotted Hidden Cove. I'll try to find out. We may have some time, but we can't count on it. Meanwhile, let's batten down. But first, let's unload the Hatteras. I had some supplies put aboard while we were adventuring in Miami. Cost a fortune!"

Yes, I thought, that's how you became a multi-millionaire, Harry. Economizing on supplies.

"Relax?" I asked.

"Why not," Diana said. "And as far as what we do next. I am going to hit the sack."

"Y yo tambien," I said, "That is once I give Enrique a hand – one hand – with the unloading."

"No," said Harry. "Enrique and I will do that. You go to bed. See whether you can sleep."

He smiled, thinking probably that I'd still be too revved up to sleep. Ah, but what several good beers can accomplish toward that goal!

Diana, the ultimate careerist, had apparently decided that neither of her stories – big as they were -- were worth getting killed. Good news, I thought. Neither of us had to try any more. I had given up already, of course, but I had been drifting. Now the drift had meaning. Why do we always believe that the next day is the one we want?

"This being a bum has its advantages," I said.

"Difference?" Diana said.

"Between a bum and a college professor? Yes. A bum doesn't have to grade papers. And a bum doesn't have to look as if he just stepped from a fitting at Paul Stuart or Ben Silver."

"That was you."

"Me and the Salvation Army. I do regret leaving all those beautiful ties behind."

"Such beautiful ties!"

"They were, Daisy. They were."

Camus says that the typical person always counts on "someday." I had thought my adventures were over and that my "someday" had come and gone. That was good in that I was no longer counting on it. I think that that attitude invited it forward to intercept my lassitude.

Happy ending? No. Not an ending. But a very pleasant present. And, although Henry Adams debated me in the forum of my mind, I figured that I had learned about what I wanted to learn. For the time being, Henry. For the time being.

The storm arrived with a hiss and then a seethe of rain and a rattle of palm trees changing directions with their airfoils in the shifting wind, and the crash of breakers trying to reclaim the land, but they were muffled sounds within the thick walls of Harry's mansion. They were good sounds within which to fall asleep. My right hand was numb. It might wake me up at some strange hour of the morning, but for now, it was a phantom limb. I hoped that the man I had hit had not suffered the fate of Frankie Campbell or Benny "Kid" Paret.

Before I did fall asleep that night, I saw forsythia exploding against the sudden green of lawns, or sometimes shining in a forest, a seed somehow having flown from domesticity. All that in some world that had disappeared, like Eden. I saw puddles at the sides of the roads. All that rain with still no place to go, except to create ghosts against the sunlight, ghosts that told where all past years had gone and all the people who had inhabited them. I saw clouds drifting in front of my eyes, obscuring the comforting concrete of runway in front of me, and the sea, boiling like a vast caldron before me, threatening to splash its scalding contents over my splinter of boat. I saw a bend in a carpeted hallway that led I knew not where. But it opened out to a new dimension in which I saw Diana's forehead, rising pale between me and the stars, moving upward to reveal her luminous eyes and, then, her smile.

fin